the
enormous
shadow

the enormous shadow

by Robert Harling

Harper & Brothers · Publishers · New York

the
enormous
shadow

1

ONLY THE BOLD MAN SAYS: *This story began at such and such a moment.* Time slips out of sharp definition. Then, too, and perhaps more to the point, I am not a bold man.

Yet having written those words, and believing them to be true, I would still be prepared to say that this record did begin, for me, at a certain time and in a certain place. For others, the story had begun long before. For others still, it will persist for years to come. Perhaps that is what the bold man sometimes forgets: that no man's story is his alone.

For me, then, this record began two years ago, almost to the day: the morning of September 15, 1954, a Wednesday, in a room on the seventeenth floor of a dingy newspaper and process engravers' building at Forty-eighth off Lexington.

That day I received Butler's cable to leave New York and get to London, *allegro con moto.* He had to have his little joke, even in costly cablese, but he was editor in chief and managing director, so why not?

Two days later, therefore, I got to London, to a land I deeply cared for but scarcely ever saw. Yet my first sight was not the most endearing: Heathrow, stretching away to the skyline, and looking, even in the morning sun, like flat, drab, bulldozed fenland.

The airport chores were swiftly done. Ten minutes later I was through the customs and out in the lobby, making for the coach, a BOAC porter puffing manfully at my side. There we were halted. A short, stolid young man, with a red face and a coxcomb of brilliantined black hair, tentatively barred our way. He introduced himself:

"I'm Moxon, sir. One of the editorial drivers. I've been told to look after you."

He was a purposeful creature and in a moment had taken hold of my two grips and directed the porter to a Humber Pullman out-

side in the car park. While he was stowing the bags I got in, alongside the driver's seat.

I vaguely remembered the face. As Moxon settled himself into the
car, I said, with that brimming bonhomie that is apt to afflict every
homing traveler, "Were you given my description?"

"No, sir. Remembered you. Been away quite a long time, haven't
you, sir?"

"Five years too long."

"New York all the time, sir?"

"Not all the time. Sometimes Washington. In fact, mostly Washington."

His disappointment was plain.

"New York always sounds exciting the way Don Iddon writes it
up, don't you think so, sir?"

"Even if you must read rival newspapers," I said, somewhat tartly,
"you needn't advertise them quite so blatantly."

His red face went redder still and he said quickly, "I see what
you mean, sir. Sorry. Not that I buy the *Mail*. Can't help seeing it
in the canteen sometimes, though."

"Well, don't break your heart. It still sells only two million copies,
doesn't it? Aren't we over three?"

"Three million four hundred and twenty-six thousand, sir."

"That's better," I said. "At least, some people might think it is."
Perhaps the remark wasn't the afterthought it seemed: it was a
thought that was often with me.

Moxon, however, took the remark as forgiveness, grinned, relaxed
and returned to what was plainly his major preoccupation in life:
passing everything on the road.

I also relaxed, gazing fondly around at the nearer fields. Yet not
for long. In a matter of minutes the fields had gone, and we were
moving into one of those approaches to great cities common to so-
called civilized lands: a long straight line of metaled road, paralleled
by billboards and wasteland dumps. Then, later, rows of sad houses
and dingy shops.

Fleet Street, too, was much the same, even after five years. Also
the London office. The same York-stoned courtway approach, not
worn noticeably smoother by the passage of many million footsteps
in the intervening years. The same wide, echoing hall with its marble

tiles, marble columns and marble counters. The same busybody bustle, so different from New York's tensile strain.

But not the same commissionaire. Instead, a tall, stiff-backed younger man in a pale gray uniform, with last-war ribbons, sending messengers upon their errands with barrack-square barks. These things I noticed in the second or so in which he took in my arrival. I had scarcely crossed the marble floor, followed by Moxon with the heavier bags, before he'd saluted me and snapped, "Boy! This gentleman to Mr. Butler. Jump to it!"

He turned to me, softening his bark to a scarcely more reassuring snap: "I'll keep your bags here, sir. Perhaps you'd put them down behind the counter, driver!"

There was no "perhaps" about it, as the driver seemed to know, for he moved to the command.

Docilely I entered the waiting lift. How easy for a commissionaire, well versed in the technicalities of his job, to become a dictator, benevolent or otherwise.

Meanwhile I was thankful that my homecoming was proving so much smoother than I had expected, and I stood there, watching the red digits on the indicator tick off the floors until they reached the top. The twelfth. The "Penthouse Paradise" as it had been known in my day.

The lift attendant with the game leg and breastful of first-war ribbons, who had been doing the same job five years before, ushered out the messenger and me. But the boy was dismissed, back into the lift, by a solemn, pale-cheeked little man, also in gray uniform, who had, it seemed, been awaiting my arrival.

It was all as smooth and painless as any trip to Cloudland ought to be, and I dutifully followed the little man along the corridor, noting only the deep, deep pile and the mirror-polished paneling in British Honduras mahogany or some other fanciful wood the Baron had chosen when he built his paper palace some twenty years before. But I put the thought aside as I fell to wondering whether my one-time editor had changed, now that he was no longer merely an editor but editor in chief. And managing director, of course.

My dragoman pushed discreetly at a flush door which opened into an ivory-and-chromium office. A dark young woman, with sharp but far from aggressive features, was seated at a desk. Alicia Gowing, the girl with all the answers and all the secrets, I surmised as she took off her spectacles. Her gentle name and fame had crossed the Atlantic.

Such creatures can be useful or dangerous in any organization, as any minion knows, and I appraised her warily as she peered, almost stared, at me in the fixed, oblivious manner of the nearsighted bereft of their glasses. Brown eyes; could be kindly, I noted for the future. With her black suit, upswept coiffure and horn-rimmed spectacles she looked more like some curious cross between governess and mannequin than P.A. to a newspaper boss. She smiled, as if I were some half-forgotten traveler from an antique land, and said benignly, "Mr. Butler is expecting you. We checked with the airport."

I followed her into a large inner office, more like a concert hall in a brave new satellite town than a journalist's workroom, but my moment of lese majesty was short-lived, for there, at the end of the room, behind a big desk, was Butler, clearly ready for any journalistic work that might come his way.

I had, as I had expected to have, that recurrent moment of foreboding I had always known in meeting him after an absence, however brief. I wish that I could define my apprehension more exactly, but I cannot. The moment passed, however, and I was almost at ease again. Yet the shock of self-revelation—that trepidation could still intrude, even after five years—persisted naggingly for several minutes.

Perhaps Butler knew this, for he did not move. He looked up as I entered the room and watched, but that was all.

His eyes held no touch, however remote, of that old-fashioned greeting the homecomer half expects as his due: the getting-up-and-coming-toward, the backslapping, the arm-gripping, the general air of welcome to the long-lost colleague. Instead, he just sat there and waited, and, as far as I could see, he hadn't changed a bit. He was still the coldest fish of all.

He moved his arm in a close, sawed-off movement toward the nearest of half a dozen armchairs set before his desk. "Take that one," he said. "Nobody else ever does. Probably too near me."

I had a moment of kinship with all those unknown creatures as I sank into the chair he had indicated. Then I looked more closely at my editor in chief. "It's pleasant to see you looking so little changed after all these years," I said, conventionally enough.

"Nobody changes much between forty and sixty," he answered evenly. "Look at all these fifty-year-old heart throbs on the screen. They still get away with it. Sixty is the cliff edge."

"There's still some way to go for both of us, then," I said. Reassuringly, I hoped.

I considered him carefully. Even at five or six feet he seemed unchanged. The same heavy jowls, the same soft lips, the same cleft, pointed chin, the same blue eyes, pale and unwavering. And the same paunchy body, slumped loosely in the big swivel chair. A few fewer hairs on the high, fair scalp were the only tribute he offered to the hurrying years.

We considered each other for a long and speculative moment. Neither gaze held friendliness or enmity, I thought. Merely an even shade of wariness.

"You've been away a long time," he said at last.

"Five years."

"Too long."

"No fault of mine."

"No," he agreed slowly. "I thought it was better that way. You were doing a good job. It was getting better all the time."

"I could have come back for a break."

"Foreign correspondents who keep coming home for breaks begin to lose their objectivity," he said in dispassionate tones. "They start getting fond of the old country again. They want to share her trials and sorrows. Worst of all, they start seeing Britain's point of view. I want a Washington correspondent who sees the American point of view. Fifty million people in this cramped bloody island see Britain's point of view. That's too many. It makes it all too damn one-sided."

He seemed to have a great deal more to say about the conduct of foreign correspondents, but suddenly he switched. "I suppose old-fashioned pride kept you from putting in a chit to come back?"

"Probably."

"That's what I reckoned on."

We were silent again.

He broke the spell. "You could have come back in any of your vacations, couldn't you? There was no one to stop you. You get six weeks." Still probing, he went on: "You're a free man. Why didn't you?"

"I had to get to know some of those forty-eight states," I said. "I wanted to get around. I needed to. I didn't want to be just another garbage can taking in all those Washington handouts. You didn't want that, did you?"

"I just said I didn't. I only wanted to know why you didn't come back in your own time, that's all."

"Well, now you do!" I said, suddenly and irritably.

I was surprised and shocked to hear my own words, but Butler seemed unperturbed by my querulous outburst. He said, "You didn't have much to come back for, anyway, did you? No people. No relations. What about that ex-wife of yours?"

"She's still around."

"Where?"

"Still in Paris."

"Still drawing alimony?"

"Till she dies."

"God is very unjust sometimes. Every day fifteen people are killed on the roads of this country."

I'd had enough of the subject and shrugged it away by asking after the Baron.

"The Chairman?" Butler amended gently. "He comes in occasionally, but he doesn't worry us as much as he used to. Perhaps it's because we've never had a better year, despite the cost of newsprint."

The newsprint reference was, presumably, the managing-director touch showing through. In the old days, when he had been just another editor, newsprint could have cost a hundred thousand dollars a reel for all he cared.

To keep the conversation away from myself, I went on with the subject of the Baron. "He used to be keener on coming in," I said. "Is he losing interest in his newspapers?"

"Any man is apt to get other interests at seventy-four rising seventy-five," Butler said, smiling thinly. "He begins to think about the other side, I'm told. He begins to wonder. The Chairman's showing an interest in the Church."

"Rome?"

"What other church is there these days?"

I didn't reply, and Butler went on: "After all, it's got everything, hasn't it? Money, power, psychology. And it's fashionable. As a religion it's made to measure for a millionaire."

"Has he really gone over?"

"Oh, God, yes," Butler said, as if already bored to death by the subject, but he still went on. "It was inevitable. All those millions. All those secrets. No wife. No children. No one to talk to. At least, not on his own level. There was only God Almighty left. And the Pope for second best."

I smiled, but Butler did not. He seemed rapt in his own words. In any case, I reminded myself, Butler had never been one to smile when others smiled.

"But I'm boring you," he said evenly.

"I'm fascinated," I said. I was—in a way.

"No you're not. You're bored to the back teeth. Religion always did bore you. Otherwise we might have had one good religious story out of you every month instead of every two years. Father Divine, Cardinal Spellman, the Mormons . . . they might all have been dead for years as far as you were concerned."

I had always been respectful of Butler's talent for remembering the minutiae of a minion's failings, and made no attempt at self-defense other than a quick side step.

"So everyone is happy," I said. "You . . . the Baron . . . who else?"

"Are you?"

" 'Busy' is probably a better word."

"It's as good as any other. You were busy over there, then?"

"Didn't it seem like it?"

He smiled. "The stuff you turned in was good. Especially toward the end. You also seemed to run the staff well. But being busy at a job's no synonym for being good at it, although, I gather, it's a belief the so-called top brass in the States is apt to have. What will you do, by the way, now you're back?"

What I'm likely to do at this precise and straw-breaking moment in Time, I thought suddenly, hating his avuncular, goading, patronizing, imperturbable guts, is to blow my top and hit the roof of this bee-utiful ivorine room. But I knew what the effect of such an outburst would be, and the knowledge lessened both my need and enthusiasm for such an outburst. Butler would be unmoved, mildly interested and secretly delighted. So I stayed my tongue and said simply, "You brought me back."

"Apart from that?"

"It depends how long I'm back for. You know that better than I do."

Butler picked up a perspex ruler from his desk and sighted along the edge to draw a bead on his gleaming brown brogues. It was an old mannerism and I had been waiting for it.

"Long enough to look around," he said. "You can even have ten days for looking around. Even a couple of weeks."

"You're too generous. And then?"

"We'll see. Probably just go back to the States, refreshed in wind and limb. And in mind, of course. Come and have lunch up the road."

2

"LUNCH UP THE ROAD" WAS THE GRILL ROOM AT THE SAVOY, AND IF that had been his daily routine during the intervening years I could see why Butler's paunch showed no signs of slimming down.

He was greeted by the staff with deference. The waiter took his order with that cosseting respect that daily usage is apt to exact.

"Do you come here most days?" I asked.

"Most working days."

"You find you work better after this?" I asked as the smoked salmon was put before us.

"My work is mainly saying 'yes' or 'no.'"

I smiled. It was difficult not to when he was in that kind of opining mood, and I was feeling less disputatious than I had been half an hour before. All that prodding was part of his technique, I told myself again. He would make a statement that could be an insult, but it was so casually made that you smiled and let it float away, refusing to react to its implications. Even when you did react, sometimes testily, he always smiled, and, in some strange way, anger died. He amused me, too. I had always been intrigued, watching him at work,

needling out the splinters of knowledge he thought he ought to have
to stay there in the job he had made his very own. Then, too, I had
watched the technique in the making. Perhaps, I thought, now that
his main job is to see that the Group goes on ticking over and ticking
up—more money, more profits—it's more than ever part of his job to
go on delving. Well, a man makes his own technique. Who was I, a
man without ambition, with no desire to rise to Cloudland, to judge
these things? Or was I holding, hidden, a bunch of large, sour grapes?

He used the same tactics of slight but telling touches throughout
the meal. "You're putting Grimston onto more and more of those
Hollywood follow-ups," he said at one point. "How much time does
he spend out there? After all, we get enough stuff free out of Hollywood without spending real dollars there."

"He was first with that new Brando story. Two days ahead of the
Express."

"That's true."

"And that wasn't his only petty triumph," I said, following up.
"He's done well on all the Audrey Hepburn stories. He only spends
a week in every month out there. It's worth it. I still use him a good
deal in New York and Washington."

"His Washington stuff's not bad. Good light relief to your own.
It's just as well. Your stories are pretty heavy going sometimes, don't
you think?"

"Capitol Hill is pretty heavy going sometimes," I said.

"True enough, but we're not what the Archbishop of Canterbury
would call a serious newspaper. Never forget that simple fact."

It was always "True enough!" as he received the bits of information, the checks and cross-checks he required.

Once again I had the impression that he was filing these items of
information in his card-index mind for later reference. He did more
than merely note, of course. That would have been too passive a
procedure for Butler. He had to add his cunning prods to pride as
well as his sowings of self-doubt. One could see the pattern clearly.
Yet I stepped into the place he had doubtless saved for me, as most
of those around him seemed to step into his patterns.

"Your Washington stuff has been pretty good, all the same," he
said, almost as an afterthought. "You made some good guesses about
McCarthy."

"It was easier there than it looked from here."

"How do things here look from there?"

I thought a bit. "Perhaps I'm not the best judge," I said at last. "I seem to know more about American politics now than British. Isn't that the way you like your Washington correspondents?"

"Try!" he said quietly.

I took a deep breath and said my piece. To me, I said, it looked as if the Tories were trying to live down the legend of the bad old days. To some extent they seemed to be succeeding, although the air of privilege still surrounded them. But they had another, tougher legend to cope with, the Churchill legend. That would cling to them for another twenty or thirty years. The sense of his greatness would diminish anyone coming after him, and would provoke, in turn, a process of denigration toward the party. For a decade after his death the Conservatives would be accused of living in his shadow and on his great renown. Many of them would come to believe it themselves. I couldn't think it was a healthy prospect. "Truman suffered from much the same kind of process after Roosevelt's death," I said. "The Democrats still suffer from it. Even a man as good as Stevenson suffered from it. The legend of a giant can grow just a bit too big for the comfort of a man-sized party."

He nodded. "And Labour?"

"To me they seem tired. Worn out. Perhaps they're not, but that's the way it seems to me. Their squabbles say the same thing. Even Bevan must be pretty tired sometimes. He's been knocking around for thirty years or more now."

"Fifty-five's not young any more," Butler said. He went on, musing. "I always think Bevan stayed a bold bad boy too long. He's never judged the right moment to stop being the *enfant terrible*. Churchill nearly had the same trouble. Right until his late middle age. That Abdication act of his was sincere, but it wasn't an act of maturity. But Bevan will probably make it all the same, the way Churchill did. Not even the worship of mediocrity that is English politics can really kill political genius, although it tries damned hard. It sometimes gets around to giving a man a chance."

"Is there anybody else?"

"There's Gaitskell and one or two others, but I'm more interested in the really young men on both sides. Men under forty. Nobody knows if they amount to anything. Why should they? They've never had a chance. Politics is a dirty old man's game. If anybody coughs up that chestnut about Pitt being Prime Minister at twenty-four you can bet it's an eighty-year-old politician putting up a smoke screen to hide the senility of the whole croaking crowd of 'em. It's a vested interest of both sides."

Butler was talking more than he used to in the old days, I thought. He had always been inclined to go galloping off on occasional hobbyhorses, but in those far-off days there had been a quorum of colleagues near enough to him to be able to scoff or laugh him down. Now there was no quorum. The higher a man climbs the fewer scoffers or laughers. At least, not to his face, I judged.

Butler's hobbyhorses had always been changeable. Apparently they still were. That day, it seemed, the subject was the antiquity of politicians. So I let it gallop. So long as it kept him off the subject of the New York office, I was prepared to be a ready companion.

"In any decently run business," he was saying, "a man is on his way to the cashier's office to see about his pension at the age these politicians start cutting their teeth. Why is it? Why does a man have to have one foot in the grave before he's considered fit to help make the laws of a great and thriving nation?"

"All other passions are dead or dying. Too old for sport, outdoor or indoor. Too old for anything but the pursuit of power."

Butler nodded. "And nobody wants to change it?"

"Only the young men."

"And me!" Butler said, smiling. He finished pecking at the partridge, which had held his keen attention despite his diatribe.

"Why the sudden interest?" I asked.

"It's got possibilities," he said. "This country isn't interested in politics as a dreary intrigue of countless parties the way the French are. Or as a great two-party personality parade the way the Yanks are. We're mainly interested in politics as a study in character. We remember our politicians for years longer than any other nation. Most of us still talk about Gladstone and Disraeli as if we'd known them. And look at the recent list: Lloyd George, Churchill, Attlee, Bevan. Nobody ever thinks of any of them in connection with any great measure. Lloyd George and pensions, perhaps. Bevan and National Health, perhaps. But I doubt it. It's character the Englishman wants."

"So long as the character is cartoonable."

"A few eccentricities, of course, but without character politics becomes an abstraction and that the English won't have at any price."

He stopped to tell the waiter he'd see the dessert wagon. The interruption seemed to stop his lecture. He turned to me. "You see what I mean?"

"Up to a point."

"Not a very distant point, it seems."

"Not very."

"We'll take it up again when you get back after this holiday I've given you."

All right, I thought, we'll take it up again after I get back, but meantime there would be other hobbyhorses. This one would have been forgotten.

But I should have known better.

3

AFTERWARD WE WENT BACK TO COURT HOUSE, UP TO BUTLER'S room again. There were a few details about the New York office to settle. For one thing, we were trying to come to something less than a cut-throat arrangement with a science-fiction syndicate; for another we were negotiating for serial rights in a new Red Army escapee story; and I had been begging for an additional secretary for months. And so on, and so on. But by four o'clock we had finished.

"See you ten days from now, then," Butler said as I stood by the door.

"Two days for each year?"

"I've always been too generous with my staff," he said complacently, "but it's a failing in the right direction, don't you think?"

I smiled. One could be angered by his bland and treacherous twists or one could accept them, even collect them. They would have made a first-class set of specimens in the art of making black look white.

"Where will you go first?" he asked.

"The theater. Then a trip round this ancient land. I come from the Cotswolds, don't forget."

"I know," he said, "Burford."

He loved to show off with those music-hall memory-man touches, and I smiled dutifully.

"No trick," he said, watching me, reading my thoughts. "Merely an association of ideas. Every time I look at you I think of those clear and innocent Cotswold streams, that's all. How will you go?"

"Hire a car."

"Put it down to the firm," he said. "And meet me at the Savoy at one o'clock, Tuesday, September twenty-eighth." He lifted his great bulk from the chair, leaned across and scribbled a note on his desk pad. Then he sank back again.

"That makes eleven days. A day extra," I said. "You're slipping."

"I know. I know," he said with mock weariness. "It's a weakness. I ought to take it in hand."

4

DURING THE DAYS THAT FOLLOWED, I FREQUENTLY THOUGHT OF Butler and all that he had said, for I did not underrate his devious, purposeful ways of thought. I sought for the motives that had prompted that political discourse, for he was not given to pointless chitterchat, and usually kept his ulterior purpose well in view.

I had often seen the more complex side of Butler at work, and watched him in tortuous, long-term plans, making every kind of allowance for the vagaries of others: the halftones of ambition, the undertones of subservience, the overtones of brashness. Yet now I could not see myself in any of those plans, but I was puzzled, all the same.

But all that could wait, I irritably told myself each time the thoughts recurred, and tried to push all memories of Butler from my mind.

The weather was reasonable, but I was prepared to take any weather as my native climate and that sufficed.

In a hired Morris I made a slow round of the Cotswolds and the West Country: Oxford, Burford, Stow-on-the-Wold, Cheltenham, then back to Winchester by way of Marlborough. Turning south, I drove down to Corfe and back by way of Salisbury, the New Forest, Horsham. A quiet and leisurely and strangely moving journey.

I had expected to have a medley of memories for company, recollections of boyhood, school and youth, but the memories were too far off, too threadbare. More recent and more violent memories pushed them out, and I gave up and stared instead. The English landscape was more rewarding.

I returned to London on the evening of the twenty-seventh of September and took a room at Athenaeum Court in Piccadilly, registering there for a week. At any moment after that I should probably be on board a plane, the Q.M. or Q.E., if Butler had his way.

But his way was different.

5

THE WEATHER WAS HOT THAT DAY. TOO HOT FOR WALKING, EVEN slowly, along the crowded Strand, I remember, and I was glad to be wearing a lightweight New York suit.

Butler was waiting in the Savoy foyer. We went straight through to the Grill Room. He ordered sherries, then luncheon, asked a few polite questions about my trip and suddenly, as if deciding to cut out all nonsense, said, "Have you thought about what I was saying last time we were here?"

"About young Grimston?"

"No, about young men in English politics."

"Not much," I lied. "Not at all, in fact."

He finished his sherry.

"It's a serious subject," he said, gazing into the empty glass.

"I'm sure it is, but it's not my headache."

"You're still a British citizen."

"I'm also three thousand miles away. You said you didn't want your overseas men to get too English."

"Don't you care about the way your country's run?"

"All politicians look alike to me. I agree with Mencken. Did you ever hear what he said? 'Any man who calls himself a politician is, thereby, a self-confessed liar, rogue, thief and scoundrel.'"

"Did he now? Say it again."

I repeated the adage. He frowned, memorizing. "He's probably right," he said, smiling, "but we've got to have 'em all the same, and I think we might as well have some young ones."

"Churchill's done something about it."

Butler pursed his lips. "Not enough. Look at the graybeards and toothless old numbers he's still got cluttered around him. Too many."

"A man prefers his contemporaries," I argued. "They talk the same language. They understand his funny ways. And he thinks he can probably trust them that much farther than he could trust the younger men."

"You're younger than I am."

"Three years."

"I have you around. I trust you. It's a gesture in the right direction."

I laughed a hollow laugh and said: "So you'd like Churchill to take on a few young chicklings, three or four years younger than himself?"

Butler smiled, but the smile faded almost as it came. He said, "Now we've had our little jokes, let's come down to brass tacks. I'm proposing to air the subject next week. One or two crusty old readers are going to break a few blood vessels, but that's good for our circulation if not for theirs. I'm going to put forward the claims of one or two promising young fellows and see what happens."

"It could be interesting. All Tories?"

"Depends," Butler said and then casually, too casually, "What would *you* suggest?"

I didn't like the sudden introduction of that word "you." I had had similar experiences before. I was watchful, but he was slicing through his *noisette de veau* as if no untoward thoughts were in his mind. Almost reassured, I said, "I'd say Tories *and* Socialists."

"I thought so, too. I thought you'd see it that way. Which would you rather do first, a Tory or a Socialist?"

I had known it ever since that word "you." "Very funny," I said, "but I made my point week before last. I know too little about English politics. I've been away too long."

"It's not a primary requirement. In fact, it's one of the things I want. It's part of the plan. You're the Englishman who's been away. He comes back and sees 'Too Few Young Men in High Places.'" He spaced out the words of the projected theme like a headline. "See what I mean? The first piece appears on Monday. Hepburn's done it. Good stuff. Then comes 'When Is a Politician an Old Man?' on Tuesday. Also by Hepburn. He's turned in two damned good pieces."

"Why can't he do the rest?"

"He's no good at these potted character studies. It's not his line. He can make any politician hopping mad with his particular brand of acid, but he's no good at getting character down in simple black and white. You know that. He never was."

I was silent.

Butler went on, explaining his scheme like a schoolmaster explaining Euclid to a dullard. "Part of Hepburn's job will be a build-up for your personality parade. You'll come in on Wednesday with the first of your pieces. You'll deal with two contrasting personalities in each piece. You can take two Tories one day, two Socialists the next, or one Tory and one Socialist each day. You've been away five years and this is your first peek at British politics. Why aren't the talents of these young men being used? You know the line. I'd like to make it half a dozen of each but we may have killed it by then. It's got its points, hasn't it?"

"How do I suggest the talents of the youthful Socialists should be used?" I asked, playing for time.

"Don't ask me. That's your job. Why aren't there any really young men in Attlee's Shadow Cabinet? And Hepburn's got quite a good crack at the middle-aged young men who make up Bevan's little set. Driberg's nearly fifty. Crossman's forty-six. That's not young. At least, it's not on any of my newspapers."

"The Baron's newspapers," I corrected.

Butler was unperturbed. "True enough," he said. "He owns 'em, I run 'em. There's something in what you say. I must get out of this possessiveness. It's a kind of paternalism. I must think up another phrase. Any suggestions?"

He smiled like a fat old friar who has scored a dialectical point over a lay pedant. But he never digressed for long from the job in hand. "Who will you start with?" he demanded.

"Don't ask me," I said irritably. "I don't even know the names of the graybeards, let alone the youngsters."

"I've got a list here," he said gently, and reached into the inside pocket of his towny tweeds to bring out a folded sheet of quarto. "Twenty names. Every one a winner. Not one out of his very earliest forties. Some of 'em even in their thirties."

"Isn't forty somewhat aged by your standards?"

"This is politics!" he said contemptuously. "How many of these have you heard of?"

I took up the sheet and considered the list with jaundiced eyes. Three of the names I knew fairly well and I vaguely recognized about half a dozen others. I intoned the score.

"Rather better than I expected," he said heartily. "After all, you're not supposed to be a regular reader of Hansard out there. In any case, I want you to come to the subject with a fairly innocent eye." He speculated upon that remark for a moment and then added, "Yes, the innocent eye, that's what I want. At least, I think I do."

"I can guarantee that all right."

"Good!"

We were silent. I said at last, "Supposing I refuse?"

"The question doesn't arise," he said. "You aren't paid to refuse."

OF COURSE HE WAS RIGHT. I WASN'T PAID TO REFUSE. IN ANY CASE I could resign. But Butler had thought well beyond those simple possibilities. He had foreseen, I have no doubt, that after initial irritation I would begin to find some attraction in the job he had thrust upon me.

In many ways it was exactly the kind of assignment calculated to interest any English journalist returning home after five years abroad. I soon began to see that clearly enough. The task would provide invaluable opportunities to see the changed political setup in England.

After all, wasn't a wish to brush up my knowledge of the British, and their peculiar beliefs and institutions, one of the reasons why I had been glad to get Butler's cable? Wouldn't interviews with half a dozen of the younger representatives of the House of Commons be a lot more enlivening than reading reports of a hundred sittings in the *Times*? I couldn't lose. I should have two weeks longer in England than I had expected, and possibly learn something to my journalistic advantage.

So my thoughts moved, dimly at first, I admit. But even there, in the Grill Room alongside Butler, I began to get faraway glimmerings of the possibilities of the job. Perhaps I should have turned and thanked him for the opportunity, but I was still too nettled by his chicanery to make so charitable a move. And he was a difficult man to thank. Something in his cold, white, affable presence dried up gratitude before it reached the tongue.

Butler was probably aware of my thoughts. He had acute intuition in such circumstances. But he showed no sign. Instead, he beckoned the waiter and asked for the dessert cart. "Pineapple for me," he said, as if confiding a secret. "No carbohydrates, my medico says."

"When did you see him last?"

"Eight or nine years ago."

"That's too long without a checkup."

"It was advice I could have given myself. Nonsensical paying out hard-earned guineas for that kind of advice. Well, what d'you think of 'em?"

He pointed to the sheet of paper still lying on the table between us. I took out a pencil and ticked four names from one side of the double-column typewritten list of names.

"I could do these without going mad," I said.

"Not bad," he said, watching the ticks. "I think I might have chosen the same lot. What about the Reds?"

"Aren't eight too many?" I asked. "Won't the public be fed up long before that?"

"You're writing them."

I smiled.

"If you turn in anything half as good as that latest Kefauver-Stassen series or your McCarthy profile of two months back, I'll be satisfied. After all, they started the idea."

"Where shall I work?" I asked, warming to the idea and doubtless flattered by his long memory.

"Where you like. Where are you staying?"

"Athenaeum Court."

"Can't you work there? You can do most of your telephoning from Court House. Rees will fix you up with a secretary if you want one. *And* with one of his staff men if you want any deviling done. You probably will. You'll be spending most of your time between your victims and a typewriter, won't you?"

"Probably," I said, but I had no plans at that stage. Butler had had quite a start.

"When will you begin?"

"If I'm to do anything of a job on it I'll have to start straightaway."

"That's what I thought. You'd better come back with me. Have you met Rees?"

"No. Is he good?"

"It depends what you mean by 'good,'" he said blandly. "By 'good' I mean a good yes man. Perhaps you don't."

"You want a caretaker, not an editor."

He reflected for a moment. "In a way, yes," he said agreeably enough. He slowly stirred his coffee and looked unseeingly at a pillar. "Yes. I think you're right. An intelligent caretaker. I might advertise for one next time. Good caretaker-editor wanted. I'll remember that."

"Why not an intelligent editor?"

"Sentiment," he said casually as he asked the waiter for the bill.

For a moment the remark seemed a *non sequitur* of a strange order. Then I said, "You! Sentiment!"

He continued to stir his coffee, unmoved by my scoffing note, and said slowly, "I made that paper. Don't forget that. It's the only paper in the Group I'm really interested in—as a newspaper. To me, the others are just money-making machines. I watch 'em, of course. I never stop watching 'em, but that's the one I love. Like a father his daughter, a miser his gold. It's in a different world. For one thing it's a bloody good newspaper—for its particular market. For another, it's the best newspaper in the Group for trying out my ideas. I propose to keep it that way."

"And Rees?"

"He fills the bill. Shrewd and capable. Prefers running a newspaper to editing one. I'm not looking for a man who wants to set Fleet Street on fire. I don't like editing by proxy, but I don't interfere much. I keep an eye on the front page and the features. Mainly the features. They make or break a paper today. At least our kind of paper."

He turned and smiled, looking like a benignant old Borgia. I smiled too. Sometimes it was very difficult to resist his disreputable honesty.

He scrawled his signature on the bill, put down his tip, thanked the waiter and pushed back the table.

Just as we were about to stand he let his plump hand fall lightly on my knee. "You haven't lost that youthful trick of trying to be funny at unfunny moments," he said. "I indulge it. I appreciate it. But your little asides could land you into trouble."

"Not big trouble."

"They're not funny enough for that. Let's go."

We went out and down to the Embankment door and waited for the car.

"Does Rees know you're putting me onto this?" I asked.

"Of course. We discussed it last week. Hence the Hepburn pieces."

"You knew I'd say 'yes'?"

"What else could you say? You were in no position to say 'no.' Allow me a modicum of psychological insight."

"What was Rees's reaction?"

"I've told you. He's a good man. He knows what's good for the paper is good for him. And I tell him what's good for the paper. It's as simple as that."

"Go on," I said, "I'm fascinated." I was.

"As a matter of fact, he jumped at the chance. What editor wouldn't? Star man from the States doing three main feature stories. You've got a following of a sort among his readers. You know you have. Be your age!"

The Bentley appeared before us. "In you go!" he said genially.

"An Indian-summer afternoon like this we ought to play hooky, but back to the grind."

7

WE WENT BACK TO BUTLER'S EYRIE FOR A HALFHEARTED CONFERENCE concerning the series. Rees and Hepburn came up and sat in two of the more distant armchairs. I sat in the chair nearest the desk. Butler insisted.

Rees was all that Butler had intimated: a short, dark, thickset Welshman with a blunt nose, dark chin, untidy collar and tie. Celtic cadences gave a softness to his comments which strangely belied the cynicism of many of his statements. It was easy to see that he might well be as much, or as little, as Butler had claimed.

From the first I was shaken. Rees accepted the series without discussion. He seemed more interested in the length of the projected pieces than in their likely contents. When he began to talk of picture and make-up, of tying the series in with the cartoon, of how much space he would give to Hepburn's pieces and my own, he seemed to come alive. He was the contemporary newspaper executive, the technician, the expert. In fact, anything, it seemed, but my somewhat antiquated idea of a journalist. *Give me the words,* he seemed to say, *and leave the rest to me. I'll put 'em across.*

I had no doubt that he could and would.

He was certainly one of the few London newspapermen who would have been at home in New York, I thought, watching him. He might well have made a sound managing editor for a New York tabloid. He could take the kernel of an idea and squeeze all there was to be got out of it, but somebody had to bring him the idea. When the bringer was Butler, then Rees was willingness itself.

I looked up at Butler and he was lazily watching Rees at work, a sardonic smile on his full and petulant mouth.

Then Hepburn began to talk. About forty, I judged, perhaps younger, perhaps older, but he would look forty for several years: a tall, dark-haired man with heavy features and a clipped, dark, quasi-military mustache. The eternal acting temporary major. His clothes were well made. He wore them with a kind of raffish distinction. That I had noticed when he entered the room. But why "raffish"? I asked myself. Was it just his foulard tie, too bold in pattern, too tightly tied, too proudly curved above the crossover waistcoat of his brown suit? Or was it the waistcoat itself?

At first sight he seemed a somewhat unneighborly character, with a flushed complexion, a defiant look about the eyes and a frequent nervous trick of a sudden hurt frown.

With certain small changes here and there, he was a newspaper type, which may vary from paper to paper but is basically always the same. I knew in my bones that Hepburn was another of those brilliant, wasted writers who work with words the way a conjuror works with colored balls. He can juggle with them so that they can mean anything an editor wants them to mean. He can write a leader, a feature story, an interview, swiftly and brilliantly, yet somehow the words will not add up to more than a demonstration of technical skill. You remember them for ten minutes. You even go out of your way to say "brilliant," but after that they are utterly dead. Nothing of the man himself comes through. The words run to seed as the man himself runs ultimately to seed. Almost every newspaper of any size carries such an expert on its payroll, and every journalist will recognize him—the man with a golden turn of phrase who carries always in his eyes a lasting query: Why the hell don't my golden phrases make up into a golden book? Why can't I write something that readers of the years to come will want to read?

My thoughts moved along those lines as Hepburn outlined the pinpricks and pinpoints of his opening piece, every detail of which was apparently known to Rees and Butler.

Within a minute I realized that I was no more than a spectator at a polite attempt to persuade me that I was being put in the picture. Almost the only thing they hadn't known in advance was the list of names I would choose. After Hepburn had said his piece Butler told them and chose the last two names himself. "Do they seem all right?" he asked.

"All right by me," Rees said. Hepburn was not so forthcoming. He frowned.

"Don't they fit in with your ideas, Hepburn?" Butler asked.

"I don't smell any trouble," Hepburn said slowly, but then, for some momentarily obscure personal reason, he began to argue about two of them.

The argument lasted for no more than two or three minutes and then, as suddenly as he had queried the names, Hepburn gave up and accepted them. His heart wasn't in the struggle. He had merely felt that he had to stand up to Butler, but it was a token stand. Already, as far as he was concerned, the little snap was over. He had kept his personal dignity. Or so he thought.

As the so-called conference broke up, Hepburn promised to let me have carbons of the pieces he had written. Rees said he would also be glad to give me what help I needed. Both seemed friendly. Neither saw in me a potential rival. After all, I was booked to be back in New York inside a couple of weeks unless Butler had another of his brainwaves. So they would co-operate.

"It's all clear, then?" Butler said as we stood up.

"I think so, sir," Rees said. Hepburn nodded.

Butler turned to me. "I'd like to see the pieces as you finish them. You'd better go through them with Hepburn before I see them, just to see you haven't canceled each other out somewhere. And he'll let you know if you've trodden too heavily on anybody's corns. Anybody who matters, that is. I think that's all, then."

Rees made no protest at this overlording of his editorship.

We went out and down to the fourth floor, along to Rees's room. There it was, the kind of room I knew too well. No touch of Rees the man. No picture, no object, no one thing to say to the visitor, *This is my room, the room where I spend one-half my waking life.* Instead, two plain desks, two armchairs, four small chairs, a red Turkish carpet over brown linoleum, a map of the world on one wall, a color rough for a double-crown poster advertising a six-day serial on the other, and a heap of newsprint galleys drooling like spaghetti over the edge of a tall oak desk. For relief I walked toward the window which overlooked the court and the playing fountains.

"Will you get those carbons, Roy?" Rees asked.

Hepburn took a packet of papers from his inside pocket and held them out to me.

"You had 'em all the time, then?" Rees said, surprised.

"If I'd brought them out we'd have been there now," Hepburn

said laconically, taking out a flat and golden cigarette case. "I've work to do."

We all lit up and Rees smiled a noncommittal smile. He was wondering where I stood. A friend of Butler's? A friend to nobody?

He took off his wrinkled jacket, hung it on a peg behind his chair and turned to me. "Miss Street next door will do all the typing you'll want. I've warned her. She's pretty good. Will you want anything more?"

"I'll want somebody who's used to making appointments. They're usually better done by a woman. Can Miss Street do that?"

"No, you'd better have Madeleine." He suddenly made a decision. "In fact, you'd better have her do everything. She's very efficient. She's more my personal assistant than a secretary. I sometimes think she really edits this bloody newspaper."

He pressed a buzzer on his desk. Almost immediately the inner door opened and a tall young woman came in. She was about twenty-five, fair haired, blue eyed, dressed in a navy sweater with white collar and a blue pleated skirt. Her demeanor was so serious that we might all have been involved in an autopsy, but I was too busy considering her English complexion to be impressed by her high seriousness. She stood there, composed and serene, awaiting Rees's instructions. Hepburn was looking her over, too. A bit too obviously and biologically, I thought, but could think of no other classification for my own staring.

Rees introduced us and then talked fast, explaining everything, succinctly and efficiently. Miss Gordon was used to this kind of thing, he said. She'd be glad to do the job, wouldn't she? "Yes, of course," Miss Gordon said demurely. Or was it so demurely?

I gave her, somewhat apologetically, Butler's list of names and asked her to try to arrange interviews during the next three days with the M.P.'s whose names we had ticked. She nodded gravely as I gave my few instructions. What she lacked in the lighter touch she seemed to make up in office efficiency. "Ring me at Athenaeum Court around six and tell me if anybody's accepted."

"They'd better," Rees said firmly, as Miss Gordon went out, and then, "Anything more?"

"I don't think so, unless you want these back." I tapped the carbons of the Hepburn pieces.

"No, I've some others upstairs," he said.

I turned back to Rees. "When will you want the first?"

"Friday midday," he said without hesitation. "Better still, late Thursday. A bit steep, I know, and I'm sorry."

It was an earlier deadline than I had been told but not much earlier than I had expected. I said I'd do my best.

"By the way," Rees said as I turned to go, "this may help. It's got a potted biography of every M.P." He handed me a copy of the *Times'* list of members of the House of Commons.

8

THAT WAS TUESDAY. AFTER THAT IT WAS HARD WORK ALL THE WAY. During the afternoon I read through the brief biographies of the M.P.'s I hoped to meet. Then I stared out of the window, across to the blessed plane trees of Green Park. Then I dozed until Miss Gordon rang on the dot of six. She had arranged four of the interviews, she said. Would I make a note of them or should she put them in the post?

"I'd better have the first, anyway," I said. "Who is he? When and where?"

"Nine-thirty. Mr. Norman Drury."

"Some of these politicos seem to start life very early. Drury is one of the Tories, isn't he?"

"Yes. The Member for Canterbury West. He apologized for starting so early, but said he had a full day's work to do before going down to the House and could only fit you in then. He's at his office from half-past eight."

"All right. Next?"

"You'll want Mr. Drury's address. Forty-eight Fore Street. A family business, apparently. Richard Drury and Sons, Ltd. Silk merchants. Fore Street is just off Cheapside."

I noted the address and asked for the next.

"Mr. Ayling. He wondered whether you would care to lunch with him at the House of Commons at one o'clock. I accepted for you."

Despite her demure approach to the job and her dry-as-dust telephone manner, I sensed that Miss Gordon had enjoyed her career as entrepreneur.

"Well done. And then?"

Surprisingly, she laughed, and said, plainly amused, "The same place for tea, I'm afraid. With Matthew Chance, the Labour M.P. I said yes, although I thought you might have had enough of the Mother of All Parliaments by then. And I've always been told that New Yorkers don't take tea."

"One, I'm not a New Yorker, Miss Gordon. Two, I drink Earl Grey tea. Regularly. I'm glad you accepted on my behalf. Two Tories, one Socialist. Any more?"

"Only one so far. But aren't three M.P.'s enough for one day? They're terrific talkers. The others seem rather elusive at the moment. While Parliament's sitting it's usually fairly easy to track them down. Especially now that pairing is rather discouraged. I'll get them tomorrow."

Even during those brief exchanges I had acquired new respect for Miss Gordon's efficiency and sense of humor. I thanked her and rang off, and took up the *Times'* list for the lives of Drury, Ayling and Chance.

Drury's record was simple and conventional. Conservative M.P. for Canterbury West. Born 1912. Wellington and Sandhurst. War Service in France, the Western Desert and Italy. (Lt. Colonel. D.S.O.) Now managing director of family mercer's business. Special subjects: army, agriculture, textiles.

Ayling seemed slightly more difficult to place. Born 1913. Educated Portsmouth Grammar School and St. John's College, Cambridge. Fellow of his College and lecturer at the London School of Economics until the outbreak of war. Then with Ministry of Economic Warfare. Now Conservative M.P. for Portsmouth, East, and a director of a publishing house.

With that background, I thought, Ayling seemed just the type to have followed Gaitskell and the other intellectuals of the Labour party. Well, it takes all sorts to make a House of Commons, and I turned to the third biography.

Chance was apparently the youngest of the trio and the least informative. The entry read simply: Born 1914. Winchester and New College, Oxford. Fought on Government side in Spanish Civil War.

War Service in Middle East, Crete, Yugoslavia. M.C. Labour M.P. for Scunthorpe and Edge End.

Ah, that's better, I thought, another Wykehamist to follow Gaitskell, Crossman, Jay, Younger *et al.* to the defense of the working classes.

9

AT THIS POINT IT IS TEMPTING TO PUT DOWN IN DETAIL SOME ACcount of my eight interviews of the next three days. Yet, although they all have some part in this record, only one is important.

Almost straightaway I discovered more pleasure in this one job than I had had in five long years of covering the American scene. It was understandable, of course. It would have been the same for an American with the situation reversed.

I had enjoyed my time in the United States, yet now I was talking to my own countrymen of my own generation or thereabouts: men in their late thirties and early forties. Intrigued as I had been by the politics of the United States, I now found a pleasurable escape in talking over Britain's problems with a group of men who seemed to have those problems very much at heart, whatever their individual politics.

Yet as the first day wore on I could begin to see the cynical truth in Butler's remark that it was a dangerous game for a foreign correspondent to return too often to his homeland. By six o'clock I was involved in what I considered Britain's major problems. I found myself waiting to play a less passive part in the way ahead, and tentatively planning other articles that I might write after I had finished this present series. Already I was prepared to decry Mencken's bitter remarks about politicians. And many of my own earlier comments on the political life seemed to have a somewhat gritty echo, too.

Meanwhile, Mr. Norman Drury, M.P.

10

FORE STREET took quite a hammering during the 1940 air raids on the City of London; little of the original street remains.

Number 48 is a square, yellow, stuccoed office *cum* warehouse standing forlornly at the corner of Fore Street and a narrow alleyway. Along the dark brown fascia board, above the frosted glass windows of the ground floor, ran the legend RICHARD S. DRURY AND SONS, LTD. ESTABLISHED 1841.

I pushed open the swing doors and stepped into a large general office. A young man with an old, sad face came to the long counter, asked my name and gloomily requested me to follow him through to an office at the far end of the room.

I was shown into a large room, without windows, blazing with daylight lamps. Three men, all standing, all looking down at a heap of silk squares carelessly arranged on a desk, turned as I entered the room. A tall, round-faced man with a thick rufous mustache looked across to me, nodded briefly, then said in a loud voice to the others, "I say the whole bloody bunch and let 'em go. What d'you say, Hughes?" He gathered up the squares—there must have been a dozen or more—and thrust them into the arms of a sedate and elderly man wearing a gray suit, high stiff collar and, I was scarcely surprised to note, a beautiful black-and-white silk tie.

Without embarrassment the old man gathered the squares together. "I'm still dubious about the new polka dot, Mr. Norman."

"Do what you like about the new polka dot, but let me know."

He crossed swiftly to the door and opened it. Mr. Hughes and his younger, tubbier, but equally smart companion went out.

We introduced ourselves. "New designs from our people up in Macclesfield," Drury said. "Get 'em down every other week. What's this your paper rang about? Your girl sounded pretty cagey. Another press stunt, I suppose?"

"Not such a stunt," I said. "We're suggesting that there's room for more young blood in fairly important posts in the government. My editor in chief thinks the Prime Minister hasn't gone far enough."

Drury grinned. "Carry on," he said. "I think your editor fellow's dead right. Had similar ideas myself recently."

"So we're proposing to run a series of about half a dozen pen portraits of younger M.P.'s who . . . you can guess the rest."

"And I'm to be one of the victims, that it?"

"More or less."

"Suits me!" Drury said briskly. "Might upset one or two of the old pundits, but fire away. By the way, I must leave here in half an hour. Absolute must. Sorry to be such a high-pressure merchant, but there it is. Afraid we all are, down there these days."

"Not everyone runs a business as well, I imagine."

"More than you'd think. Trouble here is I had a younger brother killed in the war. He'd have taken a hell of a lot off my shoulders. Even knew something about design, which is a damn sight more than I do. Always have to try things out on the wife. Sorry, you were saying . . ."

For the next half hour we talked politics in general and Drury in particular. He did most of the talking. Beneath his bold and brassy manner was a lively and inquiring mind. He talked for twenty minutes: about himself, his constituency, his special studies. He barked out his comments in a staccato, take-it-or-leave-it manner. An ingenuous shrewdness quickened all he said. "As far as I can see, we want to keep a lot of this welfare-state stuff," he said at one point. "God knows we must. Anybody'd think the Socialists had thought the whole damn thing up themselves. The trouble is these Labour johnnies think welfare's the cure-all for everything. Seem to think England's got a special dispensation from the Almighty to live on the fat of the land and not do a day's hard slogging for it. Believe me, if we don't look out, we'll have those Heinies and Japs ahead of us again. At least on price, and that's beginning to count a hell of a lot with all these millions with a little more money in their pockets. Quality's not enough. But you know all this as well as I do," and so on until he said suddenly: "I've done most of the nattering so far. Now tell me something about the States!" For the next ten minutes I had to stand up to fierce questioning. He was a listener as well as a talker, it suddenly appeared. Business, politics, personalities . . . I had to talk. At the end he looked at his watch. "Must dash now, if you'll forgive me. Very interesting getting your views. Been in the States twice since the end of the war. We do quite a good business

there ourselves. They're very fond of our club ties, y'know." He
grinned. "Sold over five hundred dozen O.E. ties in New York alone
last year. Amazing how these Etonians get around, isn't it?"

"What do the O.E.'s have to say about it?"

"Between these four walls, they don't know, old boy. Daresay
they'll find out one day. But an O.E. silk tie stands a New York club-
man in at twelve dollars, don't forget. Good for our dollar earnings.
Can I give you a lift? One thing about these blitzed sites, one can
park a car. Never could before the war."

"Ludgate Circus would suit me."

11

FROM LUDGATE CIRCUS I WANDERED SLOWLY UP FLEET STREET AND
into Court House. Out in the court, the fountains were spouting deli-
cately and brilliantly in the sunlight that balanced like a sword between the high walls of Court House and the two old houses that
the Baron let stay when he built his paper palace.

I went up to the library and sat down at a desk in one of the window recesses and scribbled out my piece on Drury. He was a natural
for an interview and the piece almost wrote itself. By midday it was
done, and I took the scribbled sheets down to Miss Gordon. I would
come back later to correct or add to the typescript.

"It will be ready in half an hour," she said as demurely yet au-
thoritatively as before.

By then it was almost time for another Tory. I went down and
out into Fleet Street and the sun, took a bus to Charing Cross and
walked slowly down Whitehall. The day held the sparkle that makes
Portland stone beautiful. The Admiralty, the Horse Guards and the
Old Banqueting Hall were pale gray under the autumnal sun. I delighted in London, watching the movement of red buses between the
old, weathered façades and the gigantic new Government blocks that
seemed to be rising all about me, and suddenly hated the idea of
returning to New York. What I want, I told myself, is winter and

summer in the Cotswolds, spring in London, the fall in New York. It was a prospect which kept me busy as I walked along Whitehall and across Parliament Square to the Houses of Parliament and the Visitors' Entrance.

12

JOHN MALCOLM AYLING, M.P., WAS SUCH AN EXTREMELY SHY young man that I wondered how he had ever been induced to stand on a platform to answer any questions more complex than his name. He was plump and short—no more than five feet five—with the remnants of sandy, curly hair topping his round head and a pink-and-white complexion that took nearly ten years off his age, despite his thinning hair. He blushed easily and frequently. The biographical note in the *Times,* I remembered, had indicated that he was barely forty, that he was a publisher and that his special study was economics.

Within five minutes I could see why Ayling, despite his obvious intelligence, would find political preferment fairly difficult. At first sight, his appearance wasn't exactly compelling, his nervousness was acute and from time to time he stumbled over trickier consonants.

I casually mentioned my New York background, my interest in his articles on economics, and then repeated the formula I had given to Drury with such success, but Ayling didn't fall for it.

"It's very flattering," he said, "and up to a point I agree with you. Not p-personally but generally. But I'm afraid I f-faced up to the fact long ago that my particular talents aren't the F-front Bench variety. Sad, of course, but there it is."

This is one of those occasions when it is more sensitive to be dull than smart, I thought, and said, obtusely enough, that I could scarcely agree with him.

He didn't take it up and we went on with our adequate lunch in the dull but snug dining room for visitors. I let him talk. The stammer was noticeable but not intrusive. I asked him about his publishing interests.

"P-publishing's a polite name for it," he said. "I was a don—economics—at Cambridge before the war. Did a spot of lecturing at the L.S.E., too. After the war—I was in Economic W-warfare, by the way —what with a wife and two k-k-kids, I was finding things a bit of a strain. I was lucky in the 1946 election, but the whole thing jolly nearly b-broke me. Then I decided that if old K-Keynes could apply his specialized knowledge to the c-c-commercial world outside, why couldn't I? After all, it's the real test. So I scraped together a few hundreds and started my so-called p-publishing house. Never had a dull day since."

"Or an unprofitable one?"

He laughed. "Oddly enough, no. It turned out to be quite a m-money spinner. More important still, we've had some quite n-notable results."

"It looks as if Keynes started something."

"I doubt whether he'd think so."

During the next quarter of an hour, while we drank our tepid coffee, he ranged knowledgeably and widely over Britain's problems in the postwar world. At the end he said, "Once I get onto that subject I'm apt to become one of the world's six m-most elemental bores."

I said, quite truthfully, that I had found his exposition engrossing. Tentatively I came back to what I termed his excessive modesty concerning the possibility of office. "I'd still like to run the article," I said.

He replied quietly, and without apparent embarrassment, "I d-don't think it's any good. Really, I don't. As you've n-noticed, I've got quite a stammer which seems to take charge at odd moments."

"I haven't noticed it unduly."

"Nice of you to say so, but t-take my word, it's there all right."

"How did you get on canvassing?"

"I'll t-tell you," he said, "but it's not a pretty story. So l-long as I have the feeling my listeners have inferior minds I'm all right. As soon as I have the slightest respect for a listener's intelligence I have to go c-careful."

"What does that make my I.Q.?"

He laughed. "Very kind, but it d-don't wash. I've noticed, if you haven't."

"You're all right on your feet in the House."

He laughed again. "I usually talk to empty benches about a d-damn dull subject and m-most of my listeners are usually asleep or don't know what I'm talking about."

"I'd still like to fly my little kite," I said.

"Well, do what you like," he said. "I've an open mind."

He walked with me through the Gallery and out into the Yard. We shook hands. "I'll let you see a draft," I said.

"Forget it," he said, laughing, and waved as he went back into the shadows. I walked out into Parliament Square, picked up a taxi to Athenaeum Court and worked on the Ayling piece for an hour or more.

The writing had its tricky moments. For a man on vacation it was like a day at the coal face, but by half-past four it was done. I rang Miss Gordon and asked her to send a messenger to collect my second piece. "I'll come in around six and go through it, if that isn't too late for you."

"I'm here till seven at least. Usually half past," she said gently. Miss Gordon had a skillful knack for replacing men in their rightful place.

I went back to my scribbled sheets, put them in an envelope addressed in bold black capitals to MISS MADELEINE GORDON: TO BE CALLED FOR and then took my second trip that day to the world's most hallowed talking-house.

13

TEA ON THE TERRACE OF THE HOUSES OF PARLIAMENT ON AN INDIAN summer's afternoon had many merits, I thought, as I relaxed into a chair and began to make the acquaintance of Mr. Matthew Chance, M.P.

I wondered why I had been singled out for such a delectable honor. The kindly September sun upon the river, the great, slow lighters and busy tugs made a mundane picture transformed into splendor by the background of Pugin's fantastic walls and windows.

Such a setting should have been reserved for the more worthy and useful members of Chance's constituency, I thought, but my host interrupted this mock-modest reverie. "I gathered from your girl that you wanted to ask a few questions. I thought this as good a place as any."

"Better than any other I can think of."

"Good. I thought it might appeal to you after your long stay in the States."

Such close knowledge of my journalistic background, I said, was a compliment indeed.

"Not really," he answered. "In some ways you're scarcely a stranger at all. I've had too much pleasure from your American notes for that. This was the least I could do. I'm very glad to meet you. Are you back for long?"

"Not long enough."

Along the Terrace the subdued chatter of hosts and guests merged with the rattle of china and tinkle of spoons; the sempiternal sounds of an English afternoon.

On opening notes as felicitous as those, I thought, the interview could scarcely go wrong.

Chance was an unusual-looking man, fairly tall, about five feet eleven or so, lean to a point of gauntness. His hair was blue-black, straight and coarse in texture. His features were strong and forceful, his nose broad yet well shaped, his chin lean and sharp. His lips were thin, and inclined, I soon noticed, to a faintly self-mocking smile. Two long lines—of laughter or tension—cut deeply into his cheeks. His eyes were intensely blue. While he talked he looked steadfastly at his listener; while he listened he looked steadfastly at the talker. This unwavering gaze was curiously emphasized by a heavy scar scored horizontally across his temple above the right eye. He wore a double-breasted blue suit, a dark red tie, white shirt, black shoes.

I might have made a guess to place him as a Guards officer, an impression probably deriving from his height and assured, almost too assured, manner. Not exactly arrogance, I thought, but near enough to cause misjudgments. His voice immediately lessened the martial impression he unwittingly gave to himself, and thus to others, for he spoke quietly and slowly, with a far-off touch of Wales overlaid by more sophisticated vowels. The so-called public-school voice is rarer than many sociologists would have us believe, and I believe that many phoneticians would bear out my words. In the case of Chance, cross-currents of upbringing had given him an unusual voice of considerable charm. As I listened, I remembered having read a forgotten gossip writer's comments: "A voice as compellingly Celtic as Bevan's, but a lot more musical," or words to that effect. Now, hearing the voice, I could echo the columnist's reaction.

I was certainly meeting some odd pieces in the British political jigsaw, I thought, both in looks and speech: the red-haired Drury with his correct, accepted vowels; pink-cheeked Ayling and his nervous stammer; and now Chance's dark arrogance and Celtic resonance. It would have been a day for Professor Higgins as well as a tiring newspaperman.

I gave Chance my hackneyed explanation concerning the series. He heard me out, watching me with that unwavering look of his.

"Who else is in the series?" he asked.

I told him. Neither Drury nor Ayling had asked that question.

"Why pick on me?" he asked.

"You seem to be making a reputation for yourself. Your name's always in and out of the newspapers. I'm afraid that's what editors look for."

"Not necessarily intrinsic merit?" he asked with his thin smile.

"Not necessarily, but, in this case, both I hope."

"What kind of questions are you proposing to ask?"

"Mainly personal. In fact, pretty well all personal. Where you grew up? What made you a Socialist? In your case, why you went to Spain? You can guess the kind of thing."

He nodded reflectively.

Over scones and butter I began to ask my questions. He answered them readily, with the assurance of a man who knows himself and his job through and through.

"The popular press is fond of referring to you as a 'Man of the People,'" I said. "Why should they single you out?"

"A catch phrase," he said. "I used it in one or two speeches I made soon after the end of the war. Then, about four years ago, the *Express* took it up, the way they're apt to take up things like that when the occasion arises, and there it was. I was labeled for keeps. After that it was too easy."

"But why should the label stick to you?"

"Perhaps because it seemed an improbable fact on the face of it," he said. "Winchester and Oxford aren't the usual background for a Man of the People. Yet I am," he added simply. "My father was a Welsh solicitor in Aberdovey. He came from nothing and made himself what he was by studying night and day. I did much the same in a softer kind of way. I went to a local school, got a scholarship to Winchester. In fact, I was a scholar, both at school and at New College."

"But that's not enough for them to pick on you and make the label stick."

He regarded me steadily. "Emphasis and contrast count in a newspaper office, don't they? Four years ago I married a well-to-do American girl. The *Standard* loves that sort of thing. 'The Londoner's Diary' even dug out an appropriate estimate of her income. Crossbencher ran it pretty hard in the *Sunday Express,* too. The Beaverbrook Press loves the chink of other people's money."

"Have you used the phrase since?"

He laughed. "A sly one," he said. "As a matter of fact I have. From time to time. It was no good giving it up, was it? Besides, a label like that does one no harm. Certainly not in the Welsh valleys. And my constituents aren't so interested in my private life as newspapers seem to be."

"Are you so sure?"

"Perhaps not," he admitted, smiling almost ruefully.

In any case, it was time to change the subject. I asked about Spain.

"It all seems so long ago," he said. "Like a dream, and for me, of course, it was nowhere near the tragedy it was for all the others. I wasn't in the International Brigade until later, you know. I'd picked up a good deal of Spanish, and pretty well became one of them and yet remained a foreigner. All that was interesting. And I admired them. They were stiff-backed, proud, willful, maddening—but so incredibly brave. All of them." He paused and then added, as if to himself: "No one can be more outside anything in this world than a foreigner caught up in a civil war."

He went on talking, almost as if he were speculating alone and aloud. "God, how ghastly the whole thing was. I saw nothing in this last war half as horrible. Almost anything is preferable to war."

I wondered whether this "Man of Peace" line was at the back of his recent speeches. I said, "Is that behind your baiting of America?"

The blue eyes considered me steadily across the table. "Do I bait?" he asked slowly, and shook his head, bringing himself back from Spain to this moment. "Perhaps, in a way, I do," he went on. "I don't think the mass of Americans want war. I'm not so sure about the American general staff. They're a very cocky lot. They really do think they know it all, don't you think?"

"They frequently give that impression," I said.

"Perhaps they're not as certain as they were two years ago. I don't know. Sometimes I think they think they've got the whole answer, and would like to see if it would work."

"You are oversimplifying things you've heard. There are many sane influences at work in the Pentagon, too, don't forget."

"Well, there it is. To me they seem to be like a lot of circus strong-arm men flexing their muscles. They think they can take on the 'whole goddam world.' One day they'll really want to try. I've heard those Pentagon characters."

"So have I. I've also heard Molotov and Vishinsky."

He nodded. "Probably," he said in a quieter voice. He seemed to close up then, and I almost regretted my comment—but not quite.

"I seem to be doing all the talking," he said. "Giving you no chance to ask your questions. I'm sorry. Fire away."

He smiled. It was a disarming smile, and I was disarmed.

The sincerity of his convictions was obvious, yet the fierceness with which he had spoken on Spain and war and the American general staff, taken with his background, scarcely added up to one's idea of a conventional pacifist. We began to speak of other things. His early life in Aberdovey. His father's determination to make him a scholar against his own inclinations to swim and sail. His scholarship from a local private school to Winchester. The unrelenting habit of work, fostered by his tutors and his father at more distant range. Then Oxford. Then Spain.

I fired an occasional question, but, like the two politicians I had already seen that day, Chance liked to hear himself talk. How they all do!

We went on talking for nearly an hour.

I could put down a detailed account of the give and take of our conversation even now, two years later, but it would draw out the record to too great a length, even though this is mainly the story of Matthew Chance.

Instead, here is the piece I wrote for Rees. He and Hepburn cut it slightly, for I had run counter to Hepburn's line in one or two of my references but, in the main, it is the piece I wrote. Judge it charitably against its journalistic place: a feature in a popular penny-halfpenny newspaper.

YOUNGER M.P.'s OF PROMISE: III

A MAN OF THE PEOPLE?

James Matthew Chance calls himself a Man of the People. Presumably he does this because, although he is a Scholar of Winchester, he was the son of a small-town Welsh solicitor, and Welsh miners put him into Parliament in 1946 and again in 1951.

Whether Chance is as much a Man of the People as he likes to think is doubtful. He is at least five inches taller than the average man of the people. He wears his dark hair rather longer than is fashionable in the Rhondda Valley. He has a rich wife. And he wears London handmade suits.

But his early history fits him for the part. He was a scholarship boy. As a young man he won another scholarship to Oxford. There he studied constitutional history, played Rugger for his College and came down with a "First." So far the story reads like that of many another Young Man of the People.

He then spent nearly a year as a schoolmaster, not exactly among the People, but at Rugby, teaching the sons of Midland industrialists and landowners the authorized versions of English history. In 1937, when he was twenty-three, the Spanish Civil War started, and Chance was one of the first of those crowds of romantic and militant young men who rushed off to fight for the Azaña Government against Franco.

Unlike so many of his fellow idealists, Chance stayed in Spain throughout the Civil War. He fought in the now almost-forgotten battles of the Guadalquivir River and Madrid and he was one of the last Republicans out of Barcelona. He was a front-line fighter. He managed, nevertheless, to contribute many articles on the war to English newspapers and magazines.

That was his life until the war ended. In September, 1939, when a bigger war began, Chance joined the British Army as a private. By 1943 he was a captain in the Rifle Brigade and in the Middle East. Later, he was sent as a liaison officer to Greece and he was in the hopeless battle that was fought in Crete. He escaped, back to Egypt, and was dropped into Yugoslavia for liaison duties with the partisan forces. By the end of the war he was a major with a decoration from Tito to wear alongside his Military Cross.

He entered Parliament in 1945, one of the many young ex-officers on both sides of the House, one of the many unknown hopes of the Labour party. He quickly made a name for himself as a biting critic of his own party's foreign policy. He was especially bitter about the handling of the Near East situation, and, later, of what he called Bevin's policy of making Britain "America's First Lackey." At first he was a lone fighter, but gradually gathered a group of younger Socialists around him. On home affairs he has been a supporter of Aneurin Bevan but a somewhat perfunctory one. He has never disguised the fact that he considers himself primarily an expert on foreign affairs.

Unlike many other critics of the Socialist approach to foreign affairs, Chance has always been listened to with respect, partly because he has actually fought in the battlefield for the causes he espouses but mainly because he has spent all the time he could spare from his Parliamentary duties in traveling abroad as a special correspondent for a Sunday newspaper. This may not give him the knowledge of a foreign office counselor, but it has given him wide firsthand experience, rare among politicians. Since 1946 he has visited the United States, the Far East and the Middle East (three times).

In any future change of power, this well-informed and independent M.P., still under forty, must receive serious consideration. Yet his undoubted talents as a debater have never yet been utilized in any official Socialist attack upon the Conservatives, his name is never mentioned in any list of likely office holders in any future Labour government. Are the Old Men of the Labour party also scared of youth, brains and political resolution?

That was the piece I wrote. It was a journalist's estimate of a man or, at least, the known facts of a man's life. But, like most journalism, it omitted a lot.

For one thing, I couldn't record the odd impression that I had had throughout my interview with Chance: that he was speaking a piece mechanically like a talking machine. He had spoken of things and happenings which should have moved him deeply, even now, all these years later. Yet he had spoken of them as a dried-up history don might have spoken of tragedy in ancient Greece. Chance had been a touch too detached. He had seemed more interested in the pattern these tragic happenings had helped to make than in the tragedies themselves. I had once tried to be a historian myself, but

I had never been able to act like an impersonal old pundit as far
as petty upsets in my own life were concerned. I still thought that the
four years I had spent in a prisoner-of-war camp had taken four years
out of my very own personal life and not just out of the world's long
history. He seemed to have none of those subjective failings. I had
the feeling that I had heard a tale told by a professional word spinner
and not by a man talking from his heart. I didn't even have the feeling that he had told me only half a story or a false story. What he
had told me was true: of that I was certain. But he had added the
facts up so that they made a story to fit a theory. Perhaps we all do
that.

But perhaps my thoughts were getting too fanciful, I told myself,
certainly too complicated. Perhaps, too, a little hindsight is creeping
into this narrative. We never know. To get back.

That brief sketch was published on the following Thursday, linked
with a somewhat shorter note on a clever but lackluster Labour member, Major Oswald Dexter, a peacetime barrister who had been a
major in the Army and couldn't forget it, despite a talent for close
legal argument far more rare than a wartime Majority. I took pleasure in a second-rate revenge for his unrelenting monologue by giving
him about half the space I gave to Chance.

But I am running ahead.

14

HEPBURN HAD WRITTEN HIS PIECES SKILLFULLY. AFTER READING
his two articles any reader would have been tempted to despise any
politician over the age of fifty. It was political pamphleteering at its
best (or worst): devilish, destructive and very entertaining to read.

My own articles carried no reference to Hepburn's attack, yet,
merely by outlining the careers (*outside* politics) of eight compara-
tively younger M.P.'s, they sustained Hepburn's argument. The reader's inference was, inevitably, that these younger men were being
kept out of office by doddering officeholders. Such an inference was

due less to any implication of mine than to the ignorance of the English electorate concerning their elected representatives. Scarcely anybody in this country, for instance, knows the names of the more important Parliamentary officeholders, still less their work and worth, a sad fact but demonstrably true. Ask any mixed company the names of holders of the following high offices in the previous and present governments: the Lord President, the President of the Board of Trade, the Minister of Transport, the First Lord of the Admiralty, the Minister for Education, the Solicitor-General.

This ignorance is also partly due to the fact that few M.P.'s manage to step out from the ranks boldly enough to become known to the Great British Public, despite the considerable newspaper space given to their activities. Out of 615 Ministers and Members, scarcely three dozen can be called well known, scarcely half a dozen make memorable impressions. Perhaps Beaverbrook is right when he says that it is easier for a mediocrity to get on in politics than in commerce.

Perhaps Butler, too, was right, and the British are interested only in manifestations of vivid personality or outstanding character in politics. Yet, as I had tried to remind him at various times, finding half a dozen first-rate men out of six hundred would be a tough task in any walk of life.

Hepburn's articles, then, caused, as they were intended to cause, some mischief, a good deal of comment and, we gathered, a certain amount of discussion in high places. More to Butler's taste, Hepburn's articles and my profiles provoked an unusual number of letters from readers, mostly approving Hepburn's critical line.

A few older readers took the attacks as grave reflections upon senility generally, and had to be answered smoothly; but most of the correspondents were far more critical (and more personal) about politicians than any newspaperman would dare to be.

My Drury-Ayling pieces duly appeared on Wednesday.

Midway through Thursday morning, Peter Winter, editor of the "Letter-Box" feature which dealt with readers' correspondence, rang me at Athenaeum Court to say that a number of letters had already arrived, some showing interest, several suggesting the names of other younger Members who might well be included in the series. Local agents, he thought, had been quick to see political advantage in having their Members publicized in this fashion, and had persuaded local sympathizers to write the letters. Whether party headquarters was as keen on the series we did not learn.

Would I care to see any of the letters? Winter asked.

I said I'd willingly leave it all to him. His success was mainly due to his skill as a journalistic *agent provocateur*. His normal technique was to quote briefly from about a dozen letters, and to this daily dozen append approving or scoffing postscripts of his own invention.

This new series was made for the "Letter-Box," for it is well known that there is no more enjoyable pastime for any newspaper reader than to join, by proxy, an attack upon established Aunt Sallys.

I was glad to hear, as any journalist would be, that my pen portraits had aroused a certain degree of interest, but I was too preoccupied with last-minute revisions to my final piece, which was to appear on the following Saturday, to bother with any "Letter-Box" complications. My last two politicians, two younger Labour M.P.'s, had proved both elusive and difficult: corrections were heavy and the whole thing was threatening to run late. Rees had a rigid timetable and I was in serious danger of upsetting it.

I told Winter something of this. He was understanding. "All the same," he added, "I think some of the letters would interest you. We're printing a selection tomorrow. The editor was saying at the conference just now that you might like to write a final piece commenting on the reaction of the public. Could be interesting."

"Could be. But what about Hepburn? Isn't that kind of thing more his line?"

"We had quite a number of letters backing him up, but, judging by the batch this morning, the public seems to like being introduced to some of its younger M.P.'s."

I promised to look in during the afternoon.

By two o'clock I had managed to clear up my outstanding queries on the Saturday article and send the corrected galleys down to Miss Gordon, asking to see revised proofs. Then I had a solitary lunch at Rule's and afterward walked slowly along the Strand toward Fleet Street and Court House. There I spent ten minutes in Winter's room, reading through some of the letters. Some were fierce, some were pathetic, a few were just plain bitter. There were also the usual madcap contributions from citizens with projects for new forms of Parliament, examinations for officeholders, payments by results and so on. I chose three or four letters from the more rational correspondents, ringed passages I thought worth quoting in "Letter-Box" in the next day's paper, discussed them briefly with Winter and left.

That was Thursday afternoon, the second day of my series, the day the piece on Chance and Dexter appeared. By then, three o'clock, I had completed my assignment: my eight "potted" biographies had either been published or the corrected galley proofs were ready for the printer. I was merely waiting for Butler's dispensation concerning my own immediate future. But he gave no word.

15

I WAITED UNTIL THE FOLLOWING MORNING, FRIDAY, AND THEN RANG his secretary, Miss Gowing. Butler was out but she said she'd ring back, so I stayed in my comfortable room overlooking Green Park, trying to absorb as much of the English scene as I could. I was engaged in the last-minute pastime of all travelers soon to return to unwanted homes-from-home, trying to engrave an ineradicable set of London images upon my mind's eye, an unforgettable gallery for the months to come.

Occasionally I turned again to the novel I was reading, but my eyes returned always to the window and the plane trees beyond. I had no wish to go out. All I wanted, or seemed to want, was the sight of this part of London I knew so well.

About noon Winter rang. "I wondered whether you might be coming in again today," he said. "Rees liked that batch of letters I put in this morning, so I thought I'd play what looks like a winning streak —with your help."

"How are your correspondents today?"

"Up to standard."

"More mad hatters?"

"The usual. One woman wants a Parliament made up of equal numbers of men and women: three hundred of each."

"Why not?"

"That's what I suggest in my footnote."

"About half-past two or three, then."

After that I went off to my luncheon date. Miss Gowing hadn't rung back.

I went down to Court House after lunching with a wartime friend, one "Cholly" Bedlington, an ex-MTB commander, now a peacetime shipowner with widespread Mediterranean interests. I found it diffi-cult to recognize, in my plump, tycoonish host, the emaciated sailor who had also been a prisoner with me in the big naval cage outside Hamburg, but I quickly recognized his irrepressible philosophy again, which even SS camp overseers had been unable to subdue. His idea of luncheon was four or five courses in the window room at Scotts. His first toast was "Ourselves and our future": his second, "À bas les Bureaucrats." He had read my articles and talked about them. Unlike most tycoons he talked about his guest first, then himself.

He was finding life profitable, he said. His eight ships were doing well. He suffered some competition from the Greeks, but "It's won-derful what some honest-to-God bribery will do, old boy, and any-way, it takes me and the missus down to Athens twice a year. All on expenses. You don't seem to have developed a New York appetite yet. No more Roquefort?"

And so on and so on. The change in men! Yet the unchanging essential core! Had not Bedlington often told us all in that faraway cage that this was exactly what he would do and be?

He gave me a lift in a new Bristol sedan as far as Fleet Street. "Always read your American stuff, old boy," he said in parting. "Bit serious sometimes. Don't take life too seriously. Not worth it, believe me."

I went up to Rees's rooms and handed the finally corrected proofs into the care of Miss Gordon. She also had my mail, about a dozen letters from the States which had been directed to Rees's office from Central Registry.

While Miss Gordon was checking my corrections I sat in a worn leather armchair reading the notes and postcards. There was also a brief letter from Chance: *I found your article entertaining and flat-*

tering. So did my wife. We are having a cocktail party here this Saturday, 6:30 to 8, and wondered whether you might care to come. Rather short notice for you, I'm afraid, and it will probably be a bit of a scrum, but you may find some of the guests quite interesting. Come in about 6 if you can and we can talk first. The address was 22 Chester Square.

There was also a note from Major Oswald Dexter pointing out an error of fact: he *had* been out of England during the war. He had visited Gibraltar on a secret mission in 1944.

Finally, a note from Ayling: *You did a tricky job very well, if I may say so.*

I dictated brief answers and an acceptance to Chance. Miss Gordon took the notes with unhurried efficiency. I finished dictating and said, "I'm just going upstairs to Mr. Winter. Could I have these to sign in half an hour?"

"But of course," she said.

There was a lot about Miss Gordon to intrigue a man.

Winter had made his choice. The letters were even more numerous, he said, and the same in tenor. They all hoped Churchill and Attlee would take the hint and throw out a few of the old deadheads.

"And what about the rest of the mad hatter's file?"

Winter grinned and passed half a dozen letters across.

"Not so many, but just as crackers—or as sane. Take your choice."

The first concerned a suggestion that no prospective M.P. should be permitted to stand for Parliament unless he could show that he had earned at least his would-be parliamentary salary in the open market. Signed, E. A. Brant, Capt. RN (retd.), Sevenoaks.

A second correspondent wanted Parliamentary sessions to be conducted on a topographical rota system: one session in Edinburgh, another in Manchester, another in Cardiff, and so on. "If it is a truly British government, why not?" asked a Miss Jean Stuart from (I scarcely needed to look) Edinburgh.

A third was scrawled on a piece of blue linen tracing cloth that draftsmen in architects' offices use. The message was simply: ASK YOUR PRECIOUS MR. CHANCE ABOUT PROFESSOR LEWIS. No name, no address, just that, in block capitals.

"This wins so far," I said.

"Oh, that!" Winter said, dismissing the scribble. "We get that kind of thing every day."

"Anonymous?"

"Usually."

"Block capitals?"

"Usually."

"Who is Professor Lewis, anyway?"

"God knows. Look him up if you're so interested."

He indicated *Who's Who* in a book trough on his desk. I took the volume and opened it to "Lewis." I began to look through the names for a professor. I came to one almost immediately: Abraham Lewis, Professor of Slavonic Studies, St. Catherine's College, Cambridge. I read through the entry and then read on. Within two minutes I had discovered that there were several other professors named Lewis. To my surprise there were fourteen entries for professors by the name of Lewis. I told Winter.

"I'm not surprised. It's a fairly common name. I met one of 'em at Cambridge once. I knew he couldn't be the chap."

"Why not?"

"Far too respectable to get mixed up with anonymous letters."

"Isn't it usually respectable chaps who do? Anonymous letters aren't much use against rogues and scoundrels."

"Perhaps you're right," Winter said absently. He was busy. Time was beginning to slip away and he wanted "Letter-Box" ready well ahead of edition time.

"Will you want me any more?" I asked.

"Not till tomorrow. And only if you think you're not wasting your time, old boy. I'm very glad to have you drop in. It's a help. Are you going to do that follow-up piece Rees was nattering about?"

"I doubt it."

"I liked the profiles."

"Thanks."

"When you going back to the States?"

"Next week, I imagine."

"Lucky devil."

After a few more words I left, saying I would come in again the next day.

I went downstairs to Miss Gordon's room. All the letters were typed, beautifully typed. I signed them and thanked her. "A pleasure," she said, without conviction. "By the way, Mr. Rees was interested in your letters. He has a penchant for looking over my shoulder."

"I see his point," I said. "And thanks for the information."

She smiled in her secretive, self-contained manner.

There was nothing more for me to do in Court House. I had no wish to meet Rees and get myself involved in another stint of hard work, so I went down and out into Fleet Street and clambered on a No. 11 bus. I had frequently promised myself a search for small pieces of antique china or porcelain I might take back to friends in New York.

I spent a pleasant afternoon wandering through Church Street into Fulham Road and bought nothing.

When I got back to Athenaeum Court the desk had a message I half expected: would I ring Mr. Butler's office immediately? The message was timed 2:30.

I rang. Miss Gowing was now less exigent. Mr. Butler had wanted to see me during the afternoon, but it was now nearly five. Perhaps it would be better the next morning.

"I'd rather come now," I said. I wanted to know my fate as soon as possible.

A moment later, rather more warmly, she said, "Mr. Butler says by all means. He'll expect you here at six."

16

BUTLER WAS SITTING BEHIND HIS BIG DESK. SOMETIMES I WONDERED whether he ever moved from that vantage point. In the old days he sometimes got up and walked to the window. As if he followed my thoughts he stood up and walked to the window. I sat down in one of the armchairs. He stood by the window for several seconds, looking down into the courtyard far below, not saying a word. Then, having made his gesture, he came back and sat in another armchair. "Tell me," he asked, "have you enjoyed doing these pieces?"

"Quite."

"No more than that?"

"I enjoyed some more than others."

"But you probably enjoyed writing about Stevenson more than writing about Stassen."

I nodded.

"It's understandable," Butler said. "It's part of the game. I enjoy doing some things here more than others. For instance, I've enjoyed having you around here. I'd rather keep you here than send you back. But there it is. I've no other man I can put in your place."

"No man is indispensable, least of all in a newspaper office," I said slowly. "I guarantee to find at least three men in this outfit who would give their eyeteeth for the chance."

"Perhaps, but I don't want a collection of eyeteeth, thank you. And wanting to do a thing is a long way from doing it. You fit, that's all."

I did not answer.

"You could leave," Butler went on equably. "You could get a job back here. Especially after the show we've given you this week. The *Mail* would take you like a shot."

"Possibly, but I lack ambition."

"Energy rather than ambition, let us say."

Again I did not answer. I had no reply but denial and I would never give Butler that petty triumph. He changed the subject. "I liked the Chance piece," he said.

"I quite liked writing it."

"What did you think of him?"

"I found him rather impressive. He had more weight than any of the others, although Ayling was impressive in his own way, too. But Chance's personality came across. He's a forceful citizen. Perhaps it was more than personality. Character, possibly."

"It's a distinction you're always trying to make."

"It's the distinction that sorts men out."

"Perhaps. What else?"

"About Chance?"

Butler nodded.

"Nothing much. I put most of my thoughts down. Did it read as if I'd kept much back?"

Butler didn't answer. Again he changed the subject, saying, "The series seems to be provoking quite a correspondence."

"So it seems."

"Have you seen any of the letters?"

"You know I have. You told Winter. Winter told you."

He smiled. "I like a newspaper to get letters. It's a healthy sign."

"Even when the letter writers are round the bend?" I asked, and quoted a few of the ideas that had been addressed to "Letter-Box."

Butler smiled and nodded. "Winter does a good job. This morning's batch was the best yet. Readable. Provocative."

"I prefer the mad ones," I said, remembering and quoting the four-ring captain's suggestion. Butler smiled. I also mentioned the reference to Professor Lewis.

"Who's Professor Lewis?" he asked.

"I don't know. I gather there's more than one. No Christian name was mentioned in this case. That was the sum total of the note."

"Where did it come from?"

"No name or address."

"Any postmark?"

"I didn't notice any envelope."

"They're always kept for a day or so. The legal department likes us to do it. God knows why. I suppose it proved useful once, forty years ago. The legal mind is like that. Ask Winter." He indicated one of the telephones on his desk.

"Is it so important?"

"There might be a story in it."

I had had wayward thoughts along the same lines during the afternoon, but I had crushed them. Following them up would mean more work.

Almost guiltily I went to the desk, picked up one of the ivory-colored telephones and asked for Winter's office. Butler crossed to the bookcase.

"What was the postmark on that note about Chance and Professor Lewis?" I asked Winter.

"Hold on a minute," he said. I heard rummaging among papers.

"A bit smudged," he said, "but I think it's Chelsea."

"What was the exact message?"

He read it out. The words were as I had remembered them, but I wrote them down.

"Anything in it?" he asked.

"I doubt it, but keep it."

With a brief "O.K." he rang off.

"Well?" said Butler. He was sitting in a chair with *Who's Who* open across his knees.

"It's no good," I said. "There are fourteen Professor Lewises recorded in that tome."

"So you *were* interested?"

"Enough to check that simple fact. Who wouldn't?"

He was silent for three or four minutes, reading through the Lewis entries, flicking over the rice-paper pages. Then he said, as if he had proved something to himself, "Well, they're certainly a mixed bag." Slowly he began to read out the entries, shortening them to names and professorships, omitting detailed careers. I watched his forefinger moving slowly down the close-set pages as he read through the list. "Abraham Lewis, Professor of Slavonic Studies, St. Catherine's College, Cambridge . . ." and then on to the others.

"Would you agree that a reference merely to Professor Lewis suggests that the writer of the note knows only one? Otherwise, wouldn't the writer include a Christian name?"

"As I seem cast to be Doctor Watson I'd say 'yes,'" I said with little interest.

"Who'd be most likely to consider his or her Professor Lewis the only boy in the world?"

"Someone very near and dear to him or somebody fairly ignorant."

"How many had you heard of?"

"Two—Day Lewis and Michael, the Dartmouth type."

"Would you term yourself 'fairly ignorant'?"

"At least I knew there was more than one," I retorted, nettled. "And at least if *I'd* been writing an anonymous note about either of them, I'd have given him a Christian name."

"Why? Supposing the writer didn't want to identify *his* Professor Lewis too clearly."

"Then why write the note at all?"

"Just to start a hare, maybe. But you're probably right. Which would you say then: someone near and dear to him or just a plain ignoramus?"

I laughed. "Either. Toss for it."

"Isn't it usually the lower orders who use block caps for anonymous messages?" Butler asked, still serious despite his attempts at humor.

"I think most people would."

He wouldn't give up. "Who would be most near and dear to a professor? Wife, mother, daughter, sweetheart or lovesick pupil?"

"Any of 'em."

"I'd plump for the lovesick pupil," Butler said decisively.

"Why?" I asked, aroused by his certainty.

"Jealousy's the great *agent provocateur* for anonymous notes."

I scoffed.

"History bears me out," he affirmed.

"All this history! How do you find time for newspapers?"

"You'll find history on our front page every morning," Butler said grandly and blandly.

"All right, how do *you* see the Professor Lewis setup, then?"

"I don't. I never romance. You ought to know that by now. I'm merely speculating, not particularly seriously. A lovesick girl, a pupil driven to distraction by the Professor's sudden interest in left-wing politics. What about that? It's about the sordid level of twentieth-century university romance, isn't it?"

I laughed outright. "Well, if it's jealousy, where does Chance come into things?"

"God only knows," he said. "Perhaps he's the left-wing beguiler. Anyway, that's for you to find out."

"Me!" I said. "My job with Chance is over."

"But I understand you're seeing him again."

"News travels fast."

"I pry in an amateurish kind of way," Butler confessed genially. "You dictated a note to Miss Gordon, Rees overheard. Now I know. Tittle-tattle plays a big part in an organization of any size. Rees was up here half an hour ago."

"Rees didn't overhear. He overread my letters, to be exact."

"It's all grist to Rees's tiny mill."

"Do I ask Chance halfway through the evening, then, if he knows a Professor Lewis?"

"Every man his own technique, but why not?"

"How would you do it?"

"I'm rusty," he said. "I've been sitting on my fat backside too long. You have to give me time to answer questions like that these days. I'd certainly memorize the details of all those Lewises so that you know which one he's talking about if the name does crop up."

"Have you ever met Chance?"

He paused for a moment. "Once upon a time I think I did," he said slowly. For a moment I thought he would not go on. Then he continued. "Long ago. In the Spanish Civil War. One of my last jobs as a special writer. Although I was editor, I thought I ought to do a stint of writing as well. Editors used to do that kind of thing occasionally in my day. Gerald Barry used to do the same kind of thing when he was editing the *News Chronicle*. Remember? He went to Spain. So I went to Spain, too. I got around quite a bit. Saw both sides. Hated 'em both. You ought to read Brennan's *Labyrinth of Spain*."

"I've read it."

"Well, that's the background, but Brennan loves all Spaniards."

"They're a remarkable race."

"Any man's entitled to an opinion. Anyway, to get back to Chance. He was quite a boy, you know. Had a terrific reputation among the Spaniards as a fighter and a rising politician."

"It didn't reach back here, did it? I don't seem to remember his name."

"Those reputations didn't cut much ice here, I know, but take my word for it, he was quite a boy. Comparable with some of the German and Italian fighters who went back with high reputations. I think our people—left- and right-wing—always considered the whole thing rather off the map, a kind of peninsular war. With one or two exceptions, of course."

"We underestimated the other peninsular war, too."

"True enough. I keep forgetting you were once historically minded."

"Chance was a Communist, I take it."

"He fought with 'em. First with one of their ragged-arsed regiments, then with the International Brigade and all that. You had that in your piece. But they weren't all Communists, you know. Far from it. Quite a lot of old-fashioned liberals joined that outfit."

"Did you ever meet him afterward?"

"I'm not sure I met him then."

"Where was it, if you did?"

"Near the end of the war. The tide was running fast against the Reds. I was taken to an airfield near Barcelona to see something of the remaining Red air force. He was there. At least, I think he was the chap. He was just being shipped out. One of a small party of

about half a dozen. They'd been flown up to Barcelona from one or
other of the crumbling fronts and were being put on board one of
those Russian tramps that were so busy in the Mediterranean in those
days. Rumor said the usual drill was by sea to Baku and then over-
land to Moscow. Early days of indoctrination courses, I suppose.
Chance was the only Englishman in that particular bunch. A Spanish
commissar type pointed him out to me, no doubt thinking I ought
to be shown an Englishman on the side of the Reds. I went up to
him and spoke but he didn't play. Shook his head and then said,
in very good Spanish, that he knew no English. Odd, don't you
think?"

"Did you tackle the Spanish commissar again?"

"I did. He'd been watching and said he must have made a mistake."

"Are you sure it was Chance?"

"Positive. I think I am, anyway. Well, that was in '37. I forgot all
about it until just before the '45 general election. Then I saw his
picture in the *Herald* one day. Only one of those simple half-column
newspaper blobs we all call halftones, but I knew straightaway it
was the chap I'd seen on the Barcelona airfield. I've been interested
in him ever since."

"But going to Moscow then doesn't prove anything. It was the great
visiting time for all the parlor pinks."

"Yes, but even the parlor pinks went as Englishmen. It wasn't
Chance's trip to Moscow that puzzled me. It was his denial of his
nationality. I call that odd. In fact, I'd go so far as to say it's an extremely rare occurrence in an Englishman, wouldn't you?"

"Perhaps you were mistaken."

"Perhaps I was. But I don't think so. You remember our man, Dick
Arnott, who got killed at Dunkirk? He was in Spain for Reuter's in
the Civil War. One day I told him about my encounter. He thought
it probably had been Chance. He'd come across him at the front.
Told me to watch him in years to come. Said he would be the English Lenin if ever there was one."

"Big words."

"So I thought at the time. Well, I've watched him on and off ever
since, but all I see is that he's sobered up like all those 1930 intel-
lectual Reds."

"What am I supposed to do now? Vis-à-vis Chance, I mean."

"Nothing, apart from finding out who Professor Lewis is."

"Nothing, eh?"

"Hang around for another week or so, anyway."

"And not go back?" Pleasure made my question eager but foolish.

"I don't see how you can do both," Butler said, grinning.

I had one last question. "If you put your cards on the table, what's the most you know about Chance and what's the worst you'd expect to discover?"

Butler laughed aloud. "The most I know about Chance is what I've told you. I think it's enough to make a man interesting. It is to me, anyway. An incident like that plus Arnott's odd words of advice stay in the mind for years. One watches a man, always hoping for an explanation for the apparently inexplicable. After I saw that picture in the *Herald* I made a point of going to one of his pre-election meetings just to see if he was the chap. I still think he was."

"Why didn't you ask him?"

"I did," Butler said quietly. "He denied the incident, of course. Perhaps I did make a mistake." He paused. "But I don't think so. Fifteen years later and I still don't think so. As for the worst I'd expect to find out, there's no best and no worst. He interests me. Isn't that enough?"

"And Professor Lewis?"

"Probably a hoax. We get enough attempts during the year."

"But you don't think so?"

"I'm open-minded."

"I'd better let Grimston know I'm hanging on here for a bit."

"I cabled him this afternoon."

"You think of everything," I said, but Butler didn't reply, merely shrugged as if such little actions were all part of his job. I added a word of gratitude for the extra days in England.

"I don't see why you should be so grateful," Butler said. "It's not a holiday I've given you; it's a job of work."

"But I like working here."

I had said the words before, I remembered, and they had proved useless.

"God knows why," Butler said. "Anyway, let me know how you get on."

17

I LAZED THROUGH THE NEXT DAY, SATURDAY, WANDERING ACROSS Hampstead, visiting Kenwood and its sad and somber mansion, afterward taking tea in Heath Street; an uneventful excursion, perhaps, but the kind of golden afternoon that proves memorable long after leaving England.

In the early evening I went down to Pimlico to the Chances' cocktail party.

The house was at the eastern end of Chester Square, a creamstuccoed façade, pleasing to the eye, scarcely distinguishable from its slightly decaying but dignified neighbors. The tall, narrow windows of the house were dark in the failing sun, the royal-blue door and brass knocker that much brighter.

Almost immediately after I rang, the door was opened by a young man in black trousers and a black-and-green striped livery waistcoat with black sleeves.

I was surprised by the speedy service, the young man and his decoratively informal uniform. Walking across Green Park I had been playing that game most of us play en route to a party: What kind of household should I find? What kind of wife? What kind of party?

I imagined a discreetly furnished home, a well-dressed hostess and a middle-aged housekeeper, the whole thing in excellent taste, quiet and orderly.

That picture was straightaway disturbed by the young butler, further disturbed by his smile and silence. He asked my name and repeated it immediately to himself, in the manner of a foreigner mastering unusual vowels and consonants. I looked again at the sallow face and somehow knew immediately that he was a Pole. He took my hat, placed it carefully on a marble-topped console set across the open doorway of a ground-floor room and led the way upstairs.

I was shown into a fairly large L-shaped drawing room. My name was announced with a precise mastery. As Chance came across the room I had time to take in further surprises. The room was scarcely the discreetly furnished, safe-but-certain background for a younger left-wing M.P. that I had half expected to find, but an enclosure of color, as brilliant as an Eastern despot's tent. The walls were Chinese red, the surface texture smooth and brilliantly reflective. The furniture was a bold assembly of black and gilt Regency and oriental pieces. The carpets were wall-to-wall mustard-yellow pile. The whole room held a concentration of color to astonish and bedazzle the eyes; yet, in the moment of entry I was absorbed into its comfort, warmed by its confident glow.

There were three others in the room, apart from Chance, standing around a black marble fireplace. Chance introduced me, first to his wife, a small, slim, pale woman of about thirty-five, with deep-set, shadowy eyes, dressed in a black ballet-length dress which emphasized her pallor. As she welcomed me, her quiet American intonation spanned three thousand miles.

The others were a married couple, Kaminetski or Karminetski by name. I forget. He was forty-five or so, with sleek, thinning black hair, and an assured, broad-chested manner. His wife was twenty years younger, also very dark, her lustrous black hair drawn back into a large bun, would-be Spanish style. Her close-fitting red dress, fortunately for her, harmonized with the walls. She was very handsome and had the unmistakable manner of someone who had been aware since childhood of that simple but important fact.

I was offered a drink and said "Sherry." Chance called, "Tadeusz!" and another pale young man, in the same rig as the butler's, appeared from the other end of the room. Another pale Pole in a House of Pallor, I told myself, enjoying my joke in the moment of taking the drink from the imperturbable, almost implacable attendant.

We all began to talk. It soon appeared that the other guest was a timber merchant in a big way of business. He had the self-made man's inevitable gambit of referring to his business background too soon, obliquely perhaps, modestly perhaps, but nevertheless too soon. He spoke of a recent visit to the States, thus showing me his knowledge of my own ground and his importance there. Chance cut into the conversation, asking me when I should be returning to the States.

"I've had a reprieve," I said. "Another two or three weeks."

"Washington or New York?"

"New York, I imagine. That's really my beat. I go to Washington when so-called human-interest stories are required. They've been getting rather frequent recently. That's why I've been there so often.

Pen portraits of politicians. A new view of Eisenhower. And so on. We have a very good regular man there, Grimston."

Chance nodded, but the plump man jumped in feet first. "I met him last summer when I was over," he said. "Found him very useful. Knows his way around. Put me onto one of the top import boys. I'm trying to get some of our West African hardwoods into the States," he added mock-modestly.

"Did you have any luck?"

"Not bad. Fifty thousand standards—that may not sound much, but it's pretty good going for a start, believe me."

"It sounds an awful lot to me, Dick," said Mrs. Chance.

We all agreed.

Having made his point the timber merchant was prepared to relax, and we began to talk fairly generally about the possibilities of an economic recession in the States.

Within ten minutes, however, I found myself alone with Chance by the window overlooking the Square. "I really want to thank you for that article," he said. "A few outside words like that can be of inordinate help in one's constituency. My agent's had fifty thousand copies run off—with your editor's permission, of course."

"The circulation manager usually tries to sell the newspapers and not reprints. Helps the net sales figures."

Chance smiled. "What kind of a man is Rees?" he asked.

"Welsh, tough, ambitious, able."

"A good journalist?"

"For this day and age, yes. Not a Delane or a Scott, of course, but ours is scarcely that kind of newspaper."

"Didn't you have an editor called Butler once upon a time?"

"We did. He's now editor in chief and managing director of the Group."

"Is he now? What kind of a man is he?"

"It would be too long a story."

"Why? Do you know him so well?"

"Nobody knows him so well. No, it's just that he's a man of legends."

"As a journalist or a personality?"

"Both."

"He doesn't do any actual editing himself now, then?"

"No."

"A kind of *éminence grise?*"

"Not so *grise*. More *noire*."

Chance smiled. "Does he take an active part in the running of the papers?"

"Fairly active, for someone weighing over two hundred pounds. Have you ever met him?"

"I don't think so. I've met many newspaper people of course, but I don't remember Butler. I must have heard his name somewhere or other."

"This series was really Butler's idea," I said, watching Chance carefully.

"Was it now? He's full of ideas, I suppose?"

"His staff seems to think so."

"And you?"

"Sometimes. There are few dull moments with him, anyway."

"You're fortunate," Chance said, almost ruefully. "In my job there are so many dull moments. They say the House of Commons is the best club in the world. I'm afraid that's true, but like most good clubs it places a high value on dullness."

"Why do you stay there, then?"

"Part duty, part drug. I persuade myself I understand my constituents as well as anyone would. I can speak for them and even fight for them, if that's not too strong a word. And I'm interested in the world we live in. I have certain ideas about Britain's job in the world. It's the only place I know where I can put those ideas forward. Occasional dullness doesn't seem too high a price to pay for the chance."

As he talked the faraway singsong Welsh note came through. Once again I thought how deep and compelling a voice it was; a voice made by many influences: Wales, Winchester, Oxford. But, unlike the voices of so many Welsh preachers, actors and politicians, his wasn't unduly self-conscious. Chance hadn't stripped his larynx bare, so to speak, and then rebuilt the vocal cords.

As he talked, I found his personality increasingly attractive. He had two rare and engaging characteristics: he was a good listener and he was modest. Unlike so many politicians he did not seem to carry around with him that conviction that in him was the answer to the world's great problems. He was also free of another occupational disease of many politicians: a sense of persecution which persuades them that they aren't being given a reasonable hearing, that someone or everyone, from constituent to Press Lord, is against them.

Although I took to him I was still vaguely conscious of his talent for talking on one plane while his mind was busy on another. He had spoken, for instance, of the dullness of the House of Commons as if he were making a plain matter-of-fact statement. Yet a man who really believes in the dullness of an institution normally derides or at least decries its demerits, affectionately or savagely, as the mood moves him. He doesn't state the fact casually, as if it were a situation that suited his purpose. Yet that was the impression I gained. He puzzled me, and perhaps that was an additional reason why I enjoyed my conversation with him, standing there by the window in the last fine dust of the fading sunny day. At one point I asked him what his immediate ambitions were.

"To travel," he answered. "No more. Possibly to write a book about my travels. And I'd quite like to write something about my war in Yugoslavia. So far, the chaps who were in Crete seem to have had it all their own way as far as writing is concerned. Leigh Fermor, Xan Fielding, half a dozen others. I should like to do something along those lines for my particular war."

Here again he spoke as if he were saying something he ought to say. Something that would fit in with a picture he had already made of himself for others. He spoke without apparent enthusiasm of his project for a book. Yet most would-be authors would have spoken with keenness of such a venture. Yet he did not give out an impression of boredom, merely of utter detachment, as if he were listening to himself make these statements.

"Apart from the book?" I asked.

"Nothing."

"In politics?"

"Not a great deal. I've very deep and probably very boring convictions about the idiocy of this country and Eastern Europe falling out. Working for that conviction is apt to prove a full-time job."

"You don't like the Americans?"

"I wouldn't say that. I don't like the Pentagon mind."

"And your wife?" It was a personal question, but justified by his attitude, I thought.

"She, too," Chance said quietly. "With her it goes deeper. Like lots of other Americans who live away from their homeland she is appalled by what she sees of dollar diplomacy, and, worse still, what she thinks it will lead to. We both think it's nowhere into its stride yet. The Americans go on paying out now and it doesn't hurt them. But if they happen to run into a slump, they'll start moaning about all that money they've spent and the lack of gratitude of all the beggar nations. The Americans will want something back. Nobody will have any dollars to cough up, so it will mean something in kind. Men, spheres of influence, concerted action, promises."

He spoke quietly and without apparent bitterness. Occasionally he smiled.

"Don't you think they write it off as they hand it out?" I said. "They're a peculiarly profligate race with their charity."

"You're too trusting."

"I don't think so. I live among them and that's the way I see them. It's in their tradition. It's almost an underlying philosophy with them. In a world as rich in natural resources as theirs they aren't so penny-proud as we are. We don't begin to understand that kind of attitude over here."

"Your beliefs do you credit," he said. "I hope you'll forgive me if I contend that you've been deceived by their individual hospitality."

"You're entitled to your beliefs. I hope you'll forgive *me* if I contend that they are warped."

We went on talking and wrangling amiably for another ten minutes. Such reasonable disagreement frequently fosters friendship more warmly than agreement. Each man grows more tolerant of the other as he sees such civilized (and unexpected) tolerance grow within himself. I liked listening to Chance's comments. His personality was elusive. I wanted to know more about him, to see more of him. He seemed at once so open yet so secretive, so kindly yet so ruthless, so compassionate yet so detached. Such contradictions and paradoxes in personality are always challenging. But our discussion for that evening ended as two cars drew up below us in the Square, and half a dozen men and women got out, looked upward and waved to Chance, who had stepped out onto the balcony.

"A pity!" he said, coming back into the room. "We must go on with this discussion some time. Sandra, my wife, also has views on this subject. You must dine here one night before you go back. One night next week."

I should be delighted, I said, which was true. He had developed the art of listening to a high degree. How rare in a politician! And how quickly we warm toward the genuine listener!

I watched him—a tall, lean man, with strong, dark features and thick black hair—walking toward his latest guests as they entered the room. He was an unusual man and a likable one. I had only seen him in these two brief encounters, yet already it seemed to me that I had known him for many years.

Sandra Chance, too, had moved away from the timber merchant and his wife to the new arrivals. She had the easy assurance of most well-to-do young American women. Young American men of the same background often remain callow beyond their years, mistaking boldness and physical vitality for assurance, but their sisters never make the same mistake. They move with a confidence and ease of manner that young Englishwomen of comparable age and wealth scarcely ever acquire. For one thing they seem unashamed of their femininity, holding themselves erect, taking pride in the curves that make them women. Perhaps their confidence derives from proven belief that this is not necessarily a man's world. Not one young Englishwoman in ten thousand seems to have had that moment of divine revelation by the age of twenty. Few enough by thirty. Forty is a different matter. English women begin to come into their own . . . but I digress.

I stood by the open window, occupying myself with these superficial speculations, looking along the Square toward St. Michael's Church. More guests arrived. The room gradually became crowded. The world outside seemed to become that much quieter as the babble rose within. "Another ten minutes," I told myself, "and then I may, with good grace, go." I stood there, puzzling over Chance, and Butler's remarks. As I began to know him better, Chance seemed unlike the character Butler had discussed. I would have put him down as a firm, resolute man, without the need to equivocate as Butler had implied.

The waiter, Tadeusz, came with more drinks, moving skillfully among the crowd. I took another sherry. "This and no more," I told myself, lighting another cigarette.

The timber merchant joined me, telling me how sensible I was to have found and kept this spot. I was inclined to agree. By then the room was crowded with thirty guests or more, and the scrum was well and truly joined. I cut my timetable, vowed inwardly to suffer the timber merchant for just five minutes more and, meantime, answered banality with banality. I gave a fleeting thought to Professor Lewis and looked around, wondering whether he might be there. Perhaps I should take the unknown correspondent's advice and ask my precious Mr. Chance. That had also been Butler's advice, I remembered. At the thought I paused, an alternative suddenly intruding. The idea was so obvious and so well worth trying that, in my eagerness, I too abruptly left the timber merchant. I could see the surprise in his eyes at this sudden boorishness.

"If you ever come to the States again," I said too quickly, "you must look me up." I moved through the crowd, gradually getting nearer Chance.

A hand grabbed my elbow. "Hey, you," a voice commanded. "Take it easy!"

I looked round into the shining, round red face of Rob Prout, a free lance I had met often in New York who was married to an ex-staff photographer from *Life*. We stood there and sought to shake hands.

"I've staked me a claim in a corner of this wall and bureau here," he said. "Come on in, pal!"

I moved with him to his hideout, three battling footsteps away. "Now tell all!" he said. "How long you've been over. What you're doing. All."

I told him and asked the same of him.

"I'm here on a kind of vacation, but I'm doing a series on the side for *Look*. Doreen's doing the pictures. You remember? She's good. We're doing a series on European folk art. Don't laugh. It's fodder. And what's more it's shaping pretty well. I can see a book in it. You know Doreen, don't you? I thought so. Well, she's gone on furniture, antiques and so forth, and she's in Brighton. A royal pavilion you've got down there or something. I got this invitation and I'm here."

"Chance's invitation or his wife's?"

"Wife's. I knew her ten years back when she was a year out of Vassar and running around the Village with more money than sense. She seems to have sobered up."

"I only met her this evening. Tell me more about her."

"I don't know everything, old pal," he said with a big grin. "When I first knew her she was just one of the crackedest Commies the Vil-

lage ever saw. Just another of these gals with too-rich poppas and a
forlorn neurotic mom. Boy, did that girl hate her poppa's fellow men!
Wouldn't take a penny off him. Lived in the Village on money she
got from an old grandma. It still wasn't peanuts."

"And then?"

"Why'm I telling you all this?"

"Local color."

"Well, she changed. Suddenly she's a poor little rich girl all over
again. Poppa dies, so she starts spending poppa's money, but not on
mink. On one of these left-wing Greenwich Village rags, published
every Friday. You know the kind of sheet. Runs it at a loss for about
a year before it folds. But it was pretty fierce stuff while it lasted. As
mean a piece of journalism as I've ever read. Well those were the
days when it was fashionable to be way over to the left, as Mc-
Carthy's finding out."

"What about since?"

"Well, she came over here just before the war, then came back to
the States and began to work for OSS in about '43. She was a bad
risk, I guess, but why not? The Russkies were our friends and allies
then, weren't they?"

"And after the war?"

"Spent most of her time over here: France, Italy, Spain."

"And Chance?"

"I don't know. Married about four years ago, weren't they? I don't
know much about the romance. He's a bit far over to the left, too,
isn't he?"

"Fairly."

"Boy, there's no such word. You're far over or you're not over at all.
At least, that's the way it is back home."

"This isn't back home. Anyway, she's settled down. You can see
for yourself."

"You mean all this?" He moved his empty glass in a close but all-
inclusive arc to take in the room, the furniture, the melee.

"More or less."

He grinned and made the familiar New York quip: "Well, it ain't
much, but it's home."

I laughed as he lowered his voice and went on. "Quite frankly, old
pal, I don't go for that settling-down line with a girl like Sandra. That
kind of woman never settles down. She's just another one of a long

list of pale, unhandsome gals who've got to keep moving or bust. You'd find, if you took 'em to pieces, they all have great turbojets pushing 'em along. Sandra's just another one of these cold, mousy Anglo-Saxon women of the Western world who've got to go on chasing something—money, fame, sex, equal rights . . ."

I interrupted. "And what do you think she's chasing now?"

"I'd have to know more about this guy Chance's sex life before I answer that. Maybe nothing at the moment, but it's still there, ticking over, waiting for another bout. For my money, she's just another cold-hearted girl with a grudge against life, the money their old dads made, the drudgery of other women's lives and Christ knows what else. She'll bust out again, brother, mark my words."

"In which direction?" I asked and looked across toward the door, to Sandra Chance. Well, she wasn't beautiful, but she wasn't "unhandsome." She had a quiet, slim grace that would have given her distinction in any crowd. Her dark brown hair was drawn back too tightly, perhaps. With a wave in that hair she might be a different woman. She did look a touch serious. But that perhaps was due to her shadowy eyes and those were beautiful, despite Rob Prout's general denigration. I needed to see more of her before passing judgment. But no such hesitations afflicted Prout.

He went on: "The same as before, old pal. We never change course after the age of seventeen. If it's money it stays money, if it's skirts it stays skirts. For me it was drink and it stays drink and I'm gonna snaffle me another Scotch before the stuff gives out. There's a lot of hard drinkers around here, I know. Can I fight your battles, too?"

"No, thanks. I'm going."

It had been good to see him again, I said. He always had such entertaining, cockeyed theories. My words were sincere.

He grinned, said farewell and stepped out into the crush.

"They may be cockeyed, old pal," he said, "but R. Prout's theories work. Just like Einstein's."

I, too, stepped out into the crowd and forced my way across to Chance, near enough to take his elbow and mutter my farewell.

"Don't forget that dinner date," he called. "Probably next Saturday. Hope you're still here. I'll drop you a note."

I went on with the tricky task of getting to the door. It was a strenuous maneuver, but even that did not account for the pounding of my heart. Out on the landing I took a deep breath and looked over the balusters to the hall below. I went very slowly downstairs, as if my feet were clad in divers' boots. The butler was alert, still smiling, coming from the small front room as if a bell had been rung to warn him of my descent. "Your hat, sir?" he said, the foreign intonation quite strong. He turned back into the room. I watched him. Two tables held a strange assembly of hats, umbrellas, walking sticks. I pointed to my hat and put a coin on the table. As he passed the hat I took a chance and said, "I couldn't see Professor Lewis here tonight. Has he come yet?"

Nervousness made me bark out the words as if they were a peremptory order. Josef almost sprang to attention. He frowned. In a gifted moment I repeated sharply: "Professor Lewis?"

Josef said, "Yes, sir. But is he not still abroad, sir?"

"I've been away. Where is he, then?"

"I do not know, sir. Abroad."

I thanked him quickly and walked out into the Square almost furtively, as if I had been guilty of some major social solecism. In reaction I sighed deeply. The tension before and during my questioning had been brief but more oppressive than I had expected or realized at the time. I put my hand to my forehead. The skin was damp with sweat. I walked on at unaccustomed speed. Not until several minutes later did I regain a sense of proportion and composure and begin to slow down.

Would this information be of any use? I wondered. Well, it was up to Butler. His minions could find the answer to a question as simple as that. Fourteen Professor Lewises: which of them is (or are) abroad? One thing was certain: the item of information I had gained could, with luck, drastically reduce the total of fourteen.

I walked into King's Road with the evening before me. For a moment I was tempted to ring Butler there and then and tell him that the remainder of the search was up to him. Instead, I walked toward Victoria. In Hobart Place I hailed a wandering taxi and to my very great surprise heard my voice giving the destination, "Court House."

18

A DAILY NEWSPAPER OFFICE ON SATURDAY EVENING IS A HOUSE OF ghosts—the ghosts of men, machines and words—and no other tomb seems so resentful of its silence.

Court House that evening seemed sullen in such a silence. I crossed the marbled hall and climbed to the fourth floor, wondering en route which room I should make my own for the hour ahead.

I decided on Winter's room, one floor down from Rees's office, and crossed to his swivel chair. He wouldn't mind. I relaxed, lit a cigarette, reached across to his book trough for *Who's Who* and turned to the "Lewis" entries.

It would be easy to make my task that evening appear to have been unusual or, at least, exciting and exacting. Alas, I cannot. It was no different from a score of such inquiries any inquisitive newspaperman is likely to make in the course of a year. Mine was, in fact, a simple, old-fashioned identity quest. First, I spoke to the switchboard supervisor, explaining my problem: "There are fourteen Professor Lewises in this country. I want to find out which of them is abroad, if any. I can give you the home addresses of most of 'em, the telephone numbers of one or two. The rest will need tracking down."

He was unperturbed. For him, too, such an inquiry held nothing out of the ordinary. He was helpful. He would depute one of his "smoother operators" for the task, he said. The operator could deal with Trunk Directory Inquiries, while I went on with my own inquiries. He switched me through to the operator, Murdoch by name.

"Make them all personal calls at first," I said. "If there's any query, or the professor isn't available, we'll drop the personal request and I'll talk to whoever's around. Give the name of the paper. Don't mention mine. If they want a name give your own. If they're suspicious, with all these burglars around, tell them to ring the paper back and reverse the charges."

"We usually do, sir, but most of 'em seem to take us at our word."

"Good! You'd better make a note of the lucky numbers in case I want them again."

"Very good, sir."

So we began. As Murdoch made his first inquiries I wrote out a list of the Professor Lewises.

First on the list was Professor Abraham Lewis, Professor of Slavonic Studies, St. Catherine's College, Cambridge. That was also his only address in *Who's Who*. Sitting there I reread the entry. Son of Rev. William Lewis, Wem, Shropshire, and Elsa Johannsen of Oslo. Educated Wem Grammar School and Balliol. Postgraduate studies, Harvard University. Lecturer, London University. Hobbies: mountain climbing, photography.

By that time Murdoch was through to the College Lodge and had switched me onto the line. No, said the sad voice of the porter, the Professor wasn't there: in fact, he didn't live in College. The voice mournfully intoned an address in Trumpington and a telephone number. I waited while Murdoch got the new Cambridge number, looking through *Who's Who*, pursuing other Lewises. An old lady's reedy voice answered. Yes, Professor Lewis did live there.

"Could I speak to him?"

"No, I'm afraid not. He's not here."

"Will he be back this evening?"

"No, I'm afraid not. He's abroad."

"Oh! I know I sound extremely inquisitive and I hope you'll forgive me, but whereabouts, may I ask?"

She seemed not to mind. "In Austria," she said simply.

Even in asking my questions I had time to be puzzled again by the readiness with which so many people answered a newspaper's queries. Those attacks upon newspapers for their intrusions into personal privacy rarely come from the so-called victims, as any reporter knows.

"Lecturing?" I asked.

"I don't know, I'm afraid. I don't think so. I think he said he was going to do some mountain climbing."

"Have you heard from him since he went? And do you know when he'll be back?"

"Yes, I had a post card yesterday to say he would be back next Wednesday." Then, in sudden panic, the quavering voice quickened. "There's nothing wrong, is there?"

I reassured her. "Nothing at all. I'm merely anxious to get in touch
with him. I'll probably ring again on Thursday or drop a note to the
College."

"Shall I say who rang?"

"No, there's no need. I'll be ringing."

We started at eight and did not finish until half-past nine. By then,
in order to pry into the lives of fourteen professors, we had made over
forty telephone calls. But by half-past nine I did have a more or less
complete dossier on the movements of ten of them.

"We'll leave the others until tomorrow or Monday," I told Murdoch. "I've got enough to work on here, anyway."

Four out of the ten names I had queried were abroad, the other
half dozen were stay-at-homes. By any laws of probability, one or
two of the remaining quartet would also be abroad. That might make
half a dozen prospects.

I looked again at my scribbled names and notes concerning the
four immediate possibles: Professors Abraham Lewis, Capper Lewis,
Keith Lewis and Nathaniel Lewis.

Mrs. Capper Lewis had answered from a number in Bangor, North
Wales. No, unfortunately her husband couldn't speak. He was in
Sweden on a short lecture tour.

"Might I ask what subject?"

"His own," she said evasively. I glanced quickly at *Who's Who*.
Born 1902. Educated, Rydal and University of Wales. Professor of
Welsh Literature, University College of Bangor.

"And that is?"

I thought she giggled. "The Bards of Wales and Bardic Studies in
Perspective are his special subjects."

"Oh, I see," I said, lamely enough.

She laughed. "I know," she said. "It doesn't seem possible, does it?
He was a bit surprised himself when he was invited to Stockholm.
But apparently there is quite an interest in these things in Scandi-
navia."

"I'm glad to hear it."

"Could I send him a cable?"

No, I assured her, the matter could wait.

Then Professor Keith Lewis. We got news of him after three calls
to various officials of Reading University, starting with a porter, end-
ing with a registrar who gave Murdoch a number in Reading.

Murdoch kept me informed of his stage-by-stage inquiry, while I mournfully studied *Who's Who*. By that time I was almost astigmatic from looking at the double-column entries.

Keith Lewis was 42. Married Julia Myfanwy Powell. No children apparently. He had been at a Caernarvon Grammar School, Bangor and London University, afterward at Bonn. Before the war he had been professor of mathematics at Manchester University. His war service had been with the Ministry of Supply. Now he was lecturer of advanced mathematics at Reading University.

From what appeared to be a boardinghouse or guesthouse, a man's Scottish voice gave his name somewhat grudgingly and dourly as "Donaldson," and only then, in answer to my direct question, said that Professor Lewis was away.

"In this country or abroad?"

"Abroad, I'm told."

"Do you happen to know whereabouts?"

"Italy, I believe."

"Lecturing?"

The Scotsman laughed shortly and suddenly mellowed. "I doubt that. He's a mathematician, ye know. Those Italians are more interested in singing and painting, I reckon, than figures."

"When is he expected back?"

As if already repenting of his loquacity the Scot returned to briefer replies. "This week, I'm told. Can I leave him a message?"

"No, I don't think so. I'll write."

"I should write to the University. He's not here a lot, you know."

Finally, Professor Nathaniel Lewis. A young girl's eager treble answered from a house near Westerham, Kent. No, Professor Lewis wasn't in. He was abroad.

"When do you expect him back?"

"Tomorrow morning. They're coming by the ferry tonight."

"Where has he been, if it's not a rude question?"

"Of course it's not. He's been in Germany."

I was sure she had blue eyes and wore pigtails.

"Lecturing?"

"How did you guess? Only for the troops, though. He's been touring with Mummy in the Black Forest. What paper did you say you were? Shall I ask Daddy to ring you?"

"There's no need. I think perhaps your father isn't my Professor
Lewis."

"Are there any others, then?"

"About a dozen."

"Are there really? I must pull Daddy's leg about that."

"How old are you?"

"Thirteen."

"You sound very bright."

"I'm supposed to be. How does one get onto a newspaper?"

I evaded that and escaped as quickly and politely as I could.

I reread Professor Nathaniel Lewis's entry in *Who's Who*. Professor
of Medieval European literature, University of London. Born 1905.
Educated Mercer's School and Magdalene College, Cambridge. Married: Mariel Anderson. One son. One daughter. Lecturer: Birkbeck
College, 1925–1935. Visiting lecturer: Grenoble University, 1935–
1937. Professorship, London University, 1937–1942. M.O.I. 1942–
1944. Address: Windrock Cottage, Nr. Westerham, Kent.

Well, there were the first four prospects, I told myself as I looked
again from my scribbled names and notes to the open pages of *Who's
Who*.

Yet the longer I stared, the more involved my quest seemed to
become. And another factor added to my difficulties. In retrospect,
that block-cap reference merely to "Professor Lewis," without the
added identification of a Christian name, did not seem so strange.
Everyone I had questioned had referred to his or her professor as
"Professor Lewis," without additional identification. That had been
left to me. Yet I had spoken to intelligent people, relations and ac-
quaintances of more than half the known total of Professor Lewises
in England. The assumption of each of them had been that there was
but one Professor Lewis, the one under discussion. The young daughter of Nathaniel, in her innocence, had epitomized the single-mind-
edness of them all. It was all quite reasonable, I reminded myself
firmly, but that didn't make my task any easier. And it would be a
titbit of information for Butler.

I copied out, in full, the biographies of the four absent professors.
It was a wearying task, but it would probably be wanted by Butler,
I reminded myself grimly. Then I rang Murdoch and told him I was

finished for the evening. By then it was half-past nine and I was very hungry indeed.

19

I DINED IN THE SPANISH RESTAURANT IN BREWER STREET AND TRIED to read the *Evening Standard* between courses, but I was too interested in my short list of gallivanting professors to be able to give more than cursory attention to the "Londoner's Diary," Beverley Baxter and the other readable attractions of that lively newspaper.

I tried being imaginative. You are given the facts, the bare skeletal facts, and you try to quicken them with life blood from your own bright, fictional mind. I tried to evoke images of Abraham, Capper, Keith and Nathaniel Lewis. It was an amusing pastime.

Waiting for *homard thermidor,* I even started on their portraits in my own ungraphical manner, putting a pencil outline round my wildest images, but very soon they all began to look alike. I could only differentiate by such drastic additions as a biblical beard for Abraham, a thin trickle of mustache for Capper, an imperial for Keith and horn-rimmed specs for Nathaniel. By the time I had finished my doodles, only Nathaniel had the slightest professorial air. A near-by diner began to whisper to his girl friend and to fidget, St. Vitus fashion, in his chair. I was plainly a portrait artist on a busman's holiday and by no means a welcome neighbor.

So I gave up.

I renewed my study of the four biographies, going back over that desultory conversation with Butler. *Who would be most likely to consider his or her Professor Lewis the only boy in the world?* he had asked. *Someone very near and dear to him or someone fairly ignorant,* I had answered.

In the light of recent knowledge some of those words had a faintly cracked and hollow ring. Not only the near and dear to any Professor Lewis disdained to add a Christian name. It seemed that all those within the professor's orbit thought of him as the only professor of that name. The more one considered the subject of professors, the more rarely did Christian names crop up. It was almost worth a thesis: An Inquiry into the Incidence (or lack of incidence) of Christian Names among Professors. Mrs. Capper Lewis hadn't asked me whether I had made a mistake, intended my questions for any other Professor Lewis. Nor the Scotsman in Reading.

So they didn't even have to be so very near and dear to him, I thought again, remembering the Scotsman's answers. I had certainly proved that minor point beyond dispute. I looked at Keith Lewis's biography. He had a wife. *Married Julia Myfanwy Powell.* No children. I had noted the Reading guesthouse number. Determined that my record be as well documented as possible against a certain interrogation by Butler, I went across to the telephone booth on the other side of the restaurant, dialed TOL and asked the operator for the number, requesting a personal call to Mr. Donaldson. Fortunately he was still in. I introduced myself and asked if Mrs. Lewis were also abroad with her husband.

"I don't know of a Mrs. Lewis," he said. "We don't know much about the Professor, you know."

Suddenly, in a rush, he became suspicious. "You'll have to ring him when he gets back and ask your own questions," he said brusquely and rang off.

There was nothing there for me, it seemed, and I returned to my table, although I still wanted to find out more about Professor Keith Lewis. His was a hazier background than any of the three who were abroad. I almost felt that I knew them.

On an impulse I went across to the booth again, switched on the light and went through the London Telephone Directory L–R. There was no entry for either Keith Lewis or Mrs. Keith Lewis. Nor for Julia or Myfanwy Lewis. I wasn't surprised. The possibilities were many. They might have separated. They might have been divorced. She might already be a Mrs. Eumophopolus or a Mrs. Postlethwaite by now. She might equally well be with him abroad, on holiday from a job of her own, joining him on this annual respite. Fresh alternatives came each moment. Nevertheless I took the directory with me back to my table. Going through the Lewis entries was an easier task when seated.

My neighbors plainly considered this the final imbecile touch after my earlier efforts as a portraitist. They tried to look away but couldn't. No professional exhibitionist could have aroused more curiosity.

There were two Mrs. K. Lewises, one Mrs. M. Lewis and one Miss K. Lewis and that was about all, but I thought I ought to ring them, preferably in the comparative comfort of my home-from-home. So I paid my bill and wandered back to Athenaeum Court.

At the desk there was a message, timed 10:25. Would I please ring Mr. Murdoch at Court House? I looked at the clock. Ten-forty.

"You were paged about two minutes ago for a call, sir," the porter said.

I took up the telephone on his counter and asked the girl on the switchboard about the call.

"Yes, sir. A lady, sir. No, she wouldn't leave a name."

I went up to my room, rang through to Court House and asked for Murdoch.

"One of the Mrs. Lewises rang and asked to speak to you. I thought I ought to let you know."

"Which Mrs. Lewis? Any Christian name?"

"I don't know, sir. Just said she was the wife of Professor Lewis and wanted to speak to you. I told her you'd gone. Said she wanted to know if anything had happened to her husband. When I said I didn't know, she said she had to have your private number. She sounded rather upset, sir. I gave her the number at Athenaeum Court. I hope I did right, sir. I'm afraid I had to give her your name, too, sir. Hope you don't mind."

"Not at all. You did well. When did she ring?"

"About a quarter of an hour ago, sir."

"It wasn't Mrs. Capper Lewis from Bangor?"

"I don't think so, sir. I'm sure it wasn't. We had no warning of a trunk call."

"It wasn't a child's voice from the Westerham number we rang?"

"I don't think so. I think it was a London call, sir. And she definitely said 'Mrs. Lewis.' Definitely."

"All right, Murdoch. Thank you. You couldn't have done more. Perhaps she'll ring here. She sounded distressed, you say?"

"A bit upset, I thought, sir."

I thanked him again and rang off.

Well, I could sit in an armchair and read. I could go to bed and read. I could go to bed and try to sleep. I could stare out of the window at the dark trees and the twinkling lights across the park. But I would wait all night for a telephone call, whatever I did. That was certain.

So I chose to lean out of the window. The evening was warm. Londoners ambled along both sides of Piccadilly. On the corner of Down Street three tarts were earnestly discussing whatever tarts do discuss. Clothes? Men? Payment by results? Half a dozen taxis stood along the rank. Cars moved fast toward Piccadilly Circus and Hyde Park Corner. The scene had the eternal allure of any street viewed from above. So I continued to lean out of the window, puzzling, staring. It was better than staring at the telephone.

A London call, Murdoch had said. Well, I had spoken to two Mrs. Lewises in London earlier that evening. One had called out to her professorial husband, summoning him to the telephone, the other had told me her husband had been playing hockey at Hampstead that afternoon and would then be going out to dinner in Belsize Park and would not be back until late. Could he ring me then?

I had thanked her and said no, I was merely trying to find a Professor Lewis now abroad. But perhaps she had become worried, afraid that her husband had become entangled with a hockey stick or a hockey blonde. Wives often worried over trifles. Yet, somehow, I doubted whether this was the Mrs. Lewis now on my trail, and I swiftly forgot her.

In any case, I reminded myself, I had the numbers of both these estimable wives. No, it was neither. And I was loath to take up the telephone. I wanted the line to be clear for the more enigmatic Mrs. Lewis.

Finally, I did pick up the telephone. "I'm expecting a call to come through here," I said to the girl on the switchboard. "I should like the call traced. See if it can be done."

She said at once, "It can be done if it's from a private number, but not from a call box. The authorities are never very keen to do it anyway."

"Will you try?" I asked. "It's very important. Give the name of my paper. Do anything."

She said that she would do her best.

"By the way," I said, "that call a quarter of an hour ago: did the woman sound upset? Can you remember?"

The girl didn't answer at once. Then she said, rather coolly I thought, "She did rather, sir."

I thanked her and rang off. She probably thought I was caught up in a big emotional moment, but she could think what she liked so long as, when the moment came, she could trace the call I so impatiently awaited.

I went back to the window and propped my chin on my elbow for another session of quiescent rubbernecking. I was there for less than ten minutes when the telephone rang. I spun round as if I had been hit in the back and took up the receiver in one sweeping move.

"Reception here, sir," the voice said. "Mrs. Lewis, sir."

Surprise makes fools of us all.

"Well, put her through!"

"She's here, sir. In the hall."

20

WE FIX OUR MINDS UPON A SINGLE OBJECT SO INTENSELY THAT ATROPHY sets in, making us incapable of seeing that same object from any other viewpoint. So with me then.

At last I had said, "Ask her up," and let the receiver drop back in its cradle.

In a daze I crossed to the cupboard, and took out a half bottle of whisky, a siphon and two glasses, put them down on the table and then went out into the corridor, along to the lift.

I had that constriction across the chest that we are all apt to get in moments of foreboding.

The lift door opened and a slim young woman, hatless and in a black, belted coat, stepped out. Her back was toward me as she fumbled the door back into working order. I moved toward her. Then she turned.

She was about five feet five, dark haired, as pale as a nun. She might have been handsome, for her nose and chin were small and finely shaped, but they seemed too sharp by reason of her pallor.

Her lips, too, were well modeled, but far too red against the white skin. Her eyes, deep set and grave, were held within shadows as large and black as Wedgwood seals. Neurotic as they come, I said to myself, and aloud, "Mrs. Lewis?"

She nodded.

I showed her the way into the room and offered her the armchair. "A drink?"

Again she nodded.

In silence I mixed a strong drink and gave it to her. She took a mouthful as if it were acid and choked.

"Take it easy," I said.

She nodded again and sat there for a minute or so, breathing deeply, coming to life and perhaps to a resolution.

"I am Mrs. Keith Lewis," she said. "You have rung my husband's lodgings in Reading twice tonight. What was it about?"

"I wanted to know if he was abroad," I said gently, and then, "Who told you I had rung?"

"The landlady, Mrs. Joynson. I used to live there with my husband until a year ago. Then I left him. She has kept in touch with me ever since. She knew my telephone number in London and rang me half an hour ago. She knows I am worried about him and thought something might have happened."

"Who is Mr. Donaldson?"

"Another guest. He wasn't there in my time. After you rang the second time he told the landlady. She rang me."

"Could you tell me why you are worried about your husband?"

"He is in danger."

"What kind of danger?"

"I don't know."

She was, I thought, no longer quite so distraught. As she began to talk so she also relaxed, infinitesimally perhaps, but enough to let her sit there with the tumbler between her hands, looking straight before her.

I was still standing. Thinking I might thus intimidate her, I sat down on the edge of the divan opposite.

"Why have you come to me?" I asked.

"Because," she said simply, "I think you might be able to help me."

"And help your husband?"

"I don't know. I hope so."

"Why pick on me?" I said, as gently as I could, but probably somewhat plaintively. "I'm almost a stranger here."

"You wrote an article about Matthew Chance, the M.P."

I nodded and said, slowly, hazarding, "*You* wrote me a note about the article, unsigned."

"Yes, I did," she said quietly.

"Why?"

"I thought if I got in touch with a journalist first I might keep things away from the police and the other people."

"How?"

"I don't know. I thought if you found things out . . . oh, I don't know." It seemed she could not go on.

"Is that why you've come here now?"

She nodded.

"It's because of that note that I rang Reading this evening. It was a roundabout inquiry but your note started it."

"I guessed that as soon as Mrs. Joynson rang. I scribbled that note on the impulse and rushed out and posted it. I was so desperate I felt I must start something going. I suppose I have now. One gets like that. I didn't know what I was doing, what I am doing. I've never been so worried. Anything is better than this."

"Where do you live?"

"In Chelsea. In the King's Road."

"You didn't go far to post your note, then?" I said, smiling, remembering the Chelsea franking, hoping to help her to relax. "Most anonymous note senders go farther afield, I'm told."

She smiled solemnly but did not answer.

I thought it best to talk plainly then, rather than later, after she had perhaps talked too much. I said, "If what you are talking about is really very serious there's nothing I can do that would finally keep it from the police. I ought to tell you that now, you know. Journalists can't go outside the law."

Again she nodded, but did not answer.

"What is it, then?" I asked.

"My husband has become a spy," she said with appalling simplicity.

I bit slowly on my lower lip and looked at her, trying, in what seemed to me a race against time, to gain some estimate of her seriousness; even, perhaps, her sanity. And all the time I was wondering what the next move might be. I remember, too, wondering whether I was awake and not dreaming, but all she did was sit there, the tumbler in her hands, considering me with her sad but steady eyes.

"That's more a job for MI5 than the police," I said at length.

"I thought it probably was," she said wearily.

"Are you sure you're not mistaken? This is a terrible accusation to make against anyone, most of all against someone you presumably love."

She nodded.

"And Matthew Chance?" I went on. "You include him in this, too?"

Again she nodded.

"You realize what you are saying?"

"I think I do."

"Aren't you sure?"

Suddenly she began to cry, quietly and agonizingly, lowering her head away from me, away from the light. Her right hand left the tumbler and moved, shakingly, across her brow, down over her face, as if molding the features of a waxen mask into a semblance of normality.

All this in silence. One minute? Two minutes? We never know.

At last she said, still looking down, "That is the terrible thing. I think I know. Yet I don't really know. That is why I left my husband. I couldn't stand the strain, the suspicion. It was driving me mad."

"What is your husband?"

"A mathematician."

"So I was told. What else?"

"That is all. But an unusual kind of mathematician, I believe."

Did I detect, far off, a touch of threadbare pride?

"He lectures at Reading University?"

"Occasionally."

"And at other times?"

"He is a consultant to the Government at Harwell."

"Ah!" I said.

We were both quiet. I broke the silence. "The Reading job is a blind?"

"Not exactly," she said. "My husband is something of an idealist. He likes teaching. He came from a provincial university himself and thinks he must give something back to the young people of the provinces. He could have gone to Oxford after the war, but he wouldn't."

Again there was that faint touch of pride in her voice as she made this, her longest statement so far.

I wanted, somehow, to make her deny all that she had already said, to give her every chance to retract, to go away. Or even, perhaps, to speak in hatred of her husband. Even that would have seemed more understandable than her sad detachment. I said, as gently as I could, "Don't you think the world today is almost predisposed to suspect a man with that kind of brain, and that kind of background? Even a wife might be forgiven for being suspicious—with all this spy talk going on. Don't you think so?"

"Possibly," she said, but her voice held no belief, not even in the remotest possibility.

After another silence I said, "How did he meet Chance?"

"I don't know exactly. At some party or other. It was one of those things that I only knew about after it was a *fait accompli.*"

"When did they meet?"

"I don't know. Sometime in late 'fifty-two or early 'fifty-three, I think."

"Did you ever see them together?"

"Yes, we went to one or two cocktail parties at the Chances' house. You know the kind of thing: writers, politicians, artists, one or two scientific people like my husband. Sometimes my husband went alone. Dinners, lunches and so on. I didn't really care for them after the first once or twice."

"Why not?"

"I'm not particularly social."

"Did your husband come up to London especially for those occasions?"

"Yes."

"Did Chance ever come to see your husband?"

"Not in Reading, but once last year, soon after I came to London, he came to my flat in Chelsea with my husband. They had been out walking, I gathered."

"Why there of all places—after you had left your husband?"

"Keith asked me if he could borrow the flat for an hour or so. I said yes. I was always hoping it would be their last meeting. I went out. I came back just as Chance was leaving."

"All this is very flimsy stuff to go on."

She nodded. "Perhaps," she said, and then softly, "I know."

"What else do you go on?"

"My husband's fear."

"When did that begin?"

"Soon after he met Chance."

"Are you sure?"

She nodded. "That's really why I stopped going with Keith. He was terrified—almost from that moment, or soon after. I couldn't bear to see it, carefully as he hid it."

"Terrified of Chance?"

"Not necessarily. No, I think that, in many ways, he liked and even admired Chance."

"Terrified of what then?"

"How do I know? Of what he had got himself caught up in? I don't know. All a wife knows is that her husband is terrified. She doesn't have to know the reason. Keith was as frightened as any man could be. When we went to the Chance house he was like a man about to be tortured. Any wife would know these things. My own belief is that he had taken one step, then another, and couldn't go back. He had to go on. Perhaps he wanted to go on, but somehow I can't believe it. I think he made the first move out of some kind of misplaced idealism or conviction. Now I think he is being blackmailed into going on." She looked up suddenly. "You don't believe me, do you?"

I acted dumb. "How blackmail?"

"Oh, come. If he had given one secret, how could he stand against them when they wanted more? He might have tried to bluff them, of course, but he isn't that kind of man. He couldn't do it."

"Couldn't it have been something else? Couldn't the meeting with Chance about that time have been just a coincidence?"

"No," she said flatly and finally.

"Did you ever have things out with your husband? I mean, discuss all that you've told me?"

"Yes," she said. "Often during the year before I left him. He said I was imagining things."

"Could he have been right?"

"No," she said again, just as flatly.

"When did you last see him?"

"Three weeks ago. Before he went abroad."

"Did you discuss this question then?"

"Yes. It always came up. All the time. It festered all the time. Every time we met, it was the subject we began with and came back to. Always."

"He denied everything again?"

She nodded.

"How was he?"

"Terrified."

"At the risk of being a bore and a boor what exactly do you mean by 'terrified'? It's that side of things I must get clear. It's not clear."

"Exactly what I say. He was tense, his mind elsewhere, jumpy. Above all, it was in his eyes."

"Couldn't his work—I imagine that's pretty exacting—have made him that way?"

"Until he got in with Chance he loved his work. In the old days, even in the most tremendous tasks, he was easy tempered."

"Will you see him after he gets back?"

"If he comes to see me."

"You have no children?"

"One. A baby girl."

"Yet, despite that, you left him?"

"I had to."

She finished the drink and gropingly placed the glass on the side table. "I had to," she said again. "I couldn't go on like that. I suppose some people—most people perhaps—would say a wife should stay with her husband whatever happens. I've sometimes wondered what the clergyman who married us—for better or for worse—would have had to say if I'd taken my little problem to him. All I know is that our real life together was finished. It had become one long hideous nightmare. If only he had told me what was happening, things might have been different, but I doubt it. I hate all this business and all it stands for. I may be old-fashioned but I could never in a million years see that this kind of thing could ever be justified. The ghastly business overshadowed everything we ever said or did or thought. You can't understand a life of lies and terror, can you?"

We all lead lives of lies and terror in some way or another, I thought, but stayed silent.

She looked ahead, not at me, not at anything. Then she said, suddenly, "I must go now. I have left my baby asleep. It's something I've never done before and I hope I shall never have to do again."

"What will you do now?"

"Now?" She half laughed, almost in desperation. "Now? Why I shall go back. The rest is up to you."

She stood up. I stood up, too, somewhat foxed and feeling rather foolish. "To me?" I asked lamely. "In what way, exactly?" First Butler left things to me. Now Mrs. Lewis.

"I told you when I first came here," she said simply. "I hoped that by telling you I might keep it out of the hands of the police. Even if you can't do that, you will at least bring things out into the open. Isn't that what newspapers are for?" She laughed, but not very cozily. "That would almost be a relief, I think. Better you should do that in your own way than I should go to the police."

"I may well find there's nothing in it, that you have been deluding yourself."

"I hope so," she said wearily, but hopelessly, as if that possibility were too fanciful even to consider. In that instant she seemed suddenly too weary to go on with the subject, even for another sentence. "Now I really must go," she said limply.

"I'll see you back."

To my surprise she did not protest.

We went down in the lift and across to the taxi rank.

"Where to?" I asked.

"King's Road. Just past Glebe Place."

We sat silent in the taxi until we were passing through Belgrave Square. Then I said, banally enough, but determined to break the silence, "How did you manage to find a flat? Isn't that rather difficult these days?"

She laughed quietly. "It's scarcely that," she said. "Two rooms in a friend's house. I lived there before I was married. It's one of those tumbledown King's Road houses, part private, part guesthouse. It's condemned and supposed to be pulled down soon. Not too soon, I hope."

"And the telephone?"

"On the landing outside my room. It's the phone for the house. I'm afraid you would have had a long job tracking me down that way."

"Ah!" I said again.

There was little else to say, but after a while I tried once more. "You don't work?"

"A little," she said. "A few drawings. No, I'm not a King's Road artistic type. I was trained as a draftswoman!"

I remembered the linen tracing paper on which the message to Winter had been scrawled.

She laughed. "I've built up quite a good connection during the past six months. It helps to keep me sane. Deciphering the average architect's scribbles and doodles keeps one's mind occupied—but one can't do that sixteen hours a day, even if there were that much work around."

We were passing through Sloane Square. I glanced at her in the lights from the Square and Peter Jones' windows. Her face was still drawn and taut. She still looked unseeingly ahead. In the shadows, her face had lost the sharp pallor that had showed so starkly under the bright light of my room. Now I could see only her profile: straight nose, sad mouth, firm chin.

I said, "I don't want to be rude and inquisitive, but are you broke?"

"Not at all," she said. "I'm not well off, but I'm far from broke. Keith does what he can. In fact, he's very generous, but government scientists aren't the best-paid people in the world. But with what he allows me and my free-lance work, I'm really fairly comfortable."

"What is your daughter's name?"

"Dinah."

"And your own? Ah, yes, I remember, Julia Myfanwy."

"How did you know?" she asked in surprise.

"It's in *Who's Who*, in your husband's entry. Julia Myfanwy Powell."

"Is it?" she asked. "I've never read it. Ridiculous name."

By then we were at Glebe Place, and the driver was asking for the number.

"Just over on the right," she said.

"When does your husband return?" I asked as the taxi swung round.

"I don't know exactly. Any day now, I should imagine."

"I'll go back," I called to the taxi driver.

I stepped out of the taxi and helped her out. "You've been very kind," she said. I made suitable self-deprecating noises, but she brushed them aside. "I shall be making myself some coffee now," she went on, and then with a last formal touch, "If that has any appeal for you, you're very welcome."

I paid off the taxi and followed her along a path into an echoing stone-flagged hall, bare and macabre under the light of a bulb that swayed in the sudden breath from the opening door. She led the way up a flight of stone stairs, also bare, to the first-floor landing and stopped before a door into a room on the left. I noticed the telephone on a ledge just outside her door, and memorized the number as she fitted her key into a lock: Flaxman 0031.

We went into a room overlooking the King's Road. Lamplight shafted into the room from the street. She switched on the light and in the sudden brightness I found the room to be unexpectedly well furnished. Unexpectedly, perhaps, because almost instinctively we are all apt to associate despair and sorrow with an equally forlorn background. Red and white print curtains and yellow loose covers on a couple of old armchairs gave color to the room. White shelves, packed with books, and odd pieces of Staffordshire, unframed drawings, blueprints and lithographs pinned on the walls added to the air of gaiety so far removed from her own despair.

She excused herself and went through a door into the room beyond. I heard murmurs of maternity and the creaking of a cot side being lowered. I walked across to the window. Saturday-night crowds from the pubs and cinemas were noisily trickling home toward Beaufort Street and Fulham. Eleven-fifteen, I noted by my wrist watch; a busy evening since six, I thought.

"Nothing untoward," she announced, coming back into the room. "But I shall never do it again. Won't you sit down?"

I crossed to one of the armchairs.

"I shall make coffee for myself," she said. "All I can offer you is a minute gin with water. Not even a tonic."

"Coffee will be better in every way."

"Don't journalists drink most of the time?" she asked, smiling.

"Only twenty-three hours a day. This is my hour for coffee."

She opened a door into a narrow kitchenette, so small that she was still virtually in the room. As she switched on the stove and reached up to the shelves she asked, unexpectedly, over her shoulder, "Are you married?"

"No. Divorced."

"Ah! I'm sorry. I was wondering whether you had children."

"No."

"That's always a good thing."

"Probably, but you wouldn't be without your daughter."

"I'm not divorced," she reminded me.

"A difference in words, surely, scarcely in estate," I said, as mildly as I could.

"Perhaps," she agreed, but not very willingly. That was plain.

"Will you go back when this is all over?" I asked.

"I hope so."

A mood of bogus lightheartedness now seemed to possess her, as if she were doing her best to persuade herself that relief had come with her confession. She spoke more casually, almost with a carefree note, but somehow it all had a hollow ring; the stress was forced, unnatural.

I said: "Have you ever told anybody else what you've told me tonight?"

"No one."

"Not your mother?"

"She died when I was ten."

"Not even that understanding landlady in Reading?"

"Good God, no."

"What do you make of Chance?"

"I don't know. As a man I like him. I think most people do. I admire him. There again, I think most people do. My husband did, and does as far as I know, enormously. He seems a strong man in a weak world. That's the way I always think of him."

"Did Chance ever seem worried when he was with your husband?"

She laughed. "Good heavens, no. He was as cool as this icebox here. I don't think he has any nerves."

"Perhaps there's no need for him to have any if you've been imagining things."

"Possibly," she said, but without belief.

"What about Mrs. Chance? Is she in on this thing you talk about?"

"I could never make up my mind. Sometimes I thought so. At other times she seemed so remote from it all, I just couldn't imagine it. She's one of those polite, inscrutable creatures one never gets to know. At least, I found her so. Somehow I think she might be. Isn't there something called 'feminine intuition'?"

"But she never seemed nervous or worried?"

"No."

"So out of the four of you, only your husband was nervous and that made you nervous. On your own admission the others didn't seem a bit tense. Odd, don't you think?"

"Put like that, yes, but Chance is a different kind of man from Keith. He's tougher, and colder. And, in a way, wiser. It's a strange word, but that's the impression he has always given me. You've met him?"

I nodded.

"What did you think of him?"

"I rather took to him. He talked a bit too much, but, after all, he *is* a politician. One half expects that. But, like you, I thought he seemed a strong-minded man in a wishy-washy world."

"Just the things which would appeal to Keith. And unlike most people who talk too much he never gives himself away. Not for a minute."

She was right in that, I thought.

"If you can be detached for a moment, how would you describe your husband, then? For instance, was he a Communist?"

She thought for a while before she began to speak, slowly and reflectively. "Yes, I suppose in a way he was a Communist. He was never a member of the party, but politically they had his sympathies. It's not unusual with scientists and technicians with his background, is it?" She looked at me for confirmation.

"It's become almost a commonplace," I said.

She went on. "But he never got himself involved in politics. Not even when he was in London. Of course, he was pro-Russian during the war, but so was everybody else. I remember we all were at school. . . ." It came as a slight shock to me to realize that someone to whom I was talking on such level terms had been a schoolgirl so recently. Recently to me, at least. ". . . but as a scientist I think Keith became increasingly perturbed by the barriers that were growing up around his work. He could never see them as British developments. To him they were part of science. International developments. Super-national, if you like . . . it was his word."

"And as a man?" I interjected gently.

"He was . . ." she began and quickly corrected her tense. "He's generous, serious, no great sense of humor perhaps, affectionate, not wildly sophisticated, utterly wrapped up in his job, a man of peace if ever there was one. Sometimes I think the great clash in his life was due to the fact that he was, at heart, a pacifist and always thought that he had dodged the real issue, which he should have settled during the war, by going on with his work as a scientist." She looked up. "That is all, I think. I've tried to be as dispassionate as I can, but it's rather difficult about someone you're fond of."

"I *still* think you may be imagining things," I said. In this mildly domestic scene I began to believe my own words and assurances.

"I hope so," she said again, but without conviction.

"Well, there's little enough to go on you'll admit. Any newspaperman would want more than this. I'm sure a judge would want a very great deal more."

"Let's forget about the judge," she said calmly, and went on, riding over my apology. "There's enough for you to start on. Just the suspicion."

She came out into the room from the small cramped kitchen. "You could work on that without going to the police, couldn't you?" she pleaded. "That's what I've hoped for all these months. That's why I wrote that ghastly anonymous note, why I rang you tonight. Don't you see? Don't you agree?"

"We'll see."

She seemed to be satisfied with even that response and went back to the percolator. To evade my insistent thoughts I took a book from the adjacent shelf. *Georgian London* by Summerson. The book had several pages of illustrations. I looked through those until she came back into the room, carrying a tray with a steaming percolator, cups and saucers.

We did not talk again about Chance or Lewis for another ten minutes. She poured coffee, looked at the book I had taken and began to talk about buildings.

In my experience it is rare for a woman to know anything about architecture, rarer still for her to be able to talk about the subject. Interior decoration, yes, but that is mainly a matter of taste and not necessarily knowledge. I must have shown surprise at one point early in the discussion, for she said, "Don't be too surprised by my *expertise*. I told you I'm a draftswoman, but I've a wider interest, too. I was at the A.A. for two years. I only left when I met Keith. He was lecturing at London University just after the war. Then we married and I turned it all in. The usual fate of would-be women architects."

"What would you have done?"

"Become a County Council draftswoman probably."

"Couldn't you do that now?"

"Not with Dinah around, and anyway, I was only halfway through the course. It's a five-year course, you know."

"I didn't know. Tell me something about your married life, if it's not too painful a subject."

"The pain gets dulled," she said simply and without self-pity. "We married in 1947, lived for a time in rooms in Gordon Square, Bloomsbury, then Keith got this job at Harwell. He was loaned by the University, of course, but Reading snapped him up when he suggested occasional lectures there. We lived at Harwell for a bit—in one of those ghastly prefabs they keep for the married scientists. Then we took rooms with Mrs. Joynson in Reading. I preferred that. Just over two years ago I began to get worried, stood it as long as I could and then left, as I said, nearly a year ago. I think it was partly the strain of that *and* having Dinah. I had her at Queen Charlotte's and came to live here. The mother of a friend of mine at the A.A. owns this house. I used to room here, as I told you. They've been very kind to me. Offered me these rooms at a cut-price rent and here I am."

"You've never even considered going back to Reading?"

"How could I? It gives me cold shivers just to think about. I told you, the last year there was a nightmare. The year here has been, too, in a way, but I do manage to put the ghastly thing out of my mind now and then. I had so much time on my hands in Reading. All I had was my thoughts. Keith spent so much time at Harwell. Here, at least, I've got Dinah and my work, for what it's worth."

She began to talk about her husband. It was plain that she was still deeply attached to him, even though she seemed to speak of him rather as a child than a husband.

His mathematical genius put him apart from other creatures, her words seemed to imply. Like most of us, she was more admiring of talents she did not comprehend than those she did. Presumably, she had some talent as a draftswoman, but this she put at naught against his understanding of the remoter realms of mathematics. Although she was obviously convinced that her suspicions were based on inescapable facts, she still did not seem to think that he had let her down in any way. All that was part of the waywardness inseparable from genius. I had come across the same tendency in wives before, but not in quite such high degree. I asked few questions. She wanted to talk. In her own mind, she had already tried Lewis and found him guilty. Now she was trying desperately to justify, or, at least, to explain or excuse the course he had taken. Partly she blamed herself, I think. Perhaps she had not understood him. Perhaps she should have directed him into industry. In a way she was also trying herself. I did not attempt to interrupt. She had kept all this to herself for two years. Now, as is so often the case, a stranger was the cause of release to the cramped, containing mind. So I let her talk.

From her words I judged Lewis to be all that she had implied: temperate, generous, even-tempered, serious, preoccupied with thoughts of the social significance of his work or discoveries, perhaps, like other scientists, persuaded that his particular kind of knowledge put him apart from his fellows, making him into one ordained to guide, to decide, to direct, doubtless in much the same way that the monastic scribes of earlier times thought that their reading and learning put them apart from their fellow men and made them logical guides for the world's immortal souls. Now, however, it was not so much our immortal souls that were at stake, but merely our quotidian lives. Perhaps we do well to be suspicious of all self-appointed guides to our destiny, here or hereafter.

Listening to Julia Lewis, I gathered that most of Lewis's life had been lived in his researches. For the rest he was a simple man of simple pleasures. Apparently he liked rock climbing, poetry, crossword puzzles, learning foreign languages, traveling abroad inexpensively. Gradually I began to make some kind of image of the man; the image still had no semblance of a traitor, but perhaps there is no known likeness. Nunn May and Fuchs, I reminded myself, had lived and worked among their colleagues for years, their loyalty unchallenged.

"Is he attached to his daughter?" I asked.

"Of course. Like most fathers, I think he would have preferred a son, but he always makes a fuss of her and brings her back presents from abroad."

"I think it's most women who would prefer a son," I said. "Don't fathers want daughters?"

She smiled remotely from superior knowledge, and I let the subject drop, asking whether her husband often went abroad.

"Fairly often, but not as often as he would like."

"Why has he gone this time?"

"An academic gathering of some kind in Milan, I believe. He is one of the representatives of the English universities. So he said. I suppose it's partly true. It's the rest I'm so doubtful of." Now she seemed able to talk calmly, but the tension was still there. Her fingers crossed and uncrossed as she talked. But I let her go on. It was best, I thought, that she should find what relief she could in talking.

Only toward the end did I ask the question that had been in my mind for the past two hours. "Mrs. Lewis," I said suddenly in a silence, "was there anything in your husband's mental make-up or behavior that would make it understandable to you why he could become a traitor?"

She thought for a long time.

"Nothing," she said at last. "Like many of his generation he was far to the left, but he never acted like a megalomaniac or schizo if that's what you mean. . . ."

"Partly."

"I must have read every word of Moorehead's book four times over this last year," she said quietly. "I see no likeness between those men and my husband."

"There was no apparent common link between the minds of the men Moorehead wrote about, yet one was there," I said gently. "And if your belief is true, your husband has something in common with them."

"I suppose so," she said at last, as if this were the final admission that she had never allowed herself to make until that moment.

"You would say that your husband was quite normal, then?"

"Is anyone normal?" she asked. "He was bitter about the world. But so are many people. The haves and the have nots. He had a tough time when young. But does that make a traitor?"

"Not often," I said, truthfully enough.

We talked on and on until midnight chimed quickly from the small clock above the fireplace. I stood up to go. "What will be the next step?" she asked at the door.

"I don't know. To try to see whether there's any truth in what you surmise, I suppose."

"And then?"

"Let us wait till then."

She nodded and gave me her hand.

I went downstairs and into the hall. Under the grim light I took out my checkbook and scribbled the telephone number on its cover. At the front iron gate I looked both ways, almost surreptitiously, half expecting to see a watcher in a doorway of one of the shops opposite, or peeping from behind a pillar of a near-by house. But King's Road remained the dowdy thoroughfare I had known so many years before. No sinister figures peered from improbable peepholes or uncurled themselves from cramped and wearisome vigil.

I walked slowly toward Sloane Square, going over the strange interlude of the past few hours. Like a man who wakes after a midday sleep in the sun, I found momentary difficulty in placing myself in time. Only five hours before, I reminded myself disbelievingly, I had still been a guest at a cocktail party given by Matthew Chance, less than half a mile away.

21

THERE WAS NOTHING I COULD DO THE FOLLOWING DAY, SUNDAY, so I ate a leisurely breakfast in bed and afterward smoked, my arms behind my head, my eyes considering the tops of the plane trees on the other side of Piccadilly, my mind brooding on the sad life of Mrs. Keith Lewis.

In the morning light, the previous evening still had an unreal quality about it, in much the same way that the morning after a battle, or a blitz, or an esoteric sexual adventure is possessed of unreality. Most of our experiences seem to evolve in sequence, one from another. Only rarely do we live through a self-contained experience, so to speak, an incident owing nothing to precedent or to any other part of our lives until that moment. My evening with Mrs. Lewis had had something of that quality about it.

But that way lies madness, and I turned to the Sunday press.

I got up about eleven, bathed and shaved and, somewhat out of character, took time choosing a tie. Some time after midday I went downstairs and out into the warm sun, intending to walk toward Piccadilly Circus. Then, on an impulse, I went back into Athenaeum

Court, looked up Butler's telephone number at Dorset House and rang.

A Germanic-sounding maid said he was away and would not be back until Monday evening. I asked for his number in the country: a Berkshire address. After a good deal of mutual misunderstanding I got the number, on the Crux Easton exchange. It was an unfair test for a middle-European.

Finally I got through and, to my surprise, Butler answered. I had always thought of him as spending Sunday mornings, somewhat ineffectually, on a local golf course. I mentioned my vivid picture.

"It's my wife who plays golf. I spend Sunday mornings reading Sunday newspapers. It's a drug. Have you seen our front page this morning? Terrible."

I said I'd only seen the *Sunday Times* and *Observer*.

"I always forget you prefer instruction to entertainment," he said. "God knows why. Why did you ring anyway? Have you found Professor Lewis?"

"Not quite. His wife."

"Ah! Jealousy. As I said. Tell me."

"Not quite."

"Pity. What is it then?"

"I wondered how soon you would be in London in the morning."

"Ten o'clock."

"Can I see you about eleven?"

"But of course. But why not now?"

"It's a bit difficult."

"Not a bit of it. My wife's playing another eighteen holes this afternoon, the crazy bitch. I'm all alone. I'll drive into Reading to meet you. It's only twenty-five miles. A mere bagatelle for the sake of the paper. Hold on, I'll get the ABC. Here it is. You can get the one-twenty from Paddington, Reading at two-five. Just a minute. Yes, it's one of these angelic iron horses that comes straight on to Newbury. I'll meet you there. I see that derisive letter 'r' in the book, so you can lunch on the train. Do me a power of good, dear boy. I'll drive you up in the morning."

I agreed, rather welcoming the prospect of escape from my own company for the day, and went back to my room, packed my shaving gear and pajamas and took a taxi to Paddington.

22

BUTLER WAS WAITING IN THE STATION COURTYARD IN HIS CAR, THE
sleek and shining Bentley I had seen before. Above a certain income
a Bentley seems to be the label of success in England nowadays.
Not a Rolls. That still seems to have an unwanted touch of reticence
about it, perhaps old-fashioned dignity, but take the same chassis, the
same body, put on a Bentley hood and the tycoon is labeled SUCCESS.
I mentioned my jaundiced views to Butler.

"You're probably right," he said. "I don't know much about cars
myself. To me it's just part of the perks. It's all on the poor bloody
shareholders and taxpayers."

He lived about eight miles from Newbury, I judged, going out
toward Hungerford, then bearing left. His house was a small and
beautiful William and Mary farmhouse set in about sixty acres, which
he let to a local farmer. Inside, the house was somewhat overfur-
nished in a chintz-and-faded-mahogany manner, but it made a pleasant background for relaxation.

"Now tell me," Butler said, placing his great bulk carefully in one
of the large armchairs, "which Lewis is it?" I told him. I also gave
him a brief outline of Mrs. Lewis's suspicions, Chance's place in
those suspicions, of Lewis's return. Butler listened attentively, asking
no more than half a dozen questions throughout my recital. At the
end he said, "Funny, isn't it? Yet somehow the Chance side of it
comes as no surprise."

"But I still think it may all be that woman's nightmare."

"Possibly, but it's rather a pleasant change, having one's own
hunches confirmed by somebody else's nightmares, don't you think?
What do you propose to do now, dear boy?"

"What do I propose!" I said in a sudden fury. "By good luck and
some small acumen I've found Professor Lewis for you. At least, his
wife. Isn't the rest up to you and your newspapers?"

"It's a bit too hot for a newspaper as it is," he said calmly. "And
too vague. We've got to blow it up so that it flies or busts. The best

way to blow it up is to tackle Lewis or Chance as soon as possible. Which?"

"Lewis," I said quickly, too quickly. It gave him the chance for disputation.

"Why? Just to give him a chance to duck on account of his forgiving wife?"

"Possibly," I said, my interest engaged again.

To my surprise Butler agreed, but for a different reason. "Judging by all his wife says—and she ought to know—he's the weaker one. If he cracks he'll probably put us onto something or somebody else. He may even come clean with the whole story if there's anything in it."

"Perhaps we could tackle both of them?"

"We're in the fortunate or unfortunate position of being able to do exactly as we damn well please," Butler said. "We've got what the generals are so happy to call the initiative. Sometimes it's a mixed blessing. It's that much easier to make a balls of things. I daresay quite a number of our most eminent generals have discovered that, too."

He sprawled there in the bulbous armchair, spilling his limbs over the cushions like an agglomeration of giant meringues. What is there, I asked myself irritably, about this big fat lout that makes him such a power in Court House? But I knew the answer even as I asked the grim, distasteful words.

"What's Mrs. Lewis like?" he asked, out of his rumination.

I described her as well as I could.

"You don't think she's part of the game?"

"Why should she tell us, then?"

"God knows. A double-cross. A smoke screen. A way to get rid of somebody somebody wants to get rid of. Isn't that a fairly frequent party line?"

"I don't think it's the case this time."

"It doesn't sound like it certainly, but real-life heroines and real-life bitches rarely look the real thing. They only look that way in Jane Austen and the Brontës. Or on the films. Is she anything to look at? As usual, you described her character, not her looks."

"It's difficult to tell. She could be quite handsome. She's as white as chalk at the moment."

"You cheered her up, no doubt?"

"I cheered her up."

"I'm very glad to hear. D'you think Chance ever made a pass at her and this is her revenge?"

"You read too many of your own newspapers."

"My newspapers, our newspapers, your newspapers, deal with life as it has been lived for at least two thousand years. So pray answer my question without these cheap asides, dear boy."

"She seemed quite detached about him. I think she genuinely thinks of him as a quite impressive figure, despite the fact that if her tale's correct, Chance is the nigger in the woodpile."

"You found him quite impressive, didn't you?"

"Yes, I'd say he's pretty impressive."

"So would I," Butler agreed. "As a matter of fact, I think he's very impressive. I'll tell you now: the whole of that series you wrote was aimed at him, written with the sole idea of getting him into it. Funny, isn't it? You fly a kite and something you never expect gets hooked onto it."

"What did you expect?"

"Nothing much. A bit more about his background and ambitions. What a man wants to do is usually more interesting than what he's done."

"Have you ever heard about Chance from any other sources?"

"Not much, apart from what poor Dick Arnott told me long ago. You remember? I told you. A word dropped here and there, that's all. Certainly not recently. But I'm built like an elephant, why shouldn't I have a memory like one?"

"What did you hear in Spain?"

"Nothing much, apart from what Arnott told me."

"Did anybody else have similar ideas about him?"

"One or two seemed to agree. His own comrades, for instance. No man is anybody's comrade in his cups. The gossip of drunks, and what's that worth?"

I was impatient. I wanted to know what to do next. As if in reply, Butler lifted his arm, took up the telephone and asked for the Court House number and a personal call to Mr. Rees. He sat waiting, silent, considering his beautiful moccasin shoes.

"You've got a stringer in Milan, haven't you, Rees?" he asked when the connection was made. "Get him and ask him to check on any international university jamboree out there and see if there's a Professor Lewis there and when he's coming back. Let me know in the morning if you get onto anything. How's the paper shaping?"

They began to talk technicalities. I got up and went to the window. The Butler garden was a picture from a nurseryman's catalogue: a dazzling concentration of chrysanthemum, Michaelmas daisies and dahlias massed in banked borders beyond a sweep of lawn, with one great cedar set in solitary grandeur in the foreground, and, beyond, tall limes and beeches, sixty or seventy feet high.

Afterward we talked again about Julia Lewis, Keith Lewis and Matthew Chance, until Joyce Butler came in, bringing with her mingled scents of the open air and Paris.

She was about ten years younger than Butler, a tall, heavy, fair-haired woman who seemed to discipline explosive energy only by considerable effort. At all times she was efficient, intelligent, tactful and friendly. In the past I had sometimes thought that, in public, she was all that Butler had trained her to be. I had also occasionally wondered about their private life, but that was restricted in any case. He was scarcely ever at home. We even went out to dine publicly that evening, to a roadhouse halfway to Reading. On those terms, private life becomes restricted to lovemaking and breakfasting, but perhaps that was enough for both of them.

Yet, watching them at dinner that night, they seemed companionable enough. She laughed at his bland, unrelenting cynicism as if she believed none of it, and he, in turn, like a cardsharper willingly outwitted by a guileless partner, smiled at the deprecating quality in her laughter.

Their relationship was interesting to watch. Also, in an odd way, quite convincing. I would even have put them down as a happily married couple. How or why, God only knows, for happiness in marriage, like life after death, is something we do well to leave without too many questions. None of the experts has yet come forward with a formula to guarantee the certainty of either.

Afterward we went back and talked for a while. I had thoroughly enjoyed my day.

23

WE LEFT EARLY THE NEXT MORNING. BY EIGHT O'CLOCK BARKER, THE chauffeur, had already brought the car round to the front door. When we appeared he was seated, somewhat forlornly, in the rear seat. He jumped out smartly to open the doors and then got back. Unwanted chauffeurs always look like peculiarly lost and ignominious souls. Barker triumphed dourly over the circumstances, sitting stiffly in the rear seat, upright and unrelaxed, rather like a piece of self-conscious royalty.

Butler drove fast and well. He chain-smoked throughout the journey, a curious habit I had noticed before. Normally he was no more than an average, twenty-a-day smoker. When driving he stared unwaveringly at the road ahead, his eyes narrowed against the smoke from his cigarette, talking and questioning, as he always did, with insatiable curiosity and no respect for privacy. When I protested he laughed. "Why not?" he said. "It's the only way we learn anything about anybody. Anybody talks, given half a chance. To a trained listener the words are plainly truth or lies. Tell me a simpler way of finding out what you want to know."

"But you only want to know about people. Never an idea."

"People are ideas," he said, "and living people at that. I'm only interested in death when someone is accused of causing it. I'm only interested in an idea when it's attached to a man or a woman, here and now. I'm not interested in the great Platonic abstractions. As far as I'm concerned, or a newspaper's concerned, no man, however great, lives beyond his obituary notice. Death plus one day is the immortality of most public figures in a newspaper. After that, a reference in the library."

"And posterity's valuation?"

"Not my concern. We deal with yesterday's history, today's if it's possible, tomorrow's if it's lucky. It's a simple ambition, perhaps, but it's clear-cut, which is more than you can say of the work of most historians."

"Perhaps that's not their main objective."

"I think it is, but it gets too complicated for 'em," he said genially. "Even a month gives time for reflection. A hundred years is fatal to the simple, clear-cut view."

"I'm still on the historian's side."

"Why not? Didn't you try to become one once upon a time? And now you're trying to be a newspaperman. I wouldn't have your inner conflicts, dear boy, not for a brand-new Bentley."

I laughed. How much of his own flumdummery did he really believe? I wondered, as I had often wondered before. Did he say these things merely for effect, to see how the listener reacted? He always made his statements as if they were pronouncements of absolute truth. Perhaps all his remarks were made with his tongue firmly in his cheek. Perhaps he even saw life like that, oversimplified into the patterns of his views. But that made him too simple and he was far from that.

Throughout the journey, from Reading to London, I answered questions about the American political situation as well as I knew how. And always he looked ahead, the cigarette smoke rising between his narrowed eyes like a fluttering veil. His probing was relentless.

Passing through Hammersmith he returned to the subject of Lewis and Chance. "What shall we do?" he asked. "Wait to see if Lewis is returning in the next day or so?"

I had also decided upon that immobile move before falling asleep the previous night, but now I said, hazarding a possibility, "Wouldn't it be worth checking all his movements in the first few days? We don't want to precipitate anything and scare him off."

"It would take too long," he said. "These things go on for years. If there's anything in what his wife says it's already been going for at least a couple of years. There's no reason why it shouldn't go on for another two, another dozen. There's probably half a dozen spy rings in the States and in this country that have been operating successfully since the end of the war."

"Senator Jenner says two dozen."

"Who's he?"

"Chairman of the Senate's Internal Security Subcommittee."

"Glad to hear I'm on the conservative side for once. One doesn't expect that from the popular press." He was silent a moment and then fired his question: "How would you, given a free hand, try to bring this little spy ring, if it is one, into the open?"

For the first time on the trip he turned to look at me as I hunted for an answer. "I'd probably try to get an interview with Lewis as you suggested last night."

"Why not with Chance?"

"That would be easier. I've at least made my number there. I think I could see him any time, but he's a tough nut. No, I'd go for Lewis."

"All right. We'll go for Lewis."

"How?"

"We'll bring him out into the open. We'll put one of the reporters onto him. If he's up to anything he'll be terrified. Secrecy is what he must have, at any price. A public figure can hide behind his public face. But to a private figure, with a secret life, the threat of publicity is terrifying. We can but try, anyway."

"And, meanwhile, what about Chance?"

"Being an M.P. he's got to stay put. He can't move. The whips will forgive an occasional pairing, but he can't disappear for more than two days without a few questions being asked. And immediately. No, we'll have 'em both under a microscope for a week or so. It should be interesting. Coming into the office or shall I drop you off?"

"Will you have had word from Milan yet?"

"Possibly, but I doubt it."

"I think I'll drop off, then. What do you want me to do?"

"Hang around."

"And what about New York?"

"It seems to be hanging together without you."

"That's true."

"Well, stay here."

He stopped at Athenaeum Court and bade me farewell, smiling his half-mocking smile as if he knew already the words I wished to hurl after him as he drove away.

24

"WE'VE GOT WHAT THE GENERALS ARE SO HAPPY TO CALL THE INITIA-tive," Butler had said the previous evening, but I wondered whether that was true after I had read the note from Chance awaiting me at the desk in Athenaeum Court. *It was pleasant to see you yesterday,* I read, *but we were both sorry we were unable to see more of you. Cocktail parties are barbaric occasions, although it's the best way for mass destruction of bores and chores. Before you go back I should like to meet again and, as I understand you were wishful of meeting Professor Lewis (I did not know that you knew him), I wonder whether you would care to dine here and meet him on Wednesday. He is expected back from Italy tomorrow, Monday. I hope you will be able to come.* Across the foot of the note he had scribbled *7:45 for 8.*

Not bad, I thought, and smiled at Butler's short-lived initiative, but in the same instant wondered what the counter to this move might be. Clearly Chance's butler had told him of my question. Nobody else had overheard. Of that I was certain.

I went upstairs and sat in the armchair by the window.

I was slightly shaken. The initiative had been mine too briefly. I gave Butler another five minutes to reach his penthouse paradise. Then I rang him. I was put through straightaway.

"Your initiative was short-lived," I said. "Chance has invited me to meet Lewis at dinner on Wednesday."

"So the servant reported all?"

"So it seems."

"Well it means that Lewis is coming back."

"Today, Chance says in his note."

"You'll go, of course."

"So it seems."

"Why not? This is better than anything we could have hoped for."

"I'm glad you see it that way."

"Well, it's movement. That's something. It's not what I'd call action but at least it's movement. I'll let you know later if we get anything from Milan." He said good-by cheerfully and rang off.

I was irritated by his cursory farewell and assumption that I should wish to go. I had thought of Chance's letter as a modest thunderbolt to toss into Butler's lap. Instead, he had shown no surprise and tossed it back to me, as if such a development had an expected place in a long-foreseen sequence of events.

I sat there moodily for a time, perhaps half an hour. Then I crossed to the telephone and asked for the Flaxman number. Julia Lewis was at home. She sounded more cheerful.

I said, "Your husband is due back today."

"Yes, I know. I had a postcard this morning."

"Will he come to see you?"

"Probably. He usually does, although not always straightaway."

"Chance knows I'm interested in your husband. He's suggested that we should meet. Dinner on Wednesday is the idea."

"Isn't that a good idea?"

"Why 'good' exactly?"

"Perhaps something will happen. Anything is better than this suspense."

"Why do you think Chance wants this meeting?"

"Probably because he wants to try to find out how much you know or suspect."

"I suppose so. Does this fit in with what you know of him?"

"I think he'd always rather face things than evade them," she said and then, as an afterthought, "Unlike most people."

I thanked her and asked after her daughter.

"She's very well," she said. "It's a pity I couldn't introduce you the other evening. Normally she's very sociable."

"I'll drop in some time and meet her."

"That would be nice," she said quickly. "We'd both like that."

She had spoken so eagerly that momentarily I was shamed by my own insincerity. After a few more politenesses I rang off. By then, thanks to the eternal inconsistency of human behavior, I was firmly convinced that I wanted to see both Julia Lewis and her daughter. I would go down to King's Road soon, I told myself, but I knew it was all self-deception. Julia Lewis's generous response to my idle words had touched my conscience. I rang the reception desk and arranged for flowers to be sent to King's Road. It was easier than visiting.

Then Butler rang. "We think Lewis gets in on the Milan flight, arriving seven-forty this evening. An Alitalia plane via Paris. It's the only Monday plane from Milan anyway. Rees is sending Sanderson down to check on him. He's done this kind of thing before."

I said nothing.

"Why don't you go down with him?" Butler said slowly, prodding at my silence. "You could at least get a peek at Lewis. That might be useful."

The suggestion made sense and I agreed, reluctantly.

"Good," Butler said quickly. "Sanderson will call for you about six."

"You're not proposing that Sanderson should interview him, are you?" I asked in sudden alarm.

"Not unless you decide to. Sanderson will defer to you in all things. It's not a bad idea, all the same. Sometimes the blunderbuss is more effective than the rapier. It might stir things up and get things going. Or am I mixing my metaphors? Please yourself."

"I don't mean to interview him myself," I said firmly. "I meant Sanderson."

"You mean you've become too big a boy for that kind of thing, is that it?" Butler said, with deliberate cussedness. I let silence grow between us and then laughed. Butler laughed too.

"Sort it out with Sanderson on the way down," he said amiably. "I leave it all to you. Your Wednesday dinner is the main thing, but it might help to enliven that occasion if you can pluck up the necessary nerve to interview Lewis tonight. The idea has its points, hasn't it? It couldn't help but bring things to the boil, and that's what we're after, isn't it?"

"Is it?" I said gloomily.

"Sort it out for yourself."

I had to admit that if Butler wanted "action," then an interview at the airport was worth considering. Lewis had lived in comparative seclusion, despite renown in his own world. An attempted interview might well provoke him to an unwise word. In such unpremeditated moments, a man can give himself away—if there is anything to give away.

"All right, I'll talk it over with Sanderson," were my grudging final words to Butler.

<h1 style="text-align:center">25</h1>

I SPENT A WRETCHED DAY, HATING THE TANGLED WEB I HAD HELPED to weave, but I was inextricably caught in its threads, and at six o'clock I was waiting in my room for Sanderson.

I went down to meet him when he was announced. He was immediately and unnervingly deferential. After five years of New York egalitarianism I was frequently disconcerted by the modesty shown by younger Englishmen toward those more experienced in their craft or industry. I told him not to call me "sir," but the usage was part of his background; he could not easily put it aside.

He was a serious, young-looking man, perhaps about thirty-two or -three, but looking no more than twenty-seven. He was tall, well built, dark haired, gray eyed, with the complexion of an open-air man. Not the russet skin of a farmer or gamekeeper, but the pink-and-white glow of a man who keeps himself in trim with a daily dozen, regular golf or Old Boy football.

We sat in armchairs by the high glass windows looking onto Piccadilly. "Are we going to interview this bird?" I asked.

"Mr. Rees said I was to leave it entirely to you, sir."

"I was afraid of that. How much do you know of the background of this story?"

"Not much, sir. I gathered that the editor thinks there may be a story in him and wants me to keep fairly close to him—if I can."

"No more than that?"

"Not really, apart from the fact that if it does come to an interview I'm to keep to this inter-universities conference he's just left."

Plainly Rees knew no more than Sanderson about the Lewis-Chance story. Butler was remaining secretive.

"All right, we'll see," I said, and got up to go.

An editorial car was waiting outside in the care of a driver I didn't

recognize. Sanderson closed the glass partition as we moved off. He
could scarcely wait before asking his first question about New York,
Washington and the North American scene. He had been six months
in the States during the war as an RAF security officer, seconded
from Scotland Yard, he told me quickly. "I got interested in the States
then," he said, "and I've stayed that way. Besides, I've got an American wife—at least, she's a Texan—and that helps to keep my interest
alive."

We talked Americana from then on.

"Have you ever thought of working there?" I asked at one point.
"Often."

"Would you like it?"

"I think so. I've no family commitments here, apart from my wife,
and she'd love it, of course."

"How does she like it here?"

"Well enough, but she'd like to be back."

As he went on I made a mental note that here was one willing
apprentice for Grimston in the U.S.A. if Butler should again raise
the subject of my future.

Well within the hour we were at London Airport. Sanderson told
the driver he could have half an hour for a meal. "The plane's due
in at seven-forty," he said. "Be back here at seven-twenty. We may
need to leave in a hurry."

We went into the airport building, through to the restaurant and
sat by the window, caught up, as the whole world is caught up, in
the routine of a modern airport, listening as attentively as children
to the globe-girdling instructions from the loudspeakers.

Through our early dinner we continued to talk, still about the
States. I found myself opining on this and that, with Sanderson frequently agreeing but also occasionally disagreeing. He skillfully com-
bined deference and firmness.

I hadn't the slightest doubt that he was already playing hard for
the high but remote stake of a place in the Washington or New
York office, but he played well, and, like all true gamesmen, occasionally lost sight of his ultimate aim in the excitement of the play. It
was a bedeviling discussion and time passed swiftly. I was surprised
and dismayed to hear the announcement of the arrival on the runway
of Flight AZ 465 from Milan.

We left so hurriedly that I grievously overpaid the waiter in our unnecessary panic. As we left the room Sanderson said, "Do we interview him or not?"

I said, in the flush of disputation and the *vin rosé*, "Yes, why not?"

"What do I ask him?"

"His views on the meeting. Results. Discussions."

"Anything in particular from yourself?"

"Nothing."

"Will you be there?"

"I don't know. My main idea was to have a look at him. I'll probably hang around like a stray dog."

We waited at the barrier at the far end of the customs hall. Sanderson said, "I'll check with one of the officials to let me know which he is. Will you wait here?"

I nodded absently, watching, more excited than I would have admitted. Sanderson returned within five minutes. "A security chap I know tipped me the wink. There he is!" He nodded toward a tall man in a brown raglan coat. In one hand he carried a small attaché case, which he put on the floor between his feet. Taking off his brown felt hat he wiped his high forehead with a colored kerchief.

I had made my image of Lewis and the reality shattered that image like a fallen mirror. I had expected to see a pale, nervous man, unmistakably a scholar, perhaps round-shouldered and shortsighted, certainly carelessly dressed and showing signs of strain. Instead, I saw a tall man, lean and tanned, with dark, receding curly hair and a dark, rather drooping mustache. A typical Celtic face, similar to many to be seen in Wales, Cornwall or Ireland, I thought, but more delicate, less earthy. He might well have been judged handsome by the knowledgeable, for his features were regular and firm, even striking, but his eyes were so deep-set that the face was as gaunt as an El Greco portrait.

He looked about with frowning intensity. He had an odd and appealing air of forlorn nobility about him.

"Are you sure that's the right man?" I said to Sanderson, but I knew I was putting off the evil moment.

"These security boys don't usually make mistakes," he said judicially.

Passengers' luggage was wheeled in and Lewis, somewhat after the others, stepped forward to indicate two canvas bags. He placed the small attaché case, unopened, on the slatted rack, and then waited patiently for inspection. I watched him, absorbed, trying to relate him to Julia Lewis's story.

He read the Notice to Travelers, nodded, smiled gravely and opened both canvas grips and the attaché case. The customs officer glanced casually at the contents, took a doll from one of the cases, asked a question, smiled in his turn and then swiftly chalked his clearance symbols on the bags.

Lewis slowly zipped the bags shut and they were caught away by a BEA porter. Lewis followed, walking slowly and reflectively.

The incident of the doll was disquieting and I liked my task even less than I had two minutes before.

Sanderson had no such hesitations. He left my side as if on skates. Unwillingly I turned and followed. As I went through the side door of the hall I almost collided with a small group. The porter had put down Lewis's bags. Sanderson was speaking to Lewis, and, for a tense moment, I thought Lewis was about to turn and run. Now I could clearly see that he was as taut as a watchspring.

Sanderson had just introduced himself and was naming his paper, then myself. I thought I saw momentary relief in Lewis's eyes and wondered whether I read his thoughts aright or too fancifully. We were newspapermen, unwanted irritants, perhaps, but still far removed from the men he had been expecting to meet him at any moment of the day or night in the many preceding months.

In those seconds I had the strange experience of sharing his sudden apprehension. This unaccountable sympathy held me from that first moment of meeting and persisted throughout my brief acquaintance with him. Perhaps most of us are moved by the sight of unguarded fear in the eyes of another human being. We all carry, within ourselves, our own brand of fear. That evening I lived in one of those rare moments when another man's protective screen falls flat.

"I wondered whether you would care to give us your comments on the congress in Milan, Professor," Sanderson said, his manner easy but purposeful. He had no doubts about himself or his assignment.

"I am afraid I have nothing to say," Lewis said. He looked around him quickly. Even a casual onlooker, I thought, would have thought him too anxious for some door of escape.

"But surely it was a meeting of some importance to all university people, particularly graduates," Sanderson went on, unperturbed.

"That may be so but I am the wrong man to ask about it."

"But you were one of the three appointed English delegates."

"I am Welsh, originally from the University of Wales," Lewis said with a sudden smile. His tension seemed to lessen as he gained in certainty that we were only newspapermen. Now, closer, I could study his face. He was younger looking than I had first thought, but the mustache was already touched with gray. *A serious, scholarly man in the mid-thirties* would have been my one-line caption.

"All the better," Sanderson was saying. "You can be detached about both your Italian hosts and your English colleagues, and we have many Welsh readers. They'll enjoy it."

Lewis smiled. "Look," he said, "I am meeting friends. I hate to be a bore like this, but I must dash."

He walked ahead. Once again the porter took up the bags. Sanderson looked inquiringly at me and I nodded. In that boorish manner, which is so often and so accurately attributed to persistent reporters, we fell into step with Lewis.

He took it, as most people take it, remarkably well.

I hated every moment. I had come into journalism too late in life to take easily to that kind of bulldozing interview, and I had, fortunately, been able to avoid its frequent necessity. An English columnist can usually pick and choose his subjects and objects. After the age of forty, such an occupational hazard as the one I now record is degrading to one's self-esteem, but I could see that Sanderson had no such qualms.

Lewis clearly thought his best course was to humor Sanderson and to ignore me. This course was fairly easy for him as I fell farther and farther behind. In this uneven manner we made our way out to the drive-in and the wide, enclosing ring of parked cars.

Lewis led the way past the cars until he stopped suddenly by a small black sedan drawn up alongside one of the dismal prefab buildings which are still an essential part of London airport. From ten yards off I heard him say, "Good-by, Mr. Sanderson," very firmly and decisively. As Lewis stopped and told the porter to put the luggage in the rear compartment, somebody in the car opened the off-side door. The porter dumped the bags inside. Lewis still carried the tiny attaché case which he had not relinquished at any moment since taking it up, opened but unexamined, from the customs bench.

As I came up to the car, Lewis was already in, alongside the driver. He slammed the door and put out his hand from the window with

the porter's tip. Sanderson was looking on, smiling quizzically, unde-
terred by the rebuff. I quickened my step as the car began to move.
As it swung round I saw, quite clearly, that the car was a Sunbeam-
Talbot and the driver was Mrs. Chance. I opened my mouth to utter
some conventional banality, but the car was gathering speed and she
was looking straight ahead. I could not even be sure that she had
seen me.

26

"WE MIGHT AS WELL GET BACK," I SAID TO SANDERSON.
   "There's no point in trying to get after them?"
   "I think I could even give you the address," I said, "but there's
still no point. It was worth it, all the same."
   "Did I imagine things, or was Lewis scared?"
   "He was scared."
   "What about?"
   "Who knows? Possibly the idea of his past catching up with his
present."
   "I suppose I'll have to admit defeat to the editor?" he asked, hop-
ing for reassurance.
   "You can tell him I was pleased with the evening's labor."
   "Thanks a lot. That's very kind."
   We were less talkative on the way back to London. I had my own
thoughts and I left Sanderson to his. My own made a strange medley.
I was trying to sort out the modest conundrum of Sandra Chance's
presence at the airport. There was the obvious explanation: that she
had picked him up and taken him back to Chester Square. Or was
there an alternative explanation, hovering in my mind from one of
Butler's earlier observations? "Jealousy, that's the great *agent provocateur* for anonymous notes," he had said. "History bears me out."
Perhaps Keith Lewis and Sandra Chance were involved in an affair.
Perhaps it had been discovered by Julia Lewis and she had sent that
note as part of a pattern of jealousy. Well, it was possible. Similar

liaisons began by the hundred thousand every day. Similar ideas of revenge wormed their way into poisoned minds. Yet somehow I still didn't think that this was one of the number. And if it were, then Julia Lewis must be one of the finest actresses I had ever seen, and I was the quintessential dupe. The possibility had to be faced. These things were by no means rare, but the picture was so depressing that I had no great wish to face it, and I tried to push it aside.

I leaned forward and opened the glass partition. "When you get to Sloane Street turn right and go through Chester Square," I said to the driver. "Slowly—from the Elizabeth Street end."

I returned to my thoughts. The possibility of an affair between Sandra Chance and Lewis still nagged. It could be the explanation of the whole patchwork story. At one stroke the bits seemed to fall into place in the puzzle. Fortunately it was a story known only to Butler and myself in Court House. And for the sake of the nation, if not for my *amour-propre*, it would be a more healthy explanation. That, at least, was some relief.

By the time we reached Chester Square I was inwardly irate, angry with myself, Julia Lewis, Butler, everyone. I had scarcely spoken to Sanderson throughout the return journey, I realized, but I was too irritable to bother with social niceties, and, instead, sat forward in the car, looking out. The Sunbeam-Talbot was outside Chance's house. I pointed to it as we passed and said, "We could get out and carry on our interview here if we liked."

"Do we?"

"I think the Professor's probably seen enough of newspapermen for one night."

"And vice versa?" Sanderson asked.

"Perhaps."

After a while Sanderson said, "Do we run anything on Lewis in tomorrow's paper? I could still get some kind of story in most of the editions."

"Forget him. You're all square with your editor?"

"Oh, absolutely. He said it was up to you."

"We'll leave it—for the moment, anyway."

He asked no more questions and I respected him for his restraint: it is always a nagging discipline for a young reporter to have to leave a story, especially a story such as this, with its unexplained undertones of fear and silence.

27

SANDERSON DROPPED ME OFF AT ATHENAEUM COURT.

"If anything develops I'll get in touch," I said. "And I'll remember your interest in the States and all things American."

He thanked me and the car moved off.

I stood there in Piccadilly, watching the car go, still disgruntled. For one thing, I was now wholly dubious of Julia Lewis's story. For another, I could see already that if I were to go on with the idea of dining with the Chances I should certainly have more than a few awkward minutes when meeting Lewis at their house, and nobody, apart from a few social buccaneers, relishes that kind of meeting.

There were three notes awaiting me at the desk. Would I ring Butler at home? Would I please ring Mrs. Lewis? And a note from Cholly Bedlington, wondering whether I would dine the following week. The first two were imperative, but for Bedlington a post card the following day would suffice. I went into the booth and rang Butler.

"Any luck?" he said.

"None." I told him briefly of the meeting with Lewis, the man's obvious fear, the rendezvous with Sandra Chance.

"Well, it fits together," he said at the end of my disjointed narrative.

"Jealousy on the part of Mrs. Lewis could make it fit together, too."

After a moment's reflection he agreed. "But I don't think so," he added. "You say he seems a decent kind of chap. Then there's the child; you say he seems fond of her. I know it's pretty flimsy stuff, but it's real. No, I think it's the big game they're playing. Anyway, you'll know by Wednesday midnight."

I laughed a hollow laugh.

"What have you done with Sanderson?"

"Sent him back without a story."

"What d'you think of him?"

"I think he might do very well in the States."

It was Butler's turn to laugh. "As your assistant or successor?"

"First one, then the other."

"No go!" he said and laughed and then, good night, he'd see me on Thursday. "You can ring me on Wednesday night here if it's worth it."

After that I called Julia Lewis. She answered immediately, almost as though she had been waiting by the door for the first ring of the telephone. "Oh, I'm so glad you've rung. Keith rang about a quarter of an hour ago. He seemed worried. Wanted to know if I had put some journalists onto him."

"And you said 'no.'"

"Of course." Her answer was a whisper.

"Shall I come down?" I asked. "I know it's past ten. . . ."

"Oh, if only you would. . . ."

"Have you had supper?"

"Yes. Just come as soon as you can."

I was at the house in ten minutes. Julia Lewis opened the door of her flat. To my surprise she seemed almost lighthearted. I had half expected to find her harassed and distressed. A dark red jersey dress brought a flush of color to her cheeks that I had not seen before.

"I can offer you coffee again," she said, showing me into the warm and colorful room.

So, once more, I sat in the armchair by the small but cheering coal fire and watched and listened and talked. Lewis must have telephoned immediately on arrival at the Chances' house. He had seemed extremely agitated, she said. How or why had the journalists picked on him? She went over their exchanges. At first she had tried to humor him, suggesting that he was now finding fame, but he had answered briefly, "Not in that way!"

"Will he come here tonight?" I asked.

"I don't think so. He'll want to see Chance who's probably not back from the House of Commons yet. Anyway, Keith likes coming in the afternoon when he can see the baby."

She changed the subject suddenly. "Were you one of the journalists he spoke about?"

I nodded.

"I thought so. How did he look?"

"Strung-up and fairly well until we began to talk to him. Then he seemed worried."

"Poor Keith," she murmured, half to herself.

"Why did you want to see me so urgently?" I asked.

She smiled before she spoke. Her answer was unexpected. "First to thank you for sending those," and she pointed to a jug of flowers. "But chiefly because of the way you seem to bring an air of well-being into my life. Perhaps it's because you're so very skeptical of everything I tell you. Perhaps it's because you're so matter-of-fact. You reassure me. After you left me the other night I had the first real night's sleep I've had in two years."

This was a new and unexpected vision of myself, and I said so, but she would not hear of it. "You are really a very reassuring person," she said again.

"Or a soporific."

She laughed. "Not really. When Keith rang this evening the whole dreadful business started up in my mind all over again. I rang you almost as a reflex action. As soon as I heard your surly voice I felt things couldn't be as grim as I really and truly know they must be."

She had started on a bantering note but ended gravely. I thought this was a moment to speak. "My managing director and editor in chief, to give him his full title, had a theory at the beginning of all this," I said slowly. "He thought a jealous woman might have sent that note to ditch her husband. A woman who'd discovered that her husband was having an affair. You, for instance. After finding out that your husband was having an affair with Sandra Chance."

I watched her take in the brutal words. She didn't answer for a second or so, then she said simply, "Well I suppose it's one way of looking at it. What do you think?"

"I don't know," I said truthfully. "I thought it might be true this evening when I saw them together. It seemed to hang together as a story."

"Did they look like lovers?"

"Not at all, but illicit lovers rarely do—in public."

"That's true." Then she said, bracing her shoulders, "Well, you *can* believe it, and, if you do, you'd believe anything!" Her voice had a high defiant ring.

"I don't believe it," I said, and in that moment truthfully.

"Now let's change the subject," she said briskly. "I don't like it. People's views are very strange sometimes."

"You can't blame them in this case," I said. "It is pretty odd, you'll admit. I may add that my editor no longer believes his theory."

But she had no wish to continue. She brushed the distasteful subject aside.

"Tell me about America," she said. "From the beginning. Your beginning, I mean. Why you went. When you went. What you do. Everything."

Under the harmless influences of near-black coffee, the warm room and the indulgent listening of Julia Lewis, I relaxed and talked, until the small balloon clock on the chimney piece again chimed midnight, quickly and shrilly like a petulant chaperone.

I had become oblivious of time and stood up with an outrush of apologies. Julia Lewis, as I now realize, had the rarest and most flattering of all qualities in a listener: she asked questions at those pauses in a narrative which merely needed another question as excuse and spur for further talk. Such a listening talent is a drug to a talker.

"Nonsense," she said to my apologies and excuses. "It is fascinating beyond words for me. It's a world I know nothing about. I enjoyed every minute."

I hoped so, indeed, but it still seemed to me a one-sided pleasure, and I said good night regretfully. We shook hands at the door.

"Lunch with me on Wednesday," I said on the moment of parting.

She thought for a moment and said, "If I can find a midday baby sitter, I'd love to."

"Is that so very difficult?"

"Not usually. My daily usually can if I give her a day's warning."

"So you will?"

"I will if I can."

Then she said in a serious voice, "It was kind of you to come. Kinder than you will ever know."

I brooded over her remark as I went downstairs and out into King's Road. A pale new moon gave the street something of the quality and clarity of an eighteenth-century print. I looked both ways. In the doorway of an antique shop on the opposite side of the road, out of the way of the cold wind, a man bent down and lit a cigarette. He stepped out of the doorway and went on, toward Fulham. I was living through such an unreal episode that I wondered momentarily whether he had been in the doorway as I came out of the front door, but it was a query without an answer, and I turned and walked briskly toward Sloane Square. There I took a taxi from the rank.

While walking, and in the taxi, I speculated upon the subject of Julia Lewis: her inner conflicts as a wife and mother; her decision to leave her husband; her looks; her view of me. I was still involved in these complex speculations when I reached Athenaeum Court.

28

THE DINNER ON WEDNESDAY WAS MY WAKING THOUGHT ON THE FOL-lowing morning, Tuesday, a thought followed swiftly by the spoken words "Damn Butler! Damn Lewis! Damn Chance!"

But before that I had a luncheon date and that prospect mollified my morbid thoughts and molten words.

I went down to Court House and spent the morning and early afternoon in the library, going through Hansard for the preceding five years, checking everything that Chance had said. Then I went across to the photographic library and went through the files there for pictures of him, possibly in Spain. There were several of him in postwar political groups and stories, but nothing earlier.

My mind kept drifting away from my self-imposed task. Finally I went out into Fleet Street and took a bus to Piccadilly Circus. Un-accountably, or perhaps not so unaccountably, I wanted desperately to go on with my conversation of the previous evening. Instead, I had to exercise unwonted self-discipline to stay myself from entering a telephone booth and ringing the Flaxman number. I was being considerate about waking the baby, I persuaded myself, but I knew that the child was left in her pram, out in the front garden, during the early afternoon. Then I remembered that Keith Lewis might well be there. I decided not to ring. I was becoming scared and wary. Worse still, it began to look as if I were getting caught up in a side issue of the story of Matthew Chance.

I derided myself for the nonsensical situation which had arisen and faced myself with an unwanted truth. I, a seemingly mature and

sophisticated man, was finding it difficult to resist telephoning a
young and virtually unknown woman. It is a situation that has faced
many men before, but to me, in those peculiar circumstances, it
looked bleak and reprehensible however I considered it. The woman
had left her husband, thinking him a spy, but she still loved him.
She lived in two rooms with a little daughter. She was a good listener with a slim figure, well-shaped features and sad eyes. Those
were the bare facts. Why not leave them in that factual form? But
that I knew I could not do, although they made a situation that was
beginning to be dangerously involved. It was all too tricky, as different as could be imagined from the somewhat tenuous relationships
that had contributed to my so-called way of life in New York City.

I tried to put aside this problem that was not yet a problem, and
need not become a problem if I behaved like a rational human being.
I tried acting rationally, by not going near a telephone, drifting, instead, into the Plaza to see a film. Only when I was in my seat did
I realize that I had already seen the film on Broadway. But—so bemused was I and so aimless was my day—I stayed and saw it through,
Vistavision, polyphonic sound and all.

Afterward I walked slowly back to Athenaeum Court. A note from
Butler awaited me: would I care to dine with him that evening at
Dorset House? Almost with relief I went up to my room and asked
the girl to get me Court House. And later, gradually and miracu-
lously, a hot bath smoothed out some of the irritabilities of aimlessness.

29

BUTLER WAS ALONE IN THE FLAT IN DORSET HOUSE. HIS WIFE HAD
gone back to Newbury, he confided as he mixed drinks.

"Some damned dog trials she's interested in. Always useful to have
one open-air and social type in the family if you live in the country.
Women's Institute, local nabobs and all the rest. What's the latest
about Chance?"

"Nothing new since yesterday."

"Tell me all about Lewis."

Once again I gave an account of events at the airport, perhaps more detailed than my telephone narrative of the previous evening.

"You think it *could* be an affair with Mrs. Chance?" he said at the end.

"I don't think so now."

"But you said so on the telephone. What's changed your mind?"

"I've seen Mrs. Lewis."

"Again?"

"Again."

"And now you're prepared to take her word for it?"

"I think so."

"But she's prejudiced, through and through."

"Probably, but I still have an odd belief that she would know."

"You're certainly working hard on this story. I take it she's not the ugliest woman in England."

"I think she could be handsome. She's rather living on her nerves at the moment."

"You've always been a peculiarly cold-blooded character where women are concerned," Butler said speculatively. "Don't tell me you're changing in your middle years."

"I've not been particularly susceptible, if that's what you mean. That's not necessarily cold-blooded, is it?"

"I'd say it necessarily was, but every man to his own self-delusions. There was that woman in the Waterman story."

He had a long memory, but it was a subject I preferred to let die. "All that was long ago," I said.

"Lots of stories about sex were long ago," he said smoothly. "Adam and Eve, for instance."

"All right, then," I said, "let's keep to stories about long ago."

He smiled and asked suddenly, "What will you talk about tomorrow?"

I was off guard and, for a moment, was confused, thinking that he had learned of my proposed luncheon with Julia Lewis, but he did not notice, and I recovered quickly enough and said that I hadn't thought about the matter. That was a lie. I had thought too much about the matter. The dinner at Chance's home was an unwelcome prospect and had scarcely been out of my mind for a moment.

"Prearranged plans seldom work," I said vaguely. "I'm trying not to think about it. It won't be a very cozy meal, that's certain."

He agreed and asked whether I thought Lewis would recognize me again.

"He must be blind if he doesn't. We met under pretty good lights, and I was introduced."

"What will you say when he asks what you were doing there?"

"I'll say I just went down with Sanderson. After all, I probably seemed to be tagging along, in any case. Sanderson did most of the interviewing, such as it was."

"It will still look extremely odd to Chance—or extremely logical." I had also thought of that. "Let's leave it until tomorrow," I begged. To my surprise he agreed.

The dinner was well cooked and well served, but I remember that we left the table, talking as if we were both involved in some marathon talkie-trance, oblivious of food. At one point I said, "I've been over here almost a month now, you know. When shall I go back?"

"Are you anxious to go back?"

"Not straining."

"Well, let it rest. The office still goes on. It's important that I should have a chance to pick your brains. Two months wouldn't be too long for you to stay here."

"Are you keeping me back just to pick my brains or to go on with this Chance business?"

"Both!" he said without hesitation. But he seemed to have put Chance out of his mind for the evening and even that reference did not provoke him into further discussion of Lewis or Chance, or, I was happy to think, Mrs. Lewis. But I was at peace too early.

The girl brought coffee into the room.

"I want more than that," he said, looking into the coffeepot. "Buckets more. Make some more and bring it in. And some bigger cups. And damned hot!"

He hurled his commands at the German girl as she moved toward the door, waving his fresh-lit Havana with an opera tenor's sweep. The girl turned and looked at him, unperturbed and amused, as if she had learned that the bark was a lot worse than the bite.

"How long before I begin to be useless as your American correspondent?" I asked. "One month? Two months?"

"Any man ought to be able to stay away from his office for two months—if he's trained his staff efficiently," Butler said portentously. "I'm not so sure about three months. That begins to be a long time. An ambitious rival might begin to get ideas. Any ambitious characters on your staff?"

"Not in that way."

"How do you know?"

I thought I knew them, I said.

"You're too trusting."

"Possibly."

"Don't you ever want to be an editor?"

"Not particularly."

"You may have to be. Getting hold of good editors is one of my major headaches. You've built yourself up some unique and valuable experience since the end of the war. We may want to cash in on it and you."

"The experience might make me a better journalist, but it doesn't guarantee I'd make a good editor."

He laughed quietly. "True enough," he said. "I wish a few more of the men on my staff had that kind of mock modesty."

Even with his so-called praise he mixed his jokes. He went on: "Does that mean you'd refuse an editorship if I offered you one?"

"It depends what you mean by editorship. Judging by your attitude to Rees we'd probably find we have different ideas about the meaning of the word, the functions of the job."

He laughed. "I'm sure we have, but I'd probably try to meet your idiosyncrasies more than halfway."

I was obstinate. Somehow I thought his probing might be serious. I had to make my stand. I said, "That probably wouldn't be far enough for an editor."

"You're not keen on this Chance job, yet you're doing it. *You're* meeting *me* more than halfway now."

"There's quite a difference between covering a story under somebody else's direction and editing a newspaper on the same terms."

He was pained. "Not direction," he pleaded. "Guidance, please."

"You can call it what you like. What you give Rees I call 'direction,' even domination."

"Harsh words!" he said, smiling, and then: "Why aren't you keen on this Chance job?"

"I think I hate investigating anybody. In this dusty world we're all too vulnerable in some way or another."

"All journalism is investigating in one way or another. If you found that Chance and Lewis were spies, would you be opposed to the idea of denouncing them?"

"I should probably denounce them, but I should ask myself 'why' all my life. We are all traitors to something or somebody."

"It's a question of degree."

"It always is," I said, almost wearily. "A man betrays his wife. It's not so heinous as a man betraying his country. Who says so? Who said so first? Who worked it out that way?"

"Logical questions don't necessarily have to have logical answers," Butler said quietly.

I went on, for I was caught up in my theme. "Perhaps Chance and Lewis—perhaps just one of them—thinks his allegiance to the world —or to an idea of one world—is greater than his allegiance to England. We know a lot of scientific creatures do think along those lines. Perhaps Lewis thinks his best way of hastening the day of that one world is to give his knowledge to all mankind, not to just one tiny part of it."

"Why not—if the tiny part is an essential part, essential to keeping all the other parts in a state of balance?" Butler said.

"There are just two parts to the world today," I said. "America and Russia. Anybody who thinks differently is a purblind ass."

"I think differently," Butler said. "You've been too long in New York and Washington. There's quite a lot of other parts and this old and decrepit nation is one of 'em. It may sound pretty old-fashioned stuff, dear boy, but I think an English scientist's duty is to England."

"And you'd shoot a scientist who sincerely held views to the contrary? Something along the lines I've just put forward?"

"Willingly. In fact, I may say I'd prove my contention with the very greatest sincerity. I'd shoot him myself. I'd probably miss, but it'd be a gesture in the right direction, you'll admit. But there's something in what you say, all the same. I know quite a number of scientists really do hold those views. God knows how or why. I find it pretty hard to understand, but I think they're sincere, even if they're all more than a bit cracked. But how is it they never do any harm on their own? How is it there's always some devious citizen

of the world around who shows the scientist the road to Moscow?
Tell me that!"

"We oversimplify the whole thing. Other men don't see issues in
that clean-cut black-and-white fashion. There are shades within
shades."

"Not for me there ain't," Butler said. "There are no shades in trea-
son. And that's why I'm after Chance. Lewis may have some of the
crackpot notions you've just put forward, but Chance don't. And he's
the bloke I'm after."

Once more we were back to the subject of Chance and we kept
to it until midnight.

30

THE NEXT DAY, WEDNESDAY, I LUNCHED WITH JULIA LEWIS.

That luncheon is now, for many reasons, difficult for me to write
about, more difficult than I had thought possible until this moment
of recollection. One simple but too-human reason is that, although
I can remember a number of details—topographical, gastronomical
and so on—there is much that is blurred beyond all hope of recalling.

I remember that I called for her at that sad and seedy house in
the King's Road. I remember that we walked, not especially talkative, along the King's Road, almost as far as Peter Jones. I remember
that from a point just short of that great glass store we took a taxi
to the Mirabelle. Those details are as clear as if they were part of
yesterday.

We were rather early, I also remember, yet we did not stay out
in the bar, but went straight through to a table I had reserved. There,
even before we had ordered our meal, we began to talk. Not the
small talk of our daily rounds, but more seriously, about ourselves.
Yet our comment was by no means heavy going. Like so many serious conversations, our exchanges were carefree and seemed to hold
much laughter. But the undercurrent was serious enough.

Within a few minutes, I knew for certain what I had already half suspected and fiercely denied to myself: I knew that I was in love with Julia Lewis. That the acquaintance already had, for me, at least, most of those paradoxical qualities which are at the heart of everything we call, with such appalling certainty, "love," I knew already. Excitement, delight, tenderness, compassion, desire: all these emotions were there, ready to be indexed had I been detached enough to label them, but I had deliberately refused to face them.

We laughed, I remember, at some overelaborate turn of phrase in the expansive menu, but then, unadventurously, ordered smoked salmon and lamb cutlets. Those are details I remember clearly. I asked about Dinah and gradually, irrevocably, we were involved in each other's lives.

She talked in that self-deprecating way reserved to mothers of young children: pride is scoffed at, yet will keep breaking through. As if she had steeled herself to put aside the temptation to dwell overlong on this favorite subject, she asked me again about America, raising queries which had come to her since our meeting two days before. Such an interest was flattering and I responded, but not for long. I was too curious about her own life.

So the beguiling shuttlecock of question and answer went on, even as I cursed myself for weakness or even madness. We talked for two hours. We also drank a very pleasant St. Emilion, I remember, and that probably helped.

By the time we came out into Curzon Street I knew that I was far more deeply involved in the life of Julia Lewis than I had been two hours before. Indeed, I knew for certain that I was far more deeply involved with another human's life than I had ever been before. I pushed the knowledge aside. Reaction is always for later on.

We walked into Piccadilly. As if made hesitant by our unabashed loquacity throughout the meal we were now silent, and took a taxi back to Glebe Place scarcely speaking a word throughout the journey. At the house I helped her down from the cab. "I will ring you this evening after the dinner, or tomorrow morning," I said. "There is a great deal more for us to talk about."

She nodded. "I had almost forgotten tonight," she said. "I wish you weren't going."

I looked down at her pale face and serious eyes and had the same thought. On a word I would have gone into the house with her, but she did not give the word. Instead, she put her hands over my own

and said, "Ring me tonight, no matter how late." Then she turned
and went along the path, indoors.

Once again in the taxi I sat back and closed my eyes, trying to
face the facts of this vast upset in my life. I tried to persuade myself that the situation was sudden and unexpected, but I had known
from our second meeting that to go on seeing Julia Lewis was to
walk, open-eyed, into serious complications of one kind or another.
Yet few men step aside from such a prospect. And few women. In
a way we invite these tribulations. Throughout my adult life I had
been wary of such possible complications, careful to a point almost
of cunning. In some ways, Butler had been right. I had perhaps been
somewhat cold-blooded in my relationships with women. Now, in
middle age, I told myself sardonically, I had cast myself, unseasona-
bly and unreasonably, in that role of folly I had so often gladly left
to others.

I looked at the simple outline of the facts and those were depressing enough. I spaced out the words in my mind: "The-wife-of-a-sus-
pected-spy-with-a-young-child." Then, in one of those moments of
masochism with which we sometimes try to exorcise a hopeless prospect which still attracts us, I repeated, "The-loving-wife-of-a-be-
loved-husband-with-a-well-loved-little-daughter."

But at such times we are beyond the pain that such cruel pre-
cision brings. Instead, a false elation upholds us. We almost convince
ourselves that all intervening obstacles can and will be overcome.

Then, too, there was another, even more disturbing consideration.
At such an early stage we rarely bother to consider whether our emotions are requited or whether they are exclusively our own. Vanity
insists that such a surfeit cannot be one-sided. Yet, in that taxi, morbid doubts began to assail me, but my ill-justified elation persisted,
despite awareness of the agonies ahead. Much of love is self-delusion.
I had had no word from Julia that she had been stirred in similar
fashion. I had only the eternal masculine belief that my own feelings
must surely be reciprocated.

Yet why should they? I asked myself. She had shown no sign that
her affection for her husband had died in despair. Then, too, she had
her husband's child. She had perhaps reacted momentarily to an escape from the chores that made her daily round, but that wasn't love.
No, I told myself, Julia Lewis had been caught immediately and
willingly into the demands of motherhood as soon as she had closed

that peeling door upon the King's Road, and had already forgotten me.

I sat throughout the afternoon at a table by the window, sometimes brooding over these sobering facts, occasionally pushing them aside to turn again to write overdue letters to colleagues in New York.

I expected to be returning within the next three weeks, I told Grimston, and proceeded to give him some account of the personalities I had met in the London office. Perhaps I wrote thus to New York in an attempt to translate myself from the dilemma in which I had become so untidily involved. Even epistolary contact with New York might bring escape from the dilemma that much nearer. We never really know the devious natures of our self-deceptions. Merged with such a desire for escape was an overwhelming desire to see more, much more, of Julia Lewis. In such ambivalent irresolutions do our lives disappear.

31

AGAINST THAT BACKGROUND I WENT DOWN TO CHESTER SQUARE THAT evening.

Again I was shown upstairs into the first-floor L-shaped drawing room. Chance, his wife and Lewis were already there.

"I think you have already met Professor Lewis," Chance said at the moment of introduction. He smiled thinly.

"Fleetingly, I'm afraid," I said, hoping that vagueness might get me over the awkward moment, but Lewis smiled.

"Your colleague was more persistent," he said quietly.

"I trust that he didn't embarrass you unduly."

"Fortunately Mrs. Chance took me out of his clutches too soon for that," Lewis said. Again he smiled as if he, too, had again disengaged himself from an awkward moment. I noted his reference, casual and natural, to Sandra Chance. If they were involved in an affair, it was extremely sophisticated and smooth in its working, but I could not see Lewis as a partner in such a liaison. Yet we are all hoodwinked daily by such things, I reminded myself firmly, but I would have wagered a lot of money on the innocence of this particular couple—on that score, at least.

We moved to sit down, Lewis and I each to an armchair, the Chances side by side on a long low settee. Lewis had certainly dealt very civilly with me, I reflected, silently thankful for the way he had glossed over our boorishness at the airport. Such restraint in an innocent and offended party is rare.

Partly to mollify him still further, partly to break a sudden silence, I asked him about Italy and the universities' convention.

He began to talk, almost eagerly, as if he, too, were anxious to hear sounds within the room, or to get away from any memory of the events of the day before. He talked jerkily but freely about his week in Milan, about his fellow scientists, about the small subcommittee he had found himself elected to, about Milan itself, its architecture, its people and their lives. I listened, relieved. Chance and his wife also listened. I wondered how we might look to a visitor, suddenly appearing. A conventional group. No tensions. No underlying fears. No mutual watchfulness. A carefree, chattering quartet. Apparently.

As Keith Lewis talked I watched him. Studying his face again, I decided that the El Greco label I had given him in the customs shed was singularly apt. His dark eyes, set within dark hollows, were strangely at variance with his tanned and bony face. The contrast was unexpected and disconcerting. This slightly Spanish look was enhanced by the drooping mustache, which gave him something of the appearance of a doleful hidalgo. At least, that is what I termed him, sitting there.

The face had a kind of tragic grandeur about it which I found strangely appealing. I had come to the house, caught up in my own problems, prepared to hate the husband of the woman I had come to love so suddenly and improbably.

. Instead, by an immediate sympathy he aroused, I found myself wishing to help this sad and serious man, if such help were within my compass.

He spoke in what I can only describe as a musical mumble. One leaned forward to catch the too-quiet words, which were uttered in a series of sudden assertions, followed swiftly by doubts and speculations.

I remembered that Julia had said that he had no great sense of humor, and I noted then that his narrative held no quirks of phrase or incident. He spoke seriously, the lecturer not far off at any moment. Yet we all listened, each of us engrossed. Occasionally he turned his eyes toward one of his listeners, but I was never certain that he saw me clearly, even when the dark eyes were so intently fixed on me. They still had too much of an inward look for easy social exchanges. After a while I tumbled to his secret: he confided rather than talked, and each of us saw himself as his sole confidant. His discourse rambled on. From time to time he hesitated as if he were afraid that his monologue might be unwanted. Then, at a question from Sandra Chance, he went on again.

I was surprised to find Chance so silent, but perhaps these traveler's tales were new to both husband and wife. Could it be that their love of assemblies, committees, came out in their readiness to listen, in their attentiveness, to Lewis's words? Yet I doubted whether either of them was as preoccupied as I by Lewis's hollow eyes and uneven narrative.

At the thought I looked up and suddenly realized that the Chances's interest in Lewis was less absorbed and more overt than I had thought. Their eyes were too fixed in their intensity. They were more like indulgent guardians, allowing a highly strung dependent to talk himself to sleep or restfulness, than attentive listeners.

With the realization, a chill seemed to move in the warm and glowing room. For me, at least, although Lewis still talked, the monologue was dead. I remember that he spoke with enthusiasm of the Italian landscape. He had motored widely, with other delegates, throughout the northern half of the country. The architecture of the hill villages had caught his imagination. "To think that Welsh villages could be like that, Chance!" he said suddenly.

"But first the Welsh have to become like that," Chance said.

"We are a race of poets!" Lewis cried defiantly.

"And Methodists!" Chance added again, smiling.

Even Lewis smiled at that and returned to the subject of the universities' convention. He had that kind of intensity which occasionally persists beyond our youth and younger manhood. I could see that, in some odd way, the Chances felt some form of protectiveness for him. I could see, too, why Julia had spoken of him as a mother might speak of a child. Despite his gaunt features and hollow eyes he had a seriousness, almost an innocence, that was strangely youthful. None of it seemed phony. Minute by minute, as I watched and listened, his wife's story seemed less and less substantial. Surely this man could not be all that she had said.

Then the butler, the man called "Tadeusz," announced dinner.

There were to be no other guests, it seemed, and we rose and followed Sandra Chance downstairs to the dining room overlooking the Square. This had been the cloakroom on the night of the cocktail party, I had to remind myself forcibly, for now the room was magically transformed from that mundane purpose and background. The circular table, and the painted Regency chairs, seemed to glow under a low-hanging brass chandelier. The curtains at the high window gave the room its final touch of sumptuousness: high, red velvet folds under ornate gilt pelmets. And all this in a room no more than twelve by twelve. Yet, as a bold and simple essay in splendor, the room had "come off," as I had heard professional New York decorators say grudgingly about their rivals' more spectacular ventures.

As I looked around I noticed that Sandra Chance was watching me.

"A beautiful room!" I said, for it seemed the only thing to say. She smiled with delight and thanked me warmly as she indicated a chair.

"I'm very glad to hear that you absolve *me* from its grandeur," Chance said in mock relief.

"It certainly lacks the austerity some of your opponents seem to find in you."

They all laughed.

"You are quite right, of course," Chance said as we sat down. "It is all my wife's achievement, and sometimes it makes things very difficult for me, politically. She likes to do this kind of thing, but there seems to be a general idea that Labour politicians ought to live in caravans, igloos or semi-detached suburban villas surrounded by chocolate-colored paint. Ever since, in a foolish moment, we invited a gossip writer here it's been implied that I live in something between the Kremlin and the Brighton Pavilion. Journalists are the most dangerous men alive."

"Always?"

"With no exceptions!" he said, politely but firmly.

I turned to Mrs. Chance. "I promise never to mention your home in any newspaper I shall ever write for."

"There are so many other things left to write about which still manage to do a lot of damage," Chance said as the butler put avocado pears before us.

"Such as?"

"Playing up a label. Look at my own. A Man of the People. It's true in one way, of course, but it's all too easy. I'm proud of the title, but it makes me sound like a tub thumper whose main interest is an extra shilling a week for dustmen. I'm all for that, of course, but I also happen to be a serious politician whose main interest is foreign affairs."

"Journalists—like cartoonists—like to have a recognizable tag," I said. "Chamberlain's umbrella, Churchill's cigar, Chance's Man of the People. You ought to count yourself fortunate."

"Possibly," he agreed, but somewhat ruefully.

"You know you'd hate it, Matthew, if you were one of the five hundred unknowns," Sandra Chance said gently.

"Six hundred," I corrected and Chance smiled as he said,

"I suppose I would, but I want a new label."

"Foreign Secretary?" I asked. His wife laughed aloud.

"Possibly," he said again, smiling. "How did you guess?" And then, more seriously, "When it comes, of course. I shan't snatch. Meanwhile, tell me, as an expert, how I can change this damned label, 'Man of the People,' into 'Man of Peace.' "

"I'm a journalist, not a publicist," I pointed out, "but I'd say that if you kept on referring to yourself as 'A Man of Peace' you'd do the job. Reiteration of a simple legend. Isn't that the first and overwhelming requirement? Hitler did it and so does every other successful advertiser. Refer to yourself by that label at least twice in every speech you make."

"Perhaps I will," he said quietly. "But was Hitler a successful advertiser?"

We laughed and went on talking, apparently lightheartedly, through the simple but pleasant meal. But it was fencing, and we all knew it, and I waited, with a sense of constraint and foreboding, for the more serious comments that I knew must lie ahead.

During the meal Chance did most of the talking. I was again a willing listener, and thus managed, I believed, to simulate an un-

concern I did not feel. Sandra Chance also seemed attentive to her
husband's views. Only Lewis was outwardly abstracted and nervous.
Before, when he had talked, he had seemed to hypnotize himself
into some kind of detachment and calmness. Now reaction had set
in. I felt sorry for him. He would look at his host as if determined
to concentrate on the words, the views, the anecdotes, and then his
eyes would look away, almost fall away, as if he were gazing inward at a distant world, infinitely removed from the table at which
he ate. Occasionally, he half closed his eyes and moved his head
slightly, like a man determined to put aside a dull ache or pain, or
thoughts that had brought him to that state. Once or twice he
frowned and slowly bit his lower lip, as if to control an apparent
agony of mind. And now, with a vacillation too human, I was inclined once again to doubts and a disturbed mind.

Perhaps I was being fanciful, I told myself, and returned to listening to my host. And each time, as I returned to this listening, I
glanced at my hostess, and each time found her eyes prepared to
meet my own, always a disconcerting reception.

These were the merest passing undertones to the pleasantries of
an excellent meal and lively conversation, for, although Chance led
and held all discussion, each of us made some contribution. And as
we all entered into general discussion I could have called my apprehensive thoughts preposterous.

Toward the meal's end, Sandra Chance left us. Chance moved a
decanter between Lewis and me. For a moment I was amused by
the thought of the Man of the People following the conventions of
a bourgeois public he affected to despise. Perhaps sensing my
thoughts, he reverted to the subject of that label.

"But as a Man of the People you're more or less alone," I warned
him. "Every other politician calls himself a Man of Peace."

"With little reason," he said; then added gaily, "Anyway a new
label is what I want. I'm tired of the old one. You change your job.
Why shouldn't I?"

"I've had the same job for five years," I pointed out.

"But you've changed it now."

"Have I?"

"I thought so. You weren't pursuing Professor Lewis in America.
Or were you?"

The fencing had ended. The moment had come a good deal earlier in the evening than I had expected.

"Am I pursuing him here, then?"

"It seems so—to him and to me," he said, a harsh edge to his voice.

Well, this is it, I remember thinking, but we'd better go on and see how far it has to go. I said, "Apart from yesterday's unfortunate episode at the airport—what gives you this odd idea?"

"Several things."

"Tell me, pray."

As I spoke, Sandra Chance came back into the room. She had taken over Tadeusz's duties, it seemed, for she put a coffee tray on the sideboard and coolly and leisurely asked each of us, "Black or white?" Chance waited, watching her, watching me, smiling slightly, apparently amused, certainly assured.

Then the cups were before us and Sandra Chance, to my surprise, once more took her place at the table.

The pause had lasted for several seconds. I wonder how many? Five seconds for each cup perhaps. One day I shall time the operation with a stop watch to see how short a time eternity can last. But an eternity is also made by other elements. Silence. The thumping of the heart. The dampness of the hands.

I was moved to sudden irritability to notice that I was fidgeting with the small spoon in my saucer, trying to balance its negligible weight on the fulcrum of my forefinger. I tried to look calm, but my features were probably fixed in some unholy grimace. One's mouth always seems to get stuck in such an asinine manner in moments of tension.

As Sandra Chance took her seat, Chance spoke again.

"Several things," he repeated calmly.

Even in a moment of stress he could not overcome the oratorical touch, for he added portentously, "They may all tot up to the long arm of coincidence, which, we all know, is pretty extensive!"

Then he left his introductory phrases and went in boldly: "I'll deal with the obvious facts. Those I know. Last Saturday, in this house, you asked the butler about Professor Lewis, implying that you knew him. You didn't know him. Next, you tried checking on his movements by ringing his lodgings at Reading. You did that the same evening, Saturday. Next, the airport on Monday. Next, you have seen his wife. At least on two occasions. Have I made out any kind of case? Or is it all just a strange series of coincidences?"

Lewis was leaning forward, staring at me, his gaze so intense that he might have been a hypnotized stooge in a variety act.

"I think you've made out a case," I said simply.

"Then what are you after?" Lewis said. His voice, much louder than Chance's or my own, burst in the room like a paper bag.

He thrust his head suddenly forward as he jerked out the words.

"Quiet, Keith!" Sandra Chance said, almost in a whisper.

"All the same, what are you after?" Chance asked quietly.

"A story," I said simply.

"Don't stall!" Chance commanded sharply.

"Remember, I'm your guest," I said.

Chance coolly considered his wrist watch. "For less than another five minutes," he said slowly.

I put my napkin on the table and made to stand up.

"I'm sorry!" he said quickly. "Not very, but I am sorry."

The thin smile was now a grim line.

"All right!" I said sitting down again. "You ask what I'm after. It's really very simple. I think you're both caught up in something that's too big for either of you or both of you, and certainly too rough for your health."

"Don't beat about the bush. You don't have to here, you know," Chance said, his voice still very quiet.

"All right, then," I said, "I think you've both got yourselves caught into a dreary piece of spying."

"You're mad!" Chance said, spitting out the words.

"That's possible. But if I'm not?"

He laughed.

"I'm sorry, but I don't see any other alternative. To me you're just plain mad. But, as a matter of grisly interest, just how did this fantastic notion get lodged in your distorted mind?"

"Like most big notions it's made up of a lot of little ones."

"Such as?"

"To you they'd all sound distorted, so let's leave them. And I'll leave, too, if you don't mind."

Then I did get up. The day was done.

Chance rose, too. Together, silently, we went out into the narrow hall. I took up my hat from a side table.

"I'm sorry this had to happen," I said, and the words were sincere.

"Bear up!" he said genially. "Madness takes many forms. Yours may be just a passing phase. The intermittent kind. Isn't that what the medicos call it? It may be just a little dangerous while it lasts. That's all. Look after yourself. Good night!"

"Good night!"

32

I WENT OUT INTO THE COOL, METROPOLITAN EVENING FROM THE strangest meal I had ever shared.

The eruption had been so sudden and so fierce that I was still dazed by the blast. I shook my head like a man coming to after an explosion, for that was the way I felt. I looked at my watch. Nine-twenty. I had arrived at seven-fifty, an hour and a half before.

Slowly and disbelievingly I made my way toward Victoria, gradually returning, step by step, into the world about me, a world I thought I knew.

From one of the telephone booths in the booking hall at Victoria Station I rang Julia.

"You're very early," she said, surprised.

I agreed. "It is very early, but that's the way it was. Can I come along later?"

"Of course. How much later?"

"Before eleven, I hope. Meanwhile you've got to stay where you are and not move. Not in any circumstances."

"Why? Has anything happened?"

"One or two things. I suppose they might be called exchanges of opinion. I don't want you to get involved, that's all. Promise?"

"Of course. You're sure that's all?"

"Quite sure. Now go and read a good book."

"Have you any suggestions?"

"*Kenilworth, Pickwick Papers, Anna Karenina.*"

She laughed good-by.

I was now far more apprehensive and perturbed than I was prepared to admit. After some fairly intensive accosting of passers-by, I changed a sixpence for coppers, and rang Butler at Dorset House.

"I'd like to come and see you *now*," I said.

"Won't it wait until the morning?"

"It probably would, but I'd rather it didn't."

"If those are your terms you'd better come now, then."

"Good. Five minutes."

"I'll expect you. I've got a canasta party here, by the way. My wife always thinks I wreck her evenings deliberately. Sometimes I'm forced to admit that the evidence points that way. But come along. D'you play the game?" he added hopefully.

"Not well enough."

"You ought to learn. It keeps me in cigars."

I took a taxi to Dorset Square from the station rank. As we were going along Grosvenor Gardens I stared out from the rear window like a nervous spinster. Was the taxi being followed? In the surrounding darkness I could see only one or two buses, a few private cars, and two innocent-seeming taxis. Idiot! I told myself. This is England. But, in the same instant, I remembered the recent dinner which had started in so civilized a manner and ended on so foreign a note.

I sat back thinking of Julia and Keith Lewis, and my thoughts were almost as confused as their lives.

Butler met me at the door and led the way along the corridor into a small workroom with a large mahogany desk, white bookshelves to the ceiling and a couple of armchairs before an electric fire.

"As I said, my wife is convinced that this is a put-up job," he said. "God knows why. I always win. Well, what happened?"

I told him.

"What now?" he said at the end.

"I don't know," I answered lamely. "If it weren't for Lewis and his jitters I should think we had been barking up a pretty wrong tree. God knows, Chance seems genuine enough."

"What d'you think they'll do now?"

"How should I know?"

"Well, make a guess. Then I'll make one. It's a way of passing the time."

"It depends how much of a panic Lewis is in. He's the weak link."

"I suppose so," Butler said ruminatively. "I suppose all this tension
and so on is new to him. Chance has had a lifetime of it. Presumably
a man develops a technique for dealing with suspense the way one
does for coping with panics in a newsroom. The question is: how do
we make Lewis really crack?"

"By hounding him and pounding him," I said without enthusiasm.
Butler nodded.

"He returns to Harwell tomorrow," I added.

"But will he? If he's as panic stricken as you say he is, he may
not go."

"Where else would he go?"

Butler did not answer, for there was no answer, a fact we both
knew. We sat there, silent.

I looked round the room, along the bookshelves, across to the neat
desk. For the first time I noticed the portable typewriter on the desk.

"You don't still use a typewriter, do you?" I asked, surprised.

"Why not?" Butler asked, unperturbed. "Everybody else has written a book on Northcliffe, why shouldn't I? I've even got a title for
it: *The Curse of Northcliffe.* He ruined the old-fashioned newspaper."

"Did you ever see one?" I asked, looking over his shoulder at the
desk and its neat accouterments. As I saw the two telephones, one
black, one red, I had the thought. I got up and walked across to
the beautiful elbow chair at the desk and sat down.

"The black one!" Butler said laconically, watching me. I dialed
the Flaxman number. After a moment Julia answered. I said, "Did
you at any time during your conversation with your husband tell
him that I had seen you?"

"Not a whisper."

"You're sure?"

"Absolutely. Why?"

"I just wanted to know. Could anybody else know?"

She was silent for a second or so. "No," she said. "I don't think
so. Nobody in the world. Not even my daily." She laughed gently.
"I've been very circumspect with your reputation, my dear."

"How would Chance know I'd seen you, then?"

She was surprised. "I can't think how," she said slowly.

"Apart from that one telephone conversation, you haven't heard
from your husband since he got back?"

"Not another word."

"I'll see you later, then."

"Not too late, please."

"Probably very soon."

I rang off and turned to Butler. He was doodling with a pencil on a blotter on his lap.

"Your voice changes when you talk to Mrs. Lewis," he said. "Ever noticed?"

"How?" I asked dully.

"The timbre. Warmer. Softer. Woolier. You ought to take it in hand. You think he had you watched, I take it."

"It looks like it."

"He probably did. How many times have you seen her?"

"Saturday night. Monday night. Lunch today."

"Not bad for a cold-blooded citizen. I occasionally wondered how fervently you were pressing your suit, to coin a phrase. When d'you think your cuckolding activities were under observation?"

"Let's keep to facts, and leave your squalid headlines out of it," I said. "Not Saturday, that's pretty certain. That would have been too soon after I asked the butler about Lewis."

"It might not have been too soon. Chance seems to work fairly quickly."

"It's possible, but I doubt it."

"You think Lewis found out that you'd rung his lodgings at Reading after he got back?"

I nodded.

"Rang his landlady, found out someone had been trying to get hold of him, then found out his wife had been told and so on?"

"Something like that."

"Mrs. Lewis knew you'd rung his lodgings. Perhaps she told Chance," Butler went on quietly.

"Not very likely."

"Your sense of detachment has gone," Butler said calmly but decisively, lumbering up from his chair.

"That's possible," I agreed.

"You still believe in this Lewis woman, then?" he said, looking down at me.

"I do now."

"All right, then," Butler said. "I'll back your starry-eyed belief. Ac-

tually, it fits in with my own notions so I'm doing nothing sensation-
ally out of character. Let's look at it like this: if she'd taken her story
to MI5 they would have done something about it. Later rather than
sooner, perhaps, although I may be maligning them. We can at least
do the same."

I sat there, looking up at him, waiting for the catch, but he went
on. "All right, we will. We'll do what we can. We'll fly a little kite."

He picked up the red telephone.

"Give me Mr. Rees," he said at the immediate click.

"Only costs fifty pounds a year," he said with relish, nodding at
the telephone, still looking down at me. "A farcical price for a special
line, I always think. Even more farcical when one thinks how little
things like that can bolster up a man's ego, apart from its occasional
uses. Extraordinary thing they're not more widely used. Hello, Rees.
Look, I've got a rather tricky piece of work for you. I want a simple
little news item planted on the front page. I want it boxed, in the
middle of column four, and set in bold face. No, I'll skip a phone
reporter this time. I'd rather you took it down. See if you've kept
your hand in. It's quite short. Here goes. Heading: 'New Spy Scare
in Britain Query.' Set that as a three-deck sans heading. Then the
credit, 'Our Washington Correspondent.' Then: 'It is rumored in
Washington that new security investigations, rivaling in importance
the Nunn May, Pontecorvo and Burgess-Maclean cases, are about
to reach a climax in England after months of joint inquiry by the
FBI and MI5. The names of an English scientist and a well-known
politician are being freely mentioned here. British residents are particularly indignant at these off-the-record disclosures and at what
they regard as yet another breach of security regulations by unof-
ficial American spokesmen jumping the gun. Stop.' That's all. For
London editions only. Send me round a dozen copies as soon as you
can. Many thanks. You'd better cable, or better still, ring Grimston
and square him. Tell him to go to earth for a couple of days and
tell him why. Read him the piece and tell him he knows nothing
about anything."

"Could I ring him?" I asked, butting in.

"All right, yes."

"When?"

"Now if you like. You'd probably catch him at the office. All right,
Rees. Forget it."

I sat staring at Butler as he replaced the telephone.

"You certainly are flying a little kite," I said.

"A kite to catch a jet," he said lightly.

"Was that touch about the scientist and the politician really necessary?"

"I thought so. We'll see."

"How?"

"We'll get copies to Chance and Lewis and see."

"It will be all round the House and Harwell by midday."

"Before, I hope," said Butler laconically.

"Shall I ring Grimston now?"

"No, I will later, or I may not. Might be interesting to see what happens in the States, too."

Always he wanted to see what would happen. Given almost any set of circumstances, with one or two unknown quantities, that was his only interest: what would happen.

We talked for about another quarter of an hour before I left. By then the anti-climax had come and I had that cold deep hole at the pit of the stomach that comes to the man whose nerve is going fast, but, as I left him, Butler was blandly unperturbed, plainly anxious to see his little kite floating in the middle of the front page of his morning newspapers and not at all keen to return to his spoiled game of canasta.

33

I WENT DOWN INTO BAKER STREET AND TOOK A TAXI TO KING'S ROAD. Now I looked over my shoulder as I entered the decaying house and went in through the bare and echoing hall. Julia was tense and nervous. As soon as she let me into the room she took my arm. "What has happened?" she asked. Her eyes were distraught.

I began to tell her about the dinner, but she interrupted me within five seconds. "Keith rang here ten minutes ago," she said. "To say good-by. He said I was to tell no one. But I can't. I must."

She began to cry. Blindly seeking, she put her arms about my shoulders. "He said he must go. Now. Straightaway. I asked him where. He said he didn't know. How could he know? He seemed almost out of his mind. Then he suddenly stopped and said good-by and the line went dead as if somebody had given him time and his time was up. He . . ."

She could not go on. I let her sink slowly down into an armchair and then took her up again, sat down in the chair myself and took her into my arms.

We sat thus for perhaps half an hour. Occasionally I whispered her name, trying to stay her words when she began her tale again. At last she got up, shook her head and rubbed her eyes as if coming from bewildered sleep. She crossed to the other chair and sat there looking across to me yet away from me, self-conscious and still deeply shaken.

"I'm sorry," she said.

I raised my hand to stop her.

"Poor Keith!" she said. "Shall I never see him again? How terrible a way to say good-by. Poor Keith. And I caused it."

I interrupted her self-accusations. "Don't blame yourself like this. Blame the world we live in if you must blame anything. He would have been caught sooner or later."

But she had to go on, into a reaction which would probably last her a lifetime through. "Poor Keith!" she murmured again and again, more like a mother whispering the name of a child, now dead forever, than a wife calling the name of a husband.

At last she came to a kind of peace and we began to talk. I told her of the dinner, Chance's outburst and then of Butler's essay in the new journalism. "It's too late," she said. "They have gone."

"Why 'they'?"

"I think they have both gone."

We were silent again.

At last she began to talk of the early days of their marriage as if that, too, were a time from another age, and, as she talked, she evoked, vividly and fearfully, the bewilderment of her recent life. She talked of Lewis tenderly but remotely, as a woman might talk of a man once loved, but long ago. At one point I said as much.

"In a way you are probably right," she said. "A part of his life seemed to go when he became so involved with Chance. Now I begin to see what really happened. He was so distracted that it probably seemed to me that I had lost him. I suppose it was then that I knew what he was doing and accused him of it. Poor Keith. He wasn't cut out for that kind of thing. Chance was."

"Yet they both believed they were doing the right thing."

"Perhaps," she said, her mind far off. "Yet I wonder whether any man really believes that is the right thing? I can't think so. Keith used to say work as a scientist made him a citizen of the world, but they were words. He loved his native Wales. Sometimes he used to hold forth about the Welsh language as if he were a bard at an eisteddfod. I used to point out the inconsistency. Before he met Chance he used to laugh. 'Welshman first! Citizen of the world second! Englishman never!' he used to shout, especially if we were on holiday in the Welsh mountains. After he met Chance all that merriment went. There were no more inconsistencies. He became so serious. Even that wasn't so bad. It was when he became frightened that I knew his heart wasn't in all the subterfuge and double-dealing. But by then it was too late, I suppose."

She talked on in a low, soliloquizing voice. I might not have been a listener. She was talking to her own distant mind. Until then I had found her somewhat reticent, preferring to listen. Now she made her own escape in words. Out of the halting monologue might come some kind of peace, I thought, even if only the peace of weariness and resignation in that bleak night.

At last, well after midnight, I rose. "Now you must sleep," I said as gently and persuasively as I could.

"I suppose so," she said. She, too, stood up. Once again her eyes held that sense of hopelessness which had shocked me when I had arrived, two hours before.

She stepped toward me and I took her in my arms.

"Don't go!" she begged. "Please. I don't think I can bear to be alone. The world is so empty."

Never justify, never explain, said a sensible man, if not a wise one, long ago. But one does justify, one does explain. Or one tries, anyway. Foolishly and unnecessarily perhaps. One tries, even in a record such as this, which is mainly the story of Matthew Chance, but also, partly, the story of myself, or something of myself.

For Julia, then, I was perhaps a comfort and refuge, however transitory, from a world grown too vast and lonely. And for me? All I knew was that I was already beyond the beginning of love. And for those who judge? They are perhaps the fortunate ones, living out their lives in tones of simple black and simpler white, strong in their virtues, prepared to judge the behavior of the rest of mankind.

Peace, then, be with all judges, their virtues, strengths and certainties. They have the weight and worth of numbers, too, for there are millions of them.

For myself, my thoughts go back often, not to the woebegone house, but to the small warm room, so improbably set within its fading walls, and of ourselves moving into a strange and sudden domesticity and tenderness.

So we slept and woke and whispered and then were silent, listening to Dinah coming expectantly awake.

As Julia stirred and left my side to tend her daughter, I thought, as millions have thought before me, of how the world must now become a different place. Not because I had slept with another woman, but because, at last, tenderness had entered in, a new experience, revealing and disturbing. For the first time I thought of one moment moving out toward a million other moments in the years ahead, wanting to share them. Before, I had thought only of escape, of the minutes and hours of boredom ahead. How soon to have the relief of the door closing behind my back. But now other thoughts, oppressive and unwelcome, crowded in, and persisted. Even as I sat opposite Julia at the table in the living room and watched Dinah, on her mother's lap, gravely test the strength of her teeth on a rusk.

Neither of us mentioned Lewis or Chance.

Later, as I left, Julia began to speak briefly of these things, but I stayed her words. "We can do nothing now," I said. "We must wait. I'll ring you later, about midday. And I shall come back this afternoon."

From then on, I thought, as I walked back toward Sloane Square, there was nothing to do but wait.

34

I DID NOT RING BUTLER THEN. I WANTED TIME TO THINK.

Not until after eleven o'clock, after I had bathed, shaved and read the morning's papers, did I ring to tell him of Lewis's farewell to his wife.

"We can't be certain it is farewell," he said. "It might well have been an act. He may have wanted her sympathy. Or to try to force her hand. Anything."

I said nothing.

"And we can't be certain he did ring," Butler went on, as if he had to make a point clear, too clear. "We've only got her word for it."

"I thought you'd decided to take her word, via mine, last night."

"I did and I do. Say ninety-nine per cent. The other one per cent comes under the general heading of keeping an open mind. That's not such a bad division of trust for someone I've never met, is it? It means I'm backing you and your so-called sanity to a greater extent than I've ever backed anyone before."

I laughed. As usual, he was wholly persuasive in his bland assertions. At least, he was persuasive enough to calm the still small voice of criticism.

"What will you do now?" I asked.

"I'll put someone onto the PRO at Harwell," he said. "D'you know Johnson—Dexter Johnson—our scientific correspondent?"

I said no.

"I've already put him on making a few tactful inquiries about Lewis's return. Checking up on facts for a story on the Milan convention and so on. We should know whether Lewis is back there by two or three this afternoon, if not before."

"And Chance?"

"He's still around."

"How do you know?"

"I had Hepburn ring him at home about an hour ago. Just to say we wanted one or two articles out of him."

"How was he?"

"Quite calm, I gather. He and Hepburn had quite a long talk. I even asked Hepburn to mention, in passing, that nasty little paragraph we carried in the later editions this morning. You've got to hand it to Chance. Apparently he asked Hepburn, strictly between their two telephones, if he had any idea who the political suspect might be. As Hepburn's completely in the dark he probably played up well."

"If Lewis has gone and Chance stays, where are we then?"

"You may well ask, dear boy. Where are we? But if Lewis really has gone, he'll be a big enough story for a few days and we ought to be able to get a few hours' lead on that. No newspaper can ask more than that in these days of unscrupulous competition, can it?" he added unctuously.

"Well, keep me posted."

"Of course."

For a moment I almost thought I caught a note of sympathy in his voice. Then he said, "You were out very early this morning."

"Very early."

"I rang you at seven."

"At seven I was out."

"I rang you again about eight."

"At eight I was still out."

"Well, keep me posted, too," he said smoothly and rang off.

35

I PULLED THE ARMCHAIR ACROSS TO MY USUAL CONTEMPLATIVE POsition by the window, sat back and looked across to the park. I must have stayed there for an hour or more, reflecting on the complications in my life. They now seemed to be increasing hour by hour, and I could not help but compare my present state with the simple pattern of my days a month or so before.

I had now been in England for just under a month. In fact, I was beginning the twenty-eighth day of my return, I computed hazily. In that time I had enjoyed a solitary meandering holiday, written a number of brief political portraits, become involved in what promised to be a world-wide front-page story and fallen in love with the wife of an alleged spy.

Put like that, the tale seemed to add up to a recital by an idiot child not to be trusted out of school. Yet, even in the middle of the sorry story, I knew that in those same twisted circumstances I had found all that I had been seeking for many years. But to admit those facts did not lessen their complexities. Indeed, they were far fewer than they promised to be within the very near future, I ruefully told myself.

I was shaken from this bitter-sweet reverie by the telephone. I took up the instrument unwillingly and answered warily.

Butler's voice said, "Well, I need hardly tell you that Lewis isn't back at Harwell yet. Apparently the citizens there are a bit surprised themselves. Johnson's *persona grata* there and they admitted off the record that they had been fully expecting Lewis back two days ago. Several dockets awaiting his comments, and so on."

"He might be at his digs in Reading," I said without belief.

"Johnson checked."

"What about parents? Any living? Oddly enough I never inquired."

"Johnson did. Lewis has no father, but an old mother living in Towyn, Merionethshire. No go."

"He might still be tucked away in Chance's house."

"I thought of that. It's more than likely, but I don't see what we can do about that. We'll have to leave it for the moment. Anyway, I thought we'd talk about things after lunch."

"We being?"

"You, me, Rees, Hepburn, Johnson. I think that's about all."

"You like being a workaday editor again?"

"It has its excitements compared with workaday, worknight editing-in-chief," he said chuckling. "I thought three o'clock. That all right for you? We should know more about Lewis by then if there's anything more to be known. My room. Come straight up."

Butler was trying hard to subdue the pleasures of activity beneath the matter-of-factness of the arrangements, but, for once, his histrionics were poor. He was plainly enjoying his day.

"How much do the others know?" I asked.

"Very little so far, but they've got to be briefed. I think we could break the story tonight. We'll take a chance, anyway."

This had been an inevitable prospect, but now that Butler spoke the words I found my hands suddenly damp. I would willingly have postponed the prospect of the story's release for many days, a strange thought for a newspaperman.

"Are you still there?" Butler asked.

"More or less."

"Tonight's as good as any time, isn't it?"

"Probably."

I could see Butler's side of the case. As far as a mass-circulation paper was concerned those few hours' start on such a story could mean fifty thousand, even a hundred thousand extra copies sold.

"Well, three o'clock then. I suppose you'll want to warn Mrs. Lewis?"

"Afterward will be time enough."

"Don't you think we should get her out of London?"

I had thought of that, even as he had been speaking.

"Are you thinking of her, or of the other papers getting at her?" I asked, more bitterly than I had intended or Butler's inquiry warranted. However dubious his intentions, it had been, at least, a charitable thought.

"Both," he answered, amiably enough.

"Where then?"

"She can go down to my place. I've squared my wife. In fact, it's partly her idea. She seems to have some kind of fellow feeling for your Mrs. Lewis. Berkshire's as safe as anywhere. No reporter from any other paper is likely to go looking for her in *my* house. D'you think you could have her ready to leave by six?"

"Probably. If she's willing to go. She may not be."

"She ought to go. For her own sake. And the child's. This is going to be a pretty dreary business for her. It's likely to be headline stuff for a few days, even weeks. Perhaps she doesn't realize that."

"I think she does."

"Have you told her?"

"Some things you don't have to tell."

"Well, do what you can. Barker can run her down. There's a guest cottage there my wife had converted from the old stables. One of her bijou additions to the place. Mrs. Lewis is welcome to it for a

week or so. In fact, for as long as she damn well likes, so my missus
tells me. I'll warn Mrs. Somerton. She's the homely kind who's used
to this sort of thing."

"You sound as if you have this sort of thing every week."

He ignored that. "You'd better take her down yourself," he said.
"She'll need someone around tomorrow morning when she wakes up
to find she's a household name."

I thanked him. The words stuck in my throat as I uttered them.
I resented his planning and replanning of other people's lives.

Perhaps he sensed my reservations.

"Don't thank me," he said. "It begins to look as if your Mrs. Lewis
has given us the biggest story we've had in years." As if to reassure
me he added, "I know she didn't mean to, but that's neither here nor
there. Anyway, I wouldn't wish the rest of the week on a woman
I hated, let alone one *you* like."

I stayed silent.

He went on: "Anyway, by the time the bloodhounds of Fleet
Street get baying around the King's Road I'd like her to be a long
way off. That's the selfish angle, of course, but it fits in with the
human side for once. Let's leave it at that."

Butler, as usual, had soon regretted the fact that he might have
shown a touch of mellowness in his relations to the rest of mankind.
He always worked hard to make himself seem that much tougher
than he was. I could never really understand why. His normal share
was as the toughness of ten.

"When do you think the conference will be over this afternoon?"
I asked.

"Why?"

"I thought I might warn Mrs. Lewis then."

"We should be through by four. What number King's Road?"

I told him.

"Six o'clock, then. Barker will be there. The rest is for you. Good
luck."

Then he added, as if by an afterthought, "I shouldn't tell Mrs.
Lewis now, old boy."

"Why not?"

"Supposing my one per cent suspicion happened to make a
monkey of my ninety-nine per cent belief. She might use the hours
between now and six to mess up the plan."

"Your one per cent works mighty hard," I said.

"Perhaps."

"You're thinking of the country's welfare, I suppose?"

"That and my newspaper," he said evenly. "Their interests occasionally coincide."

We rang off together.

I stayed in the armchair, vacillating, wondering whether to defy Butler's advice and warn Julia immediately of the projected move or to leave the news until later. As a mother with a young child, she might need the intervening hours to make arrangements for extra clothing, medicines, God knows what all. Or would it be better to present her, when I arrived at half-past four or so, with a ready-made decision and thus leave her no time for alternative plans? I left things to take their course. I was becoming a great vacillator.

I went downstairs, out into Piccadilly, and walked slowly toward the Circus, looking, I daresay, a citizen with fewer cares than most. But appearances aren't everything. In reality I knew myself to be a man about to be caught into a task that might come naturally to millions of men half my age, but which was a terrifying prospect to me: the simple task of transporting a mother and child sixty or seventy miles across country. Even with the promised aid of a chauffeur and the worthy Mrs. Somerton awaiting me at journey's end, I was filled with self-pity for the ardors ahead. I had lived too long and too comfortably alone. I had been deluding myself for years with ideas of so-called self-sufficiency. Now, in a moment of modest trial, my wholesale inadequacies in human experience were to be blatantly exposed. I walked on gloomily.

MOST EDITORIAL CONFERENCES ARE ALIKE, FOR MOST JOURNALISTS look alike. But that afternoon's conference was different. For one thing, Butler's room was different. Luxury was there, established to an oriental degree, or perhaps, more correctly, to the higher-occidental degree. And the men around him, I noticed, were that much more nattily turned out than they would have been in Rees's room. Butler certainly exacted a deference to his station.

He sprawled in his big chair, well back from the desk, one long leg scissored across the other, his plump white hands fondling an eighteen-inch perspex rule. And as we settled ourselves, like a group of unwilling choristers, he gazed upon us like a benign yet vulpine master.

Rees was perhaps less of a sartorial success than the others. He had tugged on his gray jacket with an effort at grace, but his shoulders were too ill favored for success. Hepburn looked as smooth as before. Dexter Johnson I had not previously met. He was about thirty-five, bespectacled, pale faced, blue eyed, with a high forehead, weak chin and sandy, receding hair.

Butler began. "To my mind this is an odd meeting about an odd story. On the other hand, I suppose it could be argued that it's not at all odd and has become one of the archetypal stories of our time. Anyway, I'll leave you to judge. My own belief is that it's a Pontecorvo-Nunn May-Burgess-Maclean story all rolled into one."

Even as he said the names the others began to sit up and to take very firm notice of their editor in chief. Any tendency to postprandial lethargy vanished.

Butler was moving on. "I think we've got a twelve-hour start on the story, thanks to one or two people here and elsewhere. Briefly, it's this. . . ." He went on to outline the story. He seemed to have every fact absolutely pat. In his telling it was a succinct, detailed, convincing story, appalling yet engrossing, and nobody stirred or interrupted.

Like all the more successful storytellers, Butler made his a personal narrative, speaking first of his knowledge of Chance in the Spanish Civil War, his suspicions, the hazy intentions behind the series written by Hepburn and me. "In fact," he said at that point, "it was the flimsiest journalistic kite I've ever flown."

Then he came to the pieces Hepburn and I had written, to the anonymous note and the discovery of the identity of the writer, the relationship between Chance and Lewis, the meeting at the airport, my previous night's dinner party and Lewis's farewell message to his wife.

He stopped for a moment and asked me to give a brief account of the dinner party, too near and too distant to be other than an unreal memory for me. But I gave them my recollection of the evening. As I finished, and as if my tale were merely part of the mosaic of his own story, Butler spoke again and went on to the end, summarizing his own ideas, suspicions, beliefs, and then laconically said, "Well, there it is!"

We had all listened to him in silence. The only interruption had come when he had mentioned my dinner with Chance and Lewis. Only then had the others turned their eyes from him, lolling back in his chair, toying with his rule, enjoying his recital.

Finally, he turned to me, asking for corrections and omissions, but he had left nothing out as far as I could tell, and I said so.

"Good!" he said. "Those are the facts. First, a few questions. Then to work. And, mind you, nothing outside this group in this room until the last possible moment. You'd better let the early editions go without it, Rees. I don't want anything on the streets until well after midnight. In its early stages, the story won't be much more than a note that Lewis hasn't reported back for duty. All we need do is express the nation's worry and so forth." He grinned. "Is that clearly understood?"

They all nodded.

"Good!" Butler said again. "Questions?"

"Where is Mrs. Lewis?" Rees asked quickly.

"Safe."

"Can she be reached?"

"No."

"Not by anybody?"

"No."

"Do you think there's a chance we might be jumping the gun, sir?" Dexter Johnson said, his eyes blinking fast behind his horn-rimmed spectacles.

"You say they expected him back on Tuesday. Today's Thursday. I don't call that jumping the gun. Do you think it's worth taking the risk, Rees?"

"Yes," Rees said, taking a monosyllabic cue from his master.

"If there's nothing in the story it will make my job in the future a bit tricky," Johnson said, almost plaintively. "Especially some of these

Harwell pieces. Government officials are very touchy about these things."

"I see that," Butler said slowly. "But I think it's all part of the risk."

"This story, following on that scientist and politician scare piece from Washington we ran this morning, is going to cause a good deal of speculation," Johnson persisted stubbornly.

It was plain that he did not like Butler's approach and was prepared to say so.

"Without a doubt," Butler agreed.

"There will probably be questions in Parliament," Johnson said.

"Possibly this afternoon," Butler said affably.

"If they take it seriously enough," Hepburn said contemptuously, not bothering to make clear whether he was contemptuous of politicians or journalists, or both.

Johnson spoke again. "Supposing Chance announces tomorrow morning that Lewis has been sick and staying in his house under his care. Shan't we look a pack of idiots?"

"We shall look nothing of the kind," Butler said genially. "Both Lewis and Chance will have put themselves in extremely equivocal positions. 'Why didn't they inform Harwell?' will be the immediate cry."

For a moment Johnson was halted by the logic of Butler's reply, but only for a moment. He plunged on. "And if nothing further happens by tomorrow afternoon, after our story has been current for a few hours, what then?"

"A story of that kind and that size will let loose every hound in hell," Butler said. "There's no possibility of nothing further happening. Things will begin to move at speed from about nine o'clock tomorrow morning. Probably earlier. You will have to get what sleep you can tonight, Johnson. You'll have little enough during the next week or so—or I'm a poor prophet."

A commissionaire came into the room, handed Butler a note and withdrew. Butler slit the envelope. "Chance was seen in the House of Commons ten minutes ago," he said. "Simpson's just rung."

Johnson liked things less than ever after that item of news. "Supposing Chance denies having seen anything of Lewis since his return from Milan?" he asked.

"You are forgetting, Johnson," Butler said patiently. "Two members of our staff saw Mrs. Chance meet Lewis off the plane on Monday, and one, as you've just heard, dined with them both in Chance's house *last night*. Less than twenty-four hours ago."

"That makes it seem more than ever apparent to me that we are rushing things and jumping to unwarranted conclusions," Johnson said shrilly.

At this point I noticed Hepburn nod, as if he, too, were doubtful of the need for such haste.

"All we are announcing is that Lewis has not returned to his post," Butler said. "Do you agree that it is a reasonable move to do that?"

"Yes," Johnson said, but grudgingly as if even this simple admission might be a well-sprung trap door for himself.

"What about the trimmings?" Hepburn asked aggressively.

"There'll be no trimmings, as you call them. Unlike some stories, Hepburn, this one needs no trimmings."

Hepburn flushed. Only Rees laughed. Butler went on: "What do you say, Rees?"

"Can't wait!" Rees said gleefully, almost ghoulishly. His words broke the tension which had been built up by Johnson's game persistence and Hepburn's belligerence.

"Good!" said Butler, momentary finality in his voice. "Let's meet again in this room at midday tomorrow. We may have a lot to talk about."

The meeting broke up. Butler asked me to stay behind for a moment.

"The car will be there at six," he said after the others had gone. "Did you make your arrangements?"

I shook my head.

"A pity. But you think she'll go?" he asked, the remotest touch of anxiety in his voice.

"I haven't the slightest idea. I hope she will, for her own sake, but nobody can force her."

"True enough," he said. "But if she doesn't, life is going to be pretty good hell for her." He smiled. "I know you think I'm mainly concerned with making this an exclusive story, but, believe me, it's the girl I'm thinking of. And you, of course. It won't be very cozy, dear boy, if you're not out of the way."

I was surprised by his sudden consideration, and doubtless showed my feelings, for he smiled again. "It's true. For once I'm more concerned with flesh and blood than newspapers. It's a painful—even pitiful—admission, but there it is."

I watched him warily. He continued to smile, seemingly without guile, but, as I have said before, he usually smiled when others did not. Or could not.

There was nothing more I could say or do, so I took him and his statement at their apparent worth, and went, with a mumbled word of doubting thanks. He walked with me to the door. As he opened the door he put an arm about my shoulders. "You always make me laugh. Just a little," he said. "You always spend such an inordinate amount of time looking for niggers in any woodpile I happen to build."

"It's a habit that's paid dividends once or twice."

"But people change. My woodpiles aren't so inflammable—or so nigger-ridden—these days."

"I'm a creature of habit."

He reflected upon my statement for a second or so. "You may be right," he said.

His mind moved away from such unprofitable thoughts to the task ahead. "Barker will get you back in time for the meeting here to-morrow," he said decisively. "We might lunch if you're not too busy. What's the address, by the way?"

"I told you before."

"My memory isn't what it was."

He frowned, memorizing the number. I wondered whether this was part of another game. Perhaps I was getting oversuspicious as well as oversensitive.

"He won't see a number, anyway," I said. "It's a decrepit old corner house beyond the Town Hall on the other side of King's Road. One of a tumble-down terrace, or the remains of one."

"I think I know it. Not the house, the terrace," Butler said absently.

He nodded farewell and stepped back into his room. I walked slowly along the corridor toward the lift. Despite his soothing words I was still prepared to examine, with more than normal circumspection, any woodpile Butler might build.

37

I SAT IN THE TAXI MEDITATING IMPOSSIBLY UPON THE POSSIBLE COURSE
of the next few hours. Anything could happen. That I knew only
too well. I tried to give up the speculations, but at such times of tension our mental processes are too wayward and cannot be tamed.

I reached the house about half-past four. Ninety minutes for per-
suasiveness to show results, I told myself grimly as I went along the
path to the front door. At that moment I had no confidence in my
talent or even my wish to persuade Julia to leave London. I was
weary already. I rang and Julia quickly opened the door, smiling relief as she saw me.

Once inside the room I said my piece, the words streaming out like
a repertory monologue.

At first Julia demurred. "Why should I?" she demanded. "It would
be sheer cowardice. And I brought it on myself. I went into it open
eyed. I must stay here and see it through."

"If you're here tomorrow morning by the time a score of journalists
have smoked you out—and it won't take them long—you'll know one
thing. That this wasn't what you walked into open eyed. They'll get
in by any means, even force. They'll throw question after question at
you. They'll want pictures of you. And Dinah. Flashlight pictures.
Posed pictures. Candid-camera shots and anything else they can cook
up. And it'll go on and on, all day and all night. The telephone won't
stop ringing, neither will the doorbell. You'll be given the whole
works. You'll be front-page news. We keep it that much quieter in
this country than they do in the States, but it's pretty rough going all
the same, as anyone will tell you who's been through it."

"So that's the way you earn your keep?" she said with a smile.

"I'm on an inside page."

Laughter eased things for a moment.

"I've seen some of it," I went on. "Please take my word for it."

Gradually I wore down her stubbornness.

"What about those blueprints I'm supposed to sort out and trans-

late into reasonable perspective sketches?" she asked at last, and
then I knew she was persuaded.

"Take them with you."

"How are we going?"

"In a car."

"A big car? We'll need one, you know."

"A beautiful car."

"You're coming, too?" she asked, suddenly suspicious again.

"I'm coming, too."

"Will you stay?"

"Part of the time."

"Supposing Keith rings here again?"

"*You* don't think he will. *I* don't think he will. It's a gamble we must
make. I could arrange for a reporter to stay here."

"No!" she said sharply, and went back to her earlier preoccupation, saying, "Does that mean you think Keith's already out of the
country?"

"I don't even begin to think where he might be. Nobody could."

"Will the police be involved in my removal?"

"Not so far. By nine o'clock tomorrow morning the whole world
will be involved."

She shuddered.

"Well, help me pack, then!" she said, suddenly. "Have you ever
helped pack a baby's clothes, towels and toys before?"

"A man has to start some time."

"Well, you can start with that canvas bag on top of the cupboard
if you're really a man who keeps his word. Will it really be a big car?"

"I think I can guarantee that."

"Yours?"

"I haven't one. This is a tycoon's trade-mark."

"Will there be a cot down there?"

"God knows. Perhaps I can ring."

"It doesn't matter. This one dismantles. Help me."

She walked into the bedroom. As if she had decided suddenly to
put aside dull care, she called out, "Dinah! Dinah! We're going away.
Out into the wide, wide world. Just like gypsies."

She began to pack, swiftly and purposefully. First a canvas bag,
then a suitcase, finally a wicker basket. I stood and watched, awkward, willing, but unneeded. At last, at about a quarter to six, all

was ready. Not quite all, that is, for she put on top of the wickerwork basket a small pink plastic chamber pot, a rattle and a large, unkempt Teddy bear. Then she sat down in an armchair and gravely but smilingly considered me.

"Poor dear!" she mused. "You didn't know you were letting yourself in for all this, did you?"

I took the other chair. "No," I said truthfully, "I didn't, but it still seems little enough to put against the upset to your own life."

"My life has become a continuous upset during the past year. One gets into a state of mind that takes it all without surprise or even protest."

"I suppose so," I agreed lamely.

"Does it shake you?"

"Only mildly. It's probably shaken up a few of my ideas, but that's probably no bad thing."

"I wonder," she said quietly. "I thought you winced a little when I put those childish accouterments down on the wicker basket. You probably blushed but I couldn't see. Did you?"

"Probably."

We sat there, within the darkening room, awaiting the car.

"Why should you go with me this evening?" she asked. "Is it all part of your job as a newspaperman?"

"Not exactly."

"Is it a sense of responsibility after last night?"

"Partly."

"What is the rest, then?"

"What I said last night. That I love you."

"But you can't!" she said, her voice rising. "Last night was last night!"

"What does that mean, exactly?"

"Since I met you last Saturday—less than a week ago—I have only had peace when I have been with you. I couldn't bear to let you go last night."

"No more than that?"

"Isn't that enough?"

She got up and went into the bedroom. I heard her whisper soothingly to the child. I crossed to the window. Street lamps began to space out the dusk along the King's Road. She came back into the room carrying her daughter, wrapped within a large white shawl.

The child regarded me and the world beyond the window with large, dark, unblinking eyes. Her mother said again, as if there had been no pause between us, "Isn't that enough? Millions will be lovers in the world tonight without even that. You were kind. You wanted me. I wanted you. I am a woman, after all. Perhaps we had different needs, but when we were together we both forgot the differences. Perhaps there wasn't even any difference at all. Perhaps we both wanted the same thing. It was an escape. Perhaps the only real escape for both of us."

She held the little girl close with one hand and put the other hand upon my arm. "Please, please. Leave things like that. You must."

"Of course," I said, and put my hand upon her own, but we both knew, I think, that it was not within my power of understanding to leave things like that.

The gray Bentley drew up in the street below us, on the wrong side of the road, and far too close to the bus stop for my liking.

"We must go," I said. "We don't want trouble with a bobby at this stage, parking on a bus stop."

The chauffeur had left the car and was already wandering along the street, peering at the house fronts, seeking a number.

"We are ready, aren't we, Dinah, dear?" she said.

For a moment I stood irresolutely by the pile of luggage, but, in a defiantly decisive move, I stooped and picked up the canvas case. Julia watched and laughed. "How crazy of me!" she cried. With Dinah on one arm she crossed to the kitchen and took down a big French pannier. "I can pile those oddments in here." Still holding her daughter, she began to place the oddments skillfully within the bag. "And that's not all!" she cried again, beginning to laugh. "Have you ever dismantled a child's cot?"

"Never."

"We forgot that in the rush."

"All right. What do I do? Kick it to pieces?"

"It's really quite easy. You knock the fittings out of the sockets."

I went downstairs and called Barker up to help. He showed no surprise at these extra-mobile duties. We both set to, directed by Julia, under the wide-eyed gaze of her daughter. Five minutes and we were ready. I carried the cot down to the car and stowed it in the rear compartment. Then I went back for Julia. Canvas bag in one hand, I took her by the arm, guiding mother and daughter down the darkened uneven steps, across the hall, out to the waiting car.

So we left King's Road.

38

OF ALL THE IMAGININGS I HAD NURSED IN NEW YORK CONCERNING THE nature of my holiday in England, several might have included the escorting of a young woman to a week end in the country or by the sea. None had included the escorting of a young mother *and her child* to a cottage in the country.

Yet there I was, I reflected manfully, sitting behind Barker's imperturbable back, caught into a strange improbable joke, with myself as victim. Yet, strangely enough, I had no wish to rebel. Perhaps that might come later, I thought, wary of Dinah and her ways, but she had already settled down into her mother's arms and was slipping once again into sleep.

As we drove, we talked in whispers of the day's events at Court House which had led to this journey. Julia showed no surprise that Keith Lewis had not reported back to Harwell.

"I knew it was good-by when he rang," she said. "I didn't really expect him to ring me again at the flat. When he rang I knew it wasn't a bluff. He will never come back unless he is brought back."

"Where from?"

"Shall I ever know?" she asked hopelessly. "If only one did. That would be something, but people seem to disappear and are never heard of again, only in rumors and what are they?"

"You don't think he could still be in Chance's house?"

"It's possible, but I don't think so. He spoke from a call box, I know. I'm equally sure that somebody was with him. Somebody made him ring off. Somehow I can't visualize him just leaving that house, popping down the road, ringing me and going back. It's not like him."

"Did you get any idea that he seemed to know where he might be going?"

"No inkling. He certainly didn't sound like someone lost, only desperate and terribly scared. That's all I can say for certain."

We talked round and round the subject. I spoke of Dexter Johnson's inquiries and his hesitancy at the editorial conference. He plainly had her sympathy.

"When will you have to go back?" she asked.

"There is another meeting at midday tomorrow. I ought to be there, I think."

"And Chance?"

"Yes, always Chance. Odd, isn't it? He was even in the House of Commons this afternoon, I gather."

"Why shouldn't he be? You have nothing definite against him. Only my hysterical words," she said quietly.

"Only those," I said, and put my hand upon her arm encircling the child.

We were silent for a while. Then, going through Slough, as if determined to put the subject of Lewis and Chance aside, she began to question me about our destination. I gave her some account of my week end there, but she asked for more details than I could give her concerning the house, its period and decoration. "You will see it in the morning," I said.

"And the cottage?"

"I didn't see it. I only arrived on Sunday afternoon and left Monday morning early."

"It will be strange to be in the country again," she said. "I haven't been out of London in months."

At last we were through Reading. The car moved even more swiftly and silently on this last leg toward Newbury. Within another quarter of an hour we were there. Mrs. Somerton was waiting at the cottage. Barker helped put the luggage in the narrow passage hall. After introductions, Mrs. Somerton said, "I've got supper ready here, sir. Only a light meal. I hope that's all right. Meantime, I'll show you where everything is. Then I'll be leaving you. Mrs. Butler may be telephoning."

She showed us over the cottage with pride. Evidently this was another of Mrs. Butler's essays in decoration: dining room, sitting room and kitchen downstairs, two bedrooms and a bathroom upstairs. A wood fire burned in the cast-iron basket in the sitting room, a small table was laid for a meal. The whole thing was a double-page spread from *Ideal Home*. We both exclaimed over the charms of the house to Mrs. Somerton, who, after suitable noises over the baby, and inquiries after my time of departure the following morning, left us.

I finished erecting the cot in one of the bedrooms and left Julia to her maternal duties, going down by the narrow carpeted staircase to the sitting room. It was pleasant to relax in an armchair that was perhaps a bit too small for comfort, but exactly right for the size of the room. Gradually I dozed.

"This is certainly the nicest way I've ever seen of keeping guests at arm's length," Julia called, coming into the sitting room a quarter of an hour later.

"Delicious!" I said, coming awake.

"Don't be so superior. Dinah seems to approve, so why shouldn't I? Are you ready for supper? Apparently yes."

I rose to help but was ushered back into the chair.

So we began our brief interlude. Against Mrs. Butler's chichi background we talked and ate as if we had years to live together instead of hours or days.

After supper we talked until nearly midnight. I hadn't talked so freely and so eagerly in years. Julia, too, seemed less tense than at any time since I had known her.

"One doesn't realize how essential it is to escape from dear old ghastly London until one does it," she said, sitting along the settee, which was just long enough for such disciplined relaxation.

Occasionally my thoughts wandered to Chance and Keith Lewis, and I seemed to see the scene, of which I was part, as a still clipped from a sequence of a bizarre, even macabre film. This cozy domestic interior and conversation piece, apparently serene, was permissible only because a man, whereabouts unknown, had relinquished his own domestic claims. I felt like the intruder I knew myself to be, but that melancholic mood receded: the pleasant actuality, however transient, ousted depression.

Later, upstairs, we stood on the minute landing.

"This could be an awkward moment," I said quietly.

"Why?"

"You know why. Because of last night, because of our conversation this afternoon, because of everything. Second nights are notoriously more tricky than first."

"But why?" she said. "I like you. I like myself better with you around. I've told you why. You give me the only sense of well-being I've known in all these last two years. Of course I like you. Perhaps I love you. How can I say? I love Keith, too. Does one ever stop loving people? I don't know. Let us be like this and forget the rest of the world for a while. Everything outside seems so complicated and awful. Can't we just be together now?"

She put her arms firmly about my shoulders. "Men are so extraordinary sometimes," she said laughing. "You'd hop into bed with a popsy you'd met at Bray and brought here. Even if she wasn't all that willing. But just because I'm here, a willing partner, telling you I like you, making no bones about the solace you are to me, you stand there, looking like a soulful Saint Bernard."

"Put it down to the fact I'm out of touch with the younger generation."

"I put it down to what it is," she said. "To the undying, ingrown hypocrisy of men."

I laughed, sheepishly perhaps, but protested no more.

"For over a year I've lived without a man, thanks to poor Keith," she said later. "And you've been kinder to me than anyone I've ever known. And I was curious about you. These curiosities are there, even in times of tension, aren't they? Perhaps even more then. Don't we have a dozen lives going on at any one time? At least, the psychologists say so and I believe them."

I put my hand gently over her lips.

"No more," I said. "You put my hypocritical soul to rest. Or almost."

39

MRS. SOMERTON CAME ACROSS FROM THE HOUSE ABOUT EIGHT-THIRTY to prepare breakfast, but Julia was already downstairs. "A girl can't break the habits of a lifetime just because she finds herself living among the leisured classes," she said gaily, taking plates of eggs and bacon from the minuscule kitchen to the dining room.

I hovered around the front door, wondering what chance of any newspapers in this cultivated Berkshire backwater.

Mrs. Somerton, after morning greetings to myself and then to Julia, plus an approving glance at the unexpectedly competent scene in the kitchen, said briskly, "I'll come across later, dear," and bustled off across the courtyard.

I stood there, looking across to the house, its formal elevations serene and tenuously pink in the morning sunshine. A strange background for Butler, I thought, a stranger background still for the story I was living through. Turning, Mrs. Somerton called, "I've put the papers in the sitting room, sir."

I turned and went slowly through the passageway into the room, across to the small sofa table by the window. Even as I crossed the room I could see the headline bursting from the front page, subduing even the assertive title piece.

H-Scientist Disappears

Well, it had come, I thought, looking down at the sheet before picking it up. I scanned the *Express*, the only other paper there, but there was no mention of Lewis. Butler and Rees had got away to a clear start. I read through the brief story. The whole thing had been skillfully, even damnably done. The story occupied no more than twelve lines of bold type under a subsidiary heading:

TOP HARWELL MAN

FAILS TO REPORT

AFTER JOURNEY ABROAD

Then followed a biographical outline of Lewis's career, a passing reference to his marriage ("Mrs. Lewis did not live in Reading with her husband. It is understood that she lived in a flat in London with a young daughter of the marriage."), a hazy reference to his brilliance as a mathematical scholar, a note on the recent inter-universities convention at Milan and that was all. Butler, as usual, had left his exit well and truly open. If Lewis appeared at Harwell that day, the whole story could be simply and smoothly explained away as watchfulness on the part of a great British newspaper. The welfare and whereabouts of our scientists were a national concern. Then would follow a twenty-line editorial on the necessity for such care, especially after the Pontecorvo, Burgess-Maclean disappearances, and so

on and so forth. Even with his 108-point sans serif headings, Butler
hadn't committed himself or his newspaper by a single word or
comma. I took the paper into the dining room and threw it down on
the table. "Well, here it is," I said as casually as I could.

Julia picked up the paper slowly and distastefully. As she read the
story she frowned and paled and her hands shook. I walked to the
window and looked out into the garden.

"Well, I suppose it could have been much worse," she said at last,
taking a deep breath. "Now let's eat."

I turned round and went back to the table and pulled out a chair
for her.

"How eerie it is reading about oneself in a newspaper," she said as
we sat down. "Rather like reading about someone else with one's own
blood running cold at the same time. Don't you agree?"

"I've only written about others, not been written about."

"You don't know how lucky you've been. I begin to see now why
you were so keen that I should leave London."

I began to eat. "You would have had a busy day," I said.

"Will you have a busy day?"

"That depends on 'Question time' in the House, I imagine. It could
even be an incalculable day."

"Are *you* scared in any way?" she asked suddenly.

"Only for you."

"How?"

"I don't know. But stay here, whatever you do. Promise?"

"Of course. I'm not likely to leave this haven in a hurry."

"Not even if your husband got in touch with you again?"

"How could he?"

"I don't know," I said, "but I don't rule it out as a possibility."

She was silent for several seconds. At last she said slowly, "If you
say so."

"I see Barker and the car in the drive," I said with relief.

"Don't rush!" she commanded quietly. "That's the way business-
men get ulcers, I read somewhere."

"I shan't," I said, and went on with my breakfast like a pensioner
with the rest of his life to live out at home.

"I feel like one of those house-proud little housewives one sees in
those color ads in American magazines," Julia said, getting up from

the table. "You know, seeing off hubby from the porch. Were you ever involved in little scenes like that, my dear?"

"This is the nearest I ever got to it."

She smiled and said "Touché" and then went on: "Not even when you were married?"

"That was in England. I couldn't afford a car. I lived in a flat and I usually saw myself off."

"Where was the lady?"

"In bed."

"Always?"

"Almost always."

"How did you come to make such a terrible mistake?"

"I mistook a bedtime companion for a breakfast companion."

"You'll have me in tears," she said, gently mocking.

"It's happened before—to many men," I said.

"Will it happen again—to you?"

"I doubt it," I said grimly. "Anyway, it was a long time ago. It was better that way, too. I got better breakfasts."

"Better than this?"

"Never in my life," I said truthfully.

I kissed her good-by and went out to the car. The continuing incongruities of my situation came to me at odd moments. They were with me throughout the journey back to London. Yet how easily and swiftly we make incongruities into the natural order of things.

40

I ARRIVED in Fleet Street a few minutes before midday, and went immediately up to Butler's office. I was taken straight in by Miss Gowing. Butler was standing by one of the high windows.

"I'm glad you're early," he said. "Quite a lot has happened this morning. Some of the happenings concern you."

My heart sank.

"Needless to say MI5 are in a flap," he said calmly. "I've just had an hour with Rees and one of their chaps. Here. In this room. Fellow called Myers. Wanted to know how we knew, what we knew. Everything in fact. I told him. He then came clean and told us they were about to send someone down to see Lewis—the way they sent someone down to interview Fuchs, I suppose. Hadn't they left things a bit late? I asked. He didn't think the question was funny."

"They already knew Lewis hadn't reported back?"

"Oh, God, yes. Their own men down at Harwell knew that on Wednesday morning. Apparently that was when he was due back officially."

"Did you say I'd dined with him on Wednesday night?"

"I didn't, as a matter of fact."

"How did they think we knew, then?"

"I told 'em Johnson got the story in the course of routine inquiries, trying to track down Lewis for a story about the Milan convention. It's a likely story and he fell for it."

"You must be mad!" I said in a sudden blaze of anger. "How the hell can they get to work if they don't know all the facts? Did you mention Chance?"

"Now take it easy, old boy. Again, oddly enough, I didn't. They didn't seem to have a line on Chance. I mentioned our suspicions concerning a possible connection with a politician. It was obviously a new line of inquiry for them. Chance has been lying pretty low in all this."

"We knew that!"

"Keep calm, dear boy. We'll come to that."

But I could not keep calm. I was too angry.

"Did he ask for any names?"

"He did, but I rather intimated we were pretty vague ourselves," Butler went on, unabashed.

"Why, for God's sake?"

"I'd like to take this thing a bit farther before we hand it over. Don't you agree, it's always more satisfactory to hand over a packaged job? No odd bits of string and stuff lying around cluttering up the place."

"Isn't it all a bit too important for that now?"

Butler's bland relish of his own detachment was infuriating beyond bearing.

"Possibly," he said. "We'll see what happens at the meeting this morning."

"Isn't the most important thing to try to see that Lewis doesn't leave this country? If it's not too late, that is. Isn't it?" By then I was almost shouting with anger. He shrugged. "Haven't we left that a bit late, anyway?" he asked calmly, like a judge asking advice from the so-called expert.

"How can we know? While Chance is here, it's possible that Lewis may also still be around."

"In Chance's house?"

"Not necessarily. In fact, I doubt it."

"But it looks as though Chance is going to stick it out."

"I don't see how he can," I said. "Not for long, anyway. A day or so at the outside. Once this kind of thing gets going, it goes like a prairie fire. You know that. You'll have MI5 back here within a couple of hours. They may be slow off the mark occasionally—they've a lot on their hands—but we both know that, given today's story, they'll move pretty fast. They'll have most of what they want within the next few hours."

"You're probably right," Butler said, not particularly interested in my apologia for our security services.

"Did you give them Mrs. Lewis's address?" I asked.

"It slipped my mind."

"You're mad!" I said again.

"Perhaps you're right," Butler said, but unconvinced. "I may be crazy, but I'd be crazier still giving up a really terrific—and exclusive —story at this stage. It goes against the grain."

"Not letting Lewis get away is surely all that matters."

He considered me with a long and speculative gaze, his head slightly on one side. "You remind me of one of those characters in those *Boy's Own Paper* stories I used to read as a kid," he said at last. "There was always some upright character who yearned to be on the side of the angels."

"I used to read them, too," I said. "Perhaps we never really grow up."

He laughed and said suddenly, "How is your lady friend, by the way?"

"Very comfortable, thanks to your thought and hospitality."

"Did she like my wife's ideas of decorating Honeysuckle Cottage?"

"Is that what you call it?"

"She doesn't. I do."

"It's very comfortable."

"It's hell!" he said. "And you know it."

One of the telephones on his desk rang, very quietly, and he picked up the instrument. "All right," he said, "show 'em in."

The others came in and chose their armchairs with fastidious care. They all seemed keen to leave Rees immediately opposite Butler. Rees knew his fate and took the chair.

"Any criticisms of the story as we ran it, Johnson?" Butler asked with elaborate courtesy, as soon as they were seated.

"No, sir."

"You've probably heard that MI5 thought it was discreetly written although a little premature."

"Yes, sir," Johnson said with a twisted smile.

"What shall we do now?" Butler asked. "Attack MI5 for lethargy and apathy? Or shall we start on Chance? It's a tricky proposition, but I daresay a really clever piece of writing would do it. I'm looking in your direction, Hepburn."

"Start on Chance," Rees said, without hesitation.

Hepburn smiled thinly, not averse to the flattery.

"It's been put to me this morning," Butler said slowly, "that our main object should be to keep Lewis in England."

"But he's gone," Rees protested.

"We don't know that. Myers told us this morning they've no proof that Lewis has left this country."

"That doesn't mean to say he hasn't gone."

"Yet they know the route Pontecorvo took, they know the route Burgess and Maclean took. They usually discover these things—afterward. It's easy enough to leave the country, but it's not so easy to leave without trace."

"Some of these diamond smugglers do it fairly successfully—and regularly, I'm told," Hepburn said.

"They probably have a stock of beards to put on and take off and two or three passports," Butler said. "But you think he's flown then, Rees?"

"Yes, I do!" Rees said firmly.

"How would you set about leaving the country, Rees?" Butler asked genially, beginning to enjoy himself and in no hurry.

Rees was momentarily abashed. "I'm assuming Lewis has his help-ers and fairly expert ones at that," he said.

"All right. I'll give you that. I'd assume that, too," said Butler, al-most hugging himself. "But it's still a pretty tricky operation. Come on now, what would be your first choice?"

"Air."

"Not a chance!" said Hepburn. "You don't know what you're talk-ing about, old boy!"

"But Lewis had a clear start. Nobody had anything against him up to last night," Rees protested.

"You don't know that for certain. And nobody's reported seeing him go. And where would he go? Where would you go?" Butler asked.

"Paris."

"You would!"

"Well, why not? It's as good a continental jumping-off point as any other."

"Berlin's better if you're going eastward," Johnson put in.

The meeting threatened to become a free-for-all on the subject of leaving the country unchecked and unobserved.

"I still think air is the best way," Rees protested fiercely. "A plane is checked out officially from one airport—say Croydon—lands at a prearranged point to pick up the chap, flies across Channel, dumps the chap, takes off again, lands at Orly or somewhere and reports."

"Picks him up where? Puts him down where?" Hepburn scoffed. "What about his log book? What about agricultural workers? They're usually pretty observant. What about radar? No, old boy, the main thing is to get across the Channel with the least fuss and bother. I'd take the advice of these river police characters. Jock Wilson says an old-fashioned port like London or Newhaven is still the best way out. There's no visa for France. Get to Paris and then wait."

"So you'd go to Paris, too?" Rees said triumphantly.

"For less obvious reasons," Hepburn said. "I'm on my way to Italy. I think that's a better jumping-off point."

"Cut out the party games," Butler interrupted, the party game having become too general for his solitary cat-and-mouse prefer-ences. "The security people are pretty certain nobody answering Lewis's description left this country by air or sea on Tuesday or

Wednesday and we happen to know that's true. He was here on
Wednesday night."

"Why is it so important that Lewis shouldn't leave the country,
anyway?" Hepburn asked. "I don't want to appear unpatriotic, but
why? Can you explain, Johnson?"

Johnson looked toward Butler. Butler nodded.

"Well, I'll try," Johnson said simply.

He began slowly, as if searching among a plenitude of words for
the exact few that might convey some idea of Lewis's particular
genius. "Lewis calls himself simply 'a mathematician' in much the
same way that Einstein might have called himself a mathematician
in his earliest years," he began. "He's not a human computing machine, which is the way most people regard mathematicians. The
fact is, of course, that he really is something remarkable. As far as I
can discover he's an original mathematical thinker in the most funda-
mental meaning of the phrase. He seems to be able to set other, lesser
brains onto lines of inquiry which they'd never get around to themselves in a thousand years. His lines of inquiry have had tremendous
results. I've heard on pretty sound authority that during the war he
was involved in some of the most extraordinary extensions of radar
theory and development, stuff we shan't know about, generally, for
another twenty or thirty years."

"What was he working on when he left us?" Hepburn asked. "Any
idea?"

"What most of the world's working on now. Guided missiles. I can't
say, but my guess is that he was after what the whole world's after
these days: a guided missile that can be fired by atomic means and
carries an atomic explosive or warhead. I need hardly point out both
the difficulties and attractions of such a weapon."

"That's a guess?" Hepburn asked.

"An intelligent appraisal I should prefer to call it, if you don't
mind," Johnson said tartly.

"Whatever it is, it's enough to suggest he's a man we should hate
to lose," Butler said. "I take it, Johnson, that Lewis's work, however
anonymous, would be known and followed by various boffins around
the world?"

"No doubt at all, I'd say," Hepburn said as Johnson nodded.

"And he'd be a valuable asset to a potential enemy?" Butler went
on.

"To say the least," Johnson said emphatically.

"And we'd all hate to lose the little runt," Hepburn said.

"What's got into you, Hepburn?" Butler said, amused but icy.

"I just hate his tiny mathematical guts, that's all," Hepburn said. "I've never met him and I never want to, but that's my motto. It seems a pity we have to put ourselves to so much trouble for the treacherous little bastard."

"He may have been sincere in his belief that he owes his knowledge to the world," Butler said, mildly but provokingly.

Hepburn said, "By the same token, I suppose we ought to share this story with the *Express* and the *Mirror.*"

Everyone laughed, including Butler.

"Now you're getting fanciful, Hepburn," he said genially. Hepburn laughed loudly. He had shown his independent hand, had been noticed and was satisfied. We should hear no more from him that morning.

We spent another half hour talking round the subject. With no more information to hand our follow-up story looked like being pretty thin.

"A pity!" Butler said. "A really good piece today would help those limping Saturday-morning sales."

He turned to me. "Any chance of an exclusive interview with Mrs. Lewis?"

I felt sick in the stomach at the words. I had known all along that it would have to come, sooner or later, of course: it was doubtless part of the price to be paid, now or later, for Julia's present immunity, but I didn't welcome the prospect.

"I'd rather you decided that. Once we do that, don't we put ourselves in bad, very bad, with MI5? So far, I gather, they don't know where she is."

That was momentary checkmate.

"You're probably right," he said after a moment's reflection, smiling a pouting smile at my underlying threat.

"It's a pity all the same," Rees said. "It's just what we need."

I hated him violently, even homicidally, for keeping the subject alive a second longer than necessary.

"No, I think we'll leave it for the moment," Butler said. "I think we'd better take a general line of handing out blame all round. How could he have left? What route? Who's to blame? How valuable was he? You know the drill. Perhaps Johnson could do a piece along those lines."

Rees nodded. Johnson paled, I thought.

"What about Chance?" Rees asked.

"I think we'd better let that subject rest, too," Butler said.

"It's a pretty thin prospect, then," Rees said sadly.

In a tepid kind of manner I was gradually warming toward Rees. He was so obviously keen on his paper. Little wonder he was made for Butler.

"Do what you can," Butler said almost benevolently. "Perhaps we'll have better news for you on Sunday."

Once again, as the others were going out, Butler beckoned me to stay.

"Are you going down to Berkshire tonight?" he asked.

"I thought not."

"You're not in favor of that exclusive interview, then?"

"Why should I be? Are you, frankly?"

"As a newspaperman, yes. As a man of compassion, no."

"Well, let compassion have its petty triumph today."

"It's a bad thing mixing business with bonhomie."

"I'd say it was as much common sense as compassion to let her alone for the moment."

We were both playing a double-crossing game and we both knew it. I knew he should tell MI5 of Julia's whereabouts: he knew I might do exactly that if he pressed the interview idea too far.

"All right," he said, "I'll let common sense have its petty triumph, too. Why are you staying in London?" he asked suddenly, changing, or seeming to change, the subject.

"I thought I'd try to see Chance again."

"That's not a bad idea," he said, his eyes coming craftily alive. "Not a bad idea at all." He pulled open a lower drawer to his desk and propped up his legs. "Any particular purpose in mind?"

"Nothing in particular."

"Extraordinary situation, isn't it? A scientist disappears, we don't know where, and the scallywag in chief, a well-known M.P., walks around scot free because nobody in the world, it seems, has got a thing on him."

"You don't think Myers knew more than he said, on that score?"

"I don't think so. I suppose what it boils down to is this: Chance is an old bird at this game and, as in most other games, technique counts. He saw the red light for Lewis and got him out of the country. He thinks his own tracks are covered. For a few days at least. Perhaps longer. As far as he's concerned you and Mrs. Lewis are the only really dangerous birds."

He looked up, suddenly amused. "In fact, old boy, you may be in considerable danger. Mrs. Lewis too. And all we've got down there is Mrs. Somerton and a couple of corgis."

"Very funny," I said.

"I'm sorry," he said suddenly. "In damn poor taste. What d'you think we'd better do about it? Tip off the local bobby? He's a friend of mine. I shan't have to tell him much."

"Do nothing," I said. "For one thing, I don't think this is that kind of melodrama. This is the real stuff. There's little violence to the half-dozen people primarily involved. Occasionally, but not very often. The violence comes later. Perhaps twenty years later. To ten or twenty million people. And only somebody interested in the foot-notes of history would connect the two events. Lewis and Chance today and a particularly ghastly opening phase to a war in the Middle East, say, in ten years' time."

"I always enjoy your far-fetched historical theories. This one could be worth a feature," he added, his headline mind already at work. "Care to do it?"

I laughed a falsetto laugh.

Ultimately one could never take him seriously because he was so serious, like a technical puppet jumping about on the ends of self-manipulated strings. Beneath his sly and hearty badinage, his brain worked toward only one thing: his newspapers. Perhaps he saw something of those thoughts in my eyes, for he said, "Yes, see Chance. An interview like that might be well worth having in reserve. If you could, by some remote chance, make tomorrow's paper with it, I should be very pleased."

I nodded noncommittally and then asked if he would be going down to Berkshire.

"I don't know yet. I'd like to see tomorrow's front page taking shape before I decide."

41

AFTER THAT MID-MORNING EDITORIAL CONFERENCE I WENT OFF AND lunched alone at Scotts.

I was in a taciturn mood, still brooding over Butler's remarks about the interview with Julia. The subject had only been left in abeyance. That I knew. It could be revived at any time. I hated Rees and Butler for being themselves, always a foolish pastime. Yet I persisted in the unrewarding game. Most of all, I hated Butler. I had thought his offer of the guest cottage was a sign of softness. Now I could see that it was part of the pattern of his relentless preoccupation with the one subject that had any life for him at any time.

I walked slowly back to the library at Court House and spent most of the afternoon going through the files again, tracking down Chance's speeches in Hansard, his articles in various weekly and monthly magazines, his scattered utterances and interviews. I had an impelling urge to be as well briefed as possible on the subject of Chance before I met him.

At about five o'clock I went out into Fleet Street and across to the Post Office and put through a personal call to Julia.

"Are you still comfortable?" I asked, lamely enough.

"I'm beginning to enjoy life as a rustic, if that's what you mean."

"That's more or less what I mean."

"How is that ghastly London?"

"The same. You've had no visitors or phone calls?"

"None. Why? Should there be?"

"I just wondered. No, there shouldn't be. On paper, in fact, there couldn't be. You're not to stir for anybody. You understand that, don't you?"

"Of course. You told me. I obey," she said too demurely. "But you're not expecting any surprise visitors, are you?"

"No, I'm not, but Butler put the idea into my head and I don't like it."

She said, "I see," quietly and then no more.

We talked about the weather, Dinah, Berkshire, my journey to London, when I should return.

"Probably tomorrow evening," I said.

"That's a long time. Can't you come tonight?"

I thought not, I said sadly. Then we gradually cheered up and, after a few more mutually solicitous remarks, rang off.

More relieved than I cared to admit, I walked back to Court House. The thought came to me that I had just engaged in the kind of unexciting domestic conversation that went on all the time throughout the world, but which I had never had in my life. I also remembered, with a tolerant smile, that overhearing others similarly engaged in the past, I had always felt immeasurably superior and self-sufficient. Well, those days had gone, I told myself. Now such conversations were so rewarding that I almost returned to the telephone booth. Instead, I steeled myself against such self-indulgence by buying the three London evening papers. They were all running the Lewis story with big headlines and no facts, following our lead, eking out their empty tales with rehashed references to Pontecorvo, Burgess and the others.

In Winter's office I asked to borrow his telephone and rang Chance's secretary in the House of Commons to ask for an opportunity to see him.

"He is in the Chamber, now," she said, "but I shall undoubtedly be seeing him later and could ask him to ring you."

I should probably be moving around, I said. Could she leave a message at Athenaeum Court? I would willingly come down to the House or go to Chester Square. Anywhere, in fact.

She said she'd try. More to the point, she sounded co-operative. So I went back to my hotel. Then I was suddenly tired and slept.

I came awake in a darkened world, my watch recording half-past eight. As I regained consciousness my first reaction was annoyance that Chance hadn't rung. Then I was hungry. I had a meal sent up from the restaurant and still waited, but no call came.

I read until eleven o'clock; then I went to bed and tried to sleep, but it was no good. I was wakeful and ill at ease. I thought of Julia almost continuously, speculating raggedly upon what might await us, where we should be a month from this moment, what future there might conceivably be for us. Then, as usual, my thoughts drifted back to Keith Lewis. Once again I tried to put all thoughts of him aside, but could not. I wondered, a dozen times an hour, where upon the world's wide surface he might be. That night, I remember, I thought of him for a long time. His drawn, tanned face, sad-eyed and trusting, drifted in and out of my mind like a face seeking peace that only I might give.

I breakfasted in my room, reading the morning's newspapers.

By then, Saturday, every paper was baying aloud the name of Lewis. Yesterday he had been the H-SCIENTIST. Today he was plain LEWIS in the largest display size the Ludlow machines could cast. Such is journalistic fame, such are its gradations and usages.

Rees had gone about, rather smartly, I thought, on an entirely new tack. I thought I could detect Butler's hand. The new line was

HAS LEWIS LEFT ENGLAND?

and the question strode across the full seven columns at the top of the page, followed by a three-deck, three-column subsidiary heading:

SCIENTIST DID NOT USE
NORMAL AIR OR SEA ROUTES,
TRAVEL OFFICIALS CLAIM

Then followed a neat story which added exactly nothing to the world's knowledge.

Why, asked the reporter, had Lewis bothered to return from Milan if he were proposing to vanish so soon?

Perhaps they had a new line there, I thought, and it was certainly a novel approach compared with those essayed by rival newspapers in their despairing attempts not to be out of the hunt. They had all rushed in, twenty-four hours late, with the story of Lewis's disappearance, and that was all. They could do no more.

Even the *Times* now had a circumspect single-column story midway down the main news page under a typically Printing House Square heading:

HARWELL SCIENTIST'S
UNEXPLAINED ABSENCE

How fervently I wished, at that moment, that those who directed my own group of newspapers had the same kind of reticence!

I went on to read the careful prose of the *Times* as it recorded the disappearance of Lewis, a paragraph without surmise, sensation or apparent surprise. I had almost finished when the telephone rang. I groped across the table, mumbled into the mouthpiece as the hall porter said, "Mr. Chance to see you, sir."

"Down there?" I said disbelievingly.

"Yes, sir."

"Ask him to wait. I'll be down in five minutes. No, ask him to come up."

42

I WAS UNSHAVEN AND STILL IN MY DRESSING GOWN, BUT DISADVANTAGES of that kind, I told myself firmly, had to be taken in one's stride.

Within three minutes, following a knock on the door, a porter showed Chance into the room.

He seemed considerably paler than he had been the last time we had met. Only three days before! Wednesday! I realized with astonishment.

We exchanged pretty stiff greetings.

"Have some coffee," I said. It was a relief to have an excuse to act like a civilized human being.

"Thanks, I will."

I rang for another cup and more coffee.

"You wanted to see me?" he said.

"I wanted to ask you a few questions," I amended.

He smiled his thin, sardonic smile. "Such as?" he asked.

"Well, the first is fairly obvious: where is Lewis?"

"Safe."

"That's not an answer."

"That is my answer."

"Is he in this country?"

"Look!" he said, suddenly and decisively, cutting out all flummery. "There's no answer to that. At least, there will be no answer from

me. As far as you are concerned, and this country is concerned,
Lewis has gone for good. But I wanted to see you. I was proposing
to get in touch with you this morning, in any case. Lewis may have
gone for good but there is the question of his wife."

"What kind of question?"

"I want to see her."

"I don't think she wants to see you."

"That is neither here nor there. I have a message for her."

"From her husband?"

"Who else?"

"I can deliver it."

"I'm afraid you can't. It is too important *and* too urgent for that.
In any case it's a written message. Where is she?"

"Not in London. Quite a lot of miles away, in fact."

He made a gesture of impatience. "I must still see her, all the
same."

"Why?"

"Her husband wishes her to come—to join him."

"I don't think she would want to. In fact, I'm sure she wouldn't."

"How do you know?"

"I think it's implicit in her actions, don't you? She left him a year
ago because she suspected what he is. She has now left London.
Why should she wish to rejoin him now that he's proved he's all she
suspected?"

"She left him in what was doubtless an attempt to make him
change his ways."

"Well, he didn't change them, so I imagine she still feels the same
way."

"Why? When he was still in this country she probably always had
the feeling that he might come round to knock at her door asking
for forgiveness. He will never return to this country. I have a letter
from him asking her to join him."

"Show me!"

He put his hand in his breast pocket and took out a long narrow
foolscap envelope. He held it so that I could see the words "Julia
Lewis" scrawled across the face of the envelope.

There was a knock on the door. "Come in!" I called and a pretty,
dark girl entered, carrying a tray. She came between us, for we were
both still standing on either side of the table. Each of us stepped

back and then moved toward her in an attempt to help her with the tray. But she was too efficient for us, rested the edge of the tray on the table, put down the coffeepot and then the cups. She took up the used cup and coffeepot. "More toast or rolls, sir?"

"No thank you," I said.

She regarded us in the sad, sympathetic manner that an interrupter of a scene between others often uses. Then she moved away, still watching us.

As the door closed, I growled, "We might as well sit down." Then, logically but somewhat incongruously, "Black or white?"

"Half and half."

He replaced the envelope in his pocket.

"I suppose you know the contents?" I said.

"I imagine I know the gist. As you can probably understand, Lewis is beside himself, wanting his wife and the child to join him."

"You're breaking my heart," I said. "Why didn't he think about that before?"

"I don't attempt to inquire into other people's lives."

"Liar!"

"That won't get us anywhere."

He was right in that, of course, but I felt better for my rudeness. I said, "You said Lewis *is* beside himself, as if he's still here, as if you've seen him lately. Where is he?"

Chance was imperturbable. If he had made a slip he did not show it. "He is not here," he said patiently, explaining to a child.

"Just now you also said he wishes her to 'come to him' not 'go' and then corrected yourself."

"I am not here for an exercise in hairsplitting. I wish to deliver this letter to Mrs. Lewis personally. That is all. I said I would try and I shall."

"I've given you her answer."

"So you say. What makes you so certain?"

What makes you so certain? I repeated silently to myself. Conceit, cowardice, vanity, willfulness, evasiveness? Was I really so certain that presented with the opportunity of joining her husband, with her child, with the possibility of making a new life in another land, she would flatly turn it down? Was I really so certain? And had I, in any case, the right to be so certain? Was I the keeper of her soul? Did I even begin to know what she really did want?

182   THE ENORMOUS SHADOW

Perhaps Chance saw the momentary doubt and hesitation in my eyes, for he followed up quickly, "What makes you so certain?" he asked. "Who are you to be so certain?"

"All right, all right," I said irritably. "And what is the drill if she decides to go?"

"I take her with me."

"When?"

"Now."

"Where?"

"To her husband."

"I told you, she's miles away."

"But accessible?"

"More or less."

"I must see her this morning, then."

"Why the hurry?"

He did not answer.

By then I knew that it was a decision that Julia must make herself, whatever the consequences might mean to me.

"If you'll leave the room I'll get her on the telephone and ask her," I said. "You can tell her yourself. Read her the letter."

"No, she must have this letter. Nothing I can say will make any difference to her. She does not like me. Besides, if she is to join her husband it must be now. You can realize that."

"Why should I realize that?"

Again he did not answer.

"If he's gone she can catch him up later," I said. "Mrs. Maclean waited two years before she took the long, long trail."

He remained silent.

"How would she go?" I asked again.

"That is my affair."

"Why is it especially *your* affair?"

"Because I come from her husband."

Again he used a phrase that suggested recent knowledge of Lewis.

"I'll take you to her," I said. "Are you ready to go?"

He nodded.

"Do I take it that you expect to show Mrs. Lewis the letter and that if she agrees to go, she packs and vanishes with you immediately?"

"That is roughly my plan."

"And if she refuses?"

"She refuses. That is all."

"What's the hurry?" I said again, more impatiently this time.

At last he vouchsafed an answer. "A timetable," he said simply. It was enough.

"All right," I said, "I'll shave and change. Go down and wait in the car. I'll join you in ten minutes."

"No," he said, "I'll stay here. I'm not squeamish. I've watched other men shave and change in my time. Ten minutes is too long, anyway. A man ought to be able to do all that in six minutes. You need the other four minutes to make arrangements to have me followed on my return."

"A man ought to be able to make such arrangements in two minutes," I said. "That still leaves me two minutes in hand. What should I need those for?"

"To warn your editor, perhaps?"

"You're overimaginative."

"Most would-be men of action are apt to think alike," he said. "It is more or less what I should have done in your position. May I smoke?"

Imperceptibly the emotional atmosphere within the room had changed. Our mutual liking came back. If you like a man within ten minutes of first meeting him, that liking will probably persist, more or less unchanged by passing moods, disagreement, different temperaments, for the rest of your life. That had been my experience. So it was with us then. I might loathe those characteristics in Chance which made him prefer the beliefs of another nation to those of his own, but even that was oversimplification. He might, I thought, sincerely believe that he really was working for world peace. It didn't seem possible, but who knows? Who will ever know?

I gave it up and went into the bathroom. Through the open door I saw him take up the Penguin I'd been reading, *The Woman of Rome.*

"Do you like Moravia?" he called.

"The short stories," I said. "Not that one so much. It doesn't read convincingly. Not at any point. I can't persuade myself that any man can write as a woman and get away with it."

"Defoe did it."

"Not even Defoe for me."

"You're too matter of fact," he chaffed. "Literature needs imagination from reader as well as from writer. You've got to meet people halfway."

"You're still talking about books, I take it?" I called, getting the razor under my nose.

"More or less," he laughed.

I watched him pick up other books. Scott Fitzgerald's *Tender Is the Night*, Chester Wilmot's *Struggle for Europe*, a Penguin Wodehouse.

"An odd collection," he opined.

"A traveler's collection," I said. "I buy them and then find it difficult to throw them away. They become companions. Take any you want for your journey."

"What journey?" he asked sharply, his mood of badinage falling apart like an old suitcase.

"Aren't you taking one, then?"

"Why should I?"

"Time's running out," I said, not looking round.

He was silent, so silent that I looked out from the bathroom door to see whether he had gone, but he was standing by the window, his back toward me, staring across Piccadilly at the tall and beautiful trees of Green Park. He must have sensed that I was looking at him. He said, without looking round, "My time. Your time. Is it so important? Just specks of time."

"It's a speck I'm fond of."

"Don't you ever think what a relief it will be to give the whole thing up?"

"Give me another forty years and come again."

He laughed briefly, even sadly, I thought. Then briskly, almost petulantly, he said, "You're taking longer than you should."

"I'm not the one in the hurry," I said, turning back to the mirror.

He continued by the window. Indeed, he stayed there until I had dressed and was ready to go. I could understand. It was a splendid view, one of the best in London, and I had spent hours there myself. But there was an indescribable melancholy in his stance. His broad shoulders were hunched, his hands were deep in his coat pockets. He seemed to be looking down on the scene below with unwavering concentration. Or perhaps his preoccupation was with his own sad thoughts.

As he stood there he recalled a memory to me, a memory of a solemn and silent naval captain I had served under for a short time in the war. "A melancholic with a death wish" one of my shipmates had called him, and "Death-wish Charlie" another, less romantic, had dubbed him. And the descriptions had been prophecies, too, for the man had perished off Crete. Chance looked such another as I watched him that morning, and suddenly, overwhelmingly, I was sorry for him.

Still watching him, I slowly tied my tie, put on my coat and was ready. He was still by the window. I took him by the arm. We went down by the lift and out into the morning sun.

As we reached the street I had a momentary mood of elation. A sunny Saturday morning, a fast car, the country and the sight of Julia within two hours. I put aside my deeper apprehension and took pleasure in the moment.

So began one of the stranger journeys of my life.

Strange, I reflected, as Chance slipped in the clutch and swung the car round toward Hyde Park Corner, that he had been my host in what still seemed, in retrospect, the weirdest dinner party I had ever attended. Now he was to be my companion in an equally unreal journey. At least, its purpose seemed unreal. But on that purpose I would not dwell.

"I'll drop in at Chester Square for a moment, if you'll excuse me," he said.

The car was the Sunbeam-Talbot I had seen at the airport. It was comfortable and I relaxed for the sixty miles ahead.

"Where to?" he asked.

"Make for Reading."

As we turned into Belgrave Square he said, "Will you come in for a moment?"

"Only if Lewis is there," I said as lightly as I could.

He frowned. He plainly did not like these untoward light touches. Like many other forceful men he preferred to call the moods of badinage. He had his own vulnerabilities when others called the mood.

"You can come in if you like and look in every room," he said, almost sneering. "Carry out a search without a warrant, in fact."

For a moment I was tempted to take him at his word, but the hesitation was no longer than a split second. Instead, I thanked him and declined. I knew, in my innermost bones, that Lewis was not in that house.

He went quickly into the house and was there for no longer than three or four minutes. What was he doing? I wondered. Last telephone calls? Arranging for us to be followed? I settled myself more comfortably and looked along the narrow square. The spire of St. Michael's Church, pushed away into the far corner like a poor relation, always amused me; it should have been more of a dominant architectural feature of the Square, not tucked away behind a stationer's shop. Chance came out. He seemed paler still and yet more taut and purposeful. Within a few minutes we were moving smoothly into Sloane Street, then into Knightsbridge and toward Hammersmith.

For the first half hour he drove in silence, his profile set and hard. I wondered whether anything he had heard in his house had upset him.

As we moved into the Great West Road, and he opened out the car, he seemed to relax and his mood mellowed slightly. Speed seemed to soothe his troubled spirit for a while.

I asked whether he knew the Newbury area of Berkshire.

"Fairly well," he said. "We used to take occasional holidays in Hampshire—around Alton—and some of our excursions took us as far as the Berkshire downs."

I began to ask him other questions about his boyhood. He seemed to need to talk. For over an hour he spoke as if he thought he might find, hidden in the quiet words, a key to the story of himself. Perhaps the explanation would be for me or even, perhaps, for himself. He went far back and talked of his boyhood in Wales, of his parents, his time at school, his years at Oxford, then of Spain and the 1939–45 war and his political life afterward. All this did not come as a long autobiographical record, but as a series of jerkily remembered, haltingly spoken episodes.

Before, in our meeting at the House of Commons, when he had talked of himself, he had answered a series of questions prepared by me. The answers had been factual. Now he chose his own questions and answers, and he was plainly trying to get at the influences

which had helped to make him what he was at that precise moment.
It is, I suppose, a game we all play from time to time, but I had
never seen or heard it played before with such intensity.

Finally, he spoke of books. He had mentioned a few titles during
his earlier remarks; but now he spoke of them at length.

Well, it was a subject that interested me, too, and I joined in
willingly. He said, at one point, that he had been deeply influenced
by Strachey's *Coming Struggle for Power.*

"We all were," I said. "It was heady stuff for the young."

"Not only for the young," he said.

"The young in heart, then," I amended. "What was it the old man
said? 'If a man's not a Socialist before twenty-five there's something
wrong with his heart. If he's not a Tory after he's twenty-five there's
something wrong with his head.'"

"I can't agree," he said, smiling nevertheless, "but I hadn't heard
that. I shan't give it any further currency, but let's get back to
Strachey."

"Strachey was a young man himself when he wrote the book," I
said. "Then most of us grew out of it. Who knows? He may have
grown out of it himself."

"I doubt it," Chance said, but the subject of Strachey didn't interest
him any longer. He went on, "It led me on to other things. The real
things. Strachey got his stuff out of books. I went and got them out
of life itself, fighting for them, living with them."

"Living in Russia, do you mean?"

He looked round and, as he did so, plainly put aside his first intention—to stall—and said, "Yes, Russia."

Perhaps he thought it was foolish to start lying all over again at
that late stage.

"Were you so sold on things there, then?" I asked.

He was silent for several seconds. Then he asked for a cigarette.
I lit one for him, one for myself.

"Yes, I was," he said, inhaling deeply.

"What about the graft, the strong-arm boys, the mobsters?"

"They were all there, of course," he said quietly. "They're still
there, in fact, but we've had these things in our own history. *We*
grew out of them into a society which has more to commend it, didn't
we? Why shouldn't the Russians?"

"It takes a long time," I said. "And why help them? It's their job."

"They're trying to speed it up."

"You won't be around."

"I can't help that! It's the way I think."

"Is it the way Lewis thinks—or thought?"

"Not quite," Chance said. "But he saw the glimmer."

"All by himself?"

"Mostly."

"And will he be happy there?"

"With his wife and child, yes," Chance said slowly, truthful at last.

I did not take up the words, and Chance went on: "And a genius of that kind can ultimately be happy—if that's the word—anywhere, so long as the problems are vast enough for him."

"And that can be guaranteed?"

"Assuredly."

"And will you be happy there?" I asked at a hazard.

He turned to me again, more sharply this time. "That's the second time this morning. What are you getting at?"

"Let's face facts," I said, as gently as I could. "The security people were just about to see Lewis. You don't think they're very far behind you, do you, however well you've covered your tracks?"

"I don't know," he said. He said the words uncertainly, rather like a man who has, at last and somewhat unexpectedly, lost his way through the wood. I looked from his pale face to his hands, which still gripped the steering wheel too fiercely for our moderate speed. The knuckles of his left hand showed white. The smoke from the cigarette in his right hand drifted slowly upward.

"You *do* know," I said slowly. "Any moment now, I'd say."

He said sadly, "I suppose so."

The simple statement was strangely poignant: a bitter acceptance of an unwanted destiny.

I said, "That's why you're going today, too?"

He recovered something of his earlier steeliness and did not reply, but I had got too near him to relent and I said, "You might be able to stay a day or so longer. Not much more."

Again he did not answer.

By that time we were through Reading and onto the Newbury road.

"Fork left," I said.

From then on we changed the subject, for I needed to concentrate on the road ahead. Only at one point did he query our destination.

"A cottage," I answered simply. "My one-time editor's."

"Butler's?"

"Yes. Do you know him?"

"I think I saw him once several years ago, in Spain."

"You brushed him off, he tells me."

"Did I? I might have done if he was asking awkward questions. It's a habit journalists never seem to lose."

"If you remember Butler, you remember the incident."

He smiled grimly. "What was he doing there, anyway?"

"Just looking around."

"It was no place for 'just looking around.' It was a place for taking sides. Did he?"

"Quite a lot of people wished a plague on both your houses," I said. "Perhaps Butler wished that, too. Life doesn't always have to be a battle between the Right and the Left. What about the millions in between?"

"What about them?"

"They're apt to get squeezed to death. Isn't it one of the world's tragedies that they don't have a voice any more?"

"Old stuff!" Chance scoffed. "This isn't a world for sitting on the fence."

I went on with his metaphor. "The Right and Left have knocked it down."

"It was due for knocking down."

"Yet life isn't quite as simple as either side tries so hard to make out."

He laughed, as if he were indulging a companion's earnest but inconsequential comments. "It will be time to sort out the subtleties when the Left's had a hundred years to put right the mess of a thousand years. It's not a lot to ask, is it?"

"You speak of time, but you really want space as well. You want the whole world, in fact."

He laughed. "We have to start somewhere," he said quietly.

We talked in this hopeless fashion until we turned into the drive of Westover House.

43

THE STABLE BLOCK AT WESTOVER IS ABOUT EIGHTY YARDS FROM THE
house, across a paved forecourt, with a deep border of grass, and,
beyond, an arched entrance, flanked on either side by the buildings
which have been adapted for cottages. The gardener lived in one
of the cottages; Julia was in the other.

The entrance to the house was between two crumbling stone pil-
lars surmounted by pockmarked urns. Then the drive divided: one
way leading to the house; the other to the stables.

I directed Chance to the house.

"Living in America has warped your sense of proportion if this is
what you call a cottage," Chance said.

"That comes later."

He swung the car round before the house and we both got out.
As the car doors swung to, Butler came through the open front door
of the house, out onto the top step, calling, "Good morning," apparently unruffled by our arrival. He was dressed in one of his rural
outfits: fawn cashmere cardigan, tan slacks, suede casuals—but, as
usual, he looked a big, paunchy, prosperous tycoon with no other
interests in the world but golf and money. Seeing him thus was one
of the first mistakes I had made about Butler. Many others had also
made the same mistake, but rarely more than once. I wondered
whether Chance would be similarly misguided.

"I was hoping you might be here," I said. "As you see, Matthew
Chance has given me a lift."

"A splendid idea!" Butler called. "Here for the day, I trust."

"No, alas," Chance said smiling, "I must get back."

"A pity," Butler said with easy insincerity.

"Chance has a letter for Mrs. Lewis—from her husband," I said.

"I have just been talking to the lady," Butler said affably, coming
down the worn stone steps. "Trying also to talk to her daughter, but
with scant success. They're up in the rose garden." He turned to
Chance, "I take it you would like to be alone with Mrs. Lewis?"

"Preferably."

Butler moved ahead. Like many big men he moved with surprising ease and we both had to step out following him.

The time was just after eleven. I knew that this was one of the most important hours of my life. I had the same wretched fears I had known as a wartime sailor in a foundering gunboat off the Dutch coast, aware that I should be a prisoner of war aboard the approaching flak ship within ten minutes. Once again I experienced the hopelessness with which one foresees the years of emptiness ahead. I tried to crush such thoughts, but could not, and followed Butler and Chance through a walled garden into a smaller upper garden.

Just across from the entrance was a small octagonal gazebo, three sides of which were open to the morning sun. Julia was sitting in a small garden chair, laughing down at her child, now seated on a widespread tartan motor rug. As we came through the arched gate, mother and child looked up. Julia's laughter died. She got slowly to her feet, her eyes fixed steadily on Chance. "Good morning," she said, questioningly and guardedly.

I said: "Mr. Chance has a letter for you from your husband."

She paled and moved her hands nervously against her skirt as if the palms and fingers were suddenly damp and must be dried.

Chance, tall, silent, equally pale, stood between Butler and me. He took out the letter and passed it to her.

"Should we leave you?" Butler asked.

I stood my ground as Chance nodded.

"No!" Julia cried. "You are to stay here. Both of you." She turned about and went to the far corner of the small, enclosed garden, perhaps a distance of thirty or forty feet. As she ripped open the envelope the noise exploded in the silent morning like a sneeze in a cathedral. Chance and I stood ill at ease before the smiling Dinah. Butler took command with fatuous but timely banalities.

"How long did it take you to get down?" he asked.

"An hour and fifty minutes," I said.

"Not bad. We did it in just over an hour and a half last night but it was past midnight and I know the road. Not bad. But it eats up the petrol. How many d'you get out of that Sunbeam-Talbot, Chance?"

With such conventional currency he held away the silence.

Then our words were stilled as Julia turned, as pallid as a nun. Her only words were to me. "It's no good, tell him. Now go!"

Chance stepped forward and began with the words, "But let me . . ."

She said again, "Go away, I said!" more shrilly and insistently this time. "You took my husband and made me hate all that he worked for. And now you bring me this. Go away! Please! Please!"

She turned to Butler. "Send him away, please."

Her lips trembled. She could not look at any of us. Then she turned away and walked toward the wall. Chance stood there for a moment, plainly disconcerted. It was clear that he had expected nothing like this. Tears perhaps. The need for explanation and assurance from himself perhaps. But certainly a final giving way to his wishes. Then Butler took him by the arm and said quietly, "This way."

As they left the garden I called after Chance that I should be grateful for a lift back to London if he could wait for a quarter of an hour. He nodded absently.

The child looked on, puzzled and wide-eyed, as I took Julia inside the summerhouse. It was too cool there, out of the strengthening sun, but we sat down on a rickety bench.

We stayed there for some minutes, resting against each other, saying nothing. She shed no tears, but stared unseeingly at the worn boards of the floor.

At last she moved away. "Leave me for a while now," she said quietly. "But please come back before you go. I'm sorry I behaved like that."

I was loath to go, but she was firm, and I turned and went down toward the house, seeking Butler.

44

CHANCE WAS SITTING IN THE CAR, STARING STRAIGHT AHEAD. HE nodded but did not look round as I said, through the window, that I should not be more than five minutes more.

Butler was deep in an armchair in the sitting room. "I offered him a drink," he said, "but I don't think I got the right note of conviction in my voice. He preferred to stay out there. What extraordinary birds these commissars really are! They're genuinely surprised when life doesn't fall into the patterns they've arranged. Chance was quite hurt, you know. If only he wasn't such an outsize bastard one might be quite sorry for him. How's Mrs. Lewis?"

"I think she's over the first shock. It'll take a little time for her to sort things out, but she'll be all right."

"I hope so. Bloody man!"

"Chance or Lewis?"

"Both."

"It's a bigger thing than either of them."

"I'm in no mood for metaphysical chitchat," he said. "Practicalities is what I'm after. What do we do now? Were you wise to bring that bird down here?"

"I don't think she's important to them. It was probably thought to be a good thing for Lewis's sake."

"Perhaps you're right. What next?"

"I think Lewis hasn't left yet. I think he's leaving today. Chance, too."

Butler sat up. "What makes you think that?"

"Putting two and two together. Chance said Mrs. Lewis would have to leave straightaway. When I put it to him that he was probably leaving himself he turned quite nasty. I think he knows the game's up and I don't think he wants to go."

"How d'you know that?"

"One feels these things."

"How nice to be the astrologer type!" he said. "There isn't any luggage in the car, although I haven't inspected in the trunk," he added, grinning.

"I imagine that's all sewn up."

"What do we do, then?"

"If you weren't so keen on keeping this whole thing as your own pet story, I'd say tell your friend Myers."

"Call no man from MI5 a friend of mine!" Butler said. "Aren't they too damn fond of keeping things to themselves, too? Never a decent story for a decent newspaper. All the same, perhaps there's something in what you say." He sat there for several seconds, saying nothing.

"Perhaps I ought to go back to London as well," he said at length.

"I think so," I agreed. "In fact, there's no time to waste."

"The situation's preposterous," he said, suddenly irritable. "We know it's Chance and nobody seems to have a thing on him. If we're not careful, he'll skip from under our very noses."

"Not so extraordinary," I said. "Nobody seemed to have a thing on Maclean or Burgess. Yet they skipped."

"Things were closing in on them."

"Things are probably closing in on Chance. We know they are, in fact. Why not check with Myers? If you didn't tell him everything there was even less reason for him to tell you everything."

"All right. Don't rub it in. I'll see, anyway."

He took up the telephone and asked for a Whitehall number, then sat admiring the welted toe cap of his shoe. I crossed to the bow window and stood within the warming shafts of sunlight.

The only sound in the world was a lawn mower somewhere about the grounds. Then thin, strangulated voices began to argue within the telephone receiver. Butler said, "Douglas Butler here. I was talking yesterday to Mr. Myers. I'm very keen to get hold of him again. Could you track him down and ask him to ring me at Newbury? He knows my number. Thank you. If you can't get hold of Mr. Myers perhaps Captain Walker would care to ring." He let the telephone fall back upon its cradle.

"Not in!" he scoffed. "I suppose he could be in Timbuctoo by now. I always imagine these MI5 characters skipping round the world in false beards, burnooses and sandals. Perhaps I'm wrong."

"You're as wrong as you know you are," I said. "A desk, dockets, stacks of card indexes, a brief case and a job as dreary as a pay clerk's in the army."

"Don't spoil my illusions," he said. "If we're going to London we'd better eat. I'll lay on some sandwiches or something."

"I must go now. I want to stay with Chance for as long as possible."

"All right—if you must. I'll come on later. Leave a note at the office if anything turns up."

I nodded and said good-by.

"I'll arrange with the local bobby and the gardener to have an eye kept on your Mrs. Lewis," he said. "That's usually bodyguard enough in England, isn't it?"

Grateful for his cold-blooded understanding, I gave him thanks and went out and up to the rose garden again.

Chance showed no signs of impatience as I passed the car. He still stared at the hedge beyond the drive, hunched over the steering wheel, apparently unwishful to return.

Julia was sitting in the chair by the summerhouse.

Dinah was playing with a stuffed animal on the rug.

"Why a tartan rug for a Welshwoman?" I asked.

"Mr. Butler brought it up. He says he comes of a very short line of lairds."

"Liars would be more correct," I said, as peppery as a Blimp.

"I won't hear a word against him. I'm sorry I was so foolish just now. It was a shock, presented like that, I'm afraid."

"There was no way of warning you. I thought you ought to have the letter."

"Of course."

After a moment's silence I said, "I don't want to pry, but did your husband say anything about Chance going with him?"

"Nothing! It was all about us. Us! The only thing he said about Chance was that I should put myself in his care."

"That could mean anything."

"I suppose so."

"I'm going back with Chance now."

"Must you? I was hoping you were here until Monday."

"I may come back here tonight. If I can I will. Are you still comfortable here?"

"I'm being outrageously spoiled. Mrs. Butler came over this morning. They're both so kind. He's charming, don't you think?"

"It's not the first word that springs to my lips."

She smiled. I took her by the hand and she stood up, put her arms about my shoulders and drew me close. We were there for what seemed a long time. The strangeness of the moment flickered in and out of my mind like hazy magic lantern slides. Suddenly she kissed me, finally and fiercely, pushed me away, bent down swiftly and took Dinah up from the rug. I picked up the rug and we walked slowly down through the garden, down to the old stables. There we parted. I crossed the courtyard to the car and got in. Mechanically and silently Chance pressed the starter.

Butler came down the steps, eating a sandwich. He waved a be-

neficent arm toward Chance. "Sorry my wife isn't here, by the way,
Chance. She's always got some damn thing on in Reading or Newbury or God knows where. She'll be sorry to have missed you. She's
got caught up in the human side of this Lewis story. You know what
women are."

"No," Chance said grimly, coming alive, "tell me."

Butler considered him calmly. "It's not a tale for the young, the
simple or the unsophisticated. In any case, it's a long story and I
haven't the time."

He stepped backward up the steps. Once again I had time to note
how lightly he trod. His petulant lips set in a complacent smile as
he waved again. Then he turned and went indoors.

45

WE DROVE IN SILENCE FOR MILE AFTER MILE. CHANCE KNEW THE
road and kept to a steady sixty-five as soon as we reached the Great
West Road. We both stared ahead at the road, each absorbed in his
thoughts.

By one o'clock we were moving through Slough and I was beginning to regret the sandwiches I had declined. Only another hour, I
reassured myself, but it was a dispirited reassurance.

"I'd be prepared to stop and eat," I said as we left the town.

"Where? Here?" he asked, looking around at the concrete buildings of the Trading Estate.

"Anywhere!" I said fervently. "But surely you're *persona grata* in
any canteen along here. Labour M.P. and all that."

"Five-day week," he said, smiling. "But choose your pub and I'll
stop."

"Drive on to London Airport. The food there's not so bad, I was
told by fellow travelers."

He smiled thinly and nodded.

Perhaps he was also hungry for, after leaving Slough, the speed-
ometer was needling at over seventy. I sat back, relieved at the pros-

pect of food, but skeptical of the chances of any civilized conversation across the luncheon table.

Within twenty minutes we had driven into the airport car park and were inside the restaurant.

"Be my guest," I said as we took our chairs. "I've been your guest too often."

He inclined his dark head slightly. "Far too often," he said, smiling. "In fact, I wish I'd never even met you."

"A wish heartily reciprocated."

"Even though I have been the means of introducing you to Julia Lewis?"

"Sometimes, I think, even in spite of that."

"Why?"

The waiter came. We ordered, hesitating in our choice between chops and steak, despite hunger, but at last we were through.

"Why?" Chance said, as if his questioning had not been interrupted.

"Anyone would hate to see this agony in human lives."

"Even if they saw it against a greater background?"

"Suffering makes its own background," I said. "So don't talk to me about ends and means."

"The suffering of Julia Lewis, you mean?"

"Hers. Her husband's. Even your own."

He had been at pains to give an impression of detached, casual query and occasional answer, glancing idly from time to time at the planes just beyond the high window. Now he looked up sharply. "My suffering? What on earth do you mean?"

"What I still believe. I think you're just about to leave this country. I'm certain you don't want to. Yet you must. And soon. I've come to like you in an odd kind of way and I am sorry for you. That's all."

He smiled but showed no sign that my words had touched him. Indeed, as the waiter put smoked salmon before us, he said, almost flippantly, "As you're so certain, give me some advice: how would you leave England in a hurry?"

"Do what I heard a journalist suggest the other day: get to Paris."

"From here?" he asked, indicating the runway beyond the wide windows.

"If possible."

"Were you discussing Lewis or me?" he asked, smiling.

"Lewis."

"I'm not altogether sure he's right," Chance said. "As an Englishman one would be quite conspicuous in Paris. Is *your* French all that good? Could *you* get away with it? I couldn't."

"My main object would be to get out of London. I've a healthier respect for Scotland Yard than the Sûreté-General."

"Perhaps you're right there. How would you go? Going by air assumes you've got a start. Supposing you hadn't. Suppose you knew the airports were being watched. And the seaports. What then?"

Falling in with his mood I said, "I'm assuming I've got a false passport."

"When would you book your passage?"

"As soon as I knew I had to leave. But one can sometimes pay and go straightaway."

"Would you wear a disguise?"

"Only spectacles."

"Ordinary or shaded?"

"Ordinary. Horn rimmed."

"You think that's enough?"

"I'd hope so."

He put down his knife and fork and took a pair of horn-rimmed spectacles from the breast pocket of his jacket. "Try them on," he said, smiling again.

I tried them on.

"No go," he said decisively. "You still look like the man they're looking for. And you'd aim for Paris. Why?"

"I'm assuming I've got accomplices," I said, taking off the spectacles. "If I can change my identity once again, ready for the next stage, I would more than double my chances of escape, wouldn't I?"

"It's the tricky moments here or at Northolt that would be the devil," he said. "There are some gimlet-eyed citizens around behind those little interrogating desks. I think you're underrating them."

"Surely a lot depends on where I want to go ultimately," I said. "Perhaps Paris isn't the best first stop for Moscow, although it might be for Prague. A guaranteed trip from door to door would be best."

"Of course it is, if it really is guaranteed. On the other hand, doing it in stages might help to confuse the opposition, wouldn't you think?

Each stage provokes more confusion, more people prepared to swear they've seen you."

"All right. I'd still rather do it in one easy stage. Hepburn, one of our writers, contends that an old-fashioned seaport is still the best bet."

"How did he work that out? Personal experience?"

"He says a river policeman told him so. How would you go?"

"I'd want at least a month's notice of that question," he said reflectively, but his mind was suddenly a long way off.

"I wonder how some of these smuggling fellows make their trips?" I asked, but he did not answer. His mood of badinage had passed and he was serious again. He remained silent until the steaks were brought to the table. Then he said, watching me carefully as he spoke, "Julia Lewis is an unusual woman, don't you think?"

"In what way?"

"In her strength of character."

"Like most of us she has strength and weakness. She'd be the first to agree," I said.

"Do you think it strength or weakness that she elected not to follow her husband?"

"I can't read her mind."

"Are you sure?"

I nodded.

"She left him," he said, musing, "and she's bringing up a young child on her own. I think that was strength. This, too, probably."

"Words," I said. "Strength to one, weakness to another."

"She should have followed him," he said.

"Why?"

"She is his wife."

"A husband owes certain duties, too," I said. "Some judges might say his actions amounted to cruelty. Most, I think."

"Is it cruelty to follow one's true convictions?"

"Political convictions often seem to bring cruelty to others. Sometimes to the holders of the convictions, sometimes to what one might call the holdees."

He laughed.

"You think mine have brought sorrow to Lewis and his wife?"

"I didn't say you alone had brought the sorrow."

He could not let it drop like that. Like so many self-persuaders he could only reassure himself by persuading others. "Lewis is sincere in his beliefs," he said.

"Probably."

"You don't think so?"

"How can I know? I saw him twice. He seemed a very pleasant fellow. I had no time to get to know the workings of his mind."

"Yet you think you know the workings of mine?" he said, the sneer back in his voice.

"Better," I said.

"What kind of mind do you think it is, then?"

I reflected for a minute. Then I said: "Dogmatic."

He had expected more than that, an analysis, not just one word. When I didn't go on he said, in some surprise, "No more?"

"Lots more but that mainly."

He laughed aloud.

"You're an odd bird," he said, sitting back.

"We are all odd to someone."

"I can't think why I should like you, but I do. Pigheaded but warm-hearted, I'd say."

"Possibly. Any man is entitled to an opinion."

"And you hate all you think I stand for?"

"To the bitter end."

"Why?"

"Because it means death to whatever we mean when we talk about freedom."

"Who is free today?"

"I am more free than you."

"Even if that's true—and I deny it—it's still only apparent freedom."

"I'll settle for that until the real thing turns up—and I recognize it."

"Or you're told to recognize it."

"Ah!" I said. "That's where we part company. Any man recognizes freedom without being told. It's in the air we breathe. When it be-gins to die a sickly smell begins to hover in the air. I know. I was a prisoner of war. I was also in Germany before the war. And in Italy."

He smiled sadly and looked across at me and shook his head as a tutor might over the homespun beliefs of a dull but honest pupil. We talked little more during the meal or over coffee. A few remarks about travel, airports, planes and the virtues of Boeings, Constellations, Viscounts and so on: the mild and harmless showing-off of all travelers by air. I paid the bill and followed him out through the noisy departure halls to the car park. As we stood by the car he said, "Have you ever been across to the children's playground here?"

I shook my head and he turned and walked away. Somewhat surprised, I followed. We crossed by one of the runways under the careful direction of a policeman. There, on a cindered clearing, is a barren place of pleasure for the young. In summer, at least. One day soon it will probably be engulfed by the new airport buildings. On that pleasant October day, the clearing had the sadness of a forgotten wasteland. Perhaps it was too early in the afternoon, too late in the season.

As we crossed the runway, side by side, Chance said, "As you surmised, I shall leave this country very soon. I could not stay."

He said the words in so quiet and matter-of-fact a tone that I turned quickly to see if he were smiling in mockery still, but he was staring ahead, serious and frowning. Then he turned, to see the disbelief in my eyes. He smiled and shook his head. "No," he said quietly. "In your own words, the game is up. I give myself three days, perhaps not that. What would you say?"

"Not that," I said, very quietly.

"I might have continued for many months, even years," he said as if he were soliloquizing. "I had a job to do. A job worth doing. Had you not come back and in your own bumbling way stumbled into something so much bigger than yourself, your newspaper, anything."

I was perplexed by this change of mood. Partly to play for time I said, "Julia Lewis would have told someone. She was near the breaking point. You know that."

"She would have gone with her husband had you not come back."

"She was in a desperate mood," I reiterated. "She had to tell someone."

"It need not have got to that."

"Had you decided that Lewis must go, then?"

"He was willing to go if his wife could go with him. He had made his final decision after talks in Milan. His future as a scientist was assured. Here he was beginning to be dangerous. His nerve had gone."

"And your own nerve?"

He smiled. "The question doesn't arise. This has been my life's work. A job. A belief. No more, no less."

"When did you start?"

"In the Spanish War—or very soon afterward. No, it had all started long before that. It was a world I did not like and I wished to change it. Communism is the only hope."

"Why did you inveigle Lewis into your plots and plans?"

"Because a man must work for the world he believes in. And I did not inveigle him, as you call it. Like most scientists he hated this dreary business of working for one nation. He wished to see one, peaceful world, that's all."

"Russia's world?"

"To your mind, yes," he said. "To my mind the only hope for one world." He spoke like a man who is giving himself, as well as another, a message of importance.

"It is a world that Mrs. Lewis doesn't believe in."

"So it seems, but she would have followed her husband."

"What makes you so certain?"

"There was no alternative. Until you arrived on the scene. You have changed things. One can never make enough allowances for these things. That was something I learned only this morning."

"That she prefers England?"

"Nonsense," he said, almost sharply. "There is something between you and Mrs. Lewis. That is all."

I did not reply.

"It is sad, but there it is," he said resignedly.

We walked across the cinders and then turned. A Constellation taxied in along the runway. ". . . from Buenos Aires . . ." a voice declaimed.

"Why did you start on Lewis?" I asked again, at the slight risk of being a bore.

"I did not start on Lewis, as you call it," he said. "Lewis was put in touch with me."

"And were there any Lewises before that? And others now?"

He did not answer that. Instead he said, "You will never understand. My beliefs. Anything." He spoke patiently, again like a master to an obtuse student. "I can't think why I tell you this," he went on, even as I thought, *Because you must. Because, like the rest of us, like Mrs. Lewis, like any poor wight in a confessional box. Because you must, despite the fact you think you're so much like a chunk of cold steel*, but he was going on, "Perhaps because I can't help liking you, despite your blundering, probing ways. Perhaps because you are the last Englishman of your kind I shall ever meet. You live in this petty world of England and somehow it suits you."

I started to protest, but he rode over my attempted interruption. "I know you've lived these last few years in New York, but you know what I mean. I have lived and fought for one world. It is the world's only hope. A peaceful world. You will never understand. You call it Russia's world, the Communist world. Nonsense. These are words, labels. Can't you see that your way lies another war, perhaps even half a dozen wars?"

"And your way?"

"I know, I know," he said, impatiently. "There may be wars. It is a race against time between the prospect of wars and the workers' awareness of the way they have been duped through many centuries. After I have gone I know I shall be termed a petty traitor. My name will stink to this high English heaven."

He spoke quietly, despite his touch of rhetoric. I did not interrupt. I did not wish to. He was going on. "Yet I was no traitor to the world I wanted, the world that still could be. Some few men, perhaps many men, will have to become traitors to their paltry single nations if we are to have a simpler, single world, made for all men, all races. That will be our problem, the price we shall have to pay. But it seems small enough against the ultimate gain, don't you think?"

His question came as a sudden shock. I had expected the low voice to continue for several minutes yet.

"It's too high a price for anyone I know," I said.

He laughed and put his arm about my shoulder.

"Yet it is the price I'll pay and willingly, too, my friend. Some of us must and I must be one."

For a moment he seemed slightly drunk with his own words.

"And Lewis another?" I asked.

"Not so willingly," he said ruefully. "At least not now. Once, at first, he would willingly have paid any price, but some fall by the wayside. Didn't another great innovator have that to say?"

He let his arm drop and we crossed the runway and walked toward the car. He seemed almost lighthearted as if his words, which had seemed to me like a man's own epitaph, had exorcised some devil of discontent from out his mind.

"A beautiful afternoon," he said. "They never have these afternoons anywhere in the world but this side of the Iron Curtain. Don't you agree?"

"Some of Chekhov's sportsman's afternoons were similar," I said.

"Get in," he said gaily. And so we left.

46

DURING THE REST OF THE JOURNEY CHANCE SPOKE ONLY OF THE most inconsequential things; or they seemed to me inconsequential at the time, for my mind was too taken up with all that he had said. He spoke of theaters and painting as if he were a Parliamentary man about town determined to show that not all his interests were centered on St. Stephen's.

I answered dutifully and may even have entered into one or two modest controversies, but it was a one-sided duologue. All I wanted was journey's end and the chance of sorting out my thoughts, deciding on any necessary action.

I asked to be dropped at the top of Sloane Street and this he did, swinging the car round to stop outside Harvey Nichols.

"Good-by," he said. "Our friendship has been brief but pleasant. I wish we could have seen more of each other."

I muttered my own politenesses, saying that it was still possible that we might meet again.

"You don't believe that. Neither do I," he said, smiling. "I see no possibility of such a meeting in the world as we know it."

I agreed.

We shook hands. He thanked me for my help during the day; I thanked him for the lift. It was a very English parting, I thought as I walked away. As I turned into Knightsbridge the clock above Harvey Nichols stood at half-past three. The afternoon was benign and warm. A few Saturday-afternoon saunterers looked into the tall windows. To my surprise the world moved on its accustomed weekend ways.

I walked slowly toward Hyde Park Corner, trying to get a semblance of order into my thoughts, wondering what the well-brought-up man of action would do, but I knew that I wasn't made, by nature or by experience, for decisions, a realization no man cares to face.

I crossed by St. George's Hospital and wandered into Green Park, and keeping to the grass made a slow and pleasant way, scenically, at least, toward the Mall, leaving Constitution Hill away to the right.

As I walked I came to realize that I was not only trying to avoid taking action, but hoping that action by others would make any move of mine too tardy and abortive. Like most men enclosed within unwelcome circumstances, I was hoping that my way out would be made for me, or, at worst, indicated.

My path took me, by way of Stable Yard, out into the Mall, and used the best part of half an hour. Then a cruising taxi resolved my mind for me, for I heard my voice saying, "Court House," to the driver.

I sat back in the taxi and wondered, inconsequentially enough, whether Chance had packed his bags yet. And as I thought of him I thought of his momentary silence at the airport after I had asked him how he would attempt to go abroad. I thought back over my discussion with him. There was nothing there for me. Or was there? I wondered, forcing my mind back over our exchanges word by word. His sudden silence, following his passage of badinage, worried me. What had we been talking about? I was still puzzling for the sequence of question and answer when we reached Court House.

Butler was in his room. As I entered he was sitting at his desk, the telephone wedged between his shoulder and his mouth. Weekend lassitude hung about the room like a very large cobweb.

"Take a seat," he said, waving one of his two free hands. "I'm still trying to track down this man Myers. Hitler was right. The time to invade Britain or start dropping A-bombs, H-bombs or even old-fashioned TNT is the week end. Yes? Douglas Butler here, just where I've been for the last fifteen minutes. All right, I'll hang on."

He sat back in his swivel chair, still admiring his moccasin shoe. I flopped into one of the armchairs. Then he began to speak: "Oh, hello, Myers. You remember what we were discussing yesterday? Well, as far as we're concerned things seem to have speeded up a bit in the last few hours and I wondered whether I could see you.

Yes, I think it is all that urgent. No, it's not so much Lewis, but the political figure we touched on. Oh, you didn't? Well, mine begins with C, and if it's the same you'd better get cracking. All right, if you'd rather. We may be losing valuable time, but you know best. All right. Come on round."

He put the receiver down. "We were obviously bluffing each other yesterday," he said. "He thought we had nothing. I don't think he's onto Chance yet. But all the same he doesn't want to talk about it over the telephone. These hush-hush boys distrust the instrument. Don't blame 'em. He's only at Westminster, anyway. We'll see what he's got to contribute."

I had been thinking of other things: of my conversation at the airport. Butler's words brought me sharply back into the world and the hour, but I clung vaguely to my musings.

I said, "What was the name of that river police chap somebody mentioned at the conference the other day?"

"Who mentioned?"

"Hepburn, I think. A Jock somebody or other could it have been?"

"Chief Superintendent Jock Wilson," Butler said out of his elephantine memory.

"That was it. Would there be any chance of seeing him?"

"Why, for God's sake? You don't think Lewis is doing a *Kon-Tiki* down the Thames, do you?"

I shook my head.

"We make our dates through Casey, our crime man, and a press officer at Scotland Yard."

"Could we fix it?"

"Of course. Tuesday? Wednesday? When?"

"I mean now."

"I want you here for Myers."

"You know as much as I do. Try to get me through to Wilson."

Butler growled, but snapped his house buzzer through to Daniel, the editor of one of the two Sunday papers in the group, and explained my request.

"It's rather short notice, sir," a voice croaked out of the infernal apparatus.

"I know. That's why I rang you. Say it's our Washington correspondent and all that cock."

"Yes, sir."

Butler clicked the thing shut: it was like shutting off life itself, I thought wearily.

"Why this particular venture?" Butler asked.

"I'd like to see if what Hepburn said makes sense."

"All the ports are being watched."

"I'm not concerned with ports."

"With what, then?"

"A crazy idea."

He let it go.

We sat there, saying nothing. I thought of Julia in the warm afternoon, and hated the silence and inactivity of this interlude in Court House, hated every brick in the building. Yet this was folly, and I knew it, for it was the only world I knew. I was disgruntled in the city in the sunlight.

Perhaps Butler was also wishing that he were miles away, for he moved heavily in his chair, puffed out and petulant looking, languidly holding his perspex rule, his full lips set in a childish pout. His eyes glowered wearily at the tooled-leather top of his desk.

At last he spoke. "Bloody man!" he said.

I said nothing, knowing the man's identity.

Then Daniel rang back. "Easier than I thought, sir," the flat tones muttered into the room. "All laid on. Chief Superintendent Wilson is there now. Things are very quiet and he'd be delighted. Any time from now on."

"Good man."

"Shall I lay on an editorial car, sir?"

"If you will. Many thanks. What sort of paper will you have?"

"Not bad, sir. Saturday's usual dearth of real news, of course."

"Right. I may wander down later."

"Thank you, sir."

Butler turned to me. "What's your bright idea with this Wilson fellow? Tell me."

"Nothing much. Curiosity. No more."

"You're not onto anything?" he asked suspiciously.

"Nothing. I swear."

"All right. You'd better go now. Myers will be here any moment, but why the hell I should handle him alone when you've got all the firsthand information eludes me. All right. Have a good time. You'll find the car down in Fetter Lane."

I went out, wondering why on earth a farcical idea like this should possess my mind. But I remembered Chance's remark at the airport, his hatred of the gimlet-eyed citizens at the airport interrogating desks. I wondered how deep his hatred of airports really went, and how he reckoned to spirit Julia away.

With these thoughts in possession of my mind I went down to Fetter Lane.

47

IRONGATE POLICE STATION, ALTHOUGH A TALL BUILDING, IS dwarfed within its setting: a narrow canyon of a cobbled street and towering riverside warehouses.

The station façade is plain and formal: a door at the head of a flight of stone steps, windows on either side, windows above and a blue lantern globe above the door.

I told the driver to park where he could and return in an hour.

Halfway up the steps I saw the notice ENTRANCE IN LANE AT RIGHT. I turned and went along the narrow alleyway and into an office *cum* hallway.

"Yessir?" asked a constable from behind a counter.

"I've an appointment with Chief Superintendent Wilson."

A voice from an inner glass-paneled office boomed, "Send the gentleman up, Tom, he's expected."

"Upstairs" or "aloft"? I wondered. Apparently nautical terms were kept for nautical purposes.

Chief Superintendent Wilson was standing in the large bay window of his room, overlooking the river. Here, too, a week-end torpor seemed to overhang the usually crowded scene, for nothing seemed to be moving on the drab stream. Wilson was a big man, six feet or more, broad-shouldered, but slightly stooping in stance, like a once-active man who has since spent too much time at desks. His face was bony, with a Wellingtonian nose prominent between watchful gray eyes.

We introduced ourselves.

"And what can I tell you?" he asked generously. "And do you want the information for here or America? I gather you're from Washington."

"Just generally," I said, looking around.

The room was small and snug, with an old-fashioned roll-top desk, a side table and bookcase. The walls were crowded with faded photographs, mostly of football teams and antiquated river craft. Three or four silver cups and trophies gleamed brightly within a hanging glass case.

"Are you going back to the States?" he asked.

"Probably," I said. "In fact, very soon, I imagine."

"I've got a daughter over there," he said. "Married an American airman in the war. Lives just outside New York. Place called Scarsdale. Do you happen to know the place?"

"Fairly well," I said. "One of the people in my office lives out there."

"They're both always suggesting we should go out and visit 'em."

"You should," I said. "Those New York river police have quite a job, too, you'd find."

"I daresay. I must try one day. Haven't always been river police, you know," he added quickly, as if to clarify an anomalous position. "In fact I've only been here about ten months."

I expressed surprise.

"I know," he said. "Always have to make that clear early on. Laymen are apt to think that someone like myself—someone in charge of a station like this—has grown up on the river. But the Chief Superintendent here is always a shore man, as you might say. Don't know the reason. Just one of those things. Perhaps it's thought they bring a fresh outlook. God knows. Most of the patrolmen are ex-sailors or fishermen, of course. Well, I've done enough talking about myself. Tell me something about yourself."

"It's not so much about myself I want to talk," I said, "but about a Polish ship that came into London River yesterday. Would it be possible for her to offload and leave again by today?"

He was surprised by my sudden, specific question. He had plainly expected something more general.

"A bit speedy," he said, "but there'd be nothing against it, if it was that kind of cargo."

"Have you heard whether she is leaving at all?"

"No, but that's nothing. We're not necessarily told."

"Who would know?"

"The PLA. Nobody else. I can find out for you if you like. If it's not a rude answer, can you tell me why you want to know? It might help. You don't think this Professor Lewis is on board, do you?" He laughed, humoring my curiosity.

"Would it be very difficult for anyone to leave that way?"

He laughed again. "Simplest thing in the world," he said, "if everyone were conniving: the master of the ship, the owners, the escapee. The longer I stay on this river the more surprised I am how easily such things can be worked. The wonder of it is that it's tried so rarely."

"It's not generally considered so easy."

"We don't advertise it. Look!" he said, going to the window. "See those two ships, tied up alongside there?" He pointed to a wharf about two hundred yards upstream. "Usually a couple of Dutchmen there: Amsterdam and Rotterdam craft. About three months ago a chap comes off one of the ships, wheeling a bicycle. He comes up through one of the alleys and in here to introduce himself. Turns out to be a police inspector from Amsterdam. Over here for a few weeks to study our methods. Hopped on board one of those ships as it happened to be handy. Not a bad start, I told him. He was surprised, at first. Didn't think it a bit odd. Just shows. Nice chap. Said it could happen just as easily in Amsterdam. Now, supposing we find out about that Polski. What's her name?"

"I don't know. I'm pretty vague about the whole thing."

"One of my men would know," he said, "but we'll ask the kingpin."

He picked up a telephone. "Get me the PLA duty officer, will you?" He hung on. "Oh, hello, Halliday. Chief Superintendent Wilson, Irongate, here. Can you tell me the name of the Polish ship that came in yesterday? Come again? Hold on, I'll write it down. P-o-l-s-k-i R-o-b-o-t-n-i-k, Gdynia. What's that? *Polish Worker.* Sounds like it, too. Thanks for the tip. When's she leaving?"

He listened to the other voice for several seconds, put his hand over the mouthpiece and said to me, "Not today, anyway. There's another Polski here, too, apparently." Then he spoke to his informant again. "All right, I'll take it down too. Go ahead. *J-u-l-i-u-s-z S-l-o-w-*

a-c-k-i. Who's he when he's awake? National poet, eh? How d'you learn these things? Thanks. No, nothing—just a routine query, that's all. No, thanks a lot."

He rang off and turned to me. "Neither ship is booked to leave today, it seems."

"Thanks for your help. What about tomorrow?"

"Perhaps you'd better ring here tomorrow. I'll make arrangements for the PLA people to let you know if you'd like."

I said I'd be grateful.

"Would you like to have a closer look at her, now you're here?"

"If it's not too much trouble."

"Glad of the excuse," he said, taking up a peaked cap with a heavy silver band across the peak. "Saturday's always a quiet day here. Usually my day off, but I swapped with my deputy. He wanted to watch some football match or other."

"Would you mind if we took these?" I asked, pointing to a binocular case on the side table.

"Go ahead. Hang onto them. Let's hope they show you what you're looking for."

I thanked him and took them. We went downstairs. The time was nearly half-past four by the wall clock in the outer office. Dusk would be upon the river in half an hour, I judged.

"Who's free?" asked Wilson.

"Midgley, sir."

"Tell him I want him straightaway."

"He's standing by. On the jetty, sir."

We went out from the station, through a yard crowded with wooden storeracks and oil drums, past an open workshop, onto the long jetty. Three police launches rolled to the river. A tall, burly, somber-faced sergeant, in a peaked cap, stood to attention. Wilson gave his orders. "Go up as far as Westminster and then back. Take it slowly as you get abeam of those two Polish ships above Tower Bridge, but don't get too near."

He turned to me. "Sure you'll be warm enough?"

I nodded and clambered down into the launch, remembering an injunction from what seemed long years ago that commanding officers were supposed to be last afloat, first ashore. The launch was a good deal more bare than I had expected. Like most other Londoners, I had often watched these familiar and purposeful-looking craft from the Embankment. From bridges or the Embankment they had always seemed well-equipped vessels, built for midnight duties on that great, bleak, foggy river. I had expected them to be as well-found as a naval pinnace. Instead, I found essentials: two pilots' seats, one port, one starboard, a half-covered cockpit, giving full standing shelter forward but wholly open astern, and an open after section, commodious but comfortless and seatless. I mentioned my surprise to Wilson.

"They are a bit bare," he said. "Shook me a bit when I first saw 'em, I must confess. But they're just the job for picking up would-be suicides, drifting barges and floating cargo. It's hard, wet work we get. No life for pile carpets." With a touch of Spartan pride, he added, "Only had heaters put in during the past few months, haven't you, Midgley?"

"That's right, sir."

Even the heater, installed at the side of the pilot's seat, was a most severe, utilitarian addition.

"I must compare notes and see how they treat their river police in New York and let you know," I said.

Wilson laughed. "Probably find 'em centrally heated and full of ice cream parlors."

The craft apparently carried three patrolmen. Midgley, the sergeant, was in command. Under him were two constables, each presumably able to take the wheel. The patrolman on the port side was steering. Midgley stood a pace or so aft with Wilson. I stood within the scant shelter of the half-enclosed cockpit.

Within a minute of casting off we were out in the river, moving strongly upstream. Wilson still seemed to be finding interest and novelty in his recent command, for he gazed eagerly around at the high warehouses, the lighters alongside deserted wharves, the dulled life of the week-end river.

"We'll be more or less abeam of the Polskis in half a minute, sir," Midgley said.

"Shall we go close in or stay out here?" Wilson called to me.

"Stay out here, if you don't mind."

"Right, take it easy, pilot."

I unslung the glasses, set them to suit my eyes, and then, half crouching in the cockpit, scanned first the deck of the *Polski Robotnik*, then that of the *Juliusz Slowacki*. They were both lying alongside new-looking concrete wharves and warehouses, about two hundred yards upstream from Tower Bridge, within the Pool of London.

They were almost sister ships, each about four thousand tons, I estimated, each painted in the same color scheme: dark gray topsides, pale gray superstructures, black funnels with yellow-red-yellow hoops.

Through the glasses both vessels looked extremely shipshape. A few seamen moved about the decks. I counted three in the *Polski Robotnik* and four in the *Juliusz Slowacki*.

As the figures moved within the compass of the lens, I stared fixedly, straining to mark each feature of each unknown face, but each man became another. The ships fell astern. I was bemused and depressed by the impossibility of recognizing again a face that I had seen but a few times before.

"No go?" asked Wilson, and then, as I shook my head, "Shall we come about or carry on to Westminster?"

"Westminster."

He was quick to sense my frustration, for he said in a kindly voice, "What would you really like to do?"

I was silent for several seconds. Then I said, out of my dreary thoughts, "I'd like to sit in a boat and watch those two ships every minute of the next two or three days—and nights if it were possible."

"Afraid we can't rig up any floodlighting but we ought to be able to fix something. Did you come by car?"

I nodded.

"Well, why not run the car down onto one of the wharves on the north side of the river, just this side of Tower Hill, swing it round and spend the rest of the week end there if you feel like it?"

He had been half serious, half joking in his suggestions, but I took him up on it. "It's an idea," I said.

By then we were well beyond London Bridge, coming up to Blackfriars. "All right, Midgley," Wilson said, "we'll go about now. Don't slacken speed this time as you come abeam the Polskis."

Once again I balanced myself against the deckhouse, put up the glasses and traversed the whole length of both ships, their decks, the lounging and moving members of each crew. But still they remained blue-jerseyed seamen, no more. And what more had I really expected? I thought, chiding myself for a fool.

I was silent until we got back to the pier, inwardly morose, already skeptical of my own foolish notions. I followed Wilson along the pier and into his office where I asked to ring Court House.

Wilson made as if to quit the room but I begged him to stay.

Butler was still in his office. "I suppose you've been enjoying yourself while I've been closeted here with a man no one could like, let alone love; the fate, I gather, of some unfortunate woman somewhere in the Home Counties."

"What did he have to say?"

"He knew less than I'd thought," Butler said. "I suppose we can talk on this phone? Apparently the Italian police picked up Lewis's contact in Milan. They'd been after the chap for some time. They seem to have got very little out of him, apart from a garbled, incoherent message of some kind or another, and the names of a number of other contacts, mostly Italians and Yugoslavs, I gather. The unfortunate thing is that they picked this chap up after Lewis had returned to this country. By the time they let our people know, Lewis had gone to earth."

"What about our other chap?"

"That was what caused Myers to come racing round so fast. They had references to L. and C. You know the juvenile way these underground characters always refer to each other by their own surname initials. Came out in the Hiss case. Remember?"

"Of course I remember," I said testily. "Didn't I cover the case?"

"Take it easy. I even read the articles. Well, Myers had the initials but no names. So when I mentioned C., no wonder he came round at speed. Just wouldn't believe it at first. Finally I think he did. Now he's gone racing back to his superiors who are probably sunning themselves in their country seats."

"Is Myers doing anything meanwhile?"

"I gather that C. will be under observation from this afternoon on."

"A bit late, isn't it?"

"That's what I pointed out. But perhaps we've been a bit remiss keeping these bit-bits of information to ourselves."

"We!" I almost screamed.

He was unperturbed. Indeed, he seemed to think his day was done, for he said: "What are you doing? Are you coming back to Newbury?"

"I don't think so."

"Why?" he asked, suddenly suspicious. "Anything on?"

"Nothing, alas," I said gloomily, "but I think I'll stay in London, all the same."

"I may do the same, then," he said quickly. "I'll leave a message at Athenaeum Court telling you my plans. I don't want to be absent if anything breaks on this story; it's become rather a pet of mine."

"Did Myers want to know anything more about Mrs. Lewis?"

"No, but I came clean and told him she was in our care and he could see her any time he liked."

"Good."

"By 'good' I suppose you think it's unlikely we'd ask her for that exclusive interview now I've told Myers where she is?"

"More or less."

He laughed. "Simplicity dominates the workings of your mind. What are you doing now?"

"I'm in Chief Superintendent Wilson's office. We've just been out having a look at a couple of Polish ships. I thought it a chance worth taking, but I'm afraid it was no go."

"Too bad, but never say die. Isn't that what all the admirals say? I don't see much future in that angle, all the same. Too slow. Too simple. Too obvious."

"Isn't that usually the safest way to do anything?"

"Not in this game."

"Why not?" I said, my voice rising. "And what do you know about this game, as you call it? Have you ever played it? And haven't the men who *have* left this country invariably left by simple and obvious methods? Pontecorvo. Burgess. Maclean."

"That's true."

"Of course it's true. They all used different routes but they were all pretty obvious routes, weren't they?"

"Now don't get heated and don't overplay your hand. I've already given in. And let me know how you get on," he said in parting. "Give Wilson my salutations. What are you going to do now?"

"Nothing. It'll be dark in half an hour."

"Well, keep in touch." He rang off.

He plainly had no belief in my notion. For that matter, neither had I.

I turned to Wilson. "My editor, or rather editor in chief, Douglas Butler, sends you greetings. He doesn't have much faith in my idea. In fact, I'm rather down on it myself at the moment. It seems a pretty hopeless prospect."

"I once watched a house in Maida Vale for eight weeks," he said sympathetically.

"Not for a missing scientist?"

"She had what you might call a scientific turn for blackmailing dirty old men," he said, smiling. Then he was serious again. "I couldn't help overhearing some of your telephone conversation. You really think Lewis might be on that ship?"

"No, frankly, but I'd be prepared to watch it for the chance in a million he might be."

"So would I, in similar circumstances."

He crossed to a list of telephone numbers pinned to a board above his desk, ran his finger swiftly down the list and then asked for a number on the Hop Exchange. As he waited for an answer he said, "I've thought of a better idea than the car trick."

On connection, he said, "Is that the Bridgemaster? Good. Chief Superintendent Wilson here. Irongate River Police. I want to bring a friend of mine along in a few minutes. Rather important. All right? I may want you to look after him for half an hour or so. Will that be all right? Good. Many thanks."

He rang off and turned to me, suddenly brisk, even curt, technical efficiency overriding all else. "Come with me!" he commanded. "We'll use my car. I may leave you there."

"Will I need my car at all?" I asked, puzzled by his sudden plans.

"I don't think so. No. Send him home. But you'll probably want these again," he added, picking up the binoculars and handing them into my care.

I took up the glasses with bewildered thanks, also my hat, and followed him downstairs. The driver of the editorial car was waiting in the outer office. He stepped forward expectantly, bored already, but I shook my head.

"No," I said, "I think you'd better go back to the office. It's taxis for me from now on."

Wilson spared a nod from his preoccupation.

48

WE WERE AT OUR DESTINATION WITHIN FIVE MINUTES AND WHEN WE
were there I almost laughed aloud, for we had crossed Tower Bridge
and stopped a hundred yards beyond the southern approach to
that steel-and-stone anachronism, impressive and forbidding in the
crowding dusk, despite or perhaps because of its farcical Gothic
overlay.

"See what I mean?" Wilson said, switching off the engine, watching my reaction closely.

We got out and began to walk back toward the bridge. The Chief
Superintendent was more like a schoolboy than a high-ranking police
executive.

"A better vantage point, don't you agree?" he insisted.

"If I'm allowed to go upstairs," I said.

He laughed at the phrase. "I think we can fix that," he said, march-
ing toward the first of the great bastions. Without knocking or ringing, he pushed open a small heavy door in the side of the tower. To
my great surprise the door opened into a small cell of a lobby. Two
shoulder-high wooden swinging doors faced us. Wilson pushed these
apart and we stepped into another small lobby, part of a constricted
elevator well. Narrow stairs spiraled upward, around the shaft.

"This place comes under the City of London," Wilson said. "The
Superintendent Engineer has complete jurisdiction. He really is the
bridgemaster in every meaning of the word. Absolute kingpin."

"Is it always as easy as this to get in?"

"Always," he said, pressing the button for the lift.

"Is that wise?"

"I've sometimes wondered." He made his observation with the
complacency of a man commenting on the vagaries of those outside
his province. He left me in no doubt that if Tower Bridge came
within the domain of the river police he would change the procedure
within a week. The lift descended smoothly and silently. We entered the smallest cage I have ever seen and rose quickly within the
tower.

The lift opened into a recently painted passageway, built with the compactness of a ship's bridge house. Wilson pushed open a door and we went into a long, narrow office. A fair-haired girl, sitting at a desk, looked up expectantly.

"Mr. Fellows, please," Wilson said briskly.

The girl took us straight through into a far room. Here the atmosphere of a captain's quarters in a well-run ship was even more marked, for a small, gray-haired man of about fifty-five or so, with a round, tanned face, was standing behind a long table neatly stacked with books and papers. Behind him, windows looked out into a wide world of clouds and darkening sky. Wilson introduced us. Mr. Fellows, Chief Superintendent Engineer and Bridgemaster.

I commented on the nautical planning of this eyrie.

"It's natural enough," Fellows said. "Perhaps you didn't know, but Tower Bridge used to come under the Admiralty. Once upon a time, and not so long ago at that, this whole show was run in great style by a naval officer. Four-ring captain, too."

"Now the machines are wearing out, I suppose they have to have a pukka engineer," Wilson said, grinning.

"You're talking of the machines I love," Fellows said. "They've been running well for sixty years and they're good for at least another sixty years. I won't hear a word against my dear old steam engines."

Wilson quickly explained my purpose and also made it clear the project had his blessing. I needed to watch the two Polish vessels. That was all. "Any difficulty?" he asked at the end of his outline.

"None at all. It's a bit out of the ordinary, but if you say it's necessary that's enough for me, Mr. Wilson."

"From dawn tomorrow," Wilson said. "Is that all right?"

"Quite all right."

Wilson turned to go. "I'll probably pop in and see you some time tomorrow evening before it gets dark," he said. "If that's in order with Mr. Fellows, that is. I keep forgetting I'm on foreign soil."

Fellows nodded, smiling, and Wilson bade his farewells.

"Should be my day off," he said, "but I usually wander down, and this is the most interesting sideline I've had in months."

As soon as he had gone, I knew, with a cold heart, that it had been his ebullience and interest that had carried me through the past dispiriting hour. But a man who is depressed after five minutes' observation of a ship is not in the same class as an eight-week house watcher, I told myself, and somehow felt cheered by the comparison.

In any case, I was suddenly caught up into the strange inner world of Tower Bridge.

49

"WHERE WOULD YOU LIKE TO WATCH FROM?" MR. FELLOWS ASKED AS soon as Wilson had gone.

"As near as possible. I want to see all I can of the ships."

"Those two things might easily cancel each other out," Fellows said, smiling the expert's smile. "We've got about a quarter of an hour of daylight left. You could watch from one of the control cabins, in which case you could scarcely be nearer, but you'll only see the river side of the vessels. Or you could even go up to the High Level —that's the old high-level footbridge—in which case you'd be more or less overhead. Bird's-eye view, in fact."

"Which do you suggest?"

"Try both. We'll go down and see what you think of the control cabin first."

We went down by the lift and out onto the shore span, beneath the tower, crossing the bridge to the western cabin built on the projecting piers. A uniformed attendant, standing by the curving windows, turned and gave us dutiful greeting.

"Are you on duty tomorrow, Greenway?"

"This watch, yessir."

"This gentleman may want to sit here for a while and keep an eye on those two Polish ships."

"Yessir."

"Give him what help you can and don't mention it to anyone when you go off duty."

"Well, there's that!" Fellows said. "Or perhaps you'd like to see the alternative."

I said I would.

We went out again and through a door in the nearer, south-western tower. Fellows held back a door to show me into a large lift.

Up we went, slowly and ponderously, to come out into one of the most improbable places I had ever seen: a high, bare room, more like backstage in a derelict repertory theater than the high tower of a great bridge. Fellows appreciatively watched my surprise. "When the bridge was first opened, foot passengers who didn't want to be delayed while the bridge was raised could come up here and cross by the footbridge. Didn't last long, though. Cost too much."

"They must have had wonderful views of London."

"Not so wonderful. Come this way and see for yourself."

We climbed a staircase and went through a door and out onto the footbridge high above the river.

"See what I mean?" he asked, pointing.

A high black wooden bulwark, the height of an average man, ran the full length of the footbridge, but from where we stood, between a gap in the stone of the tower and the beginning of the bulwark, I could peer down to the decks of the two Polish ships.

Despite Fellows' gloomy words, the sudden view of London was spectacular. The Tower of London, so near on the northern shore, lay below us like a boy's toy fort. Beyond the Tower, buildings merged together like a photographic montage. Slowly I began to pick out buildings that I knew. The Mint, the PLA building, St. Katherine's Dock.

"Where is Trinity House?" I asked.

"You can just see a corner of it. Or you can in daylight."

Such a topographical inquiry was beguiling, but I pulled myself back to the task in hand and looked down to the deck of the *Polski Robotnik*, then upstream to the *Juliusz Slowacki*. Men moved purposefully about the decks of both vessels or lazed by the after rails.

The *Polski Robotnik* seemed, from this high vantage point, the cleaner, newer vessel. I asked Fellows.

"I don't really know," he said. "I see a lot of Baltic vessels there but rarely get interested in any one in particular."

I took Wilson's glasses from their case and got the ships into focus. Most of the deck space seemed to come immediately under close observation, apart from sections alongside the wharf. More important, gray indistinct faces began to acquire features and personalities.

"I think I'd prefer up here," I said.

"Shall I leave you?"

"Well, I'd certainly like to stay up here for the few minutes of day-light we've got left."

"By all means."

"How shall I come down?"

"I'll come back for you in twenty minutes. Sunset's at five thirty-two. I'd rather you didn't use the lift yourself. Against regulations, in fact."

"I see."

I changed the subject. "How many times a day do you raise this bridge?"

"Between ten and thirty, say an average of fifteen."

"How long does it take?"

"About three to five minutes for the lift. As much again to clear the approaches. Each span—or bascule leaf, as we call them officially —weighs about a thousand tons."

I came back to the subject of the lift.

"Supposing I saw something I wanted to act on very quickly. What would I do about getting down then?"

He smiled at my persistence. "You hadn't really changed the sub-ject, then," he said. "All right, I'll look the other way. Mind how you use the lift. Press the button for . . . Look! Come with me!"

We walked back to the tower and went down the iron staircase to the lift, where I received instructions in handling. Then he left me. I went out to the high-level footbridge.

For twenty minutes I stood there, staring down at the two ships and their crews. Occasionally seamen moved about the decks in desultory fashion, but they were rare beings. Their shipmates were presumably ashore or below, suffering the infinite agony and bore-dom of being duty watch in port. I sympathized with them from my far-off memories.

I saw no officer. All was as quiet and uneventful as life on board any small merchant vessel in a foreign port. Yet I stayed there, taking up my glasses each time a seaman appeared or I spotted what I thought might be a new face.

By then the river was a place of mist and shadows. Lights of dis-

tant cars on Tower Hill began to distract my eyes from the scene below. The chill of the autumn evening began to steal about the bridge.

I shivered and welcomed Fellows warmly when he came to say my
time was done.

"Will you come back tomorrow?" he asked.

"With your permission."

"By all means. And if you have any time to spare you might like to
see over the bridge. We are rather proud of it."

"How is it run? What kind of power?" I said as we went down in
the lift.

For the next hour I was busy inspecting the Power House with its
great engines. "Tandem Cross Compound Steam Pumping Engines,"
I seem to remember Fellows calling them, and how willingly and
lovingly the words came from his lips! Then on to other machinery
chambers, the pumping rooms, finally to the control cabins on the
downstream side of the bridge.

Toward seven o'clock I said good-by to Mr. Fellows, said I would
be with him at dawn the following morning and left.

I walked slowly northward across the bridge, hailing a cruising
taxi at Tower Hill and went back to Athenaeum Court. I was very
weary.

I rang Julia from my room, and waited for her to introduce the
subject of Chance's visit that morning. Already that strange excursion
seemed years ago, lost in the past. I was relieved when I heard her
begin to speak of his visit so naturally. Many things of importance to
both of us were tacitly evaded, but in such evasions there is no comfort. We rang off with tender farewells, but I knew, as I went out
again into Piccadilly and began to walk toward the Circus, that those
silences, with the many unspoken words they drowned, were factors
that made me irritable, irked by complexities that I had brought
upon myself.

After a solitary meal in Soho I walked back by the way of the
quieter streets behind Oxford Street and Bond Street. Women
moved like shadows in doorways. Lovers walked blindly in their own
delight. I was despondent and tired, beset by vague forebodings and
alarms.

"Have a picnic basket and vacuum flask of coffee waiting for me

here at five in the morning," I told the night porter. He took the
order with the merest flicker of a questioning look. Service.

I went up to my room and turned in, but could not sleep for an
hour or longer. I lay within the darkened room, staring at the unseen
ceiling, thinking of the long day, of Julia Lewis, her husband, myself,
and Chance. I longed to have them there, within that room, so that
we all might talk.

Gradually I fell from that half-wakeful phantasmagoria into sleep,
equally uneasy and distressed.

50

I RETURNED TO TOWER BRIDGE THE NEXT MORNING, LATER THAN I
had intended, for I had hoped to be there soon after dawn, that is,
soon after six o'clock, but my arrival was delayed until nearer seven.
After my restless night I had been sluggish in awakening, and Piccadilly, for once, had been without taxis.

I was self-conscious about entering the door in the tower. Entry
seemed so preposterously easy. Nevertheless, I went in and swiftly
up by the lift to the offices above.

Fellows was waiting. He smiled broadly at the sight of my picnic
basket. After my apologies, which he brushed aside with the fright-
ening statement that he could never sleep after five o'clock in the
morning, he again escorted me to my lookout post on the high-level
footbridge. I put down my basket, unslung Wilson's glasses from my
shoulders and prepared, without hope, for the long vigil ahead.

Yet, although I might consider my task hopeless it had the appeal
of novelty, and, against my imminent return to the States, it promised to be yet another memory of London to add to my treasured
store.

Saturday's breeze had died, but the day held no promise of sunlight. Near and far, the wide murky stream lay dully in the thin light
of morning. The morning was cold. I was glad I had brought my
overcoat, that necessary precaution for any English picnic.

The river was heavy, motionless, like the dark sheen of a table-top setting for model ships. Wharves and moored lighters merged into a picture of dereliction. The Tower of London had the mournful beauty of all those fairy-tale fortresses we remember from a previous life. Nearer still, the towers and anchor ties of Tower Bridge rose about me like the outworks of a giant and fanciful castle.

Gradually the light strengthened and a semblance of life came to the sabbatical river: the launches of the river police upon their rounds, a single tug. But little else as I sat there shivering in the sharp morning air, watching, not needing the glasses for this quiescent prelude to the long day.

Men began to move about the decks of the two vessels soon after half-past seven. A seaman of the *Polski Robotnik*, blue-jerseyed and weary, came up from below and stumbled along the deck toward what I assumed was the galley, amidships. Within a few minutes a trail of smoke from the stack began to drift lazily above the ship, merging at last with the thin line of smoke from the funnel. Within the next half hour, other men began to drift along the decks of both ships, coming up from the fo'c'sles, moving to duties aft or to scrounge for food.

I stared down at the slothful seamen, knuckling sleep from their eyes as they came on deck and faced the daylight. My glasses moved over each figure as if I must note each limb and feature against a cross-examination soon to begin.

Later, perhaps an hour later, two men in reefer jackets and peaked caps came out from deck cabins in the *Polski Robotnik* and stood talking against the rail. One had gold braid across the peak of his battered cap, the other was smarter but unbraided. Master and First Officer, I judged. They were joined by another officer, with jagged gold braid upon his sleeve. "Sparks," I said aloud, involuntarily, swiftly bridging the years. After a brief consultation the three of them turned in through a door farther aft. Breakfast in the wardroom.

My watchfulness persisted throughout the morning. The officers of the *Juliusz Slowacki* seemed far more carefree than those of the *Polski Robotnik*. They were not on deck until after eleven. Then they walked the ship's deck with grave deliberation, a trio of portly seafarers: the Master, about fifty, with red face and sideburns; First and Second Officers, younger but as plump. A good cook or much vodka,

I surmised, but watched them carefully as they stepped out, all in animated disputation, until, their promenade finished, they disappeared within the lower bridge house.

For the rest of the morning I watched with care, swiftly taking up the glasses when a new figure or fresh bustle of movement came within my orbit. Then I put the glasses down, usually with relief. Too much staring through field glasses seems to draw out the eyes on stalks.

Gradually I began to recognize the seamen in each ship and to give them identities. One creature, with an excessively gloomy face when seen through 7 x 50 lenses, I termed "Sourpuss." Another, bowlegged and barrel chested, became, for me, "The Champ." A third, thin and emaciated, was "Scarecrow." In this way I used the hours, investing the men, their backgrounds and their hazy personalities with something of the interest of a memory test.

Soon after eleven o'clock Fellows came up with a vacuum flask of coffee, and biscuits. I thanked him warmly.

"It's a bit parky up here," he said. "Least I could do. Anything doing?"

"Nothing so far."

"Anything I can do?"

"It's just a case of watching, I'm afraid."

"Well, let me know what you're looking for if you'd like to hand over and pump ship."

I took him up on his offer and handed him the glasses.

"Just look out for any seaman or a couple of seamen, in either ship, who don't look dressed for the part or who look mildly out of things."

I walked away along the great footbridge. What a fantastic sight London seemed from this kestrel's viewpoint! Thin trails of smoke rose above the chimney pots of riverside London and beyond. Within that vast assembly of bricks and mortar, millions were now settling down to the morning papers, digesting breakfasts later and heavier than usual.

Thinking of newspapers, I wondered if the Sunday press had had any more speculations concerning the disappearance of Lewis.

On my return Fellows said cheerfully, "Everything and everyone just as you left 'em."

I thanked him, and again took up my self-appointed task of folly, as I now began to term it.

"What time is high water tonight?" I asked.

"Five fifty-three."

Partly to reassure myself, I said as he left, "Can I use the telephone in your office if necessary?"

"Of course. You're welcome. D'you expect to?"

"Only if I'm lucky."

"Well, you know how to get down now. Just make yourself at home."

We talked about the morning's news. No startling headlines, he said.

Regretfully I watched him go. His imperturbable demeanor was a sound corrective to my own depressing flights of fancy, and he was an informative guide to the bridge and its nearer world.

So the morning wore on, with no more to watch than the lethargy and aimlessness that afflict the crews of all ships in port on a Sabbath, whether the ships sail from nations of believers or unbelievers.

Soon after midday I snatched at my glasses when a seaman I had not so far seen or labeled came out of the wardroom, but he was lost to view as he moved immediately to the starboard, shore side. Part of that side of each ship was hidden from me, despite my well-nigh overhead viewpoint, and I cursed the limitations of human eyes and field glasses which fail to see around corners.

Apart from that flutter of interest, nothing.

Just before one o'clock I opened my picnic luncheon; it proved one of the most welcome and succulent meals I had eaten in years, although I seemed to alternate bites of chicken sandwich with sudden grabs at the field glasses. Seamen were again moving about the decks of both ships, preparatory to their own dinner.

About two o'clock, Fellows reappeared. I was delighted to see him. The loneliness of that high outpost was oppressive after an hour or so.

"I meant to mention the fact this morning," he began, almost apologetically, "but I usually walk my wife as far as Tower Hill on Sunday afternoons. It's rather a cramping existence for her, living this bridge life all the time. Is there anything I can do before I go? If not, my relief will be in for an hour or so and he'll look after you."

"No thanks, just mention the telephone possibility to him, that's all."

"I'll do that. Best of luck." Again he went off.

The morning had been dull and overcast. With the afternoon a
fitful sun appeared. The crews of both ships came on deck, sitting
along the port side of each upper deck, peering into the sun as if to
lose no moment of its warmth. A few talked to each other across the
rails, aft and forward of their ships.

Now, at leisure, I could range my glasses along all the men I saw,
checking their upturned faces against those I had tried to memorize
that morning. All seemed accounted for. How swiftly one begins to
memorize a group of faces within a fixed routine and setting!

At half-past three, heavy clouds moved up slowly from the west to
obscure the sun. Most of the men rose from their haunches and,
lazily and stiffly, went below.

Some time after five o'clock Fellows came out onto the footbridge
again. He was wearing a dark gray suit and a black Homburg hat,
and looked very formal and sabbatical. He placed his hat, with excessive care, upon a grimy blackened crossbeam of the footbridge.

"I hope I'm not being too inquisitive," he asked.

"Of course not."

"Any luck?"

"Not a whisper."

"When is the *Polski Robotnik* due to leave? Do you know?"

I shook my head.

"Will you come again tomorrow?"

"I doubt it, although I suppose the well-trained watchdog would."

"Most well-trained watchdogs have deputies," he said sympathetically.

We both stood there by the bulwark, looking down and across to
the ships. We were silent, each with his own speculations, for fully
ten minutes.

"You want to see it through, I suppose?" Fellows said, gallantly
making conversation.

I nodded.

As we spoke, men of the *Polski Robotnik* began to wave to those
of the *Juliusz Slowacki*, before turning from the after rail to go below.
I quickened, watching the stir that comes upon any ship in the hour
or so before leaving port. I leaned hard against the bulwark, peering
even more intently through the glasses.

"I'd offer to relieve you," Fellows said quietly, "if I knew who or what you were looking for."

I shook my head and kept to the glasses.

Shadowy movements within the bridge house of the *Polski Robotnik*, which had been deserted throughout the day, caught my eyes. I moved the glasses upward away from examination of the deck. Master and navigator, probably Second Officer, I told myself, getting charts and papers shipshape. They had presumably gone up through an enclosed companionway from the Master's cabin.

The afternoon sun seemed finally to have gone, trailing off between the clouds. I had no help there, I told myself in self-pity, even at the moment when I most needed every natural or unnatural aid. Two men, hatless and in reefer jackets, stepped from the bridge house, through an after door, onto a gangway which led to a small upper deck between the bridge house and the funnel. They remained on the gangway in an area of shadows. Even as I looked I knew, with a sudden sickness of the heart, that one was Chance. He stood there within the shadows, his back toward me, looking ashore, his hands deep in the side pockets of his reefer, his stance exactly that which I had watched in sadness the previous day in my room at Athenaeum Court: "Death-wish Charlie's" stance, in fact. I leaned forward too quickly and too far. The glasses rapped sharply against a stanchion, threatening to shatter both lens and steel.

"What is it?" Fellows asked quickly.

"One of my men, I think," I said, and then, as if to prove my words, Chance turned about and seemed to stare upward toward the sky, into the glasses that I focused so intently upon him from my high crow's nest. The other man turned, too, but of him I was suddenly doubtful. If this, indeed, were Lewis, he looked very different from the man I had met at the airport and the recent dinner party. He had certainly shaved off his mustache. Daylight was beginning to fade, and my vision was nowhere near as reliable as it had been even twenty minutes before. Life at such moments has no certainties. I stood up and handed the glasses to Fellows.

"Will you keep those two men on that bit of gangway by the funnel absolutely fixed?" I said. "I must ring. It's just possible that the bigger chap may go ashore. What's the time?"

"Just on half-past five."

"I shan't be long."

"You know the way. It's quicker by the stairs. There's only the girl down below. She may have gone."

I clattered down the stairs into the vast tower room so like a theatrical backstage. I went the wrong way. Then again. After one or two panicking false steps I found the stairs, and half fell down them. The girl had gone.

I went through the outer office into Fellows' room, took up the telephone and asked for the Court House number. As I waited I stared across the river to the scene upriver, above the berths of the Polish ships. A pleasure launch, crowded to the limit, fussed toward Westminster. Beyond that the river was more diffused and shadowy. Dusk was beginning to engulf the river. My eyes were out of shape, anyway, I told myself viciously. Fellows' room was warm but I shivered, despite my overcoat.

I got through to Court House immediately. Butler was in, downstairs in Rees's room. He said, "Hello. I'm glad you've rung. We're having a hell of a time with this story. Any fresh angle?"

"Chance is on board one of the Polish ships."

"Is he, by God? Is he sailing?"

"I haven't asked him, but the ship looks as if it could be."

"When?"

"Within an hour, I'd say. Flood tide's at six."

"You're sure?"

"I think so."

"Is that enough?"

"It's got to be."

"All right. I suppose it has."

At last Butler seemed shaken from his sempiternal calm. "It's all a bit tricky. Hold on there. I'd better get Myers. He's standing by. Not for your story, naturally. He's in touch with everybody. He seems to have the whole bloody Cabinet standing by. Between these two telephones, old boy, I think it may go to his head. Hold on."

I heard him talking into the house buzzer, into another telephone, at a secretary, but the words were mangled, indistinguishable. Then I heard the words, "I'll ask him."

He came back. "Where are you speaking from?"

"Tower Bridge."

Butler had to have his little joke. "The places you get yourself. On or under?"

"At the moment, inside the bridgemaster's office."

"You might have told me, old boy. How far are you from Wilson's place?"

"About five minutes if I can find a taxi."

"Myers says Wilson is to go aboard on any pretext whatever and hold the ship. He's to take off the pilot as a precautionary measure. Orders from absolute top level. Wilson or his deputy will get 'em himself any moment now. I suggest you get after Wilson. And keep in touch with us. Remember, this is the place that pays and cherishes you. Go to it, dear boy, and the best of luck!"

"Look!" I said, parting. "Tell Myers or somebody to tell Wilson *now*. There's no time to waste. I'm going straight back to his station, but *I* can't give him orders. Or the bridgemaster here, for that matter. He doesn't look the kind to take 'em. If Wilson's going aboard he'll want to use one of his own launches."

"All right! I see your point and quite agree. No copper worthy of the name would take orders from a newspaperman. I'll tell Myers. He'll probably have some of his own arrangements to make, although I gather it's mainly river police stuff from now on. Well, best of luck, and stay close to Wilson."

I went up to the footbridge again and explained things quickly to Fellows.

"I see," he said quietly, and then, "What would you like *me* to do?"

"I don't know," I said lamely. "I obviously don't want this ship to go if it's possible to stop it."

"I quite see that," he said. We turned away together without further word. Even in that moment of tension I took up my empty picnic basket. As we went toward the tower, Fellows said, "On the other hand, I'll have to have higher authority. You see what I mean, I hope."

"I do, of course."

"You probably think it's red tape, that I ought to take a chance," he explained carefully as we went down the stairs in a hurry, "but there's an Act of Parliament, you see. River traffic has precedence over land traffic and the bridge must be opened any hour of the day or night for any vessel making the appropriate signals."

"Don't give it another thought," I said bitterly. Yet I could see his dilemma. We turned into his office. He looked so doleful that I was moved to momentary compassion. "It probably won't arise. Anyway, it might not have been my man."

We went through the office out to the lift, and he escorted me down.

"A taxi may be a bit tricky to find just at this time on a Sunday," he said. He began to walk with me northward across the bridge, past the control cabin, toward Tower Hill. As if anxious that I should not think too harshly of him for his bureaucratic stand, he still talked of the bridge. I half listened to his facts, so patiently given, but I was preoccupied, looking over my shoulder toward Bermondsey, waiting feverishly for a taxi that seemed never likely to appear.

By that time we had left the shore spans behind and were walking alongside the high walls of St. Katherine's Dock. We must have looked like a couple of miming puppets out of some fanciful ballet: Fellows talking, explaining, gesticulating; I plunging on, unheedful of his words.

Fellows interrupted his own commentary to say, "You'll stand a better chance over there!"

We had reached the crossroads at Tower Hill, the high walls of the Royal Mint away on the right. As if from far off, handbells began to ring. "My God!" said Fellows. "A lift. Not the Polski, I hope."

We began to run back toward the bridge, but it was all too far away. Sunday-evening pedestrian and road traffic was light, and the bridge had taken no time at all to clear. Already the great bascule spans were beginning to rise.

We stood there, helpless, the great span rising against us like a gigantic, implacable hand. I knew, in that moment of bitterness and fury, that the *Polski Robotnik* was on her way. In the moment of gall I cursed Fellows, and then, in the same instant, apologized.

"I must try Wilson," I gasped, for the sprint had left me breathless.

I turned and left him and began to run back toward the Royal Mint, doubtless an incongruous figure in the City of London on an autumn evening, a running, cursing citizen in a lightweight overcoat, an empty picnic basket grasped firmly in one hand, a pair of binoculars in the other.

This time I was luckier. As I got back to the crossroads a taximan, coming fast from Cable Street, saw my flailing arms or heard my panting wail through the dusk and skidded to a stop. I half stumbled, half fell inside, gasping out, "Irongate Police Station," and then sat back to regain my breath. I was puffing like an octogenarian miler.

I had the fare and too-munificent tip ready for the driver as we neared the station, and handed them to him through the sliding window. Then, falling, running, stumbling, I made my way along the darkening passage into the station lobby.

"Chief Superintendent Wilson," I barked. "If he's in I'll go straight up. It's urgent."

"He came in three minutes ago," a constable said.

Wilson appeared on the stairs. "Hello," he called. "I was just going to ring Fellows and see if you'd left. Any luck?"

A constable from an inner room called out, "Scotland Yard, sir. On the phone, sir."

Wilson went into the inner office. I stood there, coming to, trying still to quiet my pumping heart. I heard Wilson's voice shouting, "Yessir. I understand, sir. Right."

He rang off. I heard him say, "Get Mr. Fellows, Tower Bridge."

"It's no good," I said. "She's gone."

He poked his head out from the inner office.

"O.K.!" he called to me. "The sky's the limit, it seems."

He turned back to take the telephone.

"Oh, hello, Fellows. Chief Superintendent Wilson here. I was just going to say on no account raise Tower Bridge for that Polish ship to proceed downstream, but I understand I'm late. No, nothing you can do. Nothing, I said."

He rang off and came into the outer office, saying gloomily, "We'd better go."

He marched out of the side door, along the jetty to the waiting launch. I followed, still puffing, still holding my picnic basket and his glasses. Fool, I thought, yet went on. A sergeant—not Midgley this time, I noticed—stood to attention. Two patrolmen were already in the launch.

"We have to intercept and stop the *Polski Robotnik*."

"Aye, aye, sir."

"Quickly. Has she passed?"

"No, sir," the sergeant said quietly.

"I think she's there, sir. Just ahead."

We both stood in the open cockpit aft. Almost as we left the pier and moved round into the first bend of the river, going upstream, we saw the *Polski Robotnik* bearing down on us.

By then, dusk had settled on the river.

"Signal her to halt, sergeant."

"Aye, aye, sir."

The racket of the heliograph clacking out the message took me back ten years. After a long moment's pause there was a sudden bright acknowledgment from the bridge of the Polish ship.

"Tell 'em we're coming aboard, sergeant."

Again the signal rapped out.

By that time we were almost up to the vessel. There seemed to be considerable commotion aboard, men moving about the decks on the double and a small, gesticulating group on the bridge.

"A bit of a shambles, it seems," Wilson said.

We swung round to the leeward side of the ship and, within its shelter, waited impatiently for a ladder to be slung down. We had to wait for almost five minutes before it fell, bumping and clattering against the plates.

"You'd better come along, too," Wilson said, turning to me.

I followed him up the ladder, slowly and inexpertly. Here, too, the years had taken their toll. As we reached the deck I could judge that the tide had already taken us downriver to a point beyond the station. Wilson climbed to the bridge. The Captain and two other officers were there in a close, hostile group. The pilot, a short, thick-set man in reefer and peaked cap, looked on in silence and bewilderment.

"What is this I ask?" the Captain called.

Wilson informed him lifelessly and without conviction that he had authority to search the vessel, suspecting that it might contain stolen goods. I stood by, ill at ease, an anticlimactic chill already in my bones as I began to add up my responsibility for the scene before me. I looked from the bridge out onto the deserted after gangway.

The Master listened to Wilson in surly silence, and then spat out a word of international currency not once, to my knowledge, recorded by Conrad.

Wilson ignored the outburst and turned to move down the companionway. He was followed slowly and unwillingly by the Master and his First Officer, then by me. As Wilson walked steadily after he turned to me.

"Where first, do you suggest?"

"Right round this deck, then below, to the mess decks."

"It's all a bit tricky," Wilson mumbled. It was plain that he, too, was liking no part of this unwelcome job.

Dusk was now fully about us. I looked toward the riverside as I went below. Lights gleamed from street lamps and occasional windows. Inboard, bulkhead lights stabbed bright but too-small patches in the shadows of the decks. Wilson caught his foot in the splayed base of a stanchion and cursed as he stumbled. Aft, three seamen moved about the raised poop, shadowy silhouettes hovering jerkily against the dusk, one stowing fenders, the others settling a hawser over a winch. Fanciful as it seemed, I thought I recognized the back of the man tugging a heavy coir fender farther inboard. I went up the ladder and took him by the arm. The man let go the fender and turned, fiercely shaking his arm free.

"Chance!" I said, but Chance gave no answering word or gesture. Instead, he stared blankly from Wilson to me.

"What is it you mean?" the Captain cried, coming up to us.

"This man is an Englishman and I wish to interview him ashore," Wilson said, taking his cue.

The Captain turned to the First Officer who had now joined us and was now, it seemed, to be the official spokesman. He said slowly and distinctly, as if each word must have a mathematical exactness, "It is nonsense. This man is one of the complement of this ship. He is recorded in the ship's books. One Tadeus Bronski."

He turned to Chance and spoke quickly in a foreign tongue, presumably Polish, possibly Russian.

French, German, Italian, Spanish . . . these languages most Englishmen can recognize, but are we as certain of our ear when we switch on the radio and hear a language from beyond the Elbe?

To my surprise Chance answered in a tongue that seemed to carry the same vowel sounds and consonants. Even more disconcerting was the fact that he seemed to answer fluently. I was too surprised to comprehend. Even as I remembered, from a far-off conversation with Butler, that Chance had spent a year in Russia, my nerve went. All I could understand and see, in the dusk, among that small group aft, was the look of shocked bewilderment in Wilson's face, his sudden disbelief in me and the whole sorry enterprise.

"We seem to have made a bit of a balls," he hissed in my ear.

"We have not!" I shouted irritably.

Yet he instinctively turned away. The First Officer said with a triumphant sneer, "Are you now satisfied?"

"No!" I shouted again. "Now we'll go below to the mess decks for the other man. The hell with this impostor."

The First Officer stood his ground, the others with him, as if they were about to refuse the demand. Perhaps that slight movement of resistance piqued Wilson, for he said firmly, "The mess decks, please!" Then he turned to me. "Lead on!" It was a noble utterance in a dismal moment. As we went he muttered, "There's nothing we can do at the moment, whether that's Chance or not."

I did not answer.

The First Officer had now, almost officially, taken over. He led the way forward and down into the fo'c'sle. As we descended, the nauseating yet nostalgic stench of ships below decks once again assailed my nostrils, that unforgettable miasma of oil, sweat, bilge water and the swilling sea itself.

Deliberately, unhelpfully, the First Officer went first to the quarters of the watch on deck. We stood there in the men's empty quarters, two silent, warring groups.

"Watch off duty!" I said curtly to the First Officer. He shrugged. I followed him across the deck. He moved back a sliding door and we stepped into another mess deck. In the cold gloom of a solitary blue pilot light I counted six empty bunks, six men asleep, their faces turned, as is the way of seamen, away from their shipmates to the blankness of the ship's plates.

In a moment of sudden, unwarranted decisiveness, I stepped aside and switched on the main light so that the quarters suddenly blazed with light. Not one man stirred. They might have been nailed to their bunks, so stolid was their self-control, but in that first moment of light I saw the corner of a small leather attaché case below the farthest lower bunk. I had seen that small case before, in London Airport. I leaped toward it, just as the First Officer lunged to stay me.

I grabbed the seaman in the bunk by the shoulder and tugged him hard as the First Officer got me in a second-rate football tackle. We both stumbled away, but not before I had seen the white and stricken face of Lewis, a face I shall remember till I die.

This incongruous and doubtless ignominious scene took perhaps three or four seconds, and was played out in tense silence, broken only by the sudden scuffling of the First Officer and me. Then, on a barked command or injunction from the Master, the mess deck was a shouting bedlam. Five prone men sat up and yelled. The Master, another officer and Wilson, standing by the open sliding door, seemed suddenly to be shouting each other down. Only Lewis and I were silent, staring at each other in appalled and tragic dumbness. In the pandemonium Wilson called, "I think we've had enough for one day!"

"Lewis is here!" I shouted above the din of strange tongues.

"Are you absolutely certain?"

"Absolutely."

"All right. I'll hold the ship."

From this yelling medley the five of us stumbled up on deck. Once there, Wilson said to the First Officer, "You are to drop anchor, and remain here until further notice. I will see that river traffic is warned. Let your anchor go now. D'you understand? Now! The pilot will come ashore with me."

Hatred and resistance ran between the two men like a silent flood. Then at last, after what seemed an age of defiance, the First Officer spoke to the Master, who nodded and turned away. Together they went slowly up to the bridge. The Master called his commands to the watch and we heard the great links clank out over the windlass, down and down. As the pilot descended from the bridge I went forward and watched until the anchor was safely home in the mud of the Thames, then walked back to Wilson.

"Well, there's nothing more we can do now," he said. He called up to the bridge, "I'll be back in a few minutes." Then he leaned over the side and called down, "Reynolds, come up here."

The patrolman came quickly up the rope ladder.

"Stay here, Reynolds, and stop any monkey business."

"Aye, aye, sir."

We went down by the swinging ladder into the launch. I looked across the river and we were perhaps a quarter of a mile downstream from the cluster of lights of Wilson's station. We went about and moved astern of the ship.

"You're absolutely certain now, beyond all shadow of doubt?" Wilson asked, almost begged.

"Beyond all shadow of doubt."

"What do we do now?"

"Get those men off that ship."

"It's not as easy as all that," he said. "In fact, getting a national off a foreign ship is one of the trickiest jobs in the whole world."

"They're not nationals!" I shouted.

"You bet they're down as such. And they want to go. It's not as if they're in the same boat as these chaps who jump ship and ask for political asylum."

"I tell you they were Chance and Lewis, and the main thing is to get a guard on board that ship."

The pilot stood with us, bewildered. As I mentioned Lewis's name he looked round, almost jumping round. Then he subsided again. He wanted no part of the trouble. His job was with the river, not international politics, his attitude seemed to say.

"I can send out four men until the morning," Wilson was saying. "Then it's somebody else's headache."

"It will be somebody else's headache within an hour," I said. "You don't think the authorities will let this wait till morning, do you?"

"Sir, I think that ship's slipped her cable!" the sergeant called. We all swung round. The sergeant was right. The *Polski Robotnik* was moving fast downstream.

"Holy God!" the pilot cried, at last declaring his interest.

"You were right!" Wilson said quietly.

I scarcely heard the words. They were almost a soliloquy, but in that moment he showed how deep had been his disbelief in all that I had claimed during the preceding minutes, and how resolute had been his actions.

"To the pier!" he shouted.

"Aye, aye, sir," the sergeant said, imperturbable once more.

51

BEFORE THE LAUNCH REACHED THE JETTY, WILSON AND I HAD LEAPED ashore, almost together. He was in the lead. He knew the drill. We raced along the slippery stone into the outer office. "You'll want to ring your people," he called. "Use this phone. I'll use the one in here." He stormed his way into the inner office. Constables seemed to fall away like ninepins.

I looked at the clock. Six-forty. The preceding hour had been as full of incident and surprises as a normal year. Within another minute I was through to Butler. He was back in his own office. "Tell me the worst!" he said as I began. "It wasn't Chance. It wasn't Lewis. They were two kidnaped Arsenal forwards."

I told him the story in rushed, incoherent sentences.

"It's a good story either way," he said laconically. "If we catch 'em or if they get away. Hold on, I'll tell Myers. I hope he's made all arrangements for this little change of plan."

He took up another telephone and asked for a Whitehall number.

"Myers," I heard him say, "the worst has happened. The Polski boat's slipped her cable and gone. Isn't this where you take over?"

There was a long pause and then I heard Butler's voice raised in admiring surprise. "You have! Well, well! Slow starters, quick learners. Well, best of luck. Let me know what happens. And me only, old boy. Don't forget who put you onto this. None of those other Fleet Street bloodsuckers."

He came back to me. "Extraordinary. Friend Myers has made a lot of plans in the last half hour, it seems. Arranged for a naval craft to intercept, and God knows what all."

"But where?"

"That's the kind of thing I leave to the so-called experts," Butler said. "Presumably some time before they get to Gdynia. Never know with the Navy, though. They've got some antediluvian ideas of diplomacy. Inevitable with all that cutlass-carrying. Oughtn't you to be getting after them, old son?"

"If I can borrow a craft."

"Buy, borrow, beg or steal any craft that's handy. Charge to me personally, if necessary. And those are instructions, not suggestions. Go to it!"

I rang off to find Wilson at my side.

"Apparently everything is under control," he said. "I'm to follow to see if I can be of any use. Like a lift?"

We went out along the pier again, this time picking our way more circumspectly along the greasy path.

"Downriver!" Wilson called to the sergeant. "Is the pilot still on board?"

"I'm still here," the plump man answered unwillingly.

"You'd better stay with us."

There were now three additional patrolmen also on board.

"As fast as you can, short of cracking the engine," Wilson commanded.

I stood in the stern sheets, balancing with the craft as it began to pick up speed. Wilson consulted forward with the sergeant and the patrolman.

By now the wind had begun to rise and the trip was beginning to be bumpy. The launch was taking it well. We were probably getting an extra four or five knots above our engine speed from the wind and the tide, but so was the *Polski Robotnik*.

"Will that Polski captain be able to make it, pilot?" Wilson called.

"If he's lucky. Other men have done it. I believe he's used to the river."

"And if he doesn't?"

"He'll hit something, pile up or get bogged down in Bugsby's Reach."

"We'll see," Wilson said grimly.

"What will this craft do?" I called to him.

"Seventeen knots at a pinch."

"What will the Polski do?"

"Twelve, my sergeant thinks. We might be up with them in about half an hour, forty minutes. Cold? Come forrard."

We buffeted a boisterous passage between the high warehouses off Limehouse Reach. The launch was making a sturdy battle of it. Soon the buildings on both shores could be seen only as low-lying, indistinct silhouettes. We had come round the great curve of Greenwich Reach into Blackwall, then into drearily named Bugsby's Reach. The sergeant intoned the legendary names of the reaches as we logged the miles, bravely but desperately slowly.

By then the river was dark, overshadowed by the night, and the wind was that much sharper. We huddled together within the uneasy shelter of the deckhouse.

Halfway along Woolwich Reach, Wilson said aloud, "Thank God there's no traffic."

We all probably thought the same but nobody answered.

"How long a start do you think they got, sergeant?" Wilson asked, for the third time.

"Best part of half an hour, sir."

"It couldn't have been."

"We had to go back to the station first, sir. That took ten or twelve minutes, perhaps more."

"As much as that?"

"All o' that, sir. Time flies in these things."

"Umph!"

I looked at my watch and tried to work out the simple problem of my youth: If Vessel A can do 12 knots and Vessel B 16 knots and Vessel A leaves at six o'clock and Vessel B at six-thirty when will B overtake A? I gave it up.

"But surely we ought to be up with 'em now?" Wilson almost pleaded with the sergeant as if he had read my thoughts.

"Can't say, sir. She may have a better turn of speed than I gave her credit for."

"Looks like it," Wilson said shortly. "Can't you get any more out of this tub?"

" 'Fraid not, sir."

The *Polski Robotnik* was certainly moving faster than we had judged. As a postwar vessel she was probably three or four knots faster than similar prewar cargo ships. I wondered in which yard she had been built, but even if police launches carried Lloyds Lists in their lockers, this was scarcely the moment for consultation.

We all stood together, watchful and apprehensive. Gradually— more or less at the same moment I think—the conviction came to us all that not only were we not overhauling the *Polski Robotnik*, but she was probably widening the gap between us.

So the first hour passed.

By then we were moving through Long Reach, leaving Purfleet abeam on the port side. I overheard the sergeant mutter, "Fiddler's Reach next, sir, and well outside our limits."

"You just go on," Wilson said grimly.

Occasionally craft passed us, coming upriver: low-lying sewage craft, a solitary tug, two or three coasters, even a spritsail barge un- der bare poles, her lights and silhouette a sudden and unexpected intrusion into our somber thoughts. Ahead was the unseen, widen- ing river and the distant shores, now wholly merged into the night.

Here and there, far off, the lights of lonely marshland houses pin-pricked the black hinterland, or car headlights moved in sudden curving arcs high above the marshes on either shore. We chugged on.

"What do we do if we do overtake?" I asked.

"God only knows!" Wilson said irritably. "It's the most arsytarsy jaunt I've ever been on. There's supposed to be a craft intercepting, but I hope she's got a better turn of speed than we have."

"What kind of craft?"

"God knows."

"Where from?"

"God only knows. Somewhere downriver. Sheerness perhaps. If so, we should have met 'em by now. I don't know. I tell you, I'm as much in the dark as you are." He sounded even more irritable than he had been ten minutes before. Gradually we came into the cross-river lights and traffic of the Tilbury-Gravesend ferry. I remem-bered, from years before, the frequency of the car and passenger ferries that crisscrossed the river throughout the day. Certainly that traffic would not have stopped yet. Lights burned out brightly from the Station Hotel on the northern shore, more dimly from the Graves-end pier.

"If that Polski cut across this traffic as fast as we're going through it, he's asking for trouble," said the man at the wheel, the first words he had spoken.

"Well, presumably he did, and faster, Caffrey, so cut the cackle and crash on," the sergeant said shortly.

"I can't understand it," I heard the pilot mutter to Wilson, but Wilson was silent.

By then we were across the line of the ferry traffic and into Gravesend Reach. Again we all fell silent. As we moved into the Lower Hope the wind was moving across from the starboard bow, whipping across the Kentish marshes with demoniac frenzy.

"Once round this bend and we'll have this bloody breeze right at us," Wilson said.

Then as we came toward Thameshaven, opposite Blyth sands, the sergeant said, "Sir, she's ahead and not a light aboard. He really is crazy."

I stared ahead but saw nothing.

"How far ahead, cat's eyes?" Wilson snarled.

"Three-fifty yards, sir, possibly a quarter mile."

Wilson couldn't see; I couldn't see; but we accepted the sergeant's word.

"He *is* crazy," Wilson said. He turned to me. "Now what do we do?"

"Search me!" I said. The schoolboy words came naturally to my lips and somehow sufficed at such a moment.

"Well, we *were* faster," the sergeant said with satisfaction.

"That kind of cockeyed consolation is out of place, Stokes," Wilson said. "Especially when we're as bitched as anybody could be. Well, what do we do?" he called to me again.

"Just proceed," I said. "They promised something."

"They! They! They!" barked Wilson. "Who are 'they' anyway? And where? Do they expect me to follow this bloody ship into the North Sea?"

Almost as he spoke the dazzling beam of a searchlight from another midstream craft loomed into the dark night. We stared into the blinding light. The *Polski Robotnik* stood within the glare like a black cut-out shape.

"This is 'they' I suppose," Wilson growled. "Better late than never. Now what?"

The searchlight suddenly blacked out and a signal snapped out a message in the night.

"My God, that crazy Pole is going on!" the sergeant yelled.

It was infuriating to get news at second hand, but only the sergeant had eyes for the night, especially after the blinding beam of the searchlight. The rest of us might have been blind men.

Again the searchlight swept the river and the ship.

"What craft is that?" Wilson called irritably to the sergeant.

"Frigate, sir, judging by the silhouette I got just now. Don't think she's big enough for a destroyer."

"Move up, for Christ's sake, man."

"Get a move on, Caffrey!" the sergeant called.

"I'm giving her everything we've got."

"Well, give her some more."

Perhaps we made a yard or more, for suddenly the two silhouettes also came clear to me. In the split second of recognition, I found time to be pleased that my unaided eyes had not let me down at the last.

The *Polski Robotnik* moved steadily on, past the frigate, her wake curling astern in caldron waves. We were moving on a course to starboard of her track, perhaps two hundred yards astern. In the recent moments we seemed to have made some distance.

"She's going to make a break for it!" the sergeant shouted. For a moment I thought his sympathies had suddenly switched to the Polish ship.

I tried to picture the scene on board. The tense and watchful men. The master and mate, taut and grim eyed. And Lewis and Chance? Where were they?

"The frigate's coming about, sir. Hold hard!"

The frigate coming upriver had called upon the Polish ship to heave to, the signal had been ignored, the *Polski Robotnik* had gone on and the frigate had been left astern. That we could work out for ourselves.

The frigate came about in a great sweeping curve, almost cutting us in two, and then was moving swiftly downriver in pursuit. Now, I thought, we shall miss everything, for we were yawing wildly in the whirlpool wash of the frigate, but we went on, bumping, crashing, taking it hard.

"Now what?" Wilson said, the words very quiet. "Sergeant, what about our own damned searchlight?"

"Aye, aye, sir."

Now we could see.

Like our own craft, the frigate was moving on a course well on the starboard quarter of the Pole, but the two vessels were steaming parallel courses. The frigate was moving fast and closing in. The tracks of the two vessels began to converge, slowly, inescapably.

"What on earth's he up to?" cried the sergeant.

"A boarding party?" I queried.

"Not at that speed, for God's sake."

When a plane falls from the air it seems to fall so infinitely slowly. Even a crash on a race track seems to happen at leisure. So, then, at that lesser speed, the ramming of the *Polski Robotnik* seemed to take an hour, like a sequence in slow motion.

The frigate moved in relentlessly. At the last moment I wondered whether the captain would lose his nerve, but he drove in, his angle of swift approach calculated to an inch, so that the frigate hit the Polish ship amidships at an angle of perhaps twenty degrees or thereabouts. The crunch and crashing of steel plates and timber,

buckling and splitting in collision at sea, is an awesome noise. The
nearness of the sea and the disturbing revelation that steel can fold
like tin are terrifying factors.

The noise came to us astern. In a matter of seconds we were up
with the two vessels, now locked and drifting. Shouts and curses
spilled over into the night. Steam rose between the ships in a great
hissing geyser. Men on both decks were moving fast, some with purpose, others apparently in panic. Under the impact, the *Polski
Robotnik* already seemed to be listing slightly to port.

Slowly the two ships parted like regretful partners in a macabre
dance, the frigate drawing astern into midstream, the Polish vessel
drifting downriver, moving athwart the stream, already listing omi-
nously.

The vents of these drawn-out minutes, enacted at first in utter silence and darkness, then in a furious splitting of the night, all against
the background of the estuary, had an eeriness beyond description.
Not a word had been spoken on board the launch. We were like
mute and stricken spectators of a tragedy outside our reckoning. We
could not take part and seemed unable to give voice. As the two
vessels went apart Wilson said yet again, "What now?" but only the
captain of the frigate held the answer to that repetitive query. As
his vessel stood away, his searchlight swept again over the drifting
Polish ship, and once more the black night was blindingly vivid.

We were now almost between the two vessels, slightly astern. "Let
go your anchor!" a megaphoned voice boomed out across the river
and the night.

Still the Polish vessel drifted, downriver. But the drifting was un-
cannily well controlled, I thought. The man at the wheel was holding
his own most skillfully against the wind and the tide.

He's working it, I thought. He knows what he's doing.

We were already downriver, almost half a mile from the scene of
the collision. The frigate was standing by. And still no light was to be
seen on board the *Polski Robotnik*. The bridge of the vessel moved
in and out of the searchlight with the roll of the ship. Only her starboard quarter was consistently held within the searchlight's beam.

As if in sudden decision the frigate again increased speed and
again began to move up alongside the Polski, and, just as suddenly,
as if prepared to end the day, the second anchor of the *Polski
Robotnik* went out and down with a rush.

"I'm sending a party aboard to help!" called the frigate captain's voice again.

His ship went alongside and four men went over the rails from its stern. The two vessels had much the same freeboard.

We went close, under the lee of the frigate. Wilson called, "Chief Superintendent Wilson, London river police, here! Can I come aboard?"

"Been expecting you, sir," another voice shouted.

We both went up, hand over precarious hand, from the rolling launch to the frigate's deck, thence to the bridge. The captain was a lieutenant in his late twenties, a pale, thin-faced, sharp-boned young man.

"Would you care to give me your ideas now, sir?" he asked. "I was told to do this by the Commodore, Harwich himself, sir, but I still don't believe it's true." He seemed to take my presence as a matter of course.

Wilson mumbled reassuringly, "It's true all right. A nice job."

"Thanks!" he said. "I haven't had all that practice, either, although you might think otherwise."

We all laughed.

"Much damaged yourself?" Wilson asked.

"Not all that, sir. Not below the water line, anyway."

"The other chap got it fairly badly, didn't he?" Wilson asked.

"Not too bad, but she'll make no sea passage under her own steam, that's certain. And those were my instructions."

"Presumably she'll need a tow now," Wilson said.

"I'm just getting it fixed. Where then, sir?"

"Back to Tilbury, I should think."

We waited on the bridge in the dark night while the hawsers were taken across under the steely prong of the searchlight. None of us talked. I think we were all engrossed watching the efficient naval routine. The whole of the starboard side of the *Polski Robotnik* was a shambles and looked as if a bomb had hit it. Plates were stove in, the deckhouse was split wide open, the rails were twisted like candy cane. Glass and timber were strewn around in desolate confusion. And the list was even more emphatic.

The tow was ready in a remarkably short time, despite the fact that no Polish seamen were there to help. All was done by the naval working party. Slowly the frigate took the *Polski Robotnik* in tow. Slowly the merchantman moved about.

Wilson and I scarcely spoke, and not once about Chance or Lewis. Each of us had his own thoughts for unwilling company: Wilson doubtless preoccupied with thoughts of the tricky police procedure ahead; I concerned only with Chance and Lewis. In a curious way I longed to see them. I wished, above all things, to see Lewis, to try to do something to ease his stricken mind. Yet what should I do, even if I had a fleeting chance, which was unlikely? My thoughts were unceasing queries without answers. So we all stood there, taking the swell of the tide, each watchfully alone in his mind.

Within an hour we were at Tilbury, edging in, inch by inch, toward the quay where once, long ago, before the war, I suddenly remembered in a moment of nostalgia, I had boarded a beautiful white steamer bound for Gothenberg and my first Scandinavian holiday.

Then we were alongside and, five minutes later, ashore, under the glare from shore lights above the quayside, from police car headlights and from the frigate's searchlight.

Wilson went down to the quay, across to a group of policemen in uniform. After a few muttered words with a peak-capped chief superintendent, he turned and went on board the *Polski Robotnik* by a gangway which had been rushed up from ashore. I followed him.

He went straight up to the bridge, now sloping foolishly inward toward the quayside. I still followed him, keeping so close behind him that nobody queried or attempted to bar my way.

The Master and First Officer were there, side by side, both white and drawn.

Wilson said, "This has been an unfortunate occurrence. Certain charges will have to be made against you. I therefore advise you to speak most carefully."

The Master did not answer.

"Arrangements have been made for your men to be billeted ashore for tonight," Wilson went on.

"My men will stay on board," the Master said doggedly.

"Very well. As you know, I wish to interview two men on board this vessel."

"Two of my men have been lost overboard," the Master said.

I saw Wilson stiffen and my own heart went cold.

"Which two men?" Wilson barked.

"We do not yet know," the First Officer said quietly. "Things have been difficult for us this last hour."

We were quiet. Then the Master spoke again. He timed his blows. "Also, I think, one of your own men was lost," he said slowly. "The policeman you left on board."

Nobody spoke.

"In the crash," the Master added at last. His cold eyes narrowed as he watched Wilson wilt.

"I shall send a search party on board. Immediately," Wilson said. He turned away and began to call his instructions from the sloping bridge. His voice was lifeless and hollow. The chief superintendent ashore acknowledged the words and, on the instant, policemen moved from the shadows of buildings and moved toward the *Polski Robotnik*.

There is little more to say. Even now, as I try to record those events, my pen moves slowly and unwillingly. The dread memory of the night returns too vividly.

During that night the *Polski Robotnik* was searched three times, first by the police, then twice by a party from the frigate.

But what was the use?

I watched gloomily from the quayside, weary and sickened beyond any power of my words to describe. Wilson and I both knew that no man had got ashore as the ship had maneuvered alongside. The police there had been too numerous and too watchful. No living person had gone overboard in any ship's lifeboat at any time during the pursuit, during the time of the collision or later.

Afterward we went on board the frigate, into the captain's cabin, at his invitation. There we were alone.

"Could they have gone overboard and swum for it?" I asked.

"Not unless they were well beyond Olympic standards," Wilson said. "No, we can rule that out."

By that time it was three o'clock. We were both worn out but still unable to call it a night or a day.

Yet at last, toward five o'clock, after word came to the cabin that the third search had also been made in vain, we quit, leaving the *Polski Robotnik* under the surveillance of the Essex Constabulary and the frigate's officers and men.

I traveled back to London with Wilson in his car. He had tele-

phoned Irongate from ashore an hour before. A constable, spruce
and straight-backed, an affront to our woebegone selves, was chauffeur.

We sat in the back, limp, defeated, despairing.

The car moved fast between the low fields, in company with early-
morning trucks taking produce from the Essex farms toward the London markets.

For a long time we were silent, but at last Wilson said, "I never
heard any shots, did you?"

"We would never have heard anything in that din."

"What about dumping them overboard?"

"Easy enough from the port side. That's plainly why she went on
drifting after the collision. I wondered why at the time. The whole of
the port side was as black as night. Anyone could have been mur-
dered and pushed overboard."

"It's probably what happened. To all three of them. There goes
Lewis. Did you know him well?" he asked.

"Not very. At least, not in the usual sense, but, in a strange way, I
got to know Chance very well very quickly."

"What was he like?"

"An odd man. A traitor, too, I suppose the world will call him if
the world ever gets to know. Yet I liked him. It was difficult not to
like him."

"It was difficult not to like my man, too," Wilson said grimly. "I'd
heard of Chance, of course," he said. "I suppose this whole thing is
going to make a bit of a stink in the Commons."

"If it ever comes out."

"You don't think it will?"

"I don't know. Do you?"

"I hadn't given it much thought, frankly. Doesn't it depend on
people like yourself?"

"Not always."

"I suppose not. All this comes under the heading of security, I
imagine."

After a long pause he said, looking steadily at the chauffeur's back,
"You're probably right. This whole river business will die an unnatural death. Apologies all round. Unfortunate collision. Even talk of
compensation. We shan't want it to come out. The Polskis won't.
Mark my words. You'll never be able to tell it in your paper."

I did not reply. The decision was not mine. That was up to Butler. Perhaps, for once, not even up to him.

52

I RANG COURT HOUSE FROM IRONGATE POLICE STATION. BUTLER WAS still there. He sounded tired.

"Hello, dear boy. Tell us the story. Apparently it's the most hush-hush story ever. Absolute clamp on it. Can't prize a word out of anybody. I gather there has been a little bother downriver."

"I'll come along."

"I take it you're surrounded by enemies of the press. Come along."

"Take my car," Wilson said as I put down the receiver.

I sat in the car half dozing as we moved through the gray, awakening streets. The dawn was streaked a treacherous pink. I ached with weariness, but my thoughts were stubborn and persistent, and would not let me sleep.

I thought of Chance and Lewis, of the fanaticism of the one and the ingenuousness of the other, of their preoccupation with peace and now their unpeaceful ends.

I tried to put all such images aside, but they persisted, like grim evocations, and I continued to brood over the two men I had scarcely known yet knew so well.

I thought now only of their deaths, for of their deaths I had no doubt. Had they known, in the last minutes of that pursuit and collision, that their ends were near? Chance, perhaps, for he had long known the true nature of the faith he had taken for himself. But Lewis would never have faced such facts. He had never had the need to face them. He would not have believed them, even in the moment of meeting them. His life had been lived apart from violence. He had merely put his great talents, against his wish, to the violent ends that absorb all such talents in our time. And at the end he still would not have realized that men like himself, innocent of all

evil or violent intention, can yet die evilly and violently in a world
they have so innocently helped to create.

A sudden annihilating blow? A bullet in the back? We should
never know. Weights had probably taken them to the river bed. I
shivered in the unfriendly dawn and longed to see Julia. I shivered
again and again, as if with ague.

I went straight up to Butler's room. He was lying full length along
the leather settee. All the morning newspapers were strewn on the
floor. I said "Good morning," walked across the room and looked
down at the front pages. Not one carried any hint of the story of the
Polski Robotnik. Even a paragraph about the still-missing scientist
was below the fold, a story already fading.

"Have some coffee," he said, pointing to a vacuum flask on the
desk. I poured myself out a strong long drink.

"You've got a stop on the story?" I asked.

"From top level."

"Till when?"

"Probably till doomsday. I gather it's a hot story. If you're not too
dead, tell me."

I was too dead, but I told him. Perhaps I am ungrateful. I needed
to tell someone, and Butler listened to the end, asking no questions.

After I finished he was silent for a long time. Then he said, "It's a
pity not to tell a story like that."

"Is it?"

"Would you really want to?" he asked, and considered me steadily.

"Perhaps not," I said at length, and then, "How will this Chance
and Lewis story die?"

"God knows. We'll hear. Some corny story that nobody really believes but that will serve. Then a gradual acceptance. We've been
denied great scoops before. We shall be again. I shall die a philoso-
pher yet."

For once I could not smile.

"I quite liked Chance," he said, after a time, "even though I only
knew him long enough to be snubbed by him. There was a lot there."

"I got to like him too."

"What was Lewis like?"

"Sad. Gentle." I hunted for the words. "A lost soul."

"We're all that," he said easily. "Nobody gets any extra sympathy for that. What about his wife and daughter?"

"They'll need help."

"They'll probably get it," he said, smiling.

I nodded, but still I could not smile.